Another sound car[...]
an endless depth. A [...]g[...]
and terrible, a brassy, echoing roar as harsh as
justice. He felt a tremor in the earth he knelt on, a
faint swift shiver, a pulse quite unlike the drum
high above, yet still more regular and unvarying.
The roaring cry came again, and with it a thinner,
purer call that made his skin prickle; for it brought
back the timbre of Laurin's war-trumpets, and the
crashing stride of a great army on the march, a
force of foot and horse ten or twenty times the
number he had brought to this siege. He sprang
up, hoping for an instant that it was his old host
summoned to his aid; but there was nothing of
their music in the harsh voices crying the pace.
And there was a grim note to that stride that did
not belong in his memories, a measured, inexorable pace like the action of some arcane engine
that could roll with the same relentless fervour
over land and sea alike to the wide world's end,
sweeping all from its path.

MICHAEL
SCOTT ROHAN

THE LORD OF MIDDLE AIR

VGSF

First published in Great Britain 1994
by Victor Gollancz

First VGSF edition published 1995
by Victor Gollancz
An imprint of the Cassell Group
Wellington House, 125 Strand, London WC2R 0BB

A catalogue record for this book is
available from the British Library.

ISBN 0 575 06099 9

Printed and bound in Great Britain
by Cox & Wyman Ltd, Reading, Berks

Michele Scotto fu, che veramente
Delle magiche frode seppe il giuoco . . .

Michael Scot it was, who truly
knew every trick of the magical art . . .

Dante

Of middle air the demons proud,
Who ride upon the mounting cloud . . .

Sir Walter Scott

Contents

1 🏰 The Reivers at the Ford

This was the way of it, that the stolen beasts were driven down Teviotdale and out by the Gray Hill southward. Out of the country altogether, and away towards Liddesdale, with the Colt riding hard on their track.

In hot trod, as it was called then; and with him Geordie the groom and Wat of the Homefield, two hard men and worthy, if a little solid in the skull. Riding, because the villagers had come running to the tower, and because the Colt's father was from home and few men else to take up the trail. The lifting of cattle had always been a popular sport as between neighbour and neighbour, along with the shifting of boundary stones, the diverting of streams and suchlike; but since the devastations of the late war, when all the great towns of the region had burned, it was fast becoming the daily pursuit of an increasingly lawless land. So that, as the Colt's father fulminated in his cups of an evening, there were some families in danger of forgetting that food could be gained other than from their neighbours, and of altogether losing the arts of peace and the planting and raising of seed.

This worried the Colt little, for though he was fond enough of his father, he knew well the lord was not himself averse to snapping up an unconsidered steer or two on the sly. If the arts of peace depended on him, their outlook was poor. But this continual bleeding at the herds was something else, a new thing, and the Colt fancied he could put a name to the cause. A black name, casting a sinister shadow; and the Colt would inherit these lands one day, and the wealth that grazed across them, and sprang from their soil. What was being driven away was his; and his heart burned within him.

He cast his eyes across the rising land ahead, and the rough rounded hills beyond, made hazy as the sun warmed the moist air. Normally he took delight in them in such a fresh spring dawning, the warm hues of brown and yellow bracken heath and rich green forest burgeoning after the long barren winter, glistening as if new-painted after a night's light rain. He loved the land that would be his; he knew no other, and he felt its quickening in his own blood. But now he marked only the signs of passage, the crushed grass and bracken, the hoof-scattered dung, the horseprints that wove around the central trail with a drover's hasty care; and he felt for the haft of the heavy cross-bow at his saddle.

'The spur's fresh!' snapped Wat, swinging low in his stirrups. 'They drive afoot still, the callow bastards! We'll be on them aye moment!'

'Aye,' growled Geordie through his beard, and gestured at the thickening wall of trees, oak and birch and alder, lining the shallow vale ahead. 'Yon's Allan Water, and a ford! Best we rein in, Colt, and steal up on 'em!'

'Be damned to that!' snapped the Colt, and cursed inwardly at the squeak in his voice. The men exchanged meaningful glances; the lord would have their hides if anything happened to the young man. The Colt snatched up the bow and cocked it in one motion, as Wat had long ago taught him; a churl's weapon, but even the sons of knights were best to have the use of it in these troubled times. 'We'll—'

What he intended he forgot, in the wake of what hit him. The flash sprang out of the forest shadow. The concussion made the very air a solid thing that struck him with jarring force. The trees shook and wavered, and a tide of birds billowed skyward, screaming. The horse shrilled and reared beneath him, and for a moment all sense was lost in the effort of staying in his stirrups and quelling it. Wat and the groom were no better set, wheeling and cursing their own mounts even as their ears sang with the sound. And no sooner had they got their beasts steadied than a new fright came bursting out of the trees towards them, the stolen cattle in a buffeting knot, wild-eyed, froth-nosed, lowing and bellowing, stampeding back uphill along their own tracks with no drover behind them but terror. A riderless horse, stirrups swinging, charged after them, screaming wildly, with dark streaks down its crupper, and after it, from a spot further along, another, and another, this one painfully lame yet bolting like the rest. A thin swirl of smoke twisted around the treetops.

The century was the thirteenth after Christ, the year its thirtieth. The Mongols had not yet brought the Chinese powder westward to scorch the gates of Samarkand. Neither the Colt nor his men had ever heard any such sound as this, save in the descent of lightning; and the sun stood near noon above them in a clear sky.

The Colt hesitated a second, seeing his own pallor on the walnut faces of his men. He had played at such things often enough as a child, his fancies fired by minstrel's song and nurse's story, had thought himself a brave knight stalking sword in hand into a dragon's den or outlaw's covert, unafraid and valiant. But now the very trees seemed to bristle with cold menace, and what lay behind them less known and predictable even than a dragon. Then, because he was the Colt, and was too afraid to be seen afraid, he spurred his balky mount downhill past the scattering cattle. Wat yelped and pulled at his arm, but he shook the old farmer off with an impatient snarl and grabbed a bolt from the sheaf tied at his belt. The horse shied again as the acrid, devilish smell stung its nostrils, and so did the Colt, inwardly, but he pressed on down the dung-strewn trail to the ford. Wat and Geordie, wild-eyed as the cattle, urged their panting horses after him, crossing themselves repeatedly. As he reached the margin of the trees, bow at the ready, they caught up with him, and unslung their own short longbows; but all three reined in and stopped, staring.

Allan Water ran brown but clear before them in the green-gold glade light over a bank of silted gravel that made the ford, unhurried between deep pools. The cattle had evidently crossed it; so had their thieves. They were still here. One lay at the water's edge on the far bank, face-down; he was blackened, ragged and smoking, and very still. Another stumbled about on the gravel like a blind man, clutching his face. A third was loping back across the river in great heedless splashes, oblivious to the watchers he should have feared like the hand of divine wrath. He ran straight at them, yelling wordless as a beast, and off past them into the thick wood by no path. Yet all there was to run from on the far bank was a trio of strangers, and two of them utterly unfearsome.

One was squat, with a great broad face and narrowed squinting eyes, almost a dwarf save for the heavy shoulders on him; the other was his opposite, a spindly gawk whose very eyelids seemed to droop with the effort of staying open. Both men were swarthy, not like windburned Wat or red-faced Geordie, but with the sallow yellowish colour of a hotter sun, darker men than the Colt had ever seen; and they wore livery coats brighter than bird-plumage in fantastical squares of yellow and blue. They were mounted, or perched, atop two sturdy mules, expensive beasts at the head of a small baggage train; they rode like baggage themselves. The third man, though, was more impressive. He was tall, he wore heavy robes of dark red, and he sat erect on a massive black horse of a breed the Colt didn't recognize but instantly admired. His skin was lighter, but still unusually brown, and the air of command in his bearing was unmistakable. Yet even this man looked old – ancient to the Colt's eyes, perhaps fifty, his long dark hair and short pointed beard an oddly streaked blend of white and black. The man gestured to his dwarfish servant, who sprang from his saddle, caught the stumbling man in a grip his struggles seemed hardly to disturb and, forcing him to his knees, ducked his head in the river. The reiver struggled wildly, then suddenly subsided, sobbing, as if it had brought him some relief.

The Colt, frozen by the tableau, snatched together his wits and looked around after the other. He could still hear him crashing and thrashing away through brambly undergrowth.

'You might as well leave him be!' called a very clear voice, in amiable tones. The red-robed man jerked his head slightly. 'Better to be content with rounding up your cattle, eh?'

The young man bridled. 'Who in Hell are you to be giving me orders? And what's been doing here? What have you done to these men, and by what right?' He flushed. He had been addressed in Norman French and instinctively spoken it back, instantly marking what class of person he was. That could be an unsafe thing.

'Right?' The stranger shrugged. 'The common right and duty to help in the trod. To help the rightful owner. And you would be the Colt of Branxholme, would you not? Not the lord yet, I think; not at . . . seventeen?'

'I'm Walter Scot, and my age is my own concern! I'm old enough to be sure I never saw you in my life before. So how'd you know so much of me? And I demand again, what do you here?' He hefted his bow meaningfully. 'This all stinks too much of magic to me, and we want no more of that in the Marches! We've a hot fire for any sorcerers turning this way, a stake and a tar-barrel too – or a griddle, if you'd prefer! So speak!'

The stranger threw back his head in a silent laugh. 'Sorcery, Colt! Why, what sorcery would I need simply to recognize you as your father's son? You have the self-same friendly way with you. And you had to be less than eighteen, because it is thus long since I was last in these parts, and Branxholme was not long wedded – a lovely girl! – and had no son. I have a right in these woods and on this road because they lead me to my home; and I thought to do the lord of them a favour by waylaying what were clearly thieves – Armstrong men out of Liddesdale, if I'm a fair judge. They threatened me, and that's something I do not appreciate. As for how I did it—' He gave that silent laugh again. 'No sorcery in that, young Master Scot! Merely some strong substances commonly used in alchemical investigations – and lest you balk at that, they're no secret to the better class of armourer, even. Only making them work together thus fiercely, that's a little trick they use in the far Orient – but it's one you could wield yourself if I showed you, without need of spells or incantations. And that I could prove before any judge in the land, if need be.'

Walter was silent a moment, watching the patterns of sun through the leaves, the water chattering by the stones. Against his will, he was impressed. His father, utterly uneducated himself, had taken unusual pains to give the Colt the best education these parts had to offer, at the great Grammar School of Roxburgh, and it had bred in him a strong reverence for men of

learning, and admiration for men who had seen the world –
though to that he had found exception, these last two years.
This man seemed to be both.

'Bedamned, he's the right o' it!' exclaimed Wat hoarsely at his
side.

'What? Of what?' demanded the Colt.

'Him!' hissed the old man, jabbing a thumb down at the half-
blinded thief, now kneeling miserably by the bank with the
short man's heavy hand on his shoulder. 'Him there, that's
Wullie Armstrong, Blood-Wullie's son!'

Geordie scratched his head. 'By're Lady, and is it! Blood-
Wullie that burned Hoddie Netherhope in's hoose! There's an
ill name for a Liddesdale bandit! And yon that ran by us, sure
'twas Andy Armstrong o' the Rig, that lifted above fifty head
from the Kers themselves twa months gone!'

'Andy it was, right enough,' nodded Wat. 'I kennt his mither
when she was but a wean. He had her look.'

Walter glanced at the woebegone thief; with some of the
scorching washed from his face he did have the look of an Armstrong man, right enough. 'And a hard man to meet on the
trod,' he said thoughtfully. The thief wore an armour cotte of
studded leather, with a sword and a sheaf of crossbow bolts at
his waist. The dead man had the same, and a helm, for all the
good it had done him. Two heavy pikes lay in the shallows at
the far side of the ford. 'We could have dealt with them, though.'

'Oh, aye,' said Wat, a trace too hastily.

'That's for sikker,' agreed Geordie, also hastily. 'Mind, it
wouldna' been so easy . . .'

Walter drew breath. He had known these men since they'd
dandled him on their knees as a baby. They held no secrets
from him. They had told him what he had guessed; that they
were too old and him, though he was trained in arms, too young
and untried to safely meet three hardened and heavily armed
Armstrongs in their prime. These would have been hard and
ruthless fighters, more than a match for him and his men,
maybe, even without any darker help that Liddesdale's lord
might give them. Which meant this well-spoken stranger had
done him a real service.

14

Old Wat was plucking at his sleeve. 'This yin here and his men, though, what's he? I've never clappt eyes on the like. Should we no' tak haud o' him?'

Walter would have liked to. There was too much mystery here to be let wander around unchallenged. Mystery was a danger to him and his. Yet he could not simply seize hold of the man. That would be dishonourable and inhospitable, and, besides, whatever it was had bested three Armstrongs could no doubt do as much for him. He didn't want to appear indecisive; better to sound unconvinced and stern. What would his father say? He gave a curt nod. 'Well, we can see about that. We'll have to round up the kine soon enough. But first we'll string that callant there up on a branch as a warning to his thieving kin.'

That sounded about right, and he heard Geordie grunt appreciatively; it only occurred to him a moment later that he wasn't at all eager to see a man die thus. The Colt was not especially violent, save when angry, and had little cruelty in his nature. He didn't even know how the thing was done, exactly, knots and so forth; the old fellows would, though.

The dark stranger raised an eyebrow. 'Have him, and welcome – but save him for ransom, lad, surely. The one that's dead you may gibbet if you must. It cannot hurt him further.'

Walter seized at the suggestion gratefully. 'That's so—' Then he realized he'd been called *lad*, and bridled. But the stranger was already speaking on.

'Tell me, though, first, Colt Walter – this sorcery you spoke of, and so hotly, as if eager to find it out . . . Since when was there much of *that* in these parts?'

Wat and Geordie snorted. Walter frowned. 'Since the Lord of Soulis came home from a long pilgrimage, some three years gone,' he said, still more curtly. 'Though where it took him, and to what shrine, I'd sooner not think.'

'Nor what he brought back with him,' murmured Geordie into his beard; but the dark man seemed to hear it, and raised his eyebrows.

'We've had enough of travelled men in these parts,' persisted Walter. 'You, gudeman, you'd do well to betake yourself and these your servants off to your own land by some other road.

If you're an honest soul, these parts are dangerous. And if you're not, they're more dangerous still, for honest men hereabouts have had their bellyful of black doings and thieves in the night!'

The older man laughed again, still silently, but a little sadly now, with a rueful look in his eyes. 'I don't doubt it, young sir. But that cannot be. This *is* my own land, and my home lies only a little way east, in straight sight of the Eildon Hills, as is yours. For you and I, lad, we are kin.'

Walter stared wildly, and the dark man's amusement faded into cool dignity. 'So it is. You, Walter Scot, heir of Branxholme and I, Michael Scot, lord of the honour of Oakwood and lands in Fife, formerly scholar of the universities of Oxford, Paris, Toledo, Salamanca and Bologna, besides many other noble institutions. Late physician and counsellor to the great Frederick, second of his name, King of the Sicilies, Jerusalem and Germany, Emperor of the Romans at his court in Palermo, and come straight from the See of Rome itself to sojourn in my own old home. Surely you would not deny passage to a fellow lord of your own name and blood?'

As the stately chain of titles and names rolled out like a solemn procession of the highest and greatest his world held, Walter could only gape. The man who called himself Lord of Oakwood made no apparent movement, but suddenly his horse moved forward and splashed into the stream. A huge black warhorse of a beast, keen-eyed, sleek and fast-looking with fine fringed bridle and saddle of figured leather, it moved with a high-stepping, almost ceremonial gait that spoke to Walter of courts and chivalries, quests and romances he had only dreamed of from reading the few books and hearing the scanty lays of such minstrels as reached these parts. He felt suddenly rustic, unformed, much as the farm-boys appeared to him; and with a deep burning desire he coveted that horse, too fine to be wasted on a sedate elderly scholar like this. He imagined himself riding it down into the drear mouth of Liddesdale and beating on the high gate of Hermitage, calling out its lord to single combat on the sward . . .

And being chopped into collops by de Soulis' own guard, or

simply slung from a convenient tree. He stifled a brief shudder. It had happened, and to better men than him, full-grown and war-hardened. De Soulis rarely bothered to bloody a blade; he had nothing to prove.

The man splashed across the ford and reined in facing them. Geordie stared at him, and whispered, 'Look at the face on him! Yon's a Scot, true enow, though his chops were left ower lang i' the griddle!'

'The Laird o' Oakwood Tower!' muttered Wat, the elder. 'D'you not mind him, Geordie? These twenty years gone? The scholard, the man o' cunning?'

'Mind him? Oh aye, though I never saw the man! But I heard worse names than those . . .'

That, too, the man seemed to hear. Those features, darkened by a sun Walter imagined like a lamp of hot gold in a brassy sky, twitched again in a calm grin. 'I may go on my way, then?'

Walter, unable to think of anything sensible to say, nodded like his father in a bad mood. 'I'll have that man first,' he barked.

'Assuredly. Gilbyn! Gilberto!' The man who called himself Lord of Oakwood gave a quick toss of his head, and his dwarfish servitor splashed across the stream, towing the reiver, and flung him headlong at Walter's feet. Geordie sprang down with a spare rein, bound the Armstrong's hands and ankles and heaved him over his saddlebow.

The dark man smiled amiably. 'There, then. My thanks, and my respects to Sir Robert from a kinsman – and now, if you, young Colt, would take some well-meaning advice from one, it's high time you rounded up those cattle before they spread themselves all over the Marches. Fare you well, young sir.'

Geordie swore. Walter bristled, but the man was right. 'Come on!' he called impatiently to his followers, wheeled his horse around – how awkward and weak it felt beneath him now, though it was as fine a cob as any in the Marches – and clattered up the uneven path out of the trees. Wat and Geordie followed close, as if glad to be out of that strangely oppressive sunlit glade, and the Colt found himself drinking in the clean damp air in great gulps, to be rid of that acrid smoky odour. And by all Hell, there was laughter behind them! Walter looked back with baffled fury – and then his blood ran chill again. There had been three men in that party, and no other to be seen; but in that nasty merriment there were quite unmistakably four, and one of them a deep hollow bass.

He grabbed Geordie's captive by the greasy hair. 'You! As you value your neck, how many in that party you met?'

The prisoner too was staring back, his burnt brows climbing. 'But three! I swear't! Or we'd never have challenged! And then – he threw – and it . . . it-t . . .' The hardened Armstrong dissolved in a sudden flood of wailing tears.

Geordie slapped him. 'Haud yer noise, man! Leave be, Colt, for the lord to weigh. The cattle are our concern now!'

Walter nodded and spurred his horse away, loosing the bowstring and reaching for the rope at his saddlebow. But, like some impending prophecy, the laughter followed at his heels.

2 ⛫ Ill Hand, Worse Will

The gathering of the cattle was long, but less labour than it might have been, for a few more of the Branxholme men had been summoned and sent riding hard at heel, fearful lest the Colt might come to harm in his rashness. Fearful not only for the father's wrath but for Walter's own sake; for in truth the son was more beloved of his people, and, though he did not know it, thought the better man by far. They passed the beasts by, fearing some catastrophe, but when they found him unscathed they set at once to herding and roping. They were full of praise for the young lord's daring, till they saw how it angered Walter; the feeling of bafflement and helplessness burned in him still. He would have loved to ask some of the older men if they knew anything more of this Michael, but he feared it would lower him in their eyes. When the tally of beasts was complete they watered them at the Dodburn and set off on the homeward path, with Walter riding behind rather than before, lost in dark thoughts. They left him to it.

That was how, an hour or more homeward, he was the last to notice the smoke plume over the hillcrests, till their excited shouts called it to his mind. He saw the size of it, and swore. 'More deviltry!' he snarled, swinging his horse to the head of the little column.

'Aye, so I fear,' said Wat, shading his eyes against the falling sun. 'Southeast by the Slitrig water, it'd be – and was'na it yonder the Laird was called yestre'en?'

Walter ran his fingers through his brown hair. 'Aye, he was! And will you look at the height of it? That's more than some cottar's roof caught light –'

They heard the horn, then. Not ringing, not thrilling, a thin exhausted wail that barely carried on the breeze, and was hardly stronger; but it was repeated and repeated, and from the same direction as the smoke. 'That's it!' said Walter grimly, and turned his weary horse's head. 'Follow, all of you!'

'But the beasts!' groaned one of the drovers.

'Drive them along, man!' snapped Walter. 'It's not so far, and we'll not leave them a prize for any more reivers!'

Long before they reached the last hilltop they saw the man who blew, and he them. He stared at first, unsure whether to run towards them or away, but when he saw Walter spurring ahead of the cattle he set up a great wailing outcry, and came staggering and stumbling down the sparse-grown slope with his arms flailing. When he reached Walter he was too exhausted to do more than hang at his stirrup and gasp, a lank old peasant clad in stinking sheepskins.

'Speak, man!' shouted Walter furiously. 'What's afoot?'

'Acreknowe – fired!' the man wheezed. 'Reiver bastards – the Laird's there – sieged in—'

Walter flung him sprawling from his stirrup and waved the others forward. He could guess it now, a fool could. A double thrust – the Lord decoyed from home with the bulk of his men and pinned down by a waiting force, while a few reivers struck deep into the heart of his country, stealing beasts from farms in the very shadow of Branxholme's wall, loosing more than they could steal. A move at chess, most likely; not so much for the gaining of wealth, as to show that Branxholme's shadow was no longer the sure shield it had been. A move to lessen the Lord's power and prestige. A chill thought grew on him then – a move, too, to draw out his rash heir in trod? Might there not have been another ambush waiting, some way ahead?

He flushed out the fear with deliberate anger, and spurred to the hilltop. The encounter at the ford had shaken him, moved him to reflect. He had been raised to fight, like his father before him; but he had also been schooled to think. It was upon him to show more than rashness, now. He swung from his saddle below the summit, and falling to his belly crawled forward to stare down into the vale below. Wat and Geordie, with hunters' instinct, wormed up through the dripping bracken to his side. The sight below them was grim.

The round dished vale was pleasant in the long-shadowed sunlight, a green and brown draughtboard on a dark cloth of forest, for its pieces the strips of ploughland and the round drystone beastfolds dotted here and there. At its centre, less than half a mile below, ran a strip of dark water, and along it the fermtoun, the little gaggle of steadings and shielings where the cottars lived. Walter caught the smell of the red earth freshly turned, and felt something like love for it. This was rich land, if only the little men were left in peace to till it; it was his hope when he inherited to maintain that peace, and he often imagined himself sitting sternly in judgement as his father did, or riding out to harry thieves and midnight reivers in defence of his people. Now, though, he caught another taint on the wind, and it carried the bitterness of reality.

It was from the heart of the little village that the column of brownish smoke arose, sparking and flaring at its centre. The cottars' rooftops would be all peat, few if any rich enough to afford dry thatch, still less the tiles of slate and stone that castles could command. They would burn slow, and the heavy smoke would roll among the streets and cause choking mayhem to their defenders. Clearly that was the plan of those he saw wheeling and circling around the outer walls, whooping and yelling.

Geordie unleashed a soft oath. 'All alowe! And yon's a sight more men than the Laird had word of!'

'More than he had with him!' agreed Walter softly. 'And they're stopping the ways out between the houses.'

'Like to smoking a warren!' mouthed Wat angrily.

The image made Walter wince. Sooner or later, like those rabbits, the defenders would have to break for their lives into the open, right under the hooves and blades of their foes. What plan had he?

One of the young housecarls thumped the ground. 'For why're we jist daunderin' around up here, then, Colt? Could we no'—'

'Not what?' growled Walter. 'Take them aback? All ten of us? Use your eyes, loon, there's near a hundred horse down there!' He struggled to think of the first Latin text he'd been taught from, Caesar's *Commentaries*. What would that cold clear Roman mind have done with the little he had at his disposal?

'But we canna jist—'

'Did I say we'd do naught? Back ahorse, the whole pack of you! And unrope the cattle!'

'Ye mean tether—' began Wat.

'I said no such thing! Unrope them all!'

The men stared. 'Unrope –?'

'Are ye for making Black Soulis a present, Colt?' grumbled the young servant.

'Aye!' said Walter furiously. 'A grand generous one! Drive them before us! Drive them fast!'

Intent upon the siege, the circling reivers swayed this way and that, massing wherever a breakout seemed likeliest, cutting down any who strayed beyond the sheltering walls, but wary of coming too close within the reach of pike or sword. The noise was tremendous; small wonder that they did not hear the drumming from the hillside above till it was too late. Into the dale poured some twenty-five head of weary, whip-maddened cattle, choking into the narrow level strip by the water, lowing in mindless panic as the bank-edge yawned beyond them and slipped away under their hooves. Wild-eyed, nostrils flaring and smoking in the moist air, they barged their neighbours or half-climbed each other's haunches in a parody of mating. For the second time that day they bolted, the only way they could, with tossing horn and trampling hooves into the outer flanks of the besiegers.

A man yelled; a horse was rolled over and vanished beneath the wave of glistening flanks. Another tried to leap aside, whinnied in dismay, skittered sideways, slipped and toppled into the river with a mighty splash, pinning its rider on the rocks beneath. Reivers afoot vaulted over a low stone wall as the crush came upon them, only to have it bulge and topple on their heads. A reiver yanked back his reins, his mount panicked and reared, kicking, to come down on the points of those wicked horns. Horse and rider fell, screaming together, and were gone. A man on a tall roan rose in his stirrups, warning the other riders back out of the stampede's path, then jerked and doubled over with Wat's arrow in his side. Walter fired a second later as he came within crossbow range, into a knot of startled riders; he hit no man, but the sing of the bolt before their faces set a mighty scare in them. One fell, foot still tangled in the stirrup; the others hesitated that fatal instant, colliding as they wheeled into each other. The stampede, spreading out now, ran into them and they bolted in all directions. Walter's next shot plucked one from the saddle as he went. Their companion's horse burst rearing and plunging out of the crush, saddle askew, a broken stirrup-leather flapping at its side. The stampede, maddened still further by the choking smoke and stinging sparks, plunged around the edge of the buildings and into the rest of the besiegers.

The new arrivals sent a hail of bolts and arrows after it, firing as fast as they could and whooping and bellowing to create an illusion of numbers. With such a crush there was scant need to aim, and many of their darts found a mark in man or mount. The reivers drew back in growing panic, milling uncertainly, and then had to wheel again hastily as the defenders, seeing the sudden break in their tormentors' ranks, came surging out from between the burning buildings with a triumphant skirling yell.

Walter, reining in to reload, looked on them with mingled relief and dismay. Sir Robert Scot had set out with some forty well-armed mounted troopers. Now there looked to be scarce thirty, and some afoot; but with them were the cottars and gudemen, driven by rage and desperation to arm themselves. Some had rusty old blades of long-forgotten style, but the rest bore rakes and scythes and dungforks – God help any who took a wound from those filthy tines! At last Walter saw with relief the familiar, not to say unmistakable, figure of his father atop the monstrous English carthorse of a beast that alone could bear his armoured weight, riding with his round legs stuck out from its flanks like a pair of fat hams with boots on the end. He was roaring at the least forward churls, and leaning precariously from his saddle to drive them along with slaps of his battleaxe and robust kicks. Evidently they hardly needed his encouragement; they crashed into the now broken flank of their besiegers

23

with bloodthirsty enthusiasm and laid about them with a will.

That was enough for the reivers' captain, himself now driven back against the burning buildings and blinded by the reeks he had created. He had no way to marshal a force sundered and panicked by this sudden irruption of cattle, frenzied and witless, and with God knew how many new defenders in their wake. A horn belled, loud and urgent, and before Walter and his men came within reach all the reivers who could broke off the fight and wheeled like ducks rising off a mere. Those who were cut off they made no cast to free, did not wait for stragglers but spurred their weary horses towards the village bridge and ford and the slope opposite, dropping most of the booty they'd snatched up. Walter caught up with a knot of stragglers as they crossed, felled one raw-boned blond fellow with a fine shot, slung bow to pommel and swept out his sword to meet another. But even as their blades met something hissed past, very close, and the reiver coughed horribly, rolled up his eyes and fell. Geordie, immediately behind Walter, brandished his bow with the enthusiastic air of a dog who had just defended his master.

'Damnation, man!' cried Walter, furious and humiliated at being shielded once again. He grabbed at his bow, but the reivers were already making speed up the slope. Around him the farmers and housetroops were mopping up the remnants with vicious enthusiasm. He spied his father, shaking the blood off his great Danish battleaxe, and rode joyously up to him.

'Did you see it, Father?' he yelled. 'Did you see us skelp 'em?'

Sir Robert Scot's face, shaven to the ears and above in the old Norman fashion, was even redder and more inflated than usual, suffused with furious blood as he spied his only child. He spurred towards him, puffing and blowing, and swung his stubby hand in a ringing cuff at his son's ear.

'Where in all the bowels of hell have *you* been?' bellowed the Lord of Branxholme. 'Did my word not say to come at once, hard riding? Eh? And with all you could muster from here-abouts? What's this ragtag of carls and cottars you bring me, and hours too late? Eh? Did you hope all would be done by then and me dead, is that it? Eh? Eh?' He aimed another cuff;

the young man, rubbing his reddening ear, evaded it this time with the skill of years of practice.

'But Father, hear me!' he protested. 'What word? I've had no message of yours! How could I? I've not been at home since the early hours, if it's there you sent!'

'From home – what's this? After the by'relady farmgirls again, is it? No matter!' he snapped before Walter could protest, and bellowed to his men. 'Up, Branxholmes! Up, and on their sleuth! The fewer Liddesdale sees home, the lighter we can sleep o' nights!'

Those who had horses or could seize them came milling towards the Lord as he spurred his heavy-footed mount across the little plank bridge and up the slope to the crest, slipping in the trampled mire the reivers had left. The dip in the hillside beyond was shallow and leaner than the valley, thin-soiled sheep country, a scoured vale whose rocky ribs showed through the skin. A little burn wound between the rocks, with patches of brown marshy grass among the spiky gorse. The reivers were only just crossing it. They rode fast, their leaders racing the swift cloudshadows to the further slope, but not as men do with death at their heels; they seemed in no great fear of pursuit now.

'I'll school 'em!' bellowed Robert, and setting his shield before his great-bellied armour he snatched his long ash-lance from its saddlerest and sent the monstrous horse galloping and skidding down the slope at an unstoppable pace. His troopers bayed like hounds and went crashing along in his wake. Walter and his faithful shadows, more lightly armed and mounted, had to zig-zag their way down through the tangled tussocks and thickets of scratching broom. Below him he saw the reivers turn in alarm at the steel-clad mountainslide bearing down on them, and spur their horses to scatter. But even as Robert Scot reached the valley floor a cold damp gust ruffled Walter's hair, and on its wings a deeper shadow than before came sweeping across the slope. A distant crack and rumble chilled him, and suddenly the first leaden drops of a shower. A cloudburst swept across the little vale like a drawn curtain and enveloped Branxholme and his troopers in icy, blinding water.

Walter's mount balked as thunder thudded in the clouds, but the rain was already upon them, heavy stinging drops that slapped the skin and numbed it. As through a grey veil he saw the scene of confusion below. The boggy little burn was barely a stride for a small horse to cross. Now, after the reivers had pounded through, it was a mass of puddled mire, and the rain was swelling it even as the pursuers came crashing down off the hill, collapsing crumbled banks into bubbling pools that swallowed and sucked at hooves. Horses, beyond stopping, stumbled, whinnying, and collided; men, half-blinded, toppled from their saddles into the muck and skidded there, unable to get up and in peril from the stamping, churning hooves around them. Even Walter reined in barely in time, and was almost shot from his saddle as Geordie's big mare breasted him. 'Haud hard, ye limb o' Satan!' roared the farmer over the din of the rain. 'Haud, ye corbie's bait! Haud, mear, or I'll bile ye!' Shielding his eyes, he saw Walter struggling to keep his seat, and bellowed 'I'm sair sorry, Colt! Naught tae be done wi' the beasts, they're gone gyte!'

Walter ducked down against his tired horse's neck, doing his best to soothe it as it tossed and stamped under the water's whiplash roar; it was like being under a waterfall now, and vision was cut off; even breathing seemed difficult. His ears burned and froze all at once. Then, in that grey curtain, he made out something that moved. Shielding his eyes, he struggled to see it. The hair bristled on his neck; his heart thudded. They were all around him, gliding shadows in the greyness, half-formed and terrible. They were shapes of men, or might have been; for above their bare shoulders were not the heads of men but those of beasts, with horn and tooth and antler. Perhaps they wore skins, but it was hard to be sure. They moved like hunters, cat-sleek and swift, with spears held high and bow-strings taut; the inhuman heads cast this way and that. Even as he saw them they seemed to spy him; the nearest, stag-crowned, whirled and pounced, half-crouching, jerking his spear back for a cast. The point quivered an instant before Walter's horrified eyes, long enough to see the facets of it, the glassy jagged black-ness of the flint. And just as suddenly it was gone, and the cataract was fading to ordinary windblown rain, then into irregular rippling drapes of drizzle. It unveiled a scene of miserable disorder. The charge of the Scots had foundered in the mire; and save for themselves the little valley was empty.

Above them the sky was blue again, the only clouds the white fleecy ones that had been there before, their whiteness reddening now with the evening sun, but with hardly a touch of grey. Of rainclouds there was no trace; yet the valley basin was a glittering sheet of marsh, dotted with muck-clad scarecrows picking themselves painfully out of the mire, grovelling for lost weapons or limping after skittish horses. At the head of it all stood the Lord of Branxholme, dismounted, with a great splash of mire up one side of his armour, staring up at the empty valley side. 'Dick! You there, Gawn! Help me ahorse! We can still pink their tails for them—'

But the demoralized troopers, even those still mounted, made little move to obey. 'There's scarce a spear in haund between us, Laird!' grunted Gavin of Todshaw, their sergeant. 'Our swords're sunk, our bowstrings clagged up! Let yon bastards go, lest aught else befall!'

'Else?' The Lord glared. 'What're you rabbiting about, man?'

It was Wat who said what they were all thinking. 'A worse sending, Laird!'

'Sending?' roared Robert Scot, his eyes starting.

Wat, old enough not to be daunted, glared back. 'Aye, a sending! Did ye see it comin', yon cloud? And where's it gaun tae the now? Nae common drookin', that, frae a clear sky and upon us alane! To say nae worse,' he added quietly.

'Worse!' muttered Sir Robert with apparent scorn; yet something about him gave Walter a sinister thrill of realization. His father had seen something too. And the troopers were all glancing sidelong at one another, uncertain – so had they! Only nobody wanted to be the first to admit it, and risk being tagged for a coward – least of all him.

'No, Laird.' Wat shook his head. 'There was an ill haund in this, and a worse will. Am I no' richt, Gawn? It was his doing: Black Soulis. And what mair could he no' do, the nearer Liddesdale we come?'

The Lord stood a moment. But the defeat in him was obvious. Walter felt it too, the miserable helplessness redoubled with awe and horror at the thought of a man who held the very clouds at his bidding – and worse. Thus it had been ever since young King Alexander had named the Lord Nicholas de Soulis the Keeper of Liddesdale, and hence controller of all the mischief that spilled out of it. At first there had been merely more raids, and dark rumour of what went on behind the bleak walls of the castle of Hermitage; that was bad enough. De Soulis made bitter enemies in those first years, and for all the King's favour they were gathering. He had found it convenient then to depart on his pilgrimage. The Border lords had breathed easier awhile, and set themselves to the sore task of regaining some of their own from the hard men of Liddesdale, that bleak valley with few trees and never a single church. Then de Soulis had returned, and all was worse than before, as he reached out greedy hands first this way, then that, across lands that took his fancy. For wherever his covetous glance lit there came a spate of strange and dark happenings, now no longer confined within the stronghold of Hermitage but falling across the country like a volley of venomed darts, to spread fear and terror and smooth the path of his raiding parties. Some said that his embrace was growing wide enough to encompass the whole Middle March at last, and bend the neck of knight and cottar alike beneath his cruel yoke. Till now it had been smaller men, lesser landholders in the Debatable Land, men of Eskdale and English of the Bewcastle Wastes, foresters of Kielder, who had suffered most at his hands; now, it seemed, his glance had turned northward to the more powerful lords of Teviotdale, and at their head the Scots.

Thus it had been; and with an appalling blasphemy Robert Scot hurled his lance point-down into the mud and stamped. Casting around, he saw Walter, and summoned him with a furious gesture.

Walter swung himself out of the saddle, and approached carefully. He did not greatly mind his father's blows – he knew the weight behind them was fondness far more than cruelty – but there was no sense courting them, either. Robert Scot stood waiting with his short round legs akimbo, wheezing softly with his wrath. 'You see? *You see?* An hour earlier, even – ten minutes, but, and we'd have lain hand o' them! Weighed down the trees from here to Hawick with 'em! If you hadn't been out on your damned night-flitting after some fat-arsed haywench, instead of paying the proper court to—'

'There was another raid!' snapped Walter, seeing his father raise a ham hand again, and a subject he didn't like. 'Liddesdale men, Armstrongs or their kin – they loosed cattle from a dozen steadings, ran off but twenty-five head, mostly Wat's. I rode out on hot trod with Wat and Geordie.'

The older Scot's bulk seemed to swell, but he held his hand. 'On the trod? And who said you should take such a thing upon yourself, you callow wee braggart? Eh? You damned young ninny! Armstrong reivers – what'd you think to do, then, if you caught them up? Play them at battledore? Suchlike men, they'd have slit your belly on the spot! Aye, or run off with you to sauce the bargain! A fine expense I'd have had ransoming you! It'd have been the ruin of the family! We'd have been a sight more than twenty-five kine the poorer, by're Lady, and you with worse than a skelp i' the lugs! Cheaper to wed again and raise another—'

'But we're not the poorer!'

'*What?*'

Walter grinned; he enjoyed pleasing his father. 'I got the cattle back. And I drove them down here to scatter the reivers.'

Robert Scot's eyebrows climbed. 'You— And the Armstrongs?'

'One dead, one fled, one captive, if he hasn't slipped his bonds in all this. Blood-Wullie's son, says Wat.'

'He's no gaun' far,' said Wat. 'Geordie drapped him i' the gorse yonder.'

'Wullie Armstrong's s—oho, ho!' Sir Robert Scot's mood changed, as usual, on the instant. He rubbed his hands and chortled, and shouted to all and sundry. 'Come you here, all of you, and hear this! The Colt's laid a pack of Armstrongs by the heels—'

Walter, who'd known well enough how his father would

react, stopped him. 'It's not like that, Father. It may be worse. You'd better hear it out. We caught up with them at the ford below Skelfhill – only there was this noise—'

Robert Scot listened almost in silence, which was unusual for him. The Lord of Branxholme was still in his late thirties, only a little past his prime, and despite the gross fat of his body and the swollen red cheeks that made him look like a wealthy pig farmer, he was a hard-handed man and filled with ruthless energy. And for all his lack of booklearning he was by no means stupid. Dismay grew on his once-handsome features as he heard, and he began to run an uneasy hand through the brown curls that were now his closest likeness to his son.

'Oakwood!' he muttered, when Walter had done. 'Michael of Oakwood, returned! Oh aye, that's the man all right. I mind him from when he dwelt there before – though I never laid eyes on him but once or twice, and then I was your age, or little older.' He laid an affectionate hand on his son's shoulder. 'That was an uncanny encounter, Colt. You did well not to challenge him or raise his ire, for he's a sorcerer indeed, that one.'

Walter swallowed. 'You knew him so?'

'Aye, I did. One who made the lands about too hot to hold him, and fled to England and then oversea. So he's come back, eh? That bodes little good.'

'He did help me,' Walter reminded him.

Robert shrugged, with a soggy clank. 'Aye, because it pleased his humour o' the moment, or because the Armstrongs affronted him. An unchancy spirit, was what I heard of him then. And now returned! That bodes small good to us. If de Soulis can stir up so much mischief on his own, what will two such sorcerers together not do?' Now he was tugging at his curls in real distress, and his bright eyes bulged in his cheeks. 'And godamercy, Oakwood Tower's scarce ten miles from Branxholme! Well, about de Soulis there may be little enough we can do, for now, with the King's word at his back and the King embrangled elsewhere. Marchwarden Ker's hand is held back from Liddesdale, and de Soulis has walls and men enough to make light of any common rade – to say nothing of whatever black spells he can dispose of. But this Michael, now—' He smacked mailed fist to mailed palm. 'This one we can root out before he gets well dug in, kin or no!'

'But if he's the Emperor's man—' Walter knew of the Emperor, but could hardly imagine him save as a distant vision of dazzling wealth and pomp, of glorious wars fought with infinite armies against the fiend-like Saracens, followers of false Mahound. To his father, though, the name was all but meaningless.

'The Emperor's far off,' he grunted. 'Here it's Alexander's writ that runs, if any! And he has set no shield on Oakwood that I know of, so the law may take its course. Who has greater right to set it in motion than the man's own kinsmen? Right, and duty!' He ground his gauntleted hands decisively. Walter saw how his father was turning the shame of his near-defeat and bafflement from de Soulis against the newcomer. He found suddenly that he himself wasn't quite so sure; but Robert Scot was in full flood, and there was no stopping him. He lifted his head to the evening sky.

'Tammas! Ride ahead to the Tower and tell them we're bringing in wounded! Aye, and that I'll have a pullet to my porridge the night, sauced white and dressed with buttered beans! Have them mull ale for every man's been out with me the day! And ready the irons in the undercellar for an Armstrong!'

With a mighty effort he drew his fast-sinking lance from the sucking mire. 'You, Colt, this night you'll write me a fair hand to Ker of Cessford, delating a complaint and bidding him come with soldiers. I doubt not he'll be glad enough to show the Marchwarden's hand against a sorcerer! Oh aye, we'll hold an inquisition upon Master Michael – and let us find but one small thing amiss and a good clean flame of tar will coulter the Marches of this new infection!'

3 ⛫ The Tower of Oakwood

Even this late in the morning the mists lay low along the Vale of Ettrick. The valley bottom they hid entirely, and turned the high ground into a hazy, distorted world of uncertain distances and sudden appearances. A low crude sheepfold, a stand of windbent oaks, seemed to grow solid in an instant as if newly created, as if the world were forming itself again before the horses' heads. Looking back, the rolling hilltops with their crowns of forest floated in a milky sea, through which a steel-scaled snake writhed slowly, glinting in the dim light, heading for the hidden river.

To Walter, looking back, the line seemed weak; just twenty troopers – what could be done with that? He told himself he was impatient, eager to march not just on the newcomer but upon de Soulis himself; but the truth was he was very close to being scared, and did not dare admit it. It was no help that he sensed the same nervousness in his father; the bluster was that bit louder, the oaths more frequent, the geniality more forced, as if to defy the sound-swallowing mist. Even the great Ker of Cessford seemed subdued and thoughtful, so perhaps he felt the same. Walter forced his nervousness down; this was Scotland, but it was new to him, all the more so in this dank-smelling mirk that hung like white scarves around the forest margins. He had no idea where they were, and decided that was what unsettled him.

'How far now?' he asked his father.

Robert glanced about with great casualness. 'Are you getting impatient? A mile, maybe. I reckon we'd see it from the crest of yon ridge, were it not for these bastard mists.'

'What manner of place is this Oakwood?' Walter pursued. 'Is it a stronghold?'

Robert Scot grunted. 'Oh, aye, it was once – one of the great-est of our kin, below Branxholme in size, but wanting nothing else, a tower and many lesser roofs behind high solid walls. But it's been fallen in repute for generations now, as its lords grew poorer. When last I rode this way, after the late war, it seemed half in ruins, though the English had not passed over it. Neglect by its heir, that's what brings a proud house to the ground! Small wonder, when this one was driven from the land for the evil deeds of him!'

'Evil? Hmm.' Sir Andrew Ker stroked his bushy grey beard. 'I wonder, Robert, I wonder. I knew the man, in some wise; we're much of an age. We were at Roxburgh's Grammar for our schooling, though he was a year or two behind me. He had a great name for scholarship even then, and for wisdom of a sort. And wasn't he the lad for playing strange tricks – though that could be said of many! Why, I myself . . .' He coughed hastily. 'But that's no mind. Later I met him more rarely, but once or twice, for he was so often away at his college in England. But I mind well the time he left Oakwood, when you were but the Colt in your day. As a grown man . . .' He shook his head. 'He had a great understanding upon him, and more than his share of wit. But his humours were strange, and it was ill depending on what shape they might take. Whether evil or good, though, that's a harder thing to say. He made enemies, aye, and the ignorant were feared of him; it's ever among them that the worst stories grow from the least foundation. This much is certain, that he was not forced or driven away. He went abroad of his own accord, and quietly to further his studies as he said. What's become of him, what manner of man he is now . . .' He puffed out his cheeks. 'I know no more than you. Less, since you've seen him. This encounter, though, this . . . sending that laid low three hearty Liddesdale villains at a stroke – I like that not a jot.' He glanced back at his chaplain. 'It bears hard examining.'

Robert Scot scowled. 'It does! Would we had more men to it!'

Ker scratched his bald pate. 'Well, Robert, as times are, neither you nor I have as many lances at call as we'd like. And I'm no more willing to strip my home and my people of guard than you are. Your ten, my ten, that's as much as such a quest is worth – like as not more. We'll meet no such strength at Oakwood, of that I'm certain. Why, even Black Soulis has never openly challenged the warden's men!'

'Not openly,' grunted the Lord of Branxholme, still smarting from four days earlier. 'But I'll wager he will ere long, he's but biding his by'relady time!'

'He won't until he needs to!' Walter pointed out. 'And nobody's in overmuch of a hurry to march against him, are they?'

'D'you wonder at that?' rumbled his father. 'With him squatting there in Hermitage behind the thickest walls in the three Marches, with his pack of bloody wild men from the Highlands and Isles around him, and land and gold and cattle to feed them in plenty? Not to mention all Liddesdale at his back?'

'Well?' demanded Walter, nettled. 'Worse than Hermitage has been stormed or invested! Surely men of *real* mettle—' He ducked his father's cuff.

'Don't prate like a damned bairn!' growled Branxholme. 'What d'you know of war, or of men for that matter? And besides,' he added, lowering his voice and glancing back at the troopers to see they didn't overhear, 'there's more shields than are visible around that one! The tales are that a spell surrounds de Soulis, armours him against all harm . . .'

'Aye,' agreed Walter flatly. 'I've heard tales, too, those and others. Easy enough to heed them, if you've a mind.'

His father blazed. 'You damned wee squab! When you've a home and wife and heir to mind, you'll be no more eager to put your neck on the block – though if you don't learn to mind your tongue it may come there yet!'

Ker smiled tolerantly. 'Easy, Robert, easy! It's no bad thing for a lad to have an opinion of himself, and be apt to the challenge; you were one such in your day. But mind, Colt lad, or you'll be putting your father in an apoplexy! Tales may be true or they may not, and a wise man neither believes nor disbelieves till he's tested; and when he is not sure he makes safe. So it is with your father and with me. And so it should be with you, lest you brag yourself in so deep you daren't swim free!'

Walter subsided; the Marchwarden had seen through him. He felt red humiliation burn on his cheeks. His father grunted, but Ker was merciful.

'Anyhow,' added the Marchwarden, 'there are things more certain than spells to hinder us. De Soulis is the King's kinsman and has his ear, you know that.'

'Aye, but why?' flared Walter, burning with affronted ideals. He had strong ideas about how kings should behave, mostly out of romances. 'Does the King not know what his kinsman's about? Surely if we told him, sent a deputation—'

Ker shook his head sadly. 'Alexander is beset with rebellion in Galloway under O'Neill and in the North under the Lord of the Isles, and himself hopes to reclaim Northumberland and its revenues. And on his doorstep he has the Douglases, as ever. In all this he needs, he must have for his life's sake, a calm Borderland. Which, thanks to the practices of reiving and feuding, in which we ape our heathen Dane ancestors – eh, chaplain? – neither I nor my fellow wardens can guarantee him.' The Marchwarden smiled a little sourly. 'And thanks to the Scots, among others – eh, Robert? He distrusts us. He thinks we are local lords too bound up with local interests; he looks to an outsider not caught up in family loyalties and squabbles. The more we protest, the better he thinks Soulis does his work – the more so since the bastard is careful to keep the powerful English lords quiet and the lesser ones in fear. Alexander will countenance him enriching himself at our expense, thinking that after all it is not so different from the way we live anyway. Aught worse he hears he ignores.' He tugged at his beard and sighed, then hastily resumed his public face. 'But that won't last forever! De Soulis is the King's business and his warden's, and he'll be attended to in good time, with no heed paid to his so-called magics.'

Ker caught sight of Walter's expression, and clapped the young man on the shoulder. 'Be thankful you dwell far enough from him to suffer only the odd cattle raid! In any event you shouldn't be dreaming of daredevil escapades! Not when you've a marriage to look forward to, with all its burdens – and pleasures! Eh, Robert?' He elbowed Robert Scot where his ribs might be, and the two men gave great yeasty chuckles. Walter subsided into a furious silence.

Their humour spilled bile into his mouth. Had it been his father only he might have given vent to it and taken the consequences, but he had no wish to offend Ker or appear ill before him. He admired the Marchwarden, the greatest lord he knew and a schooled and travelled man, who had been to Edinburgh and to the King's Court in Falkland, and to the English court in London, though that was all of two hundred miles away, and even to Paris, twice. Ker and his father were not exactly friends; few Border lords could be, with the continually shifting morass of disputes and blood-quarrels between families, but they had fought together in the late wars and had a degree of wary mutual respect. As the custom was, Walter had been sent to serve as page and carver in another house for a few months, to school him in manners and broaden his acquaintance; it was to Ker's house of Cessford he had gone, and had seldom been happier. Ker had a reputation for ruthless dealings, and a heavy hand in defence of his own interests, but within his own walls he was a kindly master, with more wit in him and less anger than Walter's father, and wider sympathies. His own sons were grown men, off to serve and study abroad in their turn; he had hinted that such experience would benefit any Marchland lord's son, and that he would say as much to Robert Scot. Walter had been beside himself with excitement. But then this offer of marriage had come up instead, and suddenly there was no more talk of travel or study; the alliance was too important.

And there, thought Walter, went his life. He could already see the years closing in around him like walls. Next month a bridegroom, next year a father, yet still a lesser figure at Branxholme, forever under his father's masterful thumb. Robert was only thirty-eight. He might live another twenty years yet – more, if he took after his own father. But Robert was the child of old age, and had inherited his place no older than twenty; Walter might wait till he was older than his father was now. He might have a few farms to his own, a lesser peel tower, and be left to breed children and squabble with his neighbours. He might die thus, and never inherit at all . . . Walter's thoughts ran in ever deeper furrows of gloom.

It wouldn't be so bad if the girl were at least worth it. But this primped-up little convent-mouse Margaret Douglas . . . she was not so bad-looking in her way, her bloodless little way. Like the Virgin in Ker's fine illuminated Bible. Well enough, if a virgin was what you wanted. But she was barely sixteen, damn it! A child – no, a doll, a puppet with a painted face; a vicious tongue, too, for all that. Since she'd come riding in barely a week back he'd tried to be nice to her, more than once; she'd hardly spared him a civil word, wouldn't even look him in the eye, treated him like some dung-booted oaf. Full of her own noble kinship, never missing a chance to run down him and his, or to make him look foolish – a vinegar virgin.

He couldn't understand why she was so hostile; but then he had to admit he didn't understand much about women at all. He couldn't remember his mother; he had no sisters. What little he'd found in books seemed to depict females as either untouchable goddesses or lascivious whores, neither of which fitted her. Pent up at home as he was, all his experience was of farmgirls, and anyone less like them he could hardly imagine. No bawdy giggles, no strong arms and sturdy enveloping thighs; no barnyard smells or risk of lice either, to be sure, but that was a negative virtue. Impossible to imagine her ever sharing his bed or his body, let alone anything like their lusty pleasure – hard to believe she even had the equipment. She looked as if anything so undignified as bodily functions was far beneath her, or did her best to. Hard to credit she was even the same kind of creature.

Not that he was much more at home with farmgirls, he decided unhappily – not as much as his father seemed to assume, anyhow. Oh, true, there'd been that time a year or two back when he'd first discovered how easy things came to a lord's son who wasn't altogether ill-shaped. True, he had gone a little daft in half the barns and stacks and haylofts of the wide estates; but he'd begun to think of that as childish excess. They had begun to seem all the same to him, these girls. He was wise enough, too, to know it was chiefly his rank that put them on their backs so easily, and that hurt his pride. Besides, the endless coupling was exhausting, and left him no energy for other sports. He could have more real fun going out early in the morning with his goshawk, stalking through the misty woods or racing across the wide moors, or shooting at butt with the men of the hall, or in practice of arms. A good fleshly wallowing now and again was welcome; but was that all he wanted from a woman? It didn't seem so – yet what else was there?

The other men he knew didn't seem to find that a problem, but they were landsmen themselves, good lads but no thinkers. Women bedded, cooked, kept house, raised children, shared the fieldwork in season; what was there to worry about? Walter had nobody of his own level in life he could talk to, his father least of all. He'd tentatively tried the priest, only to be treated to a ten-minute sermon on the evils of fornication until the old fellow fell down dead drunk. Walter found himself wondering sometimes if a woman could ever be anything like a companion, a friend and equal. It didn't seem possible. All that coupling, for one thing; fine, but what did that have to do with friendship? And producing children, and raising them – it was nothing he could understand. There must be something else, some other more important thing that bound men and women; but, whatever it was, his intended bride didn't seem likely to supply it.

Court her, as his father kept prodding him? Who'd want to? And how, anyway? His usual approach was an eye, a laugh, a joke or two and a tickling, exploring pursuit. It worked with the farmgirls, often enough, anyway. But try that on this purse-mouthed creature – even if he could get her away from her even tighter-mouthed old nursemaid . . . it didn't bear thinking about. Let him lay but a hand on her and ten to one she'd scream the place down, there'd be ructions, his father furious – and her damned Douglas cousins . . . It definitely didn't bear thinking about.

The path led them among trees again, up to the shallow crest ahead, passing by a massive dead ash half-fallen, the hole at its foot like an earth-mouth lined with gnarled roots and stray gummy strands. *That'll be me*, thought Walter. *Before my time* . . .

Scot, as leader, was holding up his hand. 'We're at the place!'

he said, unusually quietly, as the column clattered to an uneven halt at his back. The mists swirled about as if in answer to his gesture, and Walter saw that they were within a square of hummocks, unnaturally straight, from which whitish stones protruded, weathered and broken, like giant's teeth.

'What's this?' Walter demanded, forgetting his gloom and his bride together, and staring about for some sign of a habitable building.

Ker was also looking around. 'I know the look of these stones,' he remarked. 'There are many such in the Marches, including some in my land. They were raised by the Romans of old, like the great Wall to the south, so this unco' learned wee chaplain of mine tells – eh, Master Elwood?'

The chaplain rode gingerly forward. He was a young man new-appointed, not the whiskered ancient Walter had known, and evidently commanded less respect from his master. 'That's so, my lord. A sentry post, this, or a small fort.'

'Aye, so I've heard,' remarked Robert Scot, not much interested. 'They had a good way with stone, them. It came in handy, I'm told, having so much of it by, for the building of Oakwood – yonder.'

And as they followed his pointing finger they saw that the mists were indeed thinning in the valley below, and that through them, against the silver winding of the Ettrick Water and over the green roofs of the dense woodland that gave it its name, the great rectangular top of a tower arose. Once it must have been a proud strength indeed; but now the grey battlements were jagged and uneven, as if the relic of Rome whose stones they held had infected them with decay. The slate roof gaped open in places at either gable. Ivy and green moss patched the walls even at their tops, and in the airs around the black wings of ravens soared as they squabbled and cawed about their nests.

'A wanchancy haunt!' said Ker after a moment. 'But not a strong one. I doubt we'll find it in defence.'

Robert Scot grinned nastily. 'Maybe that's a shame to us, if so. But there's the path yonder. Forward all, and have a care, it's steep!'

Walter, jarred in his seat as his stubby mount walked sedately but awkwardly down the hill, found himself wishing for that great horse once again. But in no time at all, as it seemed, they were following the path down on to easier slopes, and around a shallow turn the outer walls of Oakwood loomed silently before them. There was a fragrance of woodsmoke in the air, but the way Robert Scot snuffed it might have been sulphur. The Lord spurred on his own big horse to the very step, and lifting his pennoned lance from its mount he beat upon the pitch-stained gate, shaking rotten splinters from its base.

'Open within!' he bellowed, scorning the use of a herald. 'The Marchwarden and the Lord of Branxholme would have words with the master of Oakwood! Open within!'

With a rasping flurry the ravens lifted in a panicking cloud, but for a long moment there was nothing more but silence within. Walter sank inwardly as he feared he might have been cozened, that this Michael might have been bound elsewhere, to Edinburgh maybe, and have misdirected them all deliberately to this old ramshackle ruin. But just as everyone seemed to be drawing breath to speak they heard clearly the grate of slow footprints within, approaching with maddening slowness. At long last a small viewport creaked rustily open in the left gate, and a dry voice spoke, so thickly accented they strained to understand.

'*Messer* Michael Scot, he say – *seigneurs* are very well–come.' But on that tongue the words sounded more like *maestro* and *signori*.

There was the sound of a long bolt being drawn, very, very slowly, and an audible grunt of effort. Nothing happened for an instant, and then with a slow grinding the left gate wobbled back on its hinges. A tall, drooping figure shuffled across the gap, black against the gleam of mist-moistened cobbles, and began to heave open the other gate.

'That's one of them!' hissed Walter. 'The servants I told you of!'

'Aye, indeed!' laughed Robert Scot, glancing around the dilapidated walls revealed. 'But not so very formidable now – why, the place is half a ruin. We could have been inside that gate with ten men!'

'Which may be why he opens it so readily,' suggested Ker. 'Such a man may have other defences than gate and guard, so do not lower yours too readily. Mind what your son saw!'

Scot snorted, but said nothing. The gangling servitor regarded them from beneath his drooping lids as they rode in, and bowed low, but so slowly they were already past. The two older men made for the mounting-block by a long stone trough. Walter slipped easily from his saddle and stood looking around. And it was as if the tower of Oakwood looked back.

All those high walls had for windows were arrowslots, streaks of blackness high in the stones. One or two had crumbled open, though, so they looked like slanted eyeholes in a blank visor; it was all too easy to imagine scornful eyes behind. He shuddered and banished the idea. The lank servant was beckoning and bowing slightly, ushering them towards the broad and well-shaped steps at the towerfoot. Ker beckoned to the chaplain, and spoke quietly to the sergeant of the troopers. Under his command the men dismounted, and began to poke rather hesitantly about the weedridden courtyard and the buildings beyond with their sad sagging rooftrees. Only then did Ker condescend to take any notice of the servant, and with the others in his wake he mounted the steps to the massive door of ironbound planking. This too creaked back before him, and the squat shape of the other servant appeared in the gap, bobbing his bows as if to emphasize his strangeness of aspect and dress. The chaplain stopped dead with a gasp; the servant grimaced with malign humour, enjoying his reaction. Ker appeared not to notice, but Robert Scot growled a trace too loudly. 'A pretty pair! Let's see what manner of lair their master inhabits!'

Walter was wondering the same. A tower so long neglected was a miserable place of chilly nitred stone and trickling damp, where the best comfort was spluttering smoky fires of un-seasoned wood; he found it hard to imagine that sunburned exotic character in such surroundings. He was surprised at the warm draught that blew around him as he passed the door, hinting at strange scents and spices, and the rectangle of golden light that opened in the ceiling at the head of the short stone

41

stair; and he was wholly unprepared for the chamber through whose wooden floor he climbed.

He stood blinking and gaping like any rustic lout at the sudden splendour into which he was transported. He was little used to bright colours, save in nature, in sunset or bird feather; the richest dyes he knew were dull by comparison, and on heavy woollens. He had seen a few brighter foreign fabrics in flashes, on the gowns Ker's lady and other women of wealth wore upon special occasions; but here the whole chamber was aglow.

Nothing of the bare stone was visible. The very ceiling was covered by a billowing canopy of silk, panelled in alternate scarlet and yellow, hung with gilded cords and sewn with glittering bullion; silver lamps hung on chains below it, others stood on tall wooden stalks, all burning sweet oil in steady flames before bright reflectors. Their light fell on the figures that rampaged through the entangling foliage of the tapestries lining the walls, dark-skinned mustachioed men in outlandish headdresses of brightly coloured cloths, fighting on horseback, running long lances at one another or cutting down at ranks of spiked helms with bright curved scimitars, brandishing short bows at strange deer and impossibly gaudy birds, feasting with bold-eyed women dressed in diaphanous costumes.

To Walter it looked like a vision of Paradise. Behind and between the tapestries ran rich brocade hangings, heavily embroidered with peculiar shapes and characters, some hanging like hooks from bars, others writ large like swift energetic slashes of a brush, yet more in thin curlicued scribbles with dots and slashes above – obviously writing, but of no meaning he could guess. Here also much of the embroidery was in gold and silver thread, and gleaming with precious stones. Only the fireplace and floor were visible; but the old stone hearth was hung about with yet more brocade, and figures carved of glossy pale stone gleamed at either side of it. The logs piled high in the fireplace burned with a fair light and sweet scents that seemed to change from moment to moment. The floorboards were bare but smooth and gapless, glistening mirror-bright with waxing, save where heaps of gaudy cushions, embroidered and tasselled, tumbled across them. By one, beneath a lamp, two or three massive books in rich bindings were piled carelessly, with tags of coloured silk protruding from their pages; Walter itched to get his fingers on them, but books were precious possessions one did not touch without leave. The air was warm and heavy as a summer noon.

Robert Scot was gazing about him, too thunderstruck even to swear. Ker was little better, for as a travelled man he had a fair idea of the wealth represented before him, and the remoteness of its origins. 'Man, what's this? What's this? The King of France himself has no chamber so fine!'

'Where would all these stuffs be from, Sir Andrew?' asked Walter. 'Those are no costumes of France in that tapestry, are they?'

Ker nodded. 'That they are not! But from where . . .' He scratched his head again. 'Some of the writings . . . I mind now, those thin curlicues, they're the script of Araby. I've seen the like on shields and writings Crusaders have brought back.'

The chaplain coughed discreetly. 'Very like, my lord. And that one there is of the Hebrew – *Aleph*, I believe.'

'Aye, maybe,' answered Ker absently. 'But these others – it seems to me I've seen the like, but only on coins, copper and silver and gold that traders have carried from afar. From Hind, or the land of Cathay, where the silk once came from before the Greeks won its secret. God alive, there's half the world here in this one room!'

'And all of it heathen!' muttered the chaplain, but Ker was turning to Walter.

'How on earth did he ever get it all here, lad? How long did you say this baggage train of his was?'

'Ten or twelve mules? Well laden, but still not enough!'

'No indeed!' said Robert Scot. 'And in so little time, a day or two, no more – how could he have done this?' The chaplain crossed himself. But Walter was not asking himself how so much as why. It did not seem in keeping, somehow, with the quiet authority of the man he had met; there was nothing quiet about this. This was all display, surely, designed to overawe and daunt simpler men. And it had certainly succeeded – but to what end? One of the white hearthside statues drew his eye; it was female, very much so, a voluptuous young girl with garlands in her hair, caught half rising as if from the bath. Her face was pure and pale in the white stone – like Margaret, thought Walter – but the firelight flushed along her bare haunches. The faint cough from behind him hardly broke into his thoughts; it sounded like the chaplain again. But the voice that followed, quiet and calm as it was, spun them all about like tops to a whip.

'I am sorry to have kept you waiting, my lords. I was occupied elsewhere.'

Andrew Ker drew a deep breath. 'That's no matter, Michael. You'd hardly have expected a visit.'

'No?' Dismounted, Michael Scot was taller than Walter had expected, of a height with Ker and topping Robert and himself, though leaner and less broad-built save at the shoulder. He looked older, too, his brown face less smooth and the lines of care deeper and more apparent, the streaks of white clearer in his long hair and beard. His teeth, though, showed unusually whole and white in his slight smile. He wore dark red again, but his loose light robe, without belt or sash, seemed plain and austere against the glittering gorgeousness of the room. His bow was impressive, though he sounded more amused than formal.

'I'm honoured by it. A long time since we met, Andrew – you become the wardenship as I thought you would. God rest your father, you've grown very like him, but wiser. Your sons fare well in the Low Countries, as I hear, and I am glad that your lady thrives. And you, Sir Robert – when I last laid eyes upon you, you were a lad as able to slip through a lady's girdle as the Colt is now. And as apt! No need to ask after your health and prosperity, for you're clearly a man of greater substance.'

He chuckled deprecatingly as Robert's nostrils flared. 'And your son, of course, I've had the pleasure of meeting. I'm glad to have helped you regain your cattle, Colt, the more so as you used them so cleverly against the reivers. Ach, but I should not keep welcome visitors afoot like a tenants' deputation! Sit you down, all, and make yourselves comfortable.'

He indicated the heaps of cushions. Ker's moustaches twitched, but he settled himself stiffly on to the nearest and sat upright, with his legs crossed, as at a campfire. Robert Scot lowered himself awkwardly on one hand, lost his battle and plumped down hard on his broad buttocks with his spurred feet sliding straight out in front of him. Walter, struggling to keep a straight face, sprawled down among his heap with boneless ease. The dark man confirmed his suspicions by drawing up a plain three-legged stool, unseen till then, and perching himself on it with austere dignity. 'You'll have some wine, of course? Excellent!' He didn't wait for an answer, but clapped his hands. '*Ehi*, Gilberto! Gilbyn! *V'apportame del vino! Da Firenze!*' He was in command, as he had been since he entered the room, wrong-footing them completely.

Ker cleared his throat tactfully, but Robert Scot boiled over and forestalled him with a blunt barrage. 'I'll wait on that wine of yours, Master Michael! I want something more from you, and that's to know what ill wind's blown you back to the March-lands, and what you mean to do hereabouts, and what's your compact with that bastard Black Soulis!'

Michael raised a quizzical eyebrow. 'A mort of questions, Sir Robert! And hardly hospitable to a stranger and a trespasser, let alone as a welcome for a kinsman returned to his own land and roof!'

Robert flushed. Hospitality was a rigid custom in these barren lands, even between enemies. But he pursued his attack all the harder. 'A welcome can give place to an honest answer! We've woes enough from one sorcerer across the hills – d'you think we're going to let another plague us on our very doorsteps? I don't give a tinker's fart for kinship if that's the matter!'

Ker's face twisted, and he caught Walter's eye. Robert had opened his mouth too wide and too soon, as usual, and made clear accusation of sorcery, before witnesses. That left Michael free to make the obvious and reasonable response. 'I'm grieved you should think that of me! What cause have you? What evil have I done you but save some twenty-five head of your tenants' best cattle, and maybe your son also? And this talk of a compact with the Lord de Soulis – I've spoken with that man but once, and that was at the court of Falkland these eighteen years gone. A scholar of parts he seemed to me, in some ways, but not a man I'd make a friend of.' He clapped one hand to his knee. 'But be that as it may, I know such charges are often laid against poor scholars who seek only the benefit of men, and I must answer them fully. You may search this worn old peel-tower of mine from top to foot and seek what proof of sorceries you may find. So, only that you keep your men in hand, and break or take nothing, I give you leave; any doors that are barred I will unlock to you. But you have had a long ride, and I ask again, will you not take some wine first?'

The ugly servant pushed his way between the hangings and proffered delicate beakers of coloured glass. Ker forestalled Sir Robert by accepting one, and the servant charged it from a heavy earthenware flask. Robert hotched and blew, held out his hand grudgingly but put the drink to his lips with a will. The chaplain, too, was eager enough, but made the cross repeatedly over his goblet, to which Michael responded with a grave *Amen!* Walter smiled to himself, enjoying their discomfiture with cheerful anarchy; at least this Michael was entertaining. He watched the dark wine flow and bubble with little interest, till he caught the aroma and sipped it curiously – then eagerly. He was used to wine that had travelled too long and too far north; it was mostly rather sour, and usually he preferred a good ale. But *this* . . . He held the glass up to the firelight and the statue caught his eye again, and held it an instant too long. He became aware of the dark man's amused glance.

'I see we have a lover of art among us! You admire the *Aphrodite Calliphygia*, Colt? It is of the old Greek fashion, though a mere Roman copy – the young goddess of love. You know of her, chaplain – and the meaning of her title?' The chaplain muttered something, and blushed an amazing scarlet. 'An appropriate interest for one to be wed so soon – to a lady of the Douglases, isn't it, Robert?' Walter wanted to sling a cushion at Ker for the look on his face.

'Daughter of Douglas of Greenshawe, God rest him!' rumbled Robert Scot with unabashed pride. The wine was mellowing him already, and the subject was guaranteed to. 'Meg, child and sole heiress! And a lovely wee thing in her person, too! It wasn't easy to bring it about, but we haggled it fast i' the end!'

Michael Scot cocked an eyebrow. 'A Douglas heiress! That's a powerful bond to bring into the family, Robert! There's few win so much from the wild Douglases – peace, alliance and a good portion with it, if Greenshawe thrives as it did!' Robert looked smug. 'I congratulate you – and you, Colt, you're a lucky man! To the wedding!'

Walter glared. Now he was tangle-footed, too. 'I thank you for that,' he muttered rebelliously, and tossed back the wine. 'A good wish is always welcome – if it comes from an honest source.'

His father chuckled approvingly. The dark man smiled, apparently unabashed, but held his peace as the leathery-faced little sergeant came clumping up the stairs. Like the others he stopped in open-mouthed shock at the splendour of the room, then gathered his wits and bowed stiffly to Ker. 'We've done as ye bade, Marchwarden. Made search of ivry outhouse and a' the walls. Found them toom as a drum, for the most part, and fall'n from use. For the rest, naethin' but what's proper, tools and tackle and sich, and nae much o' that. Nae sign of hidin' places, either, nor of aught buried; and the walls are no' sae thick they'd permit much. So there's only this tower, and the stables – they're barred tight. Shall we stave in the doors?'

'Barred,' said Michael Scot mildly, 'as is only good reason in these troubled parts, the more so with such ill-maintained walls. There's no need to go staving in any door; any and all I'll open to you, my lords. The stable first, before your men do anything hasty, and then the tower?'

The stables were set back into the slope, with high doors which looked to be the soundest in the place, and a solid and weighty lock. The key Michael drew from his robe looked complicated and heavy, but turned with silent ease. A warm waft of horsey odour drifted out into the damp air. 'It's being so much below ground that helps to keep the heat in,' he remarked. 'I could wish my forebears had done as much with the tower. I miss the warmth of the Southlands, now.'

'Or of somewhere a damned sight warmer!' muttered Robert Scot below his breath. The dark man flashed him a faint smile, and tugged the door open.

'Mother of God in his mercy!' exclaimed Robert. 'What a magnificent brute!'

The stable was a cave, probably a natural one, divided by strong wooden stalls. In some of them, along the further wall, ten mules looked up as the humans entered; finding neither the scent of food nor the jingle of tackle, they dropped their heads to eating once again. But from the first stall on the other side the great black warhorse tossed its head and stared at them all with wild rolling eyes, whinnying and stamping a greeting to Michael as he went up to it.

'Is that one of these Arab breeds I hear of?' demanded Robert.

'I got him in Spain,' said Michael, caressing the heavy black muzzle with the same air of absent-minded amusement. 'A gift, so I know little of his provenance. But at times, yes, I think there may be some Arab in him.'

'The head is larger than most Arab beasts I've seen,' mused Ker. 'And he is heavier at shoulder and thigh, too, a powerful charger. But he has all the spirit they tell of.'

'I can see that!' laughed Robert, his eyes alight. 'God, he'd be the envy of any lord in the land! Michael, man, as kinsman to kinsman, how much'll you take for him?'

Even Ker winced; Walter ground his teeth. Michael eyed the Lord of Branxholme with reproachful politeness. 'My lord Robert, it grieves me to refuse you, but this is my own mount, and I will not sell him.'

Robert's eyes screwed up in his fat cheeks. 'Come, man! I'll have no haggling over such a bargain, I'll meet your terms! Or give you mine as generous as you'd get anywhere. You may have the pick of my stable, five fine horses for that one, and a sum in gold to cap the deal!'

Michael shook his head gravely, his long hair brushing his shoulders and a strange look in his eye, amusement tempered by something darker, sadder even. 'My lord, as I said, he was a gift. Even if I wished to sell him, I am not free to.'

Robert's full mouth twitched. 'Ach, be damned to that! Who's to know, so far away? I can give you a rich price for him, enough to rebuild this old ruin! Or better than money – land enough that once was Oakwood's and passed to me, a dozen farms by

Ashkirk way and Essenside. You could be a lord as your fathers were, and not some petty scholar in the Southlands! There, that for one beast!'

Walter stared unbelieving at his father, both for the crassness of his behaviour and for the lightness with which a part of his inheritance was being tossed away. Robert Scot didn't notice, as intent on his prize as on a hunting quarry, and as voracious, almost snarling with the intensity of his wanting. The prize itself cast an opaque glance at the noisy intruder, almost as if it were amused by the row, and champed placidly away at its manger. The dark man said nothing, but slowly shook his head.

'Damn you,' choked Robert. 'I'll not be trifled with so, you haggling at me as if we were rag-arsed chapmen! I'm generous to you because you're kin – but I'll not let you say nay to me. It's my duty to have that horse, and by're Lady I mean to!'

'Your duty to have what does not belong to you, my lord?'

Robert struggled to take on a note of pleading reason. 'Think, Michael! What good's such a mount to a sedate old scholar? Such a one was formed for pride and war, for bearing great lords! It wastes away without a weight of armour on its back!'

There was a wry gentleness in the scholar's voice that some-how chilled Walter worse than any wrath could have done. 'My lord Robert, there you may be right. I doubt not many a great lord deserves to own the beast, far more than I. And believe me, I'd as soon accord you the honour as any. But it cannot be.'

'I'm warning you, Michael! I'll have that beast! I can no more see it go without its proper use than you – you—' He struggled for a comparison, and showed unusual imagination. 'Than you would see a fine rich book set to kindling!'

'I've seen books enough set to kindling, Robert,' said the Lord of Oakwood in a wintry voice. 'Many, under the pyres of those condemned as sorcerers—'

'Aye, well, that's what we're here to prevent!' interrupted Ker hastily, before Robert Scot could blurt out a reply. 'And not for horse-trading! What would you rather have, Michael, us whom you know, at least, or the commons and churchmen in a mob? It's come to that before, as well you know!'

The dark man bowed slightly. 'Sir Andrew, I'm happy in your

hands. Sergeant, would you care to cast your eye around?'

As Michael turned away Ker rounded furiously on Robert, who was still trying to talk. 'You were ever a grasping chiel, Branxholme, but you plumb the depths here! You place us so far i' the wrong we're bound now to his forbearance, and not he ours!'

Robert Scot planted his feet squarely in the stable straw. 'Say on, Ker! It'll not persuade me other! I've come a long way here today, and I'll not be palmed off by some prating old scholard! I offered him a fairer price than he'd get in Edinburgh itself, did I not? He can take that, or go without and be damned to him!'

'You came a long way?' hissed Ker. 'You came to do inquisition upon him, man! At nobody's behest than yours!'

Walter caught his arm. 'Father, leave it! Would you come to a man's house with fire and sword, and then dare to bargain for his goods? And a kinsman at that? Is that the honour of the Scots you'd pass on to me?'

Robert flushed red and shook him loose, but only lifted his arm and didn't strike. 'I offered him an honest price and more,' he said sullenly. 'He gave me insult back.'

'An it were me I'd have ca'ed the head from your shoulders!' grated Ker.

'Shall I get the beast for you, Father?' demanded Walter with a fury that surprised him. 'Shall I ride back with a few troopers this very night and set all to the sword and take what I want? An old scholard and two gowk servants, I could do it all by my own hand even. Is that a fitting gift from your son? A work such as Black Soulis might be proud of?'

The stable reek was growing strong as troopers raked through the small dungheap with wooden forks, and combed the straw from the trodden earth floor. Robert Scot thrust out his lower lip. 'Hold your tongue, boy,' he muttered. 'I offered him a price as any man might, did I say more? He was seeking to bargain, that's all. Or so it seemed. I'd no thought of, of—'

'I trust you will not, then,' said the Marchwarden quietly. 'For if there is such a reiving here, then inquisition may be marching to another door soon – the swifter if there's a new stallion behind it. Do you heed me, Robert? I cannot keep de

Soulis from his Devil's ways, but I'll not suffer others to ape him within my arm's reach – least of all those I thought had more wits and more honour.'

'Aye, aye, I hear you, I hear you,' muttered Scot. He looked at Walter. 'Go to, you're a good son; I'll not be hasty with you. It galled me to see such a beautiful beast go wasted, that was all.'

Walter contemplated the stallion flicking its tail calmly. It returned his gaze sardonically. 'Aye, Father, I longed for the creature the moment I saw it. But less so now, somehow.'

The troopers were already shovelling back the dungheap. It could have hidden little, since the stable was only recently in use again. 'That's that, Marchwarden,' the sergeant reported. 'Naught agley, it's as it should be.'

'Then, my lords, I'll show you the tower,' said Michael amiably. He eyed the troopers' dung-caked boots. 'But not the men, if you please. The sergeant will suffice to do your searching, I think.'

Most of the tower was empty, and had obviously lain so for years. In some rooms dust lay thick and untrodden, and webs garlanded the walls; in others the shutters had decayed, and leaves and other debris blown in, rotting the few poor furnishings and the floor timbers themselves in places. The sergeant, probing one such chamber, all but fell through, disappearing to the waist before Walter seized his collar; he was notably less diligent from then on. Robert Scot, stewing silently, kept his bulk firmly in the doorway, and tried every stone step before he trusted it. In the high chambers beneath the roof the ravens billowed up shrieking as old doors were forced back, and owl-chicks peeped angrily in the chimneys. The roof timbers themselves looked as if they had sprouted anew with dark quivering leaves: bats, and the floor below was dark and slimed with their stench. Only a few rooms of the tower had been cleared, a wide bare solar, devoid of furnishing, a garderobe recently scrubbed with aromatic herbs, and bedchambers for Michael and his men.

They were simple enough, the servants' rooms, with cot and chest and blanket, ewer and bowl, and a simple stool or two for furnishing. Michael's was richer, with heavy hangings and a great wooden aumbry, showing signs of recent scrubbing, in which hung a few rich robes of various hues and more simpler ones, some riding garments of figured leather, plain cottes and hose, shirts and drawers of fine linens and silks, shoes and boots of brightly coloured Cordovan leather, some with pointed or even upturned toes. Over the head of his plain cot, little better than his servants' save for the furs that strewed it, hung a massive rosary and crucifix of blue stones and gold, at which the chaplain nodded in approval and admiration. A chest beneath, well locked and chained, proved to contain a few jewels, a draft upon a Jewish goldsmith in Edinburgh, and a decent but not outrageous quantity of fine Imperial coin. All in all, much what any minor lord's chamber might contain, although Walter was slightly surprised by the massive hand-and-a-half broadsword that lay with sheath and belt across the window-seat. The only unusual note was the table beyond, laid with candle, slate and chalk and a writing-stand, and the hefty chest beside it, lined with bright carpeting and brim full of books.

'There must be well nigh twenty here!' exclaimed the chaplain, seizing one and peering at it, and then another.

'Twenty?' Robert Scot looked surprised to find there were so many writings in the world. Walter was more astonished at the idea of anyone travelling with such a valuable library. 'And what can so many books treat of?' his father demanded, snuffing like a hound on sleuth.

'Of many things,' said Michael smoothly. 'Of chronicles and the works of men, a few. Of commentaries upon holy texts, a few others. Of the processes of nature; of the ills of the human body, and their remedies. Of the philosophy of measurement and exactitude, and of right reckoning. Of maps and of voyages. Of the philosophy of the ancients, and of its relation to the study of religion. Have you Greek, chaplain? No? A shame, for you will not have heard of Aristotle, nor of Plato. Nor the Moorish tongue, I dare say. There is a man by name Avicenna . . . Many of those are renderings into our tongue of such ancient texts, made at the University of Toledo under the auspices of the archbishop, some even by my unworthy self.'

'And not one of them on, say, the processes of matter?' enquired Ker with equal calm. 'Of the Philosopher's Stone, maybe, and the alchymic work? Or of foretelling the future through the courses of the stars?'

The dark man smiled in his beard, and parried deftly. 'My noble master the Emperor Frederick, upon whom the good Lord rain blessings, has many such in his Imperial library in Palermo. I would carry no such curiosities with me. And, as you can see, I have none of the apparatus I believe such work demands. As for these books, you may copy the titles as you see them, chaplain, and send to the see of Durham to know if any are forbidden, or to Edinburgh. I believe you will find nothing amiss.'

'I believe so also,' said Ker. 'But do so, Master Elwood, nonetheless. And with that, Master Michael, I believe our search may end, for I think there is no more to be seen. Sir Robert,' he said, severely, 'you were right to bring your concerns to my attention. But I find not the slightest ground for suspicion of any wrongful practices in this kinsman of yours, and I consider we should retire with apologies.'

Sir Robert Scot had been silent throughout, as a man biding his time. Now, planting his feet as before and clasping his hands behind his back, he spoke with a barely suppressed note of triumph in his voice. 'Thus far I agree, Marchwarden: we have found nothing. But that does not mean there is nothing to be found. There remain two matters we should not leave unanswered. The first, Master Michael, is the strange means by which you hurled down the reivers my son was chasing at your first encounter. I must ask that you explain that. The second . . .' he paused, savouring his words, and the effect they would produce. 'Have you not, as I was informed by the Lord Bishop of Carlisle himself upon his Grace's spending a night at Branxholme some seven years past, written a, a *treatise* upon the art of magic? Which must mean – must it not? – that you have yourself practised it! And that must at least make you an ally of de Soulis, if not a confederate – and whom he serves, we know only too well! Riddle me that, then, Master Michael!'

Ker drew in his breath sharply, and Walter balked. Robert Scot grinned at them, a wolfish baring of the teeth; clearly he had been looking forward to this. The dark man sighed, apparently more wearied than disturbed, and leaned against the window-ledge. 'With a will, kinsman, with a will. The first, the fire I cast upon those Armstrongs – that I have already explained to the Colt. It is a simple matter of compounding ordinary substances, not unlike the Greek fire that is used by the navies of the Emperor of the East against the heathen, and is deemed a lawful and Christian weapon. I could teach you to make it, I could teach any churchman to make it, any goodwife even, as simply as bread or porridge and without any form of incantation or diabolical aid. There is some danger lest the mix take fire in the grinding of it, but no more. Compressed into an earthen vessel and lit with a wick, it shatters the pot and throws it against an enemy, with a loud report as you have heard, Colt, and a nasty smell. But except at very close range its power is more to frighten than to kill; it is less dangerous than, say, a crossbow. A little sulphur, a little charcoal made very pure, a lot of potash, that forms beneath a dunghill or grows as nitre upon the walls. Unless you get the mix just right and the ingredients pure, which one rarely does, it only sizzles fiercely. Where is the witchcraft in that?'

'None that I can see,' admitted Ker unhappily, 'though I cannot say I like the sound of it. But such tricks alone are hardly proof of evil-doing. This magical treatise, though – what have you to say to that, ey?'

'Only this – that as Sir Robert accuses me, so I did. In my youth, exploring and credulous, I did indeed dabble in the arts of divination and of necromancy – though to no ill end, seeking only to divine the secrets of the world for its benefit, and the blessing of mankind. And indeed, I made no secret of my quest, but wrote of it openly and without shame, a text which is now to be found in the universities of Toledo and Cordoba, and in Sicily, and in many other great libraries. But in the fullness of time I was convinced of my error and credulity, and I recanted and did penance for this. I have written on many other and more hallowed subjects since – on the art mathematical, upon the art physiognomical, upon the arts of healing and medicine after the Moorish masters.'

Robert Scot snorted. 'Recanted, aye – so any man may claim with the trial and the flame before him! But words are cheap, Master Sorcerer!'

'Indeed they are, cousin!' said the accused man, still mildly, and Walter saw suddenly that he too had been holding something in reserve and was enjoying it also. 'But this, now – this is beyond price!' He handed the chaplain the folded square of soft vellum he drew from the bosom of his robe. 'Will you not translate this for the others, master priest? But handle it with reverence!'

Suspiciously the young chaplain unfolded the vellum, held it up to the window light, and read *'To our trusty and well beloved servant*—' He stopped suddenly and stared at Michael. 'You are a priest?'

Michael inclined his head. 'In minor orders only, entered at Paris when I studied for the Trivium and Quadrivium.'

That was usual enough with learned clerks and scholars, but Walter knew why both Ker and his father stirred uneasily. It removed this enigmatic man one step from the everyday laws of men and into the privileged realm of the canon law, where they could not so easily pursue him. The canon read on. *'We, Hon— Honorius, by God's grace . . .'* His voice shook and faltered; the leaf quivered in his hands. He glanced quickly down the page, and as he came upon the seal at its foot he stiffened as if a lance had been thrust down his back. Honorius? Who was Honorius? Then an awful suspicion dawned upon Walter, and he leaned over the chaplain's arm to glance at that seal. There was a tall crown on it, and a bunch of keys . . .

Ker was shaking his head; Robert Scot was looking sick. The Emperor might be far away; but the Pope was here, no further than the nearest church, no further than the young chaplain beside him. And Walter suddenly felt the eye of God, who was everywhere, heavy upon them. 'This is a bull of indulgence and absolution,' said the chaplain. 'Given in due form and under the seal of His Holiness the Pope at Rome in the year 1228 to Master Michael Scot—'

'Is it valid?' enquired Ker heavily.

'It is, my lord,' said the chaplain.

'How do you know?' growled Robert. 'You new-weaned babe, with no more beard on your cheeks than the fuzz on a peach – cannot such things be falsely counterfeited, seal and writing both? Could you tell them if they were?'

'My lord, I cannot swear to it, but—'

'Of course not, you're young,' said Ker with fatal kindness. 'We'll needs send off to determine the truth of this—'

'No further than Glasgow, my lord,' said Michael with a smile. 'To Father Ambrosius, the Papal emissary to this year's diocesan synod. I met him last at Alnwick Castle when we lay there overnight on our way northward from Whitby. It was in their chapel I last took communion; and I had better welcome from the English Percys, it seems, than among my own kin.'

'You took communion in the company of the papal emissary?' demanded the chaplain. 'And you received absolution, of course?'

'He heard my confession,' said Michael humbly.

Very slowly and carefully the young chaplain folded up the vellum and handed it ceremoniously back to him. He turned to the others. 'My lords, I will write to confirm this if you think it worthwhile, but I have every reason not to doubt it. Subject to that, all is in order.' His voice took on a tinge of stony authority, as if he were savouring a mild satisfaction for past slights, even kindly meant. 'I must therefore declare under the authority of Our Lord and of his Church that this man, Master Michael Scot, cleric, is to be regarded as innocent of all charges laid against him. The inquisition is at an end. Let any question it at their peril.'

Robert opened his mouth to bellow, but no sound emerged. Ker shook his head so hard the ruff of greying curls beneath his broad dome stood out. 'That's it, Robert. Leave it, and come. You also, Walter, and you, Master Elwood; you've done your work fairly. Sergeant, go make ready our mounts!'

The Marchwarden relieved his feelings by leaning out of the window to bellow at his troopers. By the time he reached the yard they were already in their saddles, eager to leave this dismal ruin. Michael had come down to see them off with ease and courtesy, but Ker's bow to him was curt and embarrassed.

'No, I thank you, no stirrup-cup, we must ride.' He seemed about to wheel away, but thought better of it as a thought appeared to strike him. 'But, Master Michael, you say you know little of the man de Soulis and of his evil works. And yet, recanted and forgiven, you still have at least some knowledge of the arts he's reputed to practise, more than any other I can call on here. Might it not be possible that two such practitioners could grow acquaint'?'

The dark man stopped short, fingered his beard a moment, and then suddenly flashed Ker a sardonic smile. 'It might be so, perhaps. Indeed it might. Who can tell?'

'Who indeed?' said Ker dryly. 'I'm not the man to foretell the future. But if such a thing should come about, and the results profitable, I could very well ensure no further problems of this kind – say, with a populace not so obedient to the rulings of Mother Church.'

Again the smile. 'Sir Andrew, I rely upon your name in this. I will consider upon it, and send word of anything I learn.'

'Do so,' said Ker shortly. 'Master Michael, I leave you in God's grace. May I never find you otherwise.'

'Amen to that!' growled Robert Scot, and turned his mount to spur out of the courtyard, cursing as it stumbled on the uneven ground. Ker and the chaplain, riding with a new dignity, followed him, and last before the troopers Walter. And, as it is told, he looked back at the steps, where Michael Scot stood with his hand raised in benison, and above him the window of the great chamber, with all its riches. The sun, falling from the noon now, struck through it and lit a patch of ceiling and wall. It was bare. Of the silks, the hangings, the tapestries he had seen there was nothing. There was only the lime-washed stone, clean but bare.

Then Walter was hurried on out as the impatient troopers urged on their mounts. When he looked back the gates were already closing, the view hidden. What he had seen or not seen, he could no longer be sure of. Shaking his head, he turned, and catching up with his father, still silent and crestfallen, he rode with him out of the vale and to the forested heights above Ettrick.

★

But more is said of Master Scot than that, at this moment. More that must have been guessed at, as the tales go, or revealed by him, even, at a later hour. For he turned not back to his warm room above, but to the stables and the stall of his great black horse. He gazed at it a while as it browsed lazily, and shook his head. 'Ever you are the bone of contention, sowing tares where most I need the wheat!' He sighed. 'Well, well, all things are according to their nature, and that is yours.' He moved closer to the great animal and patted its neck. 'And now you must gird up your strength; for I take you soon on a little jaunt as perilous as any we've undertaken, you and I. Are you apt to that?'

The black head tossed, the white eyes stared and rolled, the huge teeth champed and foamed. A whinny rang around the stone, and the pack-mounts tugged at their tethers, teeth bared, eyes rolling. A great black hoof stamped, and the earth floor cracked; overhead the tower itself seemed to ring and shudder at the noise. And a mile hence, already, climbing the slopes of the vale into the arms of the great forest, the lords and their troopers started in their saddles and looked back, Walter longest of all.

4 ♜ The Dead Riding

The mists had lifted as the lords rode off, and the green gown
of the forest drew in around the road, each leaf jewelled and
fragrant in the pale spring sun. But the lords had no mind to
it, and rode in silence among the birdsong, unwilling to speak
lest the iron tang of failure and folly on their tongues spill out
in recrimination. Quarrels were only too easy to spark in the
Marchlands, and the Devil's own job to end; and these were
the highest of two great families, for whom a bloodfeud could
spell lasting ruin. Only the chaplain rode content. Walter saw
gladly that Ker seemed to bear him no ill will, even a sight more
regard. The man carried himself well and without fear; Walter
could respect that, too. He reserved his anger for the mocking
sorcerer; for now he was surer of the charge than ever, though
he had no better warrand for it. He longed to tell Ker of what
he had seen, or not seen; but every way he could shape it on
his tongue sounded foolish and thin, as if he were trying to
salvage some poor credit from the matter. So it was that, when
the time came for their ways to sunder, he said nothing of it,
but contented himself with thanking the warden for his trouble.

By then Ker had recovered his courtesy, and even Robert
Scot shamefacedly made his peace, promising him the fattest
acorn-fed hog from the renowned Branxholme stock when next
he passed by. The Marchwarden countered that he'd be content
with his share at the wedding feast; that somewhat restored
Robert Scot's humour, and the two men parted in another bout
of elbow-nudging. Ker and his men set off along the long path
southwest over the hills to the marches of Jedworth and the
great abbey of Jedburgh, where they must pass the night on the
road to Cessford. The Scots took their own track south.

The troopers turned merrier at the prospect of only six or

seven miles' riding to home, food and ale, but their lords rode
silent again. Robert was breathing heavily, brooding, now and
again twisting the reins in his ham hands. Walter was startled
to find himself worried about his father, as he never had been
before. He had feared for him in battle or feud, but this was
different, in a way he couldn't define. Somehow Robert seemed
smaller in Walter's eyes, a more fallible man than the harsh,
domineering giant he usually appeared, and yet, strangely
enough, one it was easier to feel fond of. He knew better than
to show it, though, except by quiet and forbearance, and attention to the needs of the journey. As they neared Branxholme,
riding by their own familiar fields and woodlands, Robert began
to recover and respond. 'A bad day's work, this, lad,' he said
heavily. 'We have shamed ourselves before a kinsman, and
before the Marchwarden – I most of all. And I have set you a
low example.'

'None I had sight of, sir,' said Walter quietly.

His father shook his head impatiently. 'And what now? Suppose we begin to have troubles with this Michael, will Ker heed
us then? For troubles we may have. Somehow I feel surer than
ever some sorcery was at work there all the time, though the
law of God and man go against it – God's wounds, that he was
laughing at us, the bastard! Sniggering up his stupid outlandish
sleeves!'

'Father, I felt the same! And yet, I don't know why, I didn't
think he had any great ill will. He just wanted to be rid of us
and in peace. But I did see one thing – nothing I could swear
to, but—'

'Aye, lad, what? Speak out, then!'

Instead Walter seized his father's arm, and pointed. At the
same moment the troopers, lifting their eyes, let out a great
groan. They had just rounded a bend in the track, from which
the next hillcrest was visible. From over its ruff of treetops thin
plumes of dark smoke threaded the air – too dark, too large,
too many.

'God's blood! More devils' work!' rumbled Robert Scot in incoherent outrage, and with no words more he waved the troopers
forward, flicked his reins against his horse's shoulder and

spurred the huge beast to a brisk cantering run. Walter did likewise, thinking chilly how Acreknowe, the little farmtown, had looked after the battle. The smokes ahead were rising from the dale of the Teviot, from the vicinity of Branxholme itself; and as they neared the rise he shrank from what he might see. But Robert reined in his horse as he reached the crest, and sat there puffing and blowing. Walter saw why at once, and together, in grim silence, they rode down into their own dale.

What had happened was clearly past, its perpetrators gone. Across the straggling village around the tower lay a long swordslash of devastation, of cot-roofs smouldering and beasts straying, of fields trampled and hedgerows torn, of still shapes grotesquely huddled around little splashes of scarlet, of women wailing. The scar of it pointed directly at the very palisade of Branxholme itself; and its gates hung broken. But Branxholme itself stood strong, rising clear of the mirk, its tall roof whole. As the riders approached a horn sounded, and Walter saw beam and bar being lifted from behind the gap; one gate was pushed wider to allow them entrance, but it creaked and twisted on its single remaining hinge, and fell askew against the wall. Voices rose in greeting, which was reassuring. Walter breathed easier as he saw the tower door intact, and no sign of fires within the wall. But Robert's face was reddening, and a vein beat visibly in his temple.

'Who was it?' was all he said to the servitors and villagers clustering around him, and his look was so fell, his voice so hollow, they stood back in fear. 'Who has dared? And how long are they gone?'

Geordie pushed his way forward. 'Never a banner among 'em, Laird! It came swift and sharp, in the cover o' mirk maybe four hour after ye rode out. They brake the gate, but we held them back frae the tower itsel'. A guid thing ye left men enow to defend her! Scant licht, and some dead that maybe could have borne better witness; but there were faces known na'theless. Heckie Croser we saw, and Jock Nixon o' Kershope wi' his sons, and Lambie Elliot from over above Redheuch leadin' a motley pack—'

Robert's fist slammed into his palm. 'Liddesdale!'

Geordie swallowed. 'That's so, Laird. But the Nixon and the Croser, they're gangrel outlaws even in Liddesdale, and Lambie Elliot's a bad man to his neighbours. And there were others, straggle-haired creatures crying wi' tongues like corbies. Tis' said—'

'Wild men out of the North, my lord,' said a quiet voice. 'I have heard their tongue before, when messengers from the Macdonald came to Tantallon. Men of the Isles, I would guess.'

Robert spun about, breathing hard, and stared at the young girl who stood there. She was very pale, but there was a flush in her cheek, marred by a smudged streak of black across it; her rich blue dress was darkened at one side by a great splashed water-stain, and there was a long naked dagger in her girdle. Her tight-bound hair was escaping in black wisps beneath her cap, and for the first time Walter saw something about her that might have stirred him. But her voice was low as ever as she made her bow to Sir Robert, her manner as frozen as always. At him she did not look.

'My lady Margaret!' choked Robert. 'You have been caught up in this, this . . . You've taken no hurt, at least?'

'None, my good lord, I thank you.' There was a careful politeness in her voice, no warmth.

'The lady's gi'en help fight the fires they set, Laird!' burst in Geordie.

Robert exploded. 'What? Who permitted it? You? I'll have the lugs off of you—'

'They could not prevent me, my lord,' interrupted the girl, still quietly. 'It would ill become even a maid of the Douglases to stand idly by in such a pass. And I had my dagger to my protection—' She broke off as a gaunt old woman came ploughing through the throng, thrusting Walter aside as if he were of no account and clucking scornfully over the young woman.

'There, my fine young mistress, and see what comes of slipping your traces and going afly off to whatever's excitement to your mind! There's your fine dress spoilt and all your hair in a muss that I took so long to put up but this morning, and before the common sort an' all! It's off to your room with you, and—'

'Aye, hale her off, away and look to her properly!' snapped

Robert. 'What do I give you lock and key for, woman, that you let your charge straggle loose among perils? Hence!'

'That I will!' snapped the nurse, unabashed. 'And better you'd save your lock and key to ward off these marauding villains, since your own arm's too weak! Pity my poor mistress come to this den of thievery, who might have had a palace to her own, indeed!' She scuttled off, shooing the crestfallen girl before her, sniffing with disdain at these Border ruffians, one as bad as another. Walter felt a momentary twinge of sympathy. He gave silent thanks his own old nurse was now kept busy as mistress in the kitchens, or she would have been after him with clean shirts and possets before the face of all.

The Lord of Branxholme slumped against the tower wall and closed his eyes, struggling to hold in his feelings. 'Even a maid of the Douglases! Had an arrow found its mark or a reiver his prize, I doubt Earl Douglas would have seen it so! Still less her cousins his braggart sons! And on top of this – men of the Isles—' He was snarling now, almost incoherent. 'De Soulis! My own village, my own damned tower, the get of a bitch! Ever nearer the heart he strikes!'

Walter turned to Geordie. 'Have we a tale of dead and scathed yet, and what was taken?'

Geordie shook his head. 'By God's mercy there was no man slain within the wall; and many got within who fled the toun. It was in the fields they butchered most, taken aback as they began their day's swink, and the auld and young who were ridden down, or burned beneath their roofs.'

'You'd better see them tallied, then,' Walter told him. 'And account made of cattle and other stock driven off or slaughtered. Find Master Steward, have him do it, if he's unhurt; and the priest, if he's sober. Any who're roofless can sleep in the stables and outbuildings here for now, and the hurt who need care . . .' He looked around. 'Where's Wat?'

'He took a spear i' the thigh, but he lives.'

'Then set another older man with some healing craft to attend to the wounded, and the priest. Have the deacon make ready burial parties. Where's the sergeant? Gawn! Do you take a party of ten, see folk gather what store of provision they can—'

'Hold your hand!' growled Robert. He clapped Walter on the shoulder. ''Tis well enough, all that, lad, but let the steward attend to it, and his boys. Our need bites deeper. Gawn! Go see a proclamation made, here and in all the farmtowns! From the first light before dawn, at our gates, every man jack able to ride, armed and weaponed with four days' meal and meat. Send out to all our brother Scots within easy ride, all who owe us allegiance; let them bring in their housetroops, all fit to bear arms!'

The sergeant's leathery face was as immobile as ever, but he was shocked rigid. Robert waved him away with a roar. 'Avaunt, Gawn, run, man! I'll hound these reivers to their gates, of Hermitage or Hell itself!'

'Father!' whispered Walter desperately. 'Is this wise?'

Branxholme's face clouded. 'Wise?' he whispered. 'D'you not see, boy, it's the only course we can run? If we don't make some show, at least, of striking back, what standing will be left us? And with standing goes our livelihood, our existence even! Will the farmers of Teviot and Ettrick pay us shield-rent for our protection any more? Should they dig into their coffers for whitemail in silver, or their herds for blackmail in cattle, if we cannot keep the hands of de Soulis out? And where then's our tryst with the Douglases, where's your inheritance, all I've been building up for you?'

His puffy face twisted into a tragic mask. 'All I've wanted and worked for! And I, I myself, I threw it away in this folly today, by my own damnfool fault! I should have known de Soulis would be spying on us somehow, that he'd wait to strike when me and my men were away – and on such an accursed fool's errand!' He caught Walter by the shoulders suddenly. 'Or – was it? If there was some compact between them, 'twixt Michael and de Soulis—'

Walter shook his head. 'Not if we were but four hours on the road, Father. The Liddesdales must have lain hid in the hills since yesterday. And at least you left enough men to hold them off. They must have seen that, and given up.' He sighed. 'Well, if you're mustering tonight, best we find food.'

'Aye, that's so,' said his father. 'And make safe other entanglements first. Go ask the lady Margaret to join us at table.'

Walter smouldered, but he had better sense than to worsen his father's troubles right now.

The women's chambers were in the best and airiest part of the tower, near the top. There the windows could be wider, and the clean breezes whirl away the myriad stinks of the village below. Walter trailed wearily up the long spiral stair, the last thing he felt like after his long ride, and paused a moment before the door. He made an obscene, tongue-lolling face at the blank wood, and knocked.

There was the usual long silence. Then the door opened a little, and the nurse's head popped around it, like a crow in a cage, and pinned him with her usual look of beady contempt. 'What'd you be wanting?' she snapped. He felt helpless before that look, a graceless hobbledehoy without even his spurs, a mere vessel for his father's ambition.

'The courtesy of speech with the lady Margaret,' he said, being careful not to add a by-your-leave to a servant. Normally he would have, to anyone; but he had learned that to her it would only be taken as gaucherie, not politeness.

'She's changing her gown and resting! She sees nobody—'

'From my father,' he added firmly.

'Oh, let the boy in, Nance,' said Margaret's clear voice from the room beyond, laden with tolerant boredom. 'He's probably come to practise inviting me down to dinner,' she added audibly, making his errand look that much more ridiculous. She was always doing that – deliberately, he was sure of that now. *Boy*, indeed! He stiffened; but the nurse was already shooing him in as if he were a gormless natural.

The chamber was large and furnished well but sparsely, with the finest hangings and druggets, and in the centre the great canopied and carven bed that had been part of his mother's dowry. Margaret sat among the cushions of the window-seat, the only one such in the tower. She wore a heavy day-robe, so large she was almost lost in it, and her hair was down on her shoulder, but hidden in a linen kerchief; the low light caught her profile in clear silhouette. 'Yes, Colt? What does your father say?'

Walter swept off his bonnet and bowed, in the single gracious motion he had learnt from Ker. 'Lady, the Lord of Branxholme and his son have the honour to request the presence of your fair self at dinner, to be served within the hour.'

'And his son?' She smiled, a sweet glacial twitch of the lips. 'That would be a great pleasure, but after the day's v–vicissitudes—'

'There are matters of moment to discuss, lady,' he said, with an impatient sternness he hadn't meant to assume. 'And there will be no time after, for we muster and ride this night.'

She looked at him sharply, more directly, maybe, than she ever had before. 'Then make answer to Sir Robert that I will come gladly.' She flapped a hand in vague dismissal. 'Oh, yes – my thanks to his son also.'

Walter smiled grimly. 'And I thought you had forgotten me, lady! I shall make of them no less than they deserve, and treasure them through our happy years ahead. By your leave—'

He took his leave smartly. He closed the door, but waited a moment. Sure enough, it slammed behind him as if somebody had kicked it. He grinned to himself as he set off down the stair again. The nurse was a fearful old gobskite, but the girl's own airs and graces somehow bothered him less now. After all, what could you expect? A lass brought up in wealth and courtliness, coming to a country barony . . .

He squashed his bonnet in his hand. 'Now hold hard a minute,' he told himself. She'd been to court at Falkland and in London, yes; she'd made sure everyone knew that – but for how long? At her age it couldn't have been much – maybe a day or two only in the south, a few weeks in the north. Long enough to learn a manner; but to grow used to high life? Where could she have done that? Greenside was prosperous, but nowhere special; its manor was little more than a good solid farmhouse with a wall around it. And Tantallon, the new Douglas stronghold, was an awesome strength, yes, but from all accounts it was scarcely more comfortable than Branxholme – a castle, not a palace, and still abuilding in parts. Her schooling, then? But that had been at a convent near Edinburgh. 'The little *bitch*!' he said softly. All that genteel long-suffering disdain put on, just to make him feel lower! Well, if he was to be pitchforked into the marriage-bed, she'd be in for a shock there, that was for sure!

Then his kindlier nature asserted itself. He remembered her earlier: half-soaked, obviously afraid but still upholding Douglas pride and defending her new home. There was something better there. An uneasy thought grew in him. Could she have been doing that all along, resisting danger? That was daft. What danger – a strange place? Branxholme was no worse than Greenside. The Scots? But Robert had treated her like spun glass every moment of the last few days.

Himself?

What had he to make her fear? He grinned, briefly. But apart from that, he wasn't going to hurt her, was he? Walter shook his head, confused. Could that be it, even so? Her manner towards him not a weapon, maybe, but a shield – he could not give the thought clear form. Trying to understand her made his head ache. But he made up his mind to attempt a different tack with her, and see if she responded.

It seemed, though, as if he might not get the chance.

'You did well in the assault, I hear, my lady,' was his first venture as she joined them at table, looking demurely pretty in a high-bosomed gown of dark green. He meant it; he was not at all sure he would have kept his head so well. But he was met with a bleak little smile, and the girl hardly raised her eyes from her food, though she barely picked at it.

'I am a lady of the Douglases, I did what was necessary. Would it had not been.'

Walter's good resolutions were melting away. He ground his teeth in anger at the snub, but Robert either chose to ignore it or more likely didn't notice it.

'Your nurse is right, nonetheless,' he rumbled, spooning in his oatmeal and beans in great mouthfuls. 'I never guessed that de Soulis would dare attack so directly and so soon. Who knows what a madman will attempt next? I'd not expose you to a moment's danger more, my lady Margaret; you must leave.'

She picked at the morsels of chicken breast in her bowl. 'I thank you for your kind concern, my lord; but if this is to be my home henceforth, then I should learn to share its perils, as all else in its daily round.'

'Mmh – nothing daily about de Soulis,' champed Robert around a mouthful. 'Something new – first foe to assail Branxholme openly 'n many a year! No—' He spluttered and swallowed with a loud grateful breath. 'Aaah! Mind's made up. Back to Tantallon you go for now, and post-haste! Your noble uncle wouldn't thank me for aught less.'

Walter felt a great tension ease within him, for a great many tangled reasons. 'I . . . will head your escort if you wish it, lady,' he offered. Robert shot him a startled glance from beneath his furrowed brows.

'You?' She dimpled sweetly. 'Why, my good Colt, I thank you; but I would not be the cause of your missing this noble expedition, and a chance to shine in the battle – even to win your spurs, maybe.'

She could hardly have made the implication clearer. Robert's frown darkened. 'He's handled himself well at the killing these last few days—'

Her smile could scarce have been milder. 'I'm sure, my lord, if it was against the breed of outlaw kerns we faced today.'

Robert flushed scarlet. 'The Colt's trained and hardy in arms, his valour's proven and his wits forbye – you might ask no more of a husband to be, or find a better. But I could not have spared him, anyhow. My officers will take you on your way, lady, by the safest route. Our path lies together, his and mine, and God grant that it lead the two of you back together again.'

She flushed slightly herself, and dropped her glance. 'God will dispose.' But she recovered her appetite then, and for all her professed attachment to Branxholme, she didn't seem unduly unhappy.

'God dispose indeed!' said Robert, as he saw the ladies to their mounts in the first grey light of dawn. 'And He may take better care of you at Tantallon than here!' Certainly Tantallon, built on a great jagged promontory split off from the mainland by an appalling gorge, would be well nigh impregnable, even to de Soulis – assuming he ever grew mad enough to challenge the Douglases, or cause trouble so close to Edinburgh even the King would have to take notice. The nurse barely bothered to conceal her satisfaction, but Walter found Margaret's face harder to read. The Scot kinsmen and retainers were already arriving for the muster, grim-faced and angry at the signs of the raid, and she watched the preparations with a strange intensity.

Robert grinned reassuringly. 'Your road lies by the eastern route to Jedburgh Abbey, well away from all such troubles – a longish ride, but you may take it as easy as you will and be well entertained at the Abbey this evening. After that all's safe enough.' He motioned to the captain of the escort, ten well-armed riders, and the little cavalcade with its two baggage ponies tripped easily out of the gate.

Margaret looked back as they passed, and suddenly she burst out, 'I wish I could go with you!'

Robert gave a roar of affectionate laughter, as if a child had said something precocious but ridiculous. 'Heaven forfend, lady!'

'But I thank you, nonetheless,' said Walter. She looked down, and did not answer.

'God be with you!' called Walter and his father together, but only the captain acknowledged it. The train of horses clipped lightly over the greying slope to the northwest, where the track wound between the trees, and away out of sight.

'And may He be with us also,' muttered Robert, looking out at his gathering force. 'At the least we'll pen that bastard in his tower a day or two, and leave scars on his lands to match our own. That'll serve to raise our banner once again, and that much I reckon we may do without grave scathe – for now.'

'May he tak' it as a schuling!' suggested Gawn with grim humour. 'Teach yon popinjay tae aim at some ither mark!'

Robert frowned. 'Or, if the lesson is not hard enough, he may strike back to raise his banner in turn. So the bitter seeds of blood-feud are sown, and they could cost us dear.'

'We'll have two hundred men at least, maybe more,' said Walter encouragingly. 'He won't have so many within Hermitage, will he?'

'Ach, no, lad, half that at most, surely, and he has no other great strength. But you can wager the dregs of Liddesdale will be at his beck, and maybe also some of the better sort, from fear of him or scent of profit. That's hard land and it grows hard men.' He smacked his mailed gauntlet against the gate. 'But iron and fire crack even the hardest rocks, in time! And we'll bring it home to him!'

By the time full day had come the muster was grown, swelled by some lesser Ettrick lords. When the column formed up at the Lord's command it numbered some two hundred and thirty mounted men; less than a hundred were fully armed soldiers, but most of the rest were seasoned fighters, skilled in the long lance that was the fast-moving horseman's favourite weapon. Walter wondered how effective it would be in a siege; but then, as Sir Robert had hinted, this might well turn out to be no more than a gesture, a swift slapping down of overweening ambition. It was a strong sight, but there was little heart in the local folk for rejoicing. Instead of cheers and the familiar boom of the gates, all that followed them as they rode out was the thin chanting of the priest atop the wall, and below him the slow thud of a carpenter's maul.

The dull sound awoke some echo in Walter's heart, and of many, to judge by their faces; and soon even that was baffled, and there was nothing but the lonely cry of peewits above the moorlands, and the harsh cawing of rooks. It was a silent force that turned south and westward towards the bleak fells and high rigs. Upon the slopes before them, under great slashing streaks of grey cloud, rose the forest the Romans of old had named Caledon, that had swallowed up many a greater force than theirs among its green shadows. Upon the farther side of that lay the way southward into the mouth of Liddesdale.

Out by the Dodburn they rode, on much the same track along which Walter had pursued the reivers; and when they came to the ford among the trees Robert peered around with an interested gleam in his piggy eyes. 'This Greek fire, or whatever the man Michael had, it would have burned fiercely, would it not?'

Walter shrugged, seizing the moment to scratch under his mailshirt. 'It stank so; and the dead Armstrong was blackened like a hearthlog.'

'And this less than a sennight gone,' said Robert. 'Yet do I see a single scorch on leaf or ground?'

'It was wet, then, with the dew and the late rain,' Walter reminded him. 'And the Armstrongs were fording the cattle, so it was towards the water it must have burnt. Did Blood-Wullie's son say more before you delivered him to Ker?'

'The less sense, the more we pressed him, but babbled like a bairn afraid. I would I'd set his ransom higher! And when we're clear of this brawl I'll see about this fire of Michael's that leaves no mark.'

Walter chuckled. 'We could use it now.'

'And soil our souls, too, with sorcery? Be damned to that! And to Black Soulis and his rainstorms! We'll see what plain fire does to the gate of Hermitage, aye, and its roof. Plainer and cleaner!'

They followed the path up from the Skelfhill, passing through tangled heather and glossy green gorse clumps with their snagging thorns, west beneath Peel Brae and the Black Cleugh, following Priesthaugh Burn to the summit of that name between the Dod Rig and Skelfhill Fell. In places the green hillside seemed but the thinnest skin over the jagged bones of the land beneath; rocks reared up to turn them from the path; smaller stones tipped and rolled to make their horses stumble. It was a rougher, steeper route than most would take, but in that lay their best hope of surprise. Here the forest that lay between them and the lands around Hermitage was narrow, and they could pass more swiftly along the ways cut by the burns in the red-brown earth. The timeless roof of oaks and ashes and tall birches would shield them. But the trail had fallen from use over the last few years, and become more and more overgrown with brush and briar and stooping branch, and the going grew harder than they had expected. When they traced the cut of the Haugh Sike that would lead them through to the steeps of Starcleugh Edge, the full-armoured knights found they must dismount. That way was a slope of riverside soil that crumbled like stale cake under laden hooves, making every yard a skidding, slithering trial for the heavy horse among the ancient knotted roots and thorn tangles. Those lighter-armed and mounted,

Walter among them, made better time along the burn's bed, though the red mud clung to hooves and boots; but many men glanced around in growing unease.

To old tales this was unchancy ground, haunted even, and if the sun shone beyond the treetops its light made little inroad into the gloom. Once, it was said, the Fair Folk rode here, and hunted through the dark with moonlit spears, a terror and a danger to any mortal rash enough to cross their path; and even those who normally scorned old tales found them easier to credit here. This was not a place for men. Limb and branch crossed the bare beast-tracks that were the only paths, raking and scratching at the unwary rider or dripping damp mould and cobweb about his neck at every turn. Clumps of holly and black-thorn scratched man and stung mount, and blowflies settled to sip the blood. The air hung heavy and laden with strange smells, but more stifling still was the sense of isolation. Nobody could see more than a few paces before or behind; the rest of the force, even the men and horses only a few places back in the line, were no more than blurs between the web of slow growth. Sound died in the steep burn cuttings, and you were never sure whether you were still part of the main band or of a tiny fragment turned aside and straying into the deeps of the wood. Surely, if the will of a sorcerer like de Soulis could hold sway anywhere, it would be here.

'It grows thinner soon enough,' Walter told some of the nearer men; though he spoke in a whisper, for no good reason he could have named. 'At the Edge it's no more than a wood, and we can strike down the easier side of the Starcleuch itself to the Braidlie Burn that flows right down into Hermitage Water. Down a deep cut beneath the steep flank of Crossbow Hill, says my father; and that'll give us good shelter for long – long enough to sneak on up and take a piss through the Hermitage keyhole, anyhow!'

The chuckle that ran back along the line reassured him some-what, but it was soon lost in the rustle and rasp of movement and the subdued ring of metal. Walter's back creaked with bending beneath the branches, so that he felt like some whiskered ancient. When he pushed through a huge patch of hawthorn that seemed able to sense every possible way through his mail-shirt, and saw a definite gleam along the stream ahead – what looked like a wide grassy bay opening between the wood's long arms and out onto the bare hillside – his relief was vast. As soon as ground and growth allowed he mounted up and followed a narrow track towards the pale patch of sunlight. But as the grinning troopers streamed out past him Walter snapped his fingers to order them back. The clearing was created by outcrops of stone, among which the trees had found no foothold and had been replaced by dense bracken thickets. 'It looks well, but we'll not go rushing out so trusting. You, you and you, Tammas, scout around there, afoot. Keep low, and off the skyline!'

The others watched in silence as the three men padded out into the open, half-crouching through the clumps of bracken, darting glances this way and that like questing dogs. This was common skill, the art of the hardened reiver spying out the country ahead, as well by moonless night as by bright day. Most of the older men were long adept in it, and even Walter could read the manner and movement of the scouts: alert, a little dubious, but not immediately alarmed. In swift silence they watched the two flankmen slink out of the bay and around the arms of the forest to either side, while the man in the centre wormed forward on his stomach to survey the open slope beyond, like an adder in the grass. In minutes only they were back, rising up as they came with little heed, and saluting Walter. He rode to meet them.

'Ne'er a soul in sight!' they said cheerfully. 'Naught but rock and tree!' But the eldest frowned.

'There has been, yet. And no' sae lang since – a main big band, I'm thinkin', passing over the slope yonder.'

'The raiders, you mean?' demanded Walter. 'They may still be on the road ahead?' He whistled softly. 'Wait till my father hears this! They can't be hurrying. We might even ride them down before they reach the Hermitage!' He looked back anxiously. Only a few of the heavy horse had kept up; he could dimly make out his father and the rest, still dismounted, picking their way around the eastern foot of Swire Knowe in single file. 'No point in blocking the paths,' he decided, plucking out a persistent thorn. 'We'll await them in clean air. Out, all!'

The men needed no telling; they mounted up and streamed past him through the bracken into the clearing, where they could straighten and stretch and the horses could browse on the sweet grass growing among the heather tussocks. As soon as he saw his father and his band come down into view, he waved and followed them out.

For an instant he thought the trumpet-blast their own; but the whole wood seemed to howl in answer. It was as if a shimmer of heat passed across his sight, as if a veil were flicked away. From among the rocks at the forest's end men sprang up, armed men with bow and long-axe, men whom some black spell had hidden from the scout's sight. Against the very flanks of the horses they rushed, thrusting left and right with their long pikes. Up and out of the shadows of the wood's end rose a wave of men who unleashed a hissing crest of arrows right down into the startled force of Scots.

'Treason and sorcery!' screamed Walter, his voice cracking as one shaft jarred across his mail and another, a crossbow bolt, thudded down into his pack. 'To me, all! Close ranks and hold them!'

His sword was in his hand before the shout had left his lips. But the men in front of him and behind, less well armoured, were already falling, transfixed by the terrible clothyard shafts of English longbows that lifted them bodily from their saddles to slump on the grass. Footmen rushed forward to hew them with pike and poleaxe. More came pouring around the arms of the trees, and the ground drummed upon the approach of hooves. Walter's sword rose and fell on the straggling crowns of the men who milled around him, clutching at his legs or stabbing with long dirks. Some were cut down, and they gave back, running apart. He saw why, as figures mailed and mounted came charging around the forest's arm with lances lowering to the ready. No time to unship his own long ash-spear; he spurred at the nearest, trampling kerns from his path, and cut hard at the shaft as it swung to face him. It shattered, and the momentum of his charge carried his sword point-on through heavy mail into the body of his enemy. The man flung up his arms with an appalling scream, but the sheer impact tore the hilt from Walter's grasp as he shot by. Walter snatched at his spear, wheeled his mount before the heavier horses could turn on him, and stabbed hard into an enemy's unprotected side, then hauled the shaft back to parry another thrust.

All was confusion, captaincy nonsense; in this deadly whirl he couldn't see who was his own, or wasn't. His leg stung, he yelled and struck down with his spear-butt, then stabbed out again as another lance ran at him. He missed, but parried and swung hard, sweeping his enemy from the saddle. That was better! A wild face screamed at him along an upraised pike; he ran the lance down into it, then jerked back the shaft as the sagging weight sought to pull it from his fingers. Again and again he lunged at figures swirling about him, scratching one, slaying another in the dreadful lottery of the fight, then turning to face a new knot of riders. They were too close already; there was a wrenching crash, but he hardly saw the great finned club as it bit through his spearshaft and left him clutching a useless truncheon. It swung up to strike, and he jabbed out in helpless defiance with the broken wood.

Then the ground seemed to quiver. A heavy lance bright with grey and white pennons took the club-wielder below the breastbone and ran right through him in an exploding shower of blood and bone and mail-rings that lifted him right out of the saddle. Walter turned to see his father, teeth bared and grimacing with the force of that fearful blow, haul back on his spear – and in the same instant, before Walter could so much as cry out, the other lance that took him in the arm, the flung axe that smashed his helmet from his head. Robert Scot's great spear, weighed down by the falling body, dropped from his hand. He swayed in his saddle, blood spurting from his riven scalp and forehead, eyes wandering. Walter reached out to support him, but Robert shook him off with a growl. He wrenched at his own great sword – it came loose, scabbard and belt and all – and he flung it into Walter's hand. 'Break, boy!' he roared. 'Break and ride for your life and our line! Gather all you can, and break —'

Another lance struck. Robert caught the shaft in his bare hands and thrust it back so hard the seasoned ash-sapling bowed and snapped. He seized the double-bladed axe at his saddle, but another spear from the ground caught him in the chest, and he gasped. Walter heard himself cry out, hauled the sword from the sheath and in the same action swung at the wielder, a bare-crowned Daneman by his look; the blond head flew from its shoulders. 'Break, I said!' roared Robert Scot, and pulled his great horse about to block the path of more riders, smashing a blow deep into their leader's helm; but in the same moment a crossbow bolt seared the beast's neck and stuck in Robert's leg. It reared, he sagged sideways and slumped, and even as his great bulk flopped on the ground two spears transfixed it. His round legs kicked absurdly in the air, and then the jackals with their raking dirks were on him.

The spearmen had no time to withdraw their weapons. Walter was upon them. With an inhuman shriek he swung and slashed one deep in the side with a spray of blood and bone, and turning on the other in the same stroke he struck through vambrace and mail to sever his arm. Then the kerns fled screaming, but Walter spared no glance for the bloody wreck on the ground. In his madness he would have cut at the next hand that reached for him, but the voice of Gawn the sergeant calmed him somewhat, though the words he hardly heard. He knew now what he must do. Calling to mind the horn by his saddlebow, he raised it and blew once, twice, louder than the shrieking tumult; he waved, a wide sweeping gesture away from the ensnaring trees towards the open slopes of Swire Knowe. He did not stop to see who heeded, but pulled his staggering mount's head around and rode full at the tangle-haired Highlandmen in his path.

The stroke of a heavy horseman's sword among heads unprotected was a terrible thing in the Marchland wars – the Lockerbie Lick, as it was named. Walter struck to the left and Gawn to the right, so that their enemies' battle fury was turned against them, for those behind pressed on so hard they left those to the fore no room to draw back; they were scythed like dry hay. Behind the two, as they guessed but dare not look, men of their own came in, ahorse and afoot, clearing room for little groups of others fighting through to them, till a broadening spearhead pressed against that side of the ambuscade. Pressed, and burst.

The oncoming ranks saw the death irresistible that bore down upon them, gave back as they should have, but too late; death was at their backs. They broke, and spilled screaming down the slopes. Walter, with an instant won, turned his mount and winded his horn again, beckoning, rallying his men one last time; then a shaft from the wood all but took the horn from his lips, and Gawn pulled him away.

Around the outer slope of the knowe they rode, where the slope grew briefly broader and the horses had firm footing, and up Windy Edge to the slopes of the Cauldcleugh hill. There Walter halted again, to rest and rally his remaining horsemen and gather in the dismounted who straggled behind with the enemy snapping at their heels. Against Gawn's protests he formed up a line of horse, some thirty or forty. The last of the foot hove into view, hunted men falling from arrow and lance, or from sheer hearts bursting as they ran. Walter sounded a charge. With the weight of the hill behind them they swept down through the fugitives, on to the straggling leaders of the hunt and over them in bloody execution. Walter gained a spear one moment, left it in another foe the next, and took a second as its owner turned to flee. The foremost hunters died like dogs beneath his hooves, and those who turned and fled spread fear in the oncomers; the hunt became a brief rout in its turn. That discouraged the enemy long enough to get the exhausted footmen around the turn of the hill and into the sheltering arms of the Cauldcleugh, that would lead them by an easier burnside back to their own territory.

Gawn, wiping other men's blood from his seamed face, looked up at the steep walls nervously, and the great gnarled oaks that made an overhanging arch at the top, stunting the waterside willows in their shadow. 'It'll speed us through,' he said, 'but an they come upon us o'er the height . . .'

'Not unless their magic wafts men through trees!' gasped Walter, wheezing with the effort to speak. 'Otherwise – from behind – or not at all. And along the cleugh here we can hold them, even ambush them at need!'

Gawn swore, and pointed. They were not yet so deep in the trees as to lose sight of the land beyond. There were no pursuers; but high on the summit of Cauldcleugh Hill a little knot of horsemen stood out against the grey sky, riding unhurriedly down towards them. One rode ahead of the rest, a bulky figure on a great chestnut warhorse, but with no sign of armour about him save the grey gleam of a light helm. Gawn's thin lips tautened to a pale slash. 'A hundred croons tae a ram's pizzle yon's Soulis himself, the get of a bitch! Come tae speir us takin' tae our heels, have ye?'

It was as if the horseman heard him, for he reined in, and, standing in his stirrups, raised an open hand. Gawn punched hand to palm furiously. 'By're Lady, the swineshite! Hellfire and damnation, can naebody gie me a bow in haund tae mark the bastard?'

Walter felt nauseous. 'Over that distance? Leave it, man—'

He stopped. There was a singing in his ears, a strange buzzing, and the saddle swayed sickeningly beneath him. Gawn caught him with an exclamation of anger.

'Could ye no' have telt me you were wounded?'

'Didn't know myself!' mumbled Walter, staring in surprise at the blood that trickled down his arm and his left side and spread stickily across his calf. 'I – *ach*!' He yelped as Gawn plucked the snapped-off arrowhead from the mail at his back, and another trickle started. Ahead of them a trooper swayed and collapsed into the burn; another sprang down to help, dragged him to the edge and then sat down dizzily, holding his own head in his hands. The burn flooded suddenly red. The sergeant blinked at the runnel of blood down his own nose.

'But that was a scratch, nae mair—' He touched it with his gauntlet, and the flow staunched. Puzzled, he looked a moment, then touched Walter's arm, then his leg. He swore and plucked the cross from about his neck, and touched that to Walter's side. A murmur of alarm ran down the column; men touched iron to their wounds, or holy signs, or crossed themselves. The man in the burn was dead already; another took his mount, and he was slung across its cruppers. Men shook their fists at the hill, and called upon the vengeance of God. But as Walter, reviving, glared back at the slope, it was empty. The watchers had gone.

Gawn shook him gently. 'Is it stopped now, the bluid, Sir Walter?'

'*No!* I mean, yes. No worse than it was, anyhow. But not that name . . . not yet.'

'Ye're the Laird now,' said Gawn grimly. 'No gainsayin' that. There's need of ye.'

The sergeant rattled on about how many wearing spurs had won them for less than his work that day, but Walter hardly took it in. The jarring sense of loss and failure was too great. He did not feel like the new Lord of Branxholme; he felt like nothing. He could have blamed his father or himself for having rushed so blindly into ambush, but he knew well enough why. They'd thought of reivers rushing home with their booty. They had not guessed – and why should they? – that de Soulis would have gone to the trouble to set such a trap, nor that it might be cloaked by his evil power. Walter remembered bitterly how he had guessed the purpose of those first raids might be to diminish the Scots. He had hardly imagined de Soulis' true purpose was to destroy them completely; yet it was clear now that he had come within a hair's breadth of succeeding. Maybe he had succeeded.

The line of men, weary and heartsick, straggled up out of the cleugh and across the western flank of the Priesthaugh, where the forest thinned again. Last of all rode Walter, and he looked up in surprise at the mass of men awaiting him there, who saluted him – grimly, but not grudgingly. There were more than he'd realized.

'Over a hundred,' confirmed Gawn. 'And mair, maybe, still lowpin' blind about the wood by ither roads. It was you brought them off.'

'It was my father,' said Walter dully. 'He bought me the way clear, striking in from the forest like that.'

'He did that,' said the sergeant. 'They struck too soon, they werena awaiting him from back i' the trees. But 'twas you seized the chance. And 'tis you've made them sweat for it, and stayed the pursuit. The Scots are no' broke yet, Laird; buckled, but no' broke.'

*

But that had yet to be proven. Walter let the force disperse on their road back, so that men weary and unhorsed need walk no further than was necessary. It was with Gawn and a few household men only that he came to the gates of Branxholme, and he left them to fend off the frantic rush of questions from Geordie at the gate and all the rest of his folk. One look made them fear to come near him. At the mounting-block he eased himself painfully from the saddle, wincing as he disturbed his wounds and weary muscles. But he turned to find Geordie hovering anxiously, and behind him a knot of young men, dark of hair and eye and with a likeness of close kin that seemed oddly familiar to Walter. Their clothes were rich but stained with rain and mud, and gold gleamed on the hilts of the swords and daggers they swung; their manner had the casual arrogance of command. Six troopers in dark livery lounged at their backs.

'They came not a hauf hour since, Laird,' stammered Geordie. 'They havena' said their business . . .'

'Our concern is with the lord and his son only,' said the tallest and evidently eldest, a scarfaced man of twenty or so. 'And with the cousin we left in your charge.'

Walter nodded. 'I should have known you at once. I'm Walter Scot—'

'So I guessed,' said the tall man, without waiting for him to finish. 'I'm James Douglas of Tantallon, and these are my brothers. Where's the Lord your father?'

'My father is dead,' said Walter, nettled at the scant courtesy of the tone. 'The Laird stands here.'

'Dead?' Douglas looked surprised, but only as he glanced about at the disorder. 'How? What's been afoot here? And where's our cousin the lady Margaret?'

'Your cousin is safe,' said Walter angrily, 'as befits our trust. We sent her away under escort, as soon as we could. It was my father's last concern before he rode out.'

'As well for you!' barked one of the younger brothers. 'We took horse at once when we had word of troubles hereabouts. We all said it was a poor match our father made, and a fool's choice to let her come here to these unchancy lands!'

'Aye!' put in another. 'And if we'd known you Scots were embroiled in your usual Marchland brawlings—'

From the Douglases, that was rich. Walter blazed despite his weariness. 'We'd no way of knowing! We were at peace, till de Soulis began this sudden raiding—'

'De Soulis? Black Soulis?' James Douglas turned sharply to look at his brothers. 'How've you been mixing it with that one?'

'In no wise,' growled Walter, 'except to take exception to his stealing our cattle and murdering our folk. Would the Douglases lie down meekly and submit to that? But it seems those were but feints, to prepare for a real stroke. The man has designs on our land, or our dominion within it, at least; and so my father was dragged down in base ambush by greater force and unmanly murdered, and I and mine scarce won free.'

There was a slight snort among the Douglases. Walter heard, but kept his head; he needed no more enemies now. 'May you never face such an occasion,' he said calmly. 'But even in adversity we're mindful of our guests. You've barely missed your cousin. If you had taken the longer road you would have met her.'

The atmosphere changed suddenly. 'The longer road, you say?' demanded James.

'That was the road we took,' said one of the youngest, his voice suddenly cracking. 'In case of just that!'

'Aye, we lay at Jedburgh last night. Surely—'

But Walter was already shouting for Gawn, over his people's protests. 'Fresh horses, and fast! And food for our guests! My lords Douglas, we are not yet so reduced, nor our grief so deep, that we forget our hospitality!'

It was a bleak meal nonetheless, for the Douglases fumed and fidgeted with little grace. Walter had his wounds washed and dressed, and felt better for that and the food and drink; but he was weak and lightheaded enough as he buckled on his father's swordbelt properly for the first time. 'Oh, Father, Father!' he muttered. 'What this match of yours might yet be costing us!' And only then for the first time did the sense of true grief overcome him and he gave way to tears; but he stifled them with cold water, as Robert would have wished with

Douglases to face. He went out to join them pale but composed.

They spared him nothing, but rode at a hard canter from the first, with scant word or regard. It seemed like an evil dream to Walter, this last unlooked-for ride, as if he were bumping his way to Hell. But he found some easing for his pain, for there were stragglers on all the roads, men of his force making their way home whom he had feared lost; and they saluted him as Laird with grave respect.

A long road might have weakened him, and yet he would have wished it longer; for it was only a little past the village of Hawick, beneath the slopes known for some old haunting as Trow Knowes, that they came upon the scene. It was the setting sun's glimmer upon a helm among the bracken that caught James Douglas's eye; a helm smashed and useless, for all the bodies had been plundered and stripped of every whole weapon, mail and other possession. The body of the old nurse lay beneath a hawthorn, thrawn and neck-snapped, ears and neck torn where rings and necklaces had been plucked loose, and a finger severed for the same fell purpose. But they found a blood-caked plaid trampled into the miry soil, as if forgotten when its owner's body was removed; and in one of the escort's corpses, below the back ribs, they found a snapped-off blade, the pattern of a Highland *skianh*. 'Mere outlaws would have taken more care, buried the bodies maybe,' said a young Douglas quietly. 'These are grown careless. But Meg – where's Meg?'

They slashed and trampled the bracken all but flat for many yards about, and searched further till it grew too dark, but there was no other woman's body there.

'Highlanders,' said James Douglas, as if it left a foul tang in his mouth. He warmed his hands at the fire Walter's men had kindled. 'And who about here recruits Northern outlaws to do his dirty bidding but de Soulis? She's carried off for ransom, I doubt not – a well laid plan, like all the rest. It's a fine hornet's nest the Scots have stirred up for themselves!'

'*We've* stirred up?' demanded Walter. 'We asked for none of this. And what about your cousin – isn't she *your* concern, too? Surely not even the Hermitage could withstand the Douglas power!'

James Douglas rounded on him. 'This is a matter for the Scots and their honour. I advise you, look to it for your own sake!'

Walter could hardly believe his ears. 'Are you telling me Douglas won't join Scot? To rescue your own dear cousin?'

James grabbed him by the collar of his mail and spat as much as spoke into his face. 'What the Douglases do or don't do is not for a Scot to say! Least of all a lousy wee lordling Scot with such a smutch on his honour! Hermitage is on your marches, not ours, and Margaret in your miserable care!'

'But to have any chance – my father's riding was desperate enough, and he had no idea how great de Soulis' forces really are! The sorcerer must have hundreds of men at his beck! No one family can muster so many, not these days!'

'Then find help where you will!' said James. 'We're charged to keep the King's peace, and de Soulis is his man. It's your honour at stake, and your problem to unravel, how you may! For I charge you, you fail upon your peril. If Margaret is not delivered or comes to harm, we will sweep the Scots out of Branxholme like so many horse-turds. And you, Sir Walter, will soon enough wish yourself in Hell!'

The tall man spat into the fire and gestured to his brothers and their men. Silently they swung themselves ahorse, then went clattering off into the night along the long road to Jedburgh. Apparently they preferred that to closer beds at Branxholme – one more snub. Out of the darkness a voice drifted back. 'So go to the Devil for your aid, if you will – but go swiftly!'

Walter motioned his troopers back to their horses and clambered painfully into his own saddle. He was lord and master of his realm now, but a fell and desperate master facing ruin and devastation at every turn. He kept his countenance before his men, but inwardly he cursed and reviled the Douglases and all their kind. Well, let them all stew together and eat one another's flesh for sustenance! A fine drizzle had come on, and it suited his mood. He felt colder and emptier than ever, a dead man riding, and his head was buzzing again. He dozed in the saddle as they rode back, as he had after those clandestine nights in barn and farmcot; and woke only when they came within sight of the lamps of Branxholme, still forlorn and despairing of mind.

He could see only one way forward, and it was bleaker and darker than the weeping night.

Suddenly Gawn, who rode beside him, thrust out a hand. They reined in sharply, their tired mounts shying and protesting. Walter heard it too, the heavy drum of hooves upon the road behind them, a strong fast canter. He smiled thinly. 'Now who else'd be abroad at this hour? The Douglases? Maybe the rain's changed their minds!'

Gawn grinned. 'And they're come back tae beg a bed? I'd like fine tae see that!' He cupped his hands to his mouth. 'Who goes?' he called. 'Who goes at Branxholme Gate? Is that a Douglas I hear?'

'It is not,' came a calm voice out of the dark. 'A fine name to put on a kinsman, indeed.'

Now they could hear there were but three sets of hooves, though one was heavy and shod as if for war, ringing on the stony ground. Walter saw the beast as it breasted the rise, black against the faint blueness in the sky, and sharper than the trickling rain was the chill that seeped through his body. He recognized that horse's high-stepping gait and the dark outline of its rider, the Master of Oakwood, Michael Scot.

5 🏰 Hermitage

Somewhere beyond the circle of light an owl hooted.

'A good evening to you, Branxholme!' said the tall man, drawing up his horse alongside. His eyes gleamed from beneath the brim of a high-crowned riding hat. 'If it's a Douglas you really want, the last I heard of were tearing up the good way to Jedworth with unseemly haste. The gudeman I had the tale of claimed he'd seldom seen braw young lads in such a sore fley.'

'Panic?' exclaimed Walter, thunderstruck.

'And why not?' shrugged the older man. 'With the Earl to explain to? And in such a way that the old villain won't lose his head and send them rushing to rescue their dear young cousin, regardless? Their fine shirts would never be the same again!'

'They're frightened,' breathed Walter, on the verge of incredulous laughter. 'Frightened! And heaping it over with arrogance, the bastards, as a cur kicks earth! I should have guessed it, when they were so eager to be gone. Stone-scared of Black Soulis!'

Michael Scot smiled thinly. 'And that surprises you? Well, indeed.'

Walter felt heat in his cheeks. 'Maybe my loss is more to me than a mere cousin is to them.'

'Ah yes.' Michael Scot regarded him an instant, and Walter thought he made out a change in the calm voice. 'I have heard that also, of course. News runs as of old in the Marches, faster than fine horses. Believe me, I am sorely sorry. I held no great grievance against Sir Robert, even some regard, though little you may credit it. He will be missed; and the manner of his death was a deadly affront. It is because of that I have turned aside from my present journey to take counsel with you. But I keep you in the cold before your gate, and it is already near dawn. Will you not go in?'

Walter looked at him an instant. He wanted desperately to go in, wanted food and bed, to drown himself in dreamless sleep. The last thing he wanted was a guest, let alone this strange creature. Gawn, his usually expressionless face suddenly twisted with alarm, was striving furiously to catch his eye. He could spurn the man from the gate, kin or no, and nobody would blame him; hospitality might extend to a murderer, but not a sorcerer. And yet, not knowing why, he shrugged gracelessly and said, 'Come, then. I cannot prevent you.'

Gawn grabbed his arm. 'If ye invite sic a one across your threshold—'

Walter smiled. 'What worse luck can he bring than what sits here grinning already? He is a Scot, after all. I'll hear his counsel, and keep my own.'

The men dispersed to quarter their mounts; Walter, heaving himself from the saddle in numb agony, handed his to Gawn. He strode into the great hall, its rushes strewn with sleeping bodies wrapped in blanket and fur, singly or together. The fire had sunk to embers and the air as usual stank. The hounds lifted their muzzles sleepily and bats were abroad in the rafters. He strode between the sleepers, ignoring muzzy protests at his spurs, and headed for the kitchen, where the turnspits and drudges were already risen and blowing up the fire for the day, under the direction of the fat cook who had once been his nurse. They froze as they saw him, but scurried like startled fieldmice from his path; the old woman, instead of bustling to exclaim over his wet clothes, only bobbed him a nervous curtsy. He was Lord here now; but it was ashes in his mouth. He missed his father's iron authority more deeply than he would have expected. He tried not to think of the body unburied that would be madness to return for; let the ravens have their due, for now. His was another road.

He tossed his sword on the great table, thumped down on a bench and called to the old woman for bread and ale and bacon. Then he sank his head in his hands – and gave a wild start as he realized Michael was still with him, and sitting down beside him. The man's two grotesque attendants crouched by the hearth, warming their chilled limbs and attracting uneasy stares from the Branxholme servants. Hospitality had its duties, and he almost automatically poured the older man ale from the great jug they brought. Michael hefted the horn beaker. 'To the late lord of Branxholme, God rest his soul!'

Walter nodded grimly, and they drank deep. Michael added, 'And in the same cup, to the new lord's better faring!' and drank his down.

Walter did slump forward on the table then, leaning on his crossed arms, staring at the sheathed sword. 'What makes you so sure of that, old man? Have you – what's the word? – cast my nativity?'

Michael helped himself to more ale, and smiled. 'Among other things, yes. Only those who have studied most deeply know how much to rely on such forecasts – or how little. So much depends upon interpretation, in which the feelings of the astrologer himself are almost bound to intrude. But I have not studied and developed the researches of the great al-Bitrugi wholly in vain. This far I will venture – there's peril ahead for you, great peril and not at all a usual kind. But there's promise also, and the same is true of that, for the sun is this month in your birthsign, and the lord of the ascendant on your behalf is Mars. For your enemy, as far as I can remember the age of the man, the lord of the seventh house would seem to be Venus, a weak and unfaithful mistress. And yet within your houses both she and the Wargod conjoin.' He chuckled. 'But then, as our pagan forefathers tell, they were always prone to that. Odd. On one level one might read that your prowess in the courts of Mars will bring you accomplishments on the couch of Venus, which wouldn't be so very surprising. But on another it might mean that you come to some compounding, understanding even, with your enemy. And, given who and what he is, I find that beyond belief.'

Walter waved the words away like buzzing flies. 'I cannot take counsel from the stars, old man,' he said grimly. 'They fear to speak clearly, lest they expose their own folly. I need no star to see my perils! How to pass them, that's what I need to know; and I doubt the answer's to be divined in a scatter of skylight, any more than a flight of swallows or a pullet's gut. I read my future in a clearer script than strings of chicken-shit!'

'Then may I ask what you find there?'

Walter spread his hands in bitter resignation. 'What more remains? A brief rest, a fresh horse, and so to Liddesdale and the Hermitage. As well meet my end honourably at Black Soulis' hands as have the Douglases butcher me like a calf to cover up their own cowardice. And, no doubt, to claim my lands after my death, in Margaret's name as my betrothed – oh aye, I see that now too.'

'Liddesdale,' said Michael easily, 'and the stronghold of the Hermitage. Now by a passing strange coincidence it was that way my feet were already turned when I heard the bleak news.'

'You should have kept on your road,' said Walter bitterly. 'No doubt they'd have held you a place at the victory feast.'

About to charge his cup again, the dark man put it down with a hollow sound, and regarded him with a strange intensity, almost of pity. 'You say these things,' he said, 'that your father might have said, copying his voice like a tame jackdaw. Yet your mind is wider and better schooled than his, and you should have enough sense to use your own judgement. As I said, the way you choose is also mine. You remember the visit that your friend Marchwarden Ker hinted I might make? It is for that I go; but *I* have every intention of coming back. And so should you, young Branxholme, if you'll but use your God-given wits. The Douglases you may worry about when the time comes.'

Walter sat bolt upright, and stared at him; but then he became aware of a delicious odour of bacon, an almost painful reminder of his hollow stomach. The old woman was hovering nervously with a great wooden ashet of bacon and peppery blood-sausage, kidneys and liver and good brown bread; but she was not looking at him at all. She was staring wide-eyed at Michael.

He inclined his head courteously, and she let the ashet sink down onto the table as if she could no longer hold it. 'Oh, sir,' she whispered to Walter, without taking her eyes off the dark man, 'be this no' Maister Michael of Oakwood they say's come again?'

Walter regarded her curiously. 'So it is, fat Jeanie. What of it?'

'Oh, maister,' she hissed, her eyes like saucers. 'My father was an Oakwood tenant these thirty years gone, and I a maidie, but one ye micht recall. D'you no' mind me, sir, wee Jeanie, Wull o' Brockhillbank's Jeanie—'

For the first time Walter saw the dark man's countenance change. The look of mild, detached amusement fell wholly away, like a waxen mask melting; and he had a sudden and almost frightening insight into the kind of countenance that must be required of an Imperial courtier, and one constantly reputed a sorcerer at that. The man's warmth was surprising as he grasped her hands. She appeared to be trying to kiss his and fall to her knees at the same time, and too flustered to manage either. 'Wee Jeanie,' he chuckled. 'I am a callous dog! I gave you no thought after you were wedded and gone, or I should have asked after you here. You look hale yet – though not so wee, eh? A good man, your Tammie Greg; still with us?'

'Alas, no,' she sighed. 'Deid of an autumn ague these five year gone; but my boys haud' the land still, from the Laird—' She stopped, and seized his hands again. 'Ye'll put paid tae his tricks, sir, will ye no'? Ye'll venge the auld laird and save my Wattie here – beg pardon, Laird!' She stammered in confusion, but Michael Scot raised her up gently.

'The lord Walter and I are not long acquaint',' he said wryly. 'I fear he doesn't trust me enough, and given the commons' name for me I can scarce blame him.'

She let go his hands in something like awe, and caught at Walter's cotte. 'Sir, sir, don't ye go believing what lies is telt about the maister here! A fine kind laird to my faither he was, and when I was like to die o' a fever he lookit in his books and socht me out a cure – and away it went in a day like a caundle-glim—' She looked down. 'Why, sir, it's yourself'll be havin' the fevers next; it's soakit tae yer skin ye are! Now ye be eatin' up yer good bacon that's gaun' cauld the while, and auld Jeanie'll fetch ye a fine dry shirt and warm it at the hearth.'

Without leaving Walter the slightest chance to speak, she waddled off. Michael reached out with an elegant eating knife and speared its thin silver blade into a chunk of sausage. 'The fever would probably have gone away anyhow; the remedy did no great harm. I have read more since, in Galen the Greek and the many Saracen healers. But knowledge has its uses, sometimes.' The ironic mask was back.

Walter looked at him. 'She trusts you – and for all her prattle, she has an eye, the old woman. She takes a kindly view, when she can; but she's not easily beguiled.'

'Yet it's little enough she's seen of me since she was a grown woman. She thanks a phantom of her childhood. What of *your* eyes, Walter Scot of Branxholme? The Colt is no more; what says the Stallion?'

Walter picked up a strip of bacon and stuffed it whole into his jaws, champing as he answered. 'That I do not trust you enough, not yet. Why should you, being who and what you are, lift a finger to help me?' He laughed, sourly. 'No, spare me an answer I might not believe. I do not trust you enough, but what the Hell does it matter? I can hardly fare worse. My life hangs loose at my belt now, to be slipped at need. I'll hear your device and, if I like it, then I care not whether you're true or false, we'll essay it.' He gulped his mouthful down, and grabbed up a kidney and another hunk of flesh. 'At least it may be a more interesting way to die.'

'Better,' said Michael, wiping his beard fastidiously with a crust of bread, 'than choking to death on bacon fat, at all events.' His hand fastened on Walter's arm with a force that startled the younger man. The fingers felt neither soft nor age-enfeebled, but hard and bony as a chicken's claw. 'So hear me well, for I'll have your whole word or none – no limping ayes, no infantile pride or high heroics that could call all Hell down upon us!'

His voice grew quick and conspiratorial. 'I believe as you do that the Hermitage now hides the Douglas maid! But at all costs and before aught else we must make sure; we must know how, we must know where. I had a plan to spy it out; but with you it will be easier. If you are bold enough, I will undertake to get you within those walls, and you must make what search you can. And . . .' He drew a deep breath, and his dark brows knitted as if in pain. 'And upon utmost hazard of my life and my soul, I will bring you forth again.'

Walter said nothing, only looked at him. His evident doubt seemed to stoke up the fierce insistency in the dark man's voice. 'I believe I can do that,' Michael continued. 'It will be perilous, yes; yet not hopeless. But only if you obey my orders, and accept my conditions. Not so much as an attempt at rescue, should you find her – no matter what her state or situation. Not yet! Later – perhaps. But for now it would call down destruction upon us all. Do you accept? Will you give oath?'

Walter gazed at him a moment. 'As I hope to avenge my father and myself,' he said evenly, 'I do, and freely.'

He expected Michael to insist, and it pleased him when the dark man merely nodded. 'Then my first command is this: get your shirt from Jeanie and your hurts tended. Eat and rest now, briefly. We should arrive at Hermitage only when the sun nears its zenith; and no later than its setting we must be gone.'

Late in the morning of the day following, a great high horse with two mules clipping along behind made their way towards the mouth of the Liddesdale, by the Whitrope Burn under Whiteknowe rather than the ill-starred eastern way of the Scots. The sky was pale and overcast, no sun to be seen; but the red robes of the leading rider glowed softly against the sparse grass and heather of the barren slopes, and the servants in their motley livery stood out still brighter – one all but a dwarf, the other somehow no longer spindly but merely lanky and long-limbed, and broad enough in the shoulder that the bright cotte hung close around him rather than flapping loose. He wore his hat tugged down low over his eyes, as one who goes against the wind.

As indeed he did; for a baleful wind freighted with rainsqualls blew out of the vale, as it often did with the scoured hills to channel it and few trees to bar it. The ancient forest was long gone from that land, if ever it had taken root there; and the high rocks poked up through the thin soil like the bones of a famine. Even in spring, scraps of snow still clung to the crests of Hawk Hill, the Maiden Paps and Hermitage Hill itself, the high doorposts of the vale. From beneath his borrowed hat Walter glanced around in mingled interest and contempt. He knew nothing of the great Ice that had shaped the land, and yet it seemed to him that he saw the passage of something like a vast hand or wing, as it might be a dark angel's, scooping out the sides of the dale into their smooth curves and scouring them of all but the barest soils to sustain life. Only sheep stirred on the higher ground here, and small scrubby ones at that; wiry, compact white cattle grazed on the little patches of bogland pasture below, and plots of kale, turnip and other vegetables ringed the occasional stonecroft, with hardly a grainfield to be seen. The only trees in the vale had evidently been planted around them as wind-breaks, and grew permanently slanted and stunted by the wind's direction.

The ugly little Gilberto grinned at Walter. *'Ancora la miseria! È un porcile, questa Scozia, no?'* He spat copiously into the thin grass.

Walter gritted his teeth and smiled amiably. The horrible little creature persisted in speaking Italian, although he knew Walter didn't; but did he know that Walter had enough Latin to guess what the little bastard meant? Probably he did; and he also knew Walter would do nothing about it, not while his fate depended on him and his master. He had been taking shameless advantage of it all the way down here, goading Walter's mule to buck, loosening his saddle-girth when they stopped to rest, subtly misadjusting his stirrups, until a sharp word from his master had put an end to it. Since then the pricking had been purely verbal; the squat serving-man seemed compounded of malice, as unable to do without it as food or breath. But again Michael's dry voice floated back.

'Pay no heed to Gilbyn. You have not seen the Abruzzi, or the mountain villages of Sicily. Nor he the rich vales of Lothian – which is probably just as well for them. Gilbyn, *basta! Finita la parola, he, piccolo ladro? È troppo cattivo qui!'* The note of authority was stern, and the little man heeded it – but not before leaning over and directing a hideous and disconcerting leer right up into Walter's face, with a belch of truly appalling breath.

A rainsquall veiled the sky ahead, a sweeping gauzy greyness;

Gilbyn pulled his hood up, cackling merrily, while Michael and Walter put up their collars and hung on to their hats. The water rattled around them with stinging force; Walter hoped it would not wash off too much of the greasy meat-juice that browned his face. That and his heavy stubble ought to conceal his Scot features from a casual glance. He was glad when the downpour quickly quietened; but as it swept past, and the keen wind cut at his ribs, he felt the warmth drain from his very bones. Ahead of them, as if taking shape and rising from the ground before him, he had his first sight of Hermitage.

He drew breath sharply. For though in those days it had not been built to the size of later years it still had the aspect of a massive strength, a threefold column of grey stone so hard and square it might have been carved of one piece by some giant mason of legend. It stood out in bare land, as if a blight had spread from it to flay the earth of all higher than grass and low green gorse; the nearest trees were the line of wind-tormented oaks that marked the course of Hermitage Water, the nearest bushes the undergrowth about their roots. The knoll on which the castle stood was higher than their highest crowns, exposed and unapproachable. The low green knowes broke like waves against the roots of its grim walls, impotent against its brutal immobility. Arches yawned in the walls from ground almost to summit, many storeys high, blank dark moaning mouths that waited without the weakness of hunger or desire, only to swallow and engulf. There was no gate behind them, only more strength, more stone around a narrow access that would hardly be worth the firing; and there were few windows, save dark slits just beneath the battlements, far above the reach of scaling-ladder or belfry. Even the low-crowned rooftops were clad in slate and lead rather than wood, dully sheened by the late rain; no fire would bite on those either. The gates in the outer wall and palisade stood open, as if to mark how unnecessary they were, like a crown upon a helm; the helm was the power, the crown only its symbol. No banner flew from the castle battlements, no splash of colour anywhere about it. Only a thread of grey smoke from the rooftop showed that mortal men dwelt within, and not some stone-trow out of old tales.

There was no village here, as there was around Branxholme and most major towers. Once there had been, for as they drew nearer Walter could make out the outlines of the walls and postholes, the scattered stones of the hearths. Now a gaggle of crude turf huts huddled some half-mile downstream like guilty beggars. All the nearer ones had been emptied or abandoned in the years since de Soulis' return, and neglect and the elements had collapsed them into mere overgrown hummocks with only a stone tooth starting here and there. Yet this was a rich settlement; for beyond those miserable huts he could see wide fields laid out, and cattle and sheep in flocks – as well they might be. There were no grainfields, though; de Soulis took much and bought more in from England, it was said, to keep the great lords on the other side of the border happy. Otherwise there could have been a wide steading here; but nothing was allowed to compromise the strength of Hermitage.

The name sat strangely on such a monstrous place. There had been a hermitage on the site, once, before the great monasteries of Melrose and Jedburgh were established, but the walls of war had long since overgrown it, and its voice had fallen silent. In all of Liddesdale there was no church or other holy place; but it was whispered that even today there were among the scanty trees a few, gnarled and ancient, upon which men might still offer up unholy sacrifices. The castle loomed like a barrier, meant to shut in such ancient evil and let it wither; but instead it shut the world out, and left what lay within to the will of its lord.

As they drew nearer they saw more signs of life, small figures that stood or lounged around the wide ring of wooden parapet, very black against the blowing clouds. Almost at once, though, these men ceased to laze, ran around and leaned out, pointing. Other specks of heads appeared on the outer wall, though no one moved to close the gates. 'Now bear yourself well, Branxholme,' said Michael softly. 'For there's no turning back here.'

'Worry about yourself!' whispered Walter indignantly, though he was fighting down his churning stomach and other irritations too. His borrowed coat was itching, and he hoped it wasn't lice. The odd flea he was used to, but not lice. 'Never doubt me!'

He looked at the vast archway in the nearest wall, piercing it almost to its summit. It looked like the jaws of Hell, yet it was meaningless, opening only on a slightly shorter wall within, and a small slot of battlement. Its design seemed to be to over-awe and diminish anyone approaching, and it accomplished that all too well for his taste. Fear and excitement were squalling children, tugging him this way and that in turn. He saw Michael examining the wall also, with almost an indulgent smile. The scholar turned his mount towards the narrow gate almost hidden in the archway-side at its foot, no more than a rabbithole by comparison and barely wide enough for a horse. There was a sharp horn note from the walls above, and another, another yet, playing a complex fanfare such as Walter had seldom heard. The sound of it stirred him, and he had to force himself to maintain his bored, slouching seat in the saddle. He fought down the urge to scratch his buttock, then realized it was wholly in character and rasped away gratefully. As the fanfare died the little port was flung wide, and a tall figure came stalking out. Walter felt his eyes widen; for in such a place and time, and in rich knightly tunic and cloak, there was little doubt who this would be. Thus he had his first close sight of the black Lord of the Liddesdale; and as it is told, he was much taken aback.

What he had expected cannot be said – a huge ogreish ruffian, perhaps, black and coarse of beard, with a devil's glint in his eye and the scorches of Hell upon his cheek, or a bent old greypate in mysterious Saracen garb, yellow-faced and de-praved. For these were the figures the romances would have shown him, and the old tales his nurse had told. In truth, though, the man Michael fitted the mould of a cunning black sorcerer far better than the genial figure that hailed them. De Soulis was a big man, true, though narrow of shoulder and somewhat run to fat, his quaggy belly billowing out his long brown tunic as he bowed to Michael. But his face was neat and plump as a baby's beneath a crop of silver hair so straight and close it looked like a steel cap, with bright apple cheeks behind which his little blue eyes wrinkled up and all but vanished as he beamed and boomed a welcome.

'*Salve magister illustrissime!* Now this *is* a great and rare honour, to have such a scholar of imperial repute and distinction arrive at my remote gate!'

'*Salve domine et magister!*' Michael swung himself easily from the saddle and returned the bow with hat on breast. 'I was on my way by these parts, and would not have missed such an opportunity even for a brief visit, Sir Nicholas. There are few enough in this my homeland with whom I share . . . a community of experience, one might say.'

De Soulis chortled deep in his throat, as if something stirred in his belly. 'Neatly put! You'll come in, of course, and rest yourself. Stay awhile! Heaven alone knows it's little enough intelligent conversation I get, surrounding myself with this band of broken sheepshaggers and fishgutters out of the Isles. And you'll not remember the old Hermitage as she is now, strong and proud; you must let me show off all my improvements. These your men? Italians? Freezing their balls off, I'll be bound. In you come, lads; dismount and mind your heads on the gate, and the narrow way behind – single file only. I find it convenient,' he added, 'to have as small a breach in my walls as possible. Keep what's in, in and what's out, out – that's what I say, ho!'

The corridor behind the little gate bent awkwardly and could be stopped by a heavy iron grille, against which a barricade could be quickly piled. Glancing up, Walter saw the roof had narrow slots in it – what were called murder-slots – and alert eyes looked back at him; he ducked his head hastily. If this was the best gate, then the place must be nearly impregnable. On this rocky knoll the walls couldn't be easily undermined, and no siege-belfry could approach, even assuming one could be built high enough. He shrivelled inwardly at the memory of his own youthful impatience, a century ago as it seemed. No wonder his father and Ker had hardly contemplated attacking Hermitage! If there was water here – and in this wet countryside there almost certainly was – and store of provision, the castle could sit tight and laugh at besiegers. That was what Robert Scot had expected it to do, allowing him a face-saving gesture; he hadn't realized the whole affair had been carefully calculated to lure the Scots to their own destruction. As it would have, if the trap hadn't been sprung too early.

Sharp fear caught at his throat. Could this be another, subtler trap? With Michael Scot as plausible bait? If it was, they would lay hands on him any moment; he had nothing but a thin Italian dagger to his belt. But nobody was paying him the slightest attention, de Soulis least of all; like everyone else he was staring at Michael's horse as his grooms led it off to the stables. 'A marvel of a creature is that!' he remarked. He made no offer to buy it, though. At last he tore himself away and ushered Michael and his followers into a pleasantly furnished chamber with cushioned chairs and a central table at which he sat Michael with great ceremony before sprawling down opposite. The cushions looked so inviting to Walter's wounds and bruises that he barely prevented himself sinking down alongside, but remembered in time to go and stand behind his 'master' alongside Gilbyn. Gilbyn trod on his toe.

A hard-faced steward brought wine in a splendid silver cruche, with silver quaich bowls to drink from instead of the horn beakers used at Branxholme, or Cessford for that matter. De Soulis poured and pledged his guest, Michael returned the pledge, and they exchanged friendly smiles. But this close Walter, studying his enemy with uneasy fascination, could see that the lids about those glittering little eyes were heavy and red-rimmed, as if from constant weeping. The pale blue pupils, almost glassy, surveyed his guests with a blankness so intense it suggested a dam over churning waters. 'A long time since we met, Michael,' he said.

'Indeed, Sir Nicholas. You've come a long way since then.'

'Not as long as yours, nor with such honour. Scholar and Imperial counsellor! I could envy you such celebrity, man!'

'I would not. Whatever's thought of me elsewhere, here in my own land I'm little known or regarded, distrusted even, whereas you are a powerful lord.'

'That's ever the way, is it not? But what is our poor Scotland, after all? When through half the colleges and courts of Europe I've heard your name resound. *Michaele Scottis sapientissime magister disciplinae*, from Spain to the Ister and beyond.'

Michael smiled. 'Then you must have been there also. You could have shone in the same line, if you chose. You had the name of a tireless seeker after knowledge.'

De Soulis laughed behind closed lips. 'I doubt that. I had something of the study, aye, but I sought knowledge not for its own sake, but that I might set it to use and profit.'

Michael's look was guarded. 'And that has also sped you along your road, as I along mine. And by strange paths, if I mistake not. The Ister, eh? And beyond. So you were at the very bounds of Christendom, the fringes of the Eastern Empire. Were you ever in Dacia?'

'Beyond the Forest? Aye, at the Seven Towers. Were you?'

'For a time. Then I think – Italy? The Scholomance? Were you ever—'

De Soulis drew breath, and glanced around. 'No. The sorts spoke against it, and the bone dice dealt me a ten on the first throw. Yourself?'

'Yes.'

'God!' It was less a word than a mere explosion of breath. 'What number were you?'

Michael's eyes closed momentarily, as if in pain. 'The sixth. And the eighth.'

De Soulis stared. 'You went twice? You went back? God! To feel that at your back – to hear . . .' He shook his head, and then, more deliberately, looked at his fingernails. 'No, not I! But were you ever in the kingdoms of Babylon?'

Michael blinked with keen interest. 'No nearer than Acre. You mean . . . Chorazin. The Black Pilgrimage—'

'Hist, man!' De Soulis leaned forward fiercely and gestured him quiet. 'Not before the men!' he added softly, glaring around at his own hangers-on.

'I can trust mine,' said Michael reassuringly.

'Maybe: they're domestics!' muttered Soulis. 'But I didn't choose mine for their softer natures. Hey, you louns! Out, avoid, get you to the buttery for a bittock bread and a stoup of ale! Master Michael and I will look over the castle. And let none disturb us; we've matter of moment to discuss!'

Michael waved casual agreement. 'Aye, Gilbyn, Gualtiero, go!'

The thuggish steward ushered Gilbyn and Walter silently out. His cotte was beginning to itch again, and he scratched irritably. That exchange had been interesting in its way, as if some subtle test of status were going on; but it was outwardly friendly, at least, and left him adrift. It seemed he could trust Michael thus far; but how about this malicious little devil Gilbyn? And when was he supposed to get his searching done, if he were stuck playing the domestic?

The bread was good, the ale strong and full and in no short supply; de Soulis could afford to feed his men well. It was this that gave Walter his idea and his opportunity. He began making a show of drinking, and to his surprise Gilbyn played along, admonishing him in Italian and explaining to their taciturn hosts that this young sprout couldn't hold his wine, or even weak Scots ale. Gilbyn's well-judged malice soon started the inevitable drinking session, and Walter was able to stagger up and demand, in fractured speech and graphic dumbshow, the urgent use of a privy. The other man would have gone with him, but Gilbyn's strong arm and stinging jibe about excuses and hasty exits pulled him back to the table. Walter reeled out into the buttery passage, not altogether acting; deep draughts of relief and new danger lightened his head as much as the ale. They would hardly be surprised if he took his time, or even fell asleep; that would be his excuse.

Now he had a whole castle to comb – no easy task. Where would an important prisoner be kept? Almost certainly in the bailey, the heart of the castle. On soft swift feet Walter padded around the inner court of the tower. It was not that big, and he found no doors that looked likely holds. There were few folk about and nobody seemed to notice him as he darted from doorway to doorway, listening and trying; he grew pleased with his new-found skill and agility. But he had to duck down hurriedly behind a well-mouth as he heard voices at a doorway, and saw de Soulis and Michael stroll past in lively and unintelligible converse, their footfalls echoing on the flagstones. Evidently de Soulis was showing off his improvements, throwing back doors here and there. One opened upon a narrow staircase that might lead to an underfloor of some kind, cellars or dungeons. De Soulis' harsh laugh seemed to suggest the more sinister end. As they passed into a door at the far side of the court Walter slunk over to the door, slid it back open and padded lightly down the stairs.

They gave upon a long, narrow corridor with two or three doors on either side, the only light in it at the further end where some kind of airshaft opened in the crudely arched roof, ancient-looking and encrusted with black mould and minerals. Evidently de Soulis had not been about his improvements here. Below the shaft stood a cask on end, evidently used as a table, with a crude fat-lamp, a beaker and some other odds and ends including what looked like twigs. Behind it sat a tangle-haired man on a low stool, his head back against the nitrous wall, his mouth open, snoring stertorously. The doors were newer-looking, solid, windowless and ironbound, with heavy bars across them and no opening except a keyhole. They could be storerooms or dungeons; but the bars and the sentry suggested the more sinister use. Nerving himself, Walter crept forward over the floor of trodden earth, put his ear to the first door and tapped gently. There was nothing, no response; but the sentry's snore did not change. Nothing happened at the next, nor at the end of that row; but at the first on the other side, nearest the sentry, Walter caught a waft of foulness at the keyhole. He tapped, gingerly; no answer. It was a carrion stink, and he shuddered. At the next there was also a smell, equally foul but privy-like; and when he tapped this time something stirred, and there was a faint clawing at the inside.

'Margaret?' whispered Walter, wincing at how loud it suddenly sounded. A low keening moan nearly made him leap away from the keyhole; but as he stilled his pounding heart he realized it was a man's voice, an old one's at that, though he could make out no words. Then the snoring broke, and he scuttled back into the stairwell, barely in time. As the moaning rose and fell the sentry stirred himself, swore, shuffled down the passage and kicked the door, shouting half in thickly accented Border speech, half in rough-sounding Erse or Gaelic of the Isles. 'Haud yer whisht, *tanamnh an Deoil!* Are ye no' deid yet, like Clem yer neighbour?'

The voice went on moaning.

'Watter ye want, iss it?' snarled the sentry. 'Stop you, and I'll gie ye watter!' He hitched up his rough kilt and pissed against the keyhole, laughing loudly. The moaning died away, and the man darted back to the barrel, seized a twig and thrust it through the keyhole, waggling it about. 'Come on then!' he hissed. 'Ye canna say we dinna feed ye!' He waited a moment, then jerked the twig back, laughing. There was a faint despairing wail from within. Walter shuddered; the bark hung from it in shreds, evidently stripped by teeth. The sentry, still laughing, went to the next cell, that Walter had not yet tried, and hammered on the door. 'You wantin' a bite too, Clem?' He hammered again, jabbed the twig through and waited; but after a minute he pulled it back, as if disappointed. He thumped, listened, then laughed. 'Iss it deid ye are, then? Aye, well, it's no' before time, ye stubborn barstid! High time we're rid o' the whole pack o' ye!' He laughed again, echoing in the stony space, and shuffled back to his barrel.

Walter crouched in silence, thinking. The creature there enjoyed persecuting his prisoners. If there had been a girl in any of the cells, he would hardly have left her out, if only with words. And there had been no response, no sense of presence behind any of the other doors. No, if she lived she was not here. This place was for the forgotten, those left to die. A valuable prisoner would be kept elsewhere. He thought of romances, of princesses held at towertops. Quickly, silently in his soft leather shoes, he stole back up the stair again.

There was only one obvious staircase rising from the courtyard, although it looked as though it branched higher up. Walter, suddenly less confident again, listened at the foot, but heard no voices or footfalls from within. Then he sprang up the stone steps lightfoot and limber, two steps at a time, pausing every so often to listen and feel for vibrations in the wooden balustrade. There were none. It didn't surprise him. This would lead to the roof, and de Soulis would have the guard on alert up there while outsiders were within; they wouldn't dare come down. He padded on up.

Doors opened off the steps at intervals, some ajar, some with voices behind them; those he dared try were not locked or bolted. The light from the narrow windows was steeply slanted and growing greyer and weaker, so that much of the castle lay already in shadow. At last he came to the level of the roof, and keeping low, with his head at floor-height, saw to his alarm that the sun was already well down the sky. For a minute its red-dening light glanced flame off a guard's spear. Sure enough, the parapets were full of men, in case the visitors tried some clever ploy with outside forces, like the Trojan Horse he had read about. He was about to give up and turn back when he realized there was one more level over his head; the stair went up into the roof above the solar. Biting his lip, he skipped lightly past the doorway and up the last few steps to a door both newer-looking and heavier than the ones below, and a very snug fit in its socket. And this one, this only, was locked.

Walter listened a moment, and heard nothing – or was that a swish of material? It was something, anyway; enough to make him greatly daring, and tap delicately. There was no response, and no more sound, yet the sense of presence grew ever more tangible, as if the whole room beyond that door were listening. So might a captured lady behave in this uncertain place. He plucked out the Italian's thin dagger, and began gingerly trying to probe the mechanism of the lock. But, just as he felt the ward start to shift, there was a sudden sharp clack and the whole door swung smoothly open. He sprang back, dagger levelled, breathing hard; had he done that?

By now Walter was so giddy with fast blood he was ready to believe it. Panther-soft, he padded up to the door and peered cautiously in. The only light was the sunset captured by a little eastward window, strained redly through its shutter; but what he saw thrilled him still further. The room was wide, with a smooth wood floor and low arched hearth like a bedchamber; but there was no bed, only a couch, bare and cushionless, with an old red nightcap lying on it. The uncovered stone wall either side of the hearth was covered with curious chalkings, mostly

half-erased; scuffs of chalk and charcoal streaked the smooth
floorboards, as if many things had been erased there also, more
thoroughly. Against the wall at angles to the couch there was
a table, a wide thing draped to the floor with a fine tapestry, its
top littered with strange-looking papers and scrolls and things
less identifiable, with a writing-stand among them topped by a
tall quill and silver sandbox. A smoky glass mirror, streaked
with soot and candle-grease, stood beside it on a tall stand, and
other peculiar instruments in chased metal and crystal stood in
a glass-sided cabinet nearby, striking glints of fire in the murky
gloom. Walter had never imagined so much clear glass could
exist, let alone bear weight. But it was the only substantial
obstacle in the empty room, and nobody could hide behind it.
Yet what had stirred? For movement he had heard. He sidled
softly up to the desk, where a half-written letter lay still sanded
on top of the writing-stand – and then hopped back with a yelp
at the sudden flurry of movement. A small, smoky-furred cat
sprang onto the desktop and spat at him.

He laughed, rather breathlessly; another like that and he
would need a privy in earnest! But he reached out, kindly
enough, to take the little beast by its scruff. It hissed and twisted
and its needle claws slashed a red streak across his hand; he
cursed and tossed it away on to the couch. Sucking his hand,
he turned back to the letter. The light was poor, the hand crabbed; he could make out only a little. But the name of Douglas,
with its soaring initial, that was clear – and there, a line or
two down, was Margaret's. All this among flowery, sycophantic
phrasings – *vraie, juste est virtueux mon Seigneur* to the point of
puking. Who would de Soulis address so?

Quite suddenly the glow went like a blown candle. Walter
looked up, alarmed; but he could still see in the gloom, and
nothing stirred. He smiled; from the couch two green gleams,
looking suddenly prominent in the surrounding greyness,
regarded him with fixed mistrust. Then his eyes focused, and
he saw that they were unusually prominent all right; they looked
larger, somehow – and, God alive, they were a hand's breadth
apart.

It took no more than that to make him break for the door,

with a stab of cold terror on his soul. He was through it and clattering down the steps, caring for concealment no longer; but something else was there at his back, landing in the doorway with a savage exhaling hiss. He sprang from one flight to the next, for his life, crashing against the balustrade, half stumbling and leaping again with dull agony in his feet and hot searing in his calves, and again. Chest bursting, legs weakening, he thought for a moment he was ahead – then something cuffed at him, tipped him over in mid-air, sent him crashing down against the wall. Even as he tried to scramble up, the great hot weight struck his back and sent him sprawling. Heavy blunt claws like a lynx's ripped at the bright livery, and he screamed and twisted violently to keep fangs from his throat. A fetid stink rolled over him, awful carrion breath. The force of his struggle dislodged them both and sent them crashing over each other to the next landing. It was none of his own doing that Walter landed on top, flattening the other with his weight and tearing free; he went rolling and bumping helplessly down the last flight into the hall. Into a wide pool of light; for there at its base stood de Soulis and Scot, with servants and lanterns. Nothing sprang after him from the stair.

De Soulis' face twisted in an ironic smile. 'Well, man? What ails you?'

Walter, gasping, remembered who he was supposed to be, and prayed that de Soulis didn't speak Italian. 'I . . . dreenk,' he wheezed, trying to imitate the lanky servant's accent. 'I . . . go pees . . . loose me . . . beest he jump me . . .'

The apple cheeks bunched up in a highly unpleasant smile. *'Bene! La tua bestia, eccola qua!'* De Soulis shouted up into the dark. 'Redcap! Redcap, come forth!'

Walter scrambled up, wincing as his wounds galled him again, expecting the pard or whatever it was to spring down on him. Or, worse, the little cat. But the feet on the steps were flatly human. What shuffled out into the light was a little old man in a grey robe like a monk's, absurdly topped by an old red stocking nightcap. He appeared to be picking his nose with a grime-grey finger. Michael's dark face was unreadable, but there was grim intensity in his gaze.

'Well, Redcap?' demanded Soulis. 'Have you been frighting this foreign lad?'

The old man inspected the result. 'Stotterin' roond privy places i' the dark!' he muttered. 'Wee limmer! He's no sair scathed, he'll be whole soon enow!'

This would have been true enough if Walter were not already wounded. His whole body felt afire, though he struggled not to show it. He shrugged and grimaced in Gilbyn's surly fashion, but he had the deadly feeling that the Lord of Hermitage saw right through him.

'Well, then,' remarked de Soulis cheerfully, 'I hold that mutual apologies are in order – eh?' Redcap shrugged in his turn, blew his nose noisily on his thumb, and held out his hand to Walter, who took it shrinkingly. It felt rough and hot.

'Grand, eh? Grand!' exhaled de Soulis. He seemed hugely pleased about something. 'So now, what about a spot of dinner, eh?'

Michael spread his hands in courteous regret. 'I fear not, much as I have enjoyed the visit. I must ride on tonight.'

'What?' exclaimed de Soulis. 'But you've scarcely arrived, it's miles back to Oakwood, you'll not be there before morning. No, you must eat and sleep here, I insist, it's my duty. Why, there's a night full of broken men and other riff-raff out there—'

He pressed the courtesies home with gleeful force, but Michael was equally pleasantly obdurate. Finally de Soulis yielded, and had their horses brought out, staring in fascination at the stallion once again; it stamped and snorted as it saw him, its hooves booming on the flags of the yard, and nickered till the walls rang.

'A fine art you must have to tame that callant, Michael lad!' said de Soulis wryly.

Michael Scot smiled. 'It is not so hard, once mounted. Would you care for a ride, perhaps?'

De Soulis's look became a touch glassy. 'Ha! Another day, perhaps! I'll not hold you back now. No indeed! But I am glad that you're in this land once again, and I trust we'll meet ere long. There may be matters of mutual profit to concern us!' They took long-winded and courteous leave of one another, with much bowing and scraping, and the visitors led their horses through the narrow port once again. De Soulis came out to wave them farewell. And even as the light faded, and the castle became a single black crag against the last streaks of colour in the sky, Walter seemed to feel those pale greedy eyes following at his back.

He shifted in his saddle. 'Master Michael!' he hissed. 'Are we away?'

'Aye, barely. Did you—?'

'A moment!' exclaimed Walter, slipping from his stirrup and disappearing behind a convenient clump of gorse. Gilbyn gave a great crow of malevolent laughter.

'So,' remarked Michael when Walter reappeared plucking painful sprigs of gorse from his hose, 'you did not find the privy. Aught else?'

'Naught!' spat Walter. 'Save a fright and a shaming!' He poured out the tale of the sinister sights in the dungeon, of the tower stair and his failure and humiliation; but when he came to the letter Michael was greatly interested. He halted him, looking back at the battlements of Hermitage, and bade him save the tale till they were further on.

At last, as darkness and the slope of the hills cloaked them, Michael glanced back, bade Gilbyn have a care for watchers, and remarked softly, 'That's an unexpected gain! You know to whom it was written, of course.'

'Somebody important,' suggested Walter lightly. 'If not . . .' His voice faded.

'The King,' nodded Michael. 'There's dark work in hand here, yoked as much to the Douglases as yourselves. Alexander wishes to control the Douglases and the whole land of reivers at this his southern gate, to tap the power and the wealth they dispose of to feed his own armies. It's clear enough de Soulis has sold him the idea he can deliver such a thing – and a wealthy Douglas wedding would be a fine start.'

'*What?*' howled Walter, appalled. 'You tell me the King would so countenance brigandage and murder and the black art? And sanctify rape?'

'Not at all,' said Michael judiciously. 'But he might not inquire too deeply into de Soulis' methods.'

Walter shivered. 'D'you know what he unleashed on me up there? It wasn't that dirty old sot that got me screighing down that stair – it was some beast out of Hell, first a wee kittie and then a damned great lion or pard or something of the sort! And then he calls out that dirty old loun – why? What was he, its keeper or what? Anyhow, that was the limit of my searching. Much good I made of it! She might have been behind one of those dungeon doors, but I think not.' He shivered. 'I hope not! I pray not, passing foul as they were!'

'The old monks' cells, they were,' said Michael reflectively, 'of the hermitage that stood there these three centuries past. So he told me, along with more than I wanted to know. He held nothing back; he showed me the castle from top to bottom, openly. We were just going to look at the tower when you saved us the trouble. Open as the day.'

Walter eyed him keenly. 'You mean – as you did? The same trick you played on my father and the warden?'

'Ah, you see that, do you? By showing all, you control the search. He was laughing at us, in open defiance, to sow doubt – either that he might have no hand in Margaret's vanishing, or that she is being held elsewhere, if she still lives.'

'Laughing,' said Walter heavily. 'Then we've failed.' He felt heavy with uselessness. 'You kept faith, anyway. You gave me a slim chance, and I threw it away.'

The dark man shook his head, looked back over his shoulder into the night, and permitted himself a brief chuckle. 'Not a bit of it, lad. You did exactly what was required of you. You searched well, but not too well. I expected you'd trip some manner of sorcerous trap, though I admit none so fierce, and that also you did. De Soulis, detecting one clumsy searcher, would feel all the cleverer and suspect the true one less. That was why he seemed so pleased. Meanwhile Gilbyn was searching in his own manner.'

Walter swivelled in his saddle, forgetting his pains. '*Gilbyn*? He never stirred—'

The squat man cackled. 'Through the minds and souls of those

I drank with,' he said, in perfect Norman French. 'Such small minds! Such black and shrivelled little souls, as if the fires already licked at them!'

'He— You found something out?'

Michael Scot shook his head, his black locks invisible now, merging with the falling night. 'No. Their master had already detected Gilbyn, though more subtly; it took him a while with me distracting his mind. Gilbyn learned much of interest, but of Margaret naught.'

'Then—'

'No. Gilbyn too was a distraction from the real searcher. Him we have yet to hear from, and it is well past time.' Michael's voice took on a sharp note of question. *'Well?'*

Walter stared around wildly, expecting perhaps the servant whose role he had usurped; but the sky was quenched now, black as the earth, and he could not even make out the road beneath him.

Then he jumped violently and almost fell from his saddle. A voice spoke in the darkness. An awful voice: inhuman – deep and dark and resonant as lightless pits in stone. But it had a place, and breath, and that place was right beside him in the darkness – far too close.

'I hear, Magister!' it said, and it spat out its words like gobbets of lead. *'I hear, I speak, I serve! Within the earth the echoes talked, they told many things. Below the passage of the cells another lies, that was the crypt and undercroft of the hermitage of old. Beyond light and hope there, a young woman kneels. Bread she eats, water she sips and no chains clink, on mats she lies and not bare stone; of comfort or company she has nothing else. Save for the presence of the dead she is utterly alone; and she cries aloud, or prays for the soul of poor Margaret.'*

6 🏰 The Riding of the Night

'Well,' said Walter harshly, 'you've been true to your word thus far, wizard, I'll give you that. But, lord God, I don't doubt now why my father thought of you as he did! Or what risks I run in keeping such unchancy company!' He shivered, and tossed the ale back straight from the jug, then wheezed with pain. 'That voice – Christ, the hollowness of it! As if an open grave spoke, and offered counsel!'

All that long road back in the dark, bedevilled by the picture it had painted him, shaken from the strange attack and the pain of his maltreated wounds, he had ridden with his back icy and the hair starting on his head, wincing at the touch of every twig, thinking each leaf a clammy finger, each thorn a claw, and hating himself for it. Cowardice was dishonour, by every particle of his upbringing; yet he could not charge headlong at what he feared, as his father had, like the wild boars he hunted. In Walter there was too much thought for that, and so he struggled to persuade himself the voice was a jongleur's trick, the page Gilbyn or even Michael himself casting the voice as Irish tumblers did. That had helped. All the same, the moment they came within Branxholme gate he had run to rouse the old priest and have himself shriven and blessed, even as he shed his borrowed livery and had his wounds tended. And, that done, he had turned to the new-cleared hall for food and ale – especially ale.

'But the voice told you what you needed to know!' said Michael. 'And you have seen your enemy now, and the strength of his hold. Even a battery of mangonels and the finest siege engines Douglas or Percy could field would hardly suffice to break down the walls of Hermitage, if there were no greater power behind them. And power there is.'

Walter frowned with sudden aggression. 'De Soulis? Not

feared of him. He's been a fierce man in his day, no doubt; but he's old. Aye, he has men enough, but take them away and—' He gestured dismissively, and tilted the jug. 'I could see him down soon enough! Or,' he added hastily, ashamed of his own arrogance, 'a knight of more proof and experience surely could – my father, had the bastard but dared face him! But certainly I might venture, strength for strength.'

'No!' said Michael, and there was that about the word which made Walter lower the jug.

'You mean to say—'

'I do. The tales about him are no less than truth. Strong forces wind and coil around him and through him like smoke in ceaseless flow, for those who have eyes to see. They would let no blade pass, no brand burn, no rope tighten, no water fill his lungs. With their force to stiffen his sinews his strength would surely surpass yours.'

Walter set down the jug slowly. The drink had blunted the throb of his own wounds, but only a little. 'Then what, wizard? Has your stratagem won me nothing but a stay? Have I still no hope but to go seek my death at Soulis' gate?'

Michael's intense eyes fixed the younger man. 'Did I say so? I would not have led you into such peril merely to waste time. Nor myself! I also went into danger yesterday, do not forget that; and perhaps I have more to lose. This is a world of balance, birth and death, winter and spring, cycle and anticycle beneath the commanding planets that shape our destinies in ways dark and faint. Do we see the stars by daylight? Yet when the sun falls, and petty torches are quenched, they shine out in majesty beneath the regal moon. For every power there is a counter, for each act a recoil, for each object an opposite, though it may lie hid from us for a time, maybe forever if we know not how to seek it. There are means to defeat even such a hardened sorcerer as de Soulis, and one such you can set hand to – with my help.'

Walter slapped his hand flat down on the table with stinging force. 'Then find me one! There's worth enough yet in Branxholme's coffers to buy—'

Michael shook his head gravely, lifting an admonitory hand like a saint in a painting. The low early sun streaming through the open door caught it, and for an instant the tanned and weathered fingers shone with gold. 'It is not for the asking, nor the buying neither. It must be won, and hard-won – in foreign service, in another land.'

'Abroad? As in a Crusade, you mean?'

Suddenly Walter was all alive with interest, the tales he had heard and the bold ballads surging up in his beer-muddled mind. To see other lands, other lives as he had longed to since Ker suggested it – *that* drove fright and desperation from his mind. 'But the maid? I would be a year gone! Maybe even three. How can I leave her in thrall for so long? And my demesne and people? By then de Soulis would have swallowed up her and the Scots altogether, and be going on to gather the Marches under his sway!'

Michael's dark face grew pensive. 'It is for no such time I would have you gone. In any event the lady Margaret is reasonably safe, for now. De Soulis wants an alliance with the Douglases under a shield of seeming legality he can display before the King. He is not yet ready to seek marriage by force, or to hold her open hostage and in deliberate torment. He will strive to haggle, to agree, to strike a bargain with her people. That will take time, and he will not be hasty. For as a pawn in the gaming and a seal on the agreement he needs her whole and in health.'

Walter glared into space. 'F'that's true, then the Douglases can redeem her even without a fight! I've half a mind to let them! God knows, I wish the maid no ill, but 's not as if I care a whit for her – still less she me! Help if she needs it, but just to save the Douglases' honour – shit! Let 'em try their worst against me, if it's no more 'n force they respect!'

'Of course,' added Michael, 'he may seek to break her spirit, but only by circumstance, not pain; and I guess she will not break so readily. But *not yet* is not *never*. If he cannot compound with the Douglases – after that, what?'

Walter snarled in beery revolt. 'Yes! I know, all too well I know! What my honour cannot permit while I live! What the Douglases insist I remedy alone! I weary of Douglases, do you know that, wizard? And even of honour!' He sagged, and slumped back against the table, wincing as he hit a bruise a spearpoint had left in his side. 'Honour, honour will not let me be. Will not. And . . .' He drank again, could not articulate what he felt. 'There is more. Much more.'

He stared muzzily around him at the familiar warmth of Branxholme hall. After the last day's horrors it seemed kindly and accustomed, with long shafts of sunlight sparkling down through the dusty sunshine. Sleepy flies were already beginning to buzz around the platter with the remains of his breakfast. He waved them away almost genially. This hall, this manor, his home – it was his now to defend, and he could not imagine wanting anywhere else. But how long would he have quiet enjoyment of it, or his folk of even their poor huts, if de Soulis weren't stopped?

'How long,' he demanded carefully, 'would this quest of yours take me away?'

Michael shrugged. 'Who can say? Not long enough to damage your cause, if you are the man I think you. But the sooner we leave, the better.'

Walter sat up. 'You also?' He licked his lips. 'So be it. When, then?'

'Are you so ready? *Now.*'

Walter reached nervously for the beer-jug, around whose rim a fly was circling hopefully, but Michael impatiently drew his hand away. 'Come!' he commanded, and his hand clasped tight around Walter's arm. Too stunned to resist, or too drunk, the young man rose, and Michael drew him towards the sunlit door.

The bailey court was empty, except for Michael's great dark horse, tethered by the water trough, still saddled and bridled. The low sun gilded its flanks and flashed fire on the ornate trappings; it gleamed entangled in the heavy mane it tossed, as fresh and eager as if those long miles the night before were no more than a dream. Walter turned to the stable to call his grooms for a fresh horse, but Michael stopped him. 'No. This is no road for any ordinary horse to tread. Algol will bear us both.'

Walter chuckled. 'Algol? Is that the beast's name? A fine out-landish ring—' He stopped, and his laughter died. He pulled his arm free in sudden flaring distrust. 'And what manner of outlandish road would it be that only a warlock's horse can tread?'

Michael Scot looked up at the sun for a moment, letting it bathe his face, and flashed one of his sudden smiles. 'Not to Hell, Walter, if that's what you fear.' And he sang in a low voice a short snatch from a familiar old ballad:

> I'll tak' ye where the white lilies grow,
> On the banks of Italie.

'Italy?' Walter stood a moment in swaying astonishment, his mind muddied by drink and exhaustion. In that state it all seemed sensible enough to him, being where Michael had lived; and into his mind came the thought of Rome the Holy City, and the launching of Crusades, and the tales of the paladins and the ancients, Julius Caesar and Charlemagne all muddled up together, the Pope and the Holy Roman Emperor. The sun shone ever warmer on his head, and he thought of all the tales he had heard, of a land where it never grew cold, of rich strong wine and bright colours and towering timeless palaces, and proud courtiers and lovely women bright as exotic birds. This man had awoken all those images in Walter's dreams; now he would take him to see them. Very natural, very reasonable; and when his mind cleared he was already mounting up behind Michael's saddle.

'Wait!' he croaked. 'I must have some clothes packed, and food – I've nothing save my sword about me—'

'You need no more!' said Michael sternly, restraining him as he was about to dismount. 'No more than your blade and your courage. Be sure and not let either slip by the way. All else we will find, and more! But this I charge you – hold fast to my saddle, or at need my shoulder, and otherwise do nothing, say nothing, till I give you leave. You understand?'

His eyes glittered with a ferocity that belied his usual calm. Walter swallowed, and nodded. Michael turned away. '*Avanti!*'

His grip on Walter's arm was unbreakable, and with his other hand he flicked the reins, hard. Walter felt the surge of force in the muscular back beneath his thighs, the thrill of a strength

113

that seemed limitless lent to his own limbs. The black horse swung about and whinnied aloud, a daunting sound. Walter waved to the sentries guarding the half-mended gate, but never had a chance to see their answer. The gate swung wide, the great horse surged forward like a fierce spring gust, and wall and gate whirled by in a blur as it sprang for the open road beyond. Down it galloped past cot and farmstead, past field and sheepfold with the forest gate before it, and the rolling heights above. The wind stung tears in Walter's eyes, so that when he twisted around for a parting look at Branxholme he saw only distant blurs; next moment he had to turn back and fight for balance as the slope grew steep beneath them. Then they were upon the trees of the ancient forest, and among them. The sun was still too low to spear down between their dense-woven boughs; their shadow turned the way to gloom, for all the glowing sky above. The paths were many, the ways mazy and entwined; yet not for an instant did the magnificent beast's relentless pace falter under Michael's firm hand, guiding it ever deeper into the dark.

The trees grew straight by the older and well cleared ways, where the pressure of their fellows was relieved; but on the roads Michael chose the oak and the chestnut, even upright birch and ash, grew ever more gnarled and bent, tangled in tortuous embrace. Walter was forever ducking to avoid a clutching bough or sweeping veil of leaves, till he lost all sense of their direction. At last it was as if the trees joined fingers overhead, closing out the last glimmer of open sky and leaving the riders in darkness; but the black horse rushed on unchecked. Walter hunched down, lest branches unseen sweep him from the saddle, but Michael remained upright as ever, and from that moment on there were no more. They might as well have been racing down a tunnel carven in rock – or up, for Walter could find no sense of his bearing in the gloom. It closed in about him like a fist, but he held to Michael's charge and spoke no word. The horse bore him easily and without strain. The jolting of its stride was slight, but the effort of staying upright was no less, the fear of falling great. And eventually even a slight jolting may become a torment by repetition, as a myriad gentle pressures may crush a man. He swayed, feeling his wounds burn, his bruises protest; but he held fast to the saddle, and his strength did not fail. After a while he lost all sense of time; there might never have been a world of light or air, never another life, only an eternity of smooth, tireless running beneath him, and rushing air above.

It was a shout from Michael that jolted him awake. 'On, on! Make speed! How fast do you go?'

With the coming of the answer Walter all but lost his hold and fell.

'*As fast as the wind I fare, Michael.*'

'Not enough!' cried the wizard, and Walter felt him urge the creature on. 'Not near fast enough; you do but canter as if this were a lady-ride! Race, lest we founder at the fords and be swept away! Faster!'

Walter felt the burst of energy in the great body, the rush of air redouble to a speed he had never thought any horse could reach; but he swayed on his seat, sick with dread and horror, greater than that of falling into the rushing dark. What manner of back bore him he dared not guess; but there had been no mistaking that awful voice, or, this time, its origins. He felt faint and dizzy, his blood sang in his ears.

But before he had time to think further there was a sudden flurry of sound beneath him. The onrush never slackened, the fall of the hoofbeats faltered not the slightest, but their sound became a splashing spattering he knew well, thick and heavy with the weight of marshland. Splashes of the muck thrown up slapped against his boots; he braced himself for the chill clammy impact of marsh-water. But when a greater splash struck his leg he yelled aloud and almost let go in his shock. It clung, and flowed down stickily, and it was searing hot as he brushed it off. And the stink of it – no marsh-waft, more a sickliness he'd smelt all too often of late. His drink-filled guts rebelled, and he had to choke them down. A great flood was welling around the horse's belly, lapping at his boots with a strong slow surge. The brute was hip-deep and still pushing remorselessly on through what must be fords, breasting a vast sluggish weight of current; but in what? The stench rose up in suffocating, sickening waves.

He jerked his boots free of it in horror. They were riding through a river of hot blood.

Abruptly he felt a change, a slight leaning, heard the awfulness beneath froth and bubble around those muscled pillars of legs. A sudden thrust, a splashing, spraying sound, and they were racing free; but foulness clung and clotted on Walter's boots and hose, and he shuddered at the touch.

'On now!' cried Michael aloud. 'On!'

The beast sprang away on to solidity once again, on to clean earth perhaps; but all was darkness yet, and to Walter it was on the road to Hell. He clung with all the strength he had, but he no longer knew why; darkness reigned, and the onrushing wind.

Suddenly Michael shouted again, harsh and angry. 'You! What kind of speed d'you call this, you idling corbie's bait? What way d'you think you're making now?'

And again that terrible voice spoke, and Walter had to fight not to clamp his hands over his ears.

I outstrip the wind that blows behind me, Michael, and overtake that which blows before.

'Jade!' yelled the wizard. 'Halting naig! Is it the spur you're lacking? Make haste, fly, lest we be o'erwhelmed!'

Walter would not have thought those hoofbeats could grow faster; but they did, and merged into one single horrendous drumming that awoke pounding resonances all around them. The chill wind was flaying his cheeks now, and he huddled further down into his collar; but it found every cranny and seam in his clothing, and drank out the heat through every one. His pulse pounded and roared in his ears, his breath rasped in his throat; yet despite them, because of them almost, he seemed to catch another change in the drumming, a subtler one that swirled and shifted the windrush till it was as much before him as about him, and growing louder. A pulse grew in it, a slow, heavy rumble, and he thrilled as he guessed at it. A second later and he was sure, though he had seen the sight only twice in his life. It was the crashing of waves upon a shore, and their splashing, bubbling return, as the great ocean-beast drew breath. Any moment now he hoped he might at least make out their white crests glimmering like the manes of a great riding; but though the sea-tang flew in his face, the dark was unbroken.

'You gangrel geld-mare!' screamed the wizard, and lashed the rein-ends about. 'Is't a coulter you'd pull, that you linger so? Shall I set a brechan 'bout your neck to draw a cart? Race, rogue that you are! Make gledes of your hooves if you will, or feel fire lash your laggard houghs! Faster! Faster yet, and yet!'

The rumble of the hooves became one single sound, a thudding no longer but a singing, sizzling whine like water drops gliding on hot iron. For the first time Walter felt the flanks beneath his thighs expand and pant for breath. All of a sudden a spark flared in the blackness, hotly red; an eye glowed by its own light, as though coals burned within. 'Faster!' screamed Michael, so his voice raked in his throat; the beast's sides heaved. More light awoke. The black horse's nostrils flared wide and sprayed out two tearing tongues of red flame. They lit up its whole head, tossing and frenzied against the blackness, and shone on its rider's distorted face, grimacing with the effort of will and expense of spirit. 'Now how fast?' Michael yelled like a man possessed.

'No less fleet than the thought of a girl between her two lovers, Michael!'

He let loose a wild laugh that shook the saddle. 'Well enough at the last! Go now! Go!'

Walter clung and shook to the deeps of his soul, as afraid of man as mount. He knew now the source of that midnight voice, for he had felt every booming word of it vibrate against him, the mighty cage of ribs reverberating with the force of straining lungs. He had heard the Highland tales of the kelpie, the each uisge they named it, the devilish water-horse that rode forth from fall and pool to bear off mortals on its back. By some such demon was he borne off. And what of its rider?

Suddenly a stinging spray struck him, fiery hot; he slapped it from his face and hair, and it smelt like sand. Then the thunder of surf was suddenly all around them, the awful song of the hooves lost all solidity and dwindled to a light hissing, bouncing note, with the hint of splashing at its edges; and he imagined them, horse and riders, flung skipping like a child's flat stone over some waste of darkling waters towards a shore of endless night.

It startled him all the more, then, when after a time he began to fancy he saw something ahead, a faint charcoal lightening in the blind dark. Soon there was no doubt of it; the night was wearing thin. A transparent greyness returned, and with it a sense of space, of earth and sky divided, the one still shadow-deep, the other flooded with mild milky light. And where they met there rose the dark silhouettes of a line of rolling hills. Blinking, Walter looked down, expecting to see the swell of ocean beneath hooves that flashed like arrows. Instead he saw thin wisps of mist, and beyond them pale sparkling sand, in which the great hooves had sunk to the feathers. They were still, and at rest.

'You may dismount a while,' said Michael Scot.

Walter slewed sideways and fell heavily into the sand. He lay with his eyes closed, and rejoiced in the solidity of it, trickling it through his fingers with blessed ease, rejoicing in the silence. A light warm breeze sang in his ears, tinged with sweet fragrance. He reopened his eyes and found himself gazing up at a high bank of long green grass, filled with white lilies; the breeze whispered among them, and the lilies nodded and bobbed agreement. All else was quiet, save for the muted thunder of the ocean. Above the bank was only the mist.

Gradually, unbelieving, he rose to his knees, then hauled himself up by Michael's stirrup and stood panting for breath. The air was warm and humid. He stared up at his guide; the older man looked pinched and grey, but unbent. 'That—' Walter breathed. 'That was . . . fearful. Past all nature. That was a journey through Hell!'

'It was not,' said the other with crisp certainty. 'A river of blood streams within your own veins, rushes and roars within your own ears, when they are not filled with foolish distractions. And within the tears of suffering mankind is an ocean salt and infinite.'

Walter shook his head, uncomprehending. He managed to straighten up and look around. In front of them the bank divided, and a narrow sandy path led up from the beach, splitting into ways that wound among green slopes which gleamed wetly beneath their mist-drapery.

'Mount now,' said Michael curtly. 'Our way is the middle-most. Ask not of the rest.'

Walter looked with deep distrust at the peaceable horse, and a chill in his marrow: should a man cast up by a raging river eagerly wade in again? But he knew well enough he had no choice. 'Have we far to go?' he grunted painfully, feeling every wound swear as he struggled to haul himself up astride those massive haunches. The beast looked around at him with mild concern, as horses do.

Michael's hand plucked him up, light as a child. 'No further than a space of your thought,' he said, and smiled.

'Good!' said Walter, shifting uneasily. He felt battered and bruised, and still more than somewhat drunk. 'I hope there's water to be had, and clean clothes.' Even as he said it he wiped hand to thigh; and what he felt made him look down. Hose and boot were fresh and clean, free of the slightest trace of blood.

The path, narrow at first, opened out as the ground rose to an open lea. Thus much Walter glimpsed, a rich grassy country that made his own fells look windswept and wasted. The sky was a louring grey, not cool like Scottish airs but warm and oppressive, the lily-scented breeze weighing on the breath like a promise of midsummer thunder. The track they rode was a faint scar running dead straight across the lea's broad back, its only interruption till the eye reached dark distant streaks that surely marked the margins of dense forests. Thus much, before pale fingers of mist sponged away the landscape like paint from a board. They too were warm, stifling almost, quite unlike the chill dankness of his homeland; and they bore a new heavy, heady scent, musk and roses and something sharper. All the same, they brought back the ride to Oakwood, and how far away he was from everything he understood. He looked at Michael Scot, placidly guiding the great horse onward, as confident as if the scholar were on the path to his own front door. It infuriated him somehow, and he wanted to jar that complacency.

'Mist again!' he said bitterly. 'Do you always move in haze and haar, Master Michael?'

'Which of us does not?' responded Michael seriously. 'At every step it closes behind us, and opens before. Are we not confined forever, my young lord, in the narrow conduit through which time flows from future to past? Small wonder we see it hung about with vapours and choked with cloud. But on a plane less philosophical, such weather is quite normal in – these remote climes. We shall be out of it soon.'

Even as he spoke Walter realized the angle of the land had changed, was now directing them steadily downhill. The horse's hooves clattered on something harder than earth, and looking down Walter was startled to make out the shapes of smooth yellow stones between the drooping grass tussocks. This, the whole road behind and before, was a made way, a pavement even, from out of the deeps of time. It was not unlike the ancient fragments dotted about his own country; but of a vast length and surely long neglected. He was about to ask about it when quite suddenly Michael reined in, and the great horse whinnied softly. A mighty sense of awe flooded out all other thought.

The horse stood poised at the crest of a low rise, bordering a wide, shallow vale. Its bowl was milky with thin mist, but through it shone the metal of a broad river, and on the far bank, whiter yet, a high straight wall. Massive and strong it must be, Walter realized, and yet, graceful in its proportions, it hardly seemed so, crowned with low turrets, braced with slender buttresses. A bridge of the same white stone and pattern swooped across the river towards it, like an arrow's flight made solid, and where they met rose the pillars of a noble gate. That alone would have awakened his wonder; but from their vantage they could see beyond its summit to the city that lay behind.

The low-gabled roofs were tiled, most in dull red but some in green or blue that gleamed as if glazed. Near the wall the rooftops were all they could see, but beyond this the city rose up the further slope, and its frontages stood out proudly, even and well shaped to Walter's keen eye, their painted walls glowing softly in pinks and reds and yellow and austere white, set with windows closed by contrasting shutters, lined with airy colonnades and high-roofed porches, all placed and proportioned with careful balance and measure. Yet still greater balance showed in the nature that offset all this cool craft: spaces and fields shone yellow-green with grass; tall thin trees like green-flamed candles ran in rows alongside the houses and marked the wider ways. Lower, shady forms spread great fans of branches over the spaces between, and slowly stooped to brush the rooftiles in the languid air.

Walter had never seen anywhere remotely like this. His mind had been fettered by the narrow confines of the Marches and their few towns, the grim towers and gaunt walls that dominated a hard fierce land. As a child he had imagined even the gates of Heaven framed in the rough reddish stone of Carlisle's castle, the largest building he knew, and the Heavenly City as a slightly larger version of Jedburgh's great abbey. Now those fetters shattered, and he gaped like a peasant boy at a riding of knights. Only in the minute images on illuminated leaves had he ever so much as glimpsed anything comparable. Frantically he tried to imagine where this might be. The only possible place he could conceive of in such splendour was the Holy City, Rome itself. 'Is this – is this where the Pope dwells?' he blurted out, and then shrivelled at how stupid it sounded.

But the face Michael turned on him was suddenly creased and twisted with something he might easily have called terror. The deepset eyes glittered as he thrust a finger to his lips. 'Shht! No more! That name you must never mention here, nor that of the Deity nor of – of Jesus, nor any other holy word or title within that wall! Never – nor unsheathe that steel sword by your side. Never, save in utmost peril of your life!' The black horse whinnied suddenly, as if in distress.

'Michael!' Walter was suddenly stone-cold sober. He clapped a hard hand on the older man's shoulder, swung him round again to look him hard in the eyes. 'Where is it you've brought me? Are we among the enemies of God and man?'

Michael met his gaze, unperturbed now. 'Not enemies, no. Call them rather neutrals, who pay the price for their neutrality and guard it all the more jealously. At times they can be man's friend or his enemy, but in the end there is only one side they are on, and that is their own.' His eyes dropped. His face seemed less set, less sure than Walter had ever seen it, though his voice was if anything more sardonic. 'A strength and a weakness both. I do not suggest you imitate it. Come, Algol!'

The way to the bridge was short, shorter than it looked. Very soon their ancient road joined another that was more in use and better tended, and that in turn another of paler cobbles that was all but weedless, solid and smooth. Walter couldn't imagine how it was done or maintained – not that there seemed to be much traffic. In fact, there was nobody about, though it must be almost dawn by now. After a while that made him anxious. He looked for guards or toll-collectors as they approached the bridge, but there were none. The pale road continued on unbroken between its high pillars, capped with images of fantastical beasts, and there was no hollowness in the footfalls; it might as well have been solid ground beneath them. Walter looked at the turbid swell of water beyond the parapet. There were little sparkles within it, as if the invisible sun were breaking through. Certainly the light was clear enough, despite the mists; the parapets almost glowed in their whiteness, veined with only the faintest greenish streaks. Walter guessed this must be the marble he'd read about, a finer version of the streaked black stone they had in the great hearth at Cessford. The wall was of the same, and the high pillars of the gate that opened ahead; but the two statues that stood before it, of fantastic beasts like great cats, with flaring manes and paws outthrust in clawing warning, were in pure white stone, with never a vein. The regality of them made him draw his breath; this was how a great lord's hall should be approached. The gates were mere cages of painted metal, festooned with leaves and stems so cunningly wrought that he felt they should have trembled even in the faint breath of the breeze. They didn't look capable of keeping anyone out, and it came to him that this might be a land without enemies, a land where a man need not fence his own against his neighbour. Nevertheless, they were shut, and he made ready to call a guard; but as the horse Algol drew nearer they parted and swung back upon silent hinges, and Michael rode in without hesitation. Walter was too busy gaping to be afraid. Only the sharp jangle of their closing caused him a sudden pang of doubt.

He looked back sharply, but there was nobody in sight. In fact, the streets within the walls seemed to be as empty as the roads – except that somewhere there was something like music playing, a faint sweet-toned jingling and singing on the ear that came and went. That, and a sense of watchfulness that seemed to lie in the blank windows themselves, though their shutters were wide, and flowers glowed softly in little wooden troughs and earthen pots upon their sills – a fashion that amazed Walter, but gradually pleased him, as he caught their thousand scents on the air. He thought how fair a woman's rooms might be made with such living ornaments, beauty adorned with beauty, and how fresh – better than strewing herbs, even. He found himself imagining what kind of beauties might live behind such windows; it made him at once more excited and more at ease. 'Who lives here, wizard?' he demanded. 'And what have we to do with them?'

'People, for the most part,' responded Michael, turning his mount's steps into a wide sloping avenue, flanked with a double row of the tall candle-trees. 'People with their own hopes and fears and concerns, joys and sorrows, even if they are not altogether like your own. Think of yourself in a foreign land, not wholly unfriendly but proud and quick to take offence, and bear yourself accordingly. Your speech will be understood. We are going to ask a favour of them – or, to be more precise, the chance to earn one. Be the Lord of Branxholme you are, and let me be your ambassador. Follow my lead and breathe no word without it. You have the wits; look to them!'

Walter gazed in great wonder on the building that rose before them in the heart of the hillside. He had seen it from beyond the wall, its triple porticoes enclosed by ornate columns, without perceiving it was one edifice; nor how large those columns were. Fluted at the flank, encrusted with carved vegetation at the top, they towered easily ten times his own height in that glowing white stone, as fresh and clean as if cut only yesterday. The whole place was sheathed in it, held and framed in the centre of the hillside by lesser halls above and below like a pearl in a precious setting, its lustre redoubled in their reflection. It was no seat of war; yet Walter felt in his bones that even the maddest Border warlord would shrink from challenging the power and authority it embodied. Hard Tantallon itself on its riven outcrop of cliff held no such promise of strength as this defenceless hall. The floor of the portico was mosaic of grey and black, set between strips of still blacker stone, and the great hooves skidded and found no grip on its mirror surface as Michael rode calmly in.

And suddenly there were men around them, men in robes, men in short coats and hose, all of the same softly striped pattern; livery, so these were servants. They bowed deferentially to Michael as he dismounted, and hailed him with soft liquid greetings in a tongue strange to Walter, yet with touches of maddening familiarity. They were strange-looking men enough, many of a recognizable type or kin, dark-haired and sallow-skinned, cleanshaven despite the heavy blueing of beard upon their strong jaws. He looked at them with deep suspicion before he slid down, aching and unstable and feeling his inflamed wounds grate against his clothes. They all seemed adequately human, as far as the shadows in the porch would allow; he saw no sign of horn or tail or hoof or feral pointed ear. And some of them were lighter, one or two of them tall and yellow-haired with square hard faces not unlike the Norse pedlars he sometimes encountered, close kin to his own folk. Only the gloom put an unnatural lustre in their watchful eyes, as they ushered the newcomers through the wide outer doors of bronze, panelled with entwined reliefs of revel and procession.

Others came out into the dim hall to see these newcomers, others whose garb was not that of service. Grave older men, in ear-flapped caps and long ruffed robes of sombre richness, hung about with chains of silver and gold; tall young men, with trailing hair and tight gaudy hose, often boldly striped, cat-lithe in short jackets and codpieces of bold contrasting colour. Gold-gleaming swords or long jewelled daggers were slung at their thighs. They stood with arms folded, barely bowing to Michael and not at all to Walter, sizing him up with insolent calm; he was almost tempted to let his hand slide toward his sword, but heeded the wizard's word and merely returned the stare.

And in doing this he became aware of other eyes in the background – wider, darker, bold, framed in dark curls or long silken swathes around faces that were pale heart-shapes in the shadowy hall. Somehow what light there was from the high-set windows contrived to gather itself around them, so that he saw clearly their straight noses and high brows, soft reddened lips and breasts half-bared beneath translucent folds of patterned and embroidered silk. They were young, those who came into the light, and their gaze also weighed him. Half-grown and graceless he felt before it, the gaping ploughboy again, scattering clods of dung as he hobbled along. Lords, ladies all of this all too foreign land, and what was he among them?

He was Lord of Branxholme, that was what. He bore a good name, fair schooling and, if he limped, it was with honourable wounds. He gritted his teeth and walked straight with hand easily upon his sword's pommel; let them see a poor warrior of Scotland could have his own proper pride. To his surprise the women's gaze grew bolder. To his greater surprise he began to enjoy it. But he remembered Michael's warning, and forbore to swagger. As well so; for, as bronze doors boomed like gongs and turned upon sunken pivots, it came to him again that he was entering a place that brooked no challenge.

It was a throne-room; and the throne was occupied. It was much as he'd imagined the court at Edinburgh to be, or Westminster Hall or Paris perhaps, save for the purplish-grey light; but he had an uneasy feeling that in reality they would fall far short of this sombre splendour. Gold glowed in the walls and over them, in the veined inlay and the threads of tapestries. Through their heavy folds of fabric, wars and hunts twisted and turned, with golden armour and silver spears and blood in glittering streams of dyed silk and garnets. Not even that day at Oakwood had he seen the like, and that splendour, he felt sure, was only a glamour set upon it by the mind of Michael, inspired, perhaps, by the court of his Imperial master.

Or was it by this hall? For Michael evidently knew here and was known. He strode confidently up to the great black dais beneath three high windows, and bowed low first before the high-backed chair set thereon, and the one within it, and again to the one who stood by. And though the first held Walter's gaze in awe and in courtesy, thenceforth none but the other one held his thought; and all in a moment he was limed, taken and enthralled.

'*Salve, o Re!*' declared Michael in a loud clear voice. 'Hail, King Laurin, child of Filarin, child of Alferon of the mighty line of Elphicleos! Again I return to your realms, as once you made me free to.'

The one he addressed sat with lowered head, lips resting lightly on his steepled hands, his long hair, the shade of ashes shot with silver, shadowing his face; yet even thus a sense of contained power dwelt in him. At Michael's salutation he looked up, and smiled slightly. The voice was light and dry, ironic and challenging in its detachment, yet not without a certain respect. 'I see you, *Messer* Michele! I did so, and find no reason to repent of it. Go freely among us as ever. Yet you never come without cause, in quest of trouble, or trailing it in your wake. To what do we owe this renewed honour?'

The face the light fell upon was as human as the rest, lean, beardless, of no particular age, alert and commanding and fine of feature. Yet it was now at last that Walter truly knew whither he had been brought, and felt a gulf of worlds between him and his homeland. Hermitage itself was more natural to him than this fair palace, beneath that cold regard.

It was not a closed countenance; there were many things there for Walter to read. Sorrow sat upon that brow, sorrow unending, suffering and loss, loss regal, loss endured and yet to come; yet also there was majesty. This was a king undaunted, to whom rule and order were not conveniences or ideals but a vision as vital and natural as breath, a king out of a storybook, a ruler such as men found at best once in a generation. The eyes were dark, darker than Michael's and with the curious slight sheen he was to come to know well, like a bloom on metal or a beetle's wingcase. It was the look in them, as if they would outstare eternity at need, that made the King altogether unhuman. Walter read remoteness there, distance, and alien concerns, so alien he might have felt more kinship with a beast or bird. What attention this being would spare him he must earn.

126

As Michael evidently had. He smiled in answer. 'I bring you a great champion, oh Laurin! A young warrior among men, Gualtiero, Lord of the family of Scot and the honour of Branx-holme, but lately come into his own. I have brought him here for the healing of his wounds, and to serve you against your foes.'

The dark eyes looked at Walter, mildly enough but straight through him. Other eyes pierced him more deeply. 'How were these wounds come by?'

'Honourably,' said Michael, 'while taking command of a force surprised by treachery and overwhelming odds, after the fall of its captain his father, and by his skill and main force bringing away the greater part safe.'

'That is well,' nodded King Laurin. 'Better a brave retreat than a foolish end. The Lord Gualtiero is welcome. For the rest – we will see. But healing, that is easy enough to bestow, for here no mortal ill can long endure.' He raised a hand. 'Astrafiammante, daughter, pledge our guests their health.'

The dark girl who stood by his side bowed. From the tray a servitor brought she took up a goblet like a bubble of light, and filled it from a golden jug. Dark wine foamed briefly through the clear glass, and settled. She tripped forward, to Walter's eyes almost gliding, and stepped off the dais to stand before him. He would have knelt before her, but she swiftly raised the goblet in cupped hands to his height. As if in a dream he saw her black curls swirl around her white throat, the lift of her breasts beneath the thin court costume, her long slender fingers clasped around what seemed to be a floating jewel.

'Drink, guest, and be healed!' she said, and her voice was soft and delicate, accented only in its very precision. He did not know whether the heady scent of flowers he breathed came from the wine or her. Fragments of Jeanie's tales flew through his mind, about boys and girls decoyed into strange realms, being offered food and knowing they must not take it; and momentarily he thought of looking to Michael Scot. But that might cause offence, and Michael had already warned him against touching their pride. In truth, anyway, he could hardly have refused her anything, even if he was lost forever; he already felt it. He closed his own hands gently about the fragile-looking glass, touching and restraining hers as they slipped free, and fought for the fragments of formal courtesy he had been taught.

'Will you not taste first, lady?' he asked. He had a momentary twinge of horror that she might think he feared poison; but no, she lowered dark eyes, like her father's and yet so unlike, and even in this greyness he could see a faint flush against her cheekbones. She sipped delicately, and pressed it back to him; and he was suddenly aware of raging thirst and shaking weakness.

'Hail, King!' he said. 'And hail, Lady! Your health!' He dared add no blessing, and it pained him. The wine was a cooling flood, spreading over cracked lips, easing a dry throat, warming a hunger-chilled stomach. It seemed to swirl and vibrate even as he swallowed, heartening, thrilling through him with such vigour and warmth that he felt it might burst out of his ribs and invade the room, like a torch flaring into crackling life. He drained the cup, and drew breath; and for the first time since the battle it no longer hurt to do so. He flexed his arm; he clasped his side; he cautiously twisted his back. Nothing, not the slightest pain; only a lingering weakness.

The girl set the empty cup on the waiting tray and offered him a bowl of fruit that chilled the air between them, cooled in icewater. His hand trembled as he took a slice of some yellow thing that seemed to dissolve in his mouth, sharp and faintly resinous, immensely satisfying. Another, and he felt the tang of it throughout his limbs, spreading as if the juice pulsed through his heart and veins, chilling yet satisfying as it went. He drew in the warm air gratefully now, and smiled at the girl.

She returned it gravely. 'Are you healed, guest?'

He had never seen anyone like her, he told himself; his mouth seemed dry all over again at the sheer beauty she embodied, supple, flower-graceful yet keenly alive. This much of the storybooks was no lie; he could believe this one capable of heroic deeds, if her will so drove her. She made every other girl he had trifled and tumbled with seem fat and grubby, or pale and insipid at best; he could hardly remember what they looked like. He recalled everything Michael had told him about these people's pride; he could guess the wrath of which Laurin was capable. None of it, nothing could hold him back. 'Alas, no, lady,' he said softly, and he bowed to her. 'All the wounds I bore with me are vanished, but a worse one has taken their place.'

There was a single swift intake of breath in the hall. She said nothing, but only bowed in return. Michael's sardonic voice broke abruptly into his thrall. 'And did nobody ever tell you the fable of Persephone and the seed of pomegranate? Aye well, well, never mind. Where blood leads, thought must halt after.'

Face aflame, Walter glared at him, then remembered his peril and bowed silently to Laurin. The King's face creased into graceless amusement, and his voice was harsh. 'And for exactly which of my most deadly of enemies does this cub of men consider himself a match – to Alberic the Black, for one, or King Huon, who was once a mortal also, or Lord Midir of the Sidh? For know, young lord of men, that in this land there are kingdoms also, and borders and boundaries over which blood is spilt, rivalries between lords of power as fierce as in the fields you know. Against which shall I test your sword?'

'Against King Andvari of the North!' replied Michael with ringing firmness before Walter could get a word in. 'The Otter-Lord, master of your great rivers and the gold therein. Give him but a hundred of your knights, and myself for counsellor, and he will deliver you of this annoying thorn!'

Laurin's eyes opened suddenly wide in the gloom, catching an eerie light. 'Master of nothing! Incursor, thief and usurper!' He thumped the throne-arm with the flat of his hand. 'Let this mortal boy but recover some of the ravished gold, and he will be of service. Let him destroy the Otter-Lord, or even deprive him of his sword, and I will need no greater champion!'

There was laughter in the hall at that; but it died suddenly as Walter whirled and went down on one knee before the throne of Laurin. He would have drawn his sword, but remembered in time, unbuckled it and presented the gilded hilt, still sheathed, to Laurin. 'My lord King, this is my father's sword that he gave me on his dying field. May I prove worthy of it in your service, or may I never return!'

He was aware of Michael at his side, nodding wryly as if at some jongleur's clever turn of phrase; but Walter paid him no heed at all. There had been nothing of cleverness or of gesture in what he did. He had followed his feelings; were they not the only guides a man could trust among such folk? His heart seemed to twist within him. And then, only a little unwillingly, Laurin reached forward and, a trace hesitantly, touched the sword's gilt. 'So be it, mortal! Go on as you have begun, and you will fare nobly! But a hundred of my knights, that is a strong force to ask of me. I will see what I can manage. Some among my esquires may—'

'No!' The voice was the girl's, low but decisive. 'He shall have followers of mine! You, Arianno, Ghismondo, Egisto—'

Young men burst from the crowd, loud in protest, snatching their high caps from their heads and dashing them to the mosaic, hands straying to dagger and sword as they confronted Walter. But the icy juice still ran in his veins, and he rounded on them, raised the sword before them. Michael's hand clamped on his arm, but he shook it off, prepared to draw – and at the first faint gap between crosshilts and scabbard they hurled themselves back in disordered fright. Walter turned his back on them. 'My lady, whatever you give, I shall take in honour. It is more than I could ask!'

'For now!' she said, and for the first time met his glance fully. 'But when you return, you may find you have greater liberty.'

With that she made her bow to her father and her guests, and left the dais with her women gathering about her in a rustling, murmuring pool of silk and black curls. She swept from the hall, and did not look back.

7 ▉ King's Ransom

Hung with bells, the bridles jingled softly all along the narrow path, and every so often one of the beasts whinnied softly, or snorted swirls in the mist. Walter cursed, but quietly. *'Manfredo!'* he hissed at one of the loudest offenders. 'Can you not keep your beasts quiet?'

The lean young creature behind him shrugged. 'What would you? They are the mounts of knights of the Fair Realm. They are used to riding boldly into battle beneath bright banners, not this skulking fashion of mortal warfare.'

'Aye, well, they'd make a poor show lifting kine out of Tyne-dale, that's for certain,' Walter whispered with grim intensity. 'But try to hold your damned noise, at least! It's nobody's lives but your own you're risking!'

Except mine, and maybe even Master Michael's, he thought grimly.

Manfredo shrugged again, his heavy brows louring. 'What are our lives to our honour? We are not footpads or masterless men to lurk in ambush for our foes! We ride boldly to meet them—'

'I know! I know! Beneath bright banners, as you keep saying, and what good's it done you? These Otter people have just massacred any small bands Laurin sent out, head-on, and ducked back into the fenlands every time a bigger force came near! Anyhow, nobody's asking you to do any lurking. Just to choose your own ground of battle for once, and your own time to be brave. That's the whole point of all this tramping through the mires and middens – to outflank them, to come upon them from a way they don't expect and can't run away from! Pass that down the line, in case anyone's forgetting!' He went padding back up to the head of the column, where Michael Scot was leading both their mounts.

The wizard regarded him with mild amusement. 'You would sooner be leading a band of mosstroopers?'

Walter looked back sourly as somebody stepped into a squelching boghole and cursed vociferously. 'On such a quest as this? Aye, I would. Any day! You know, old Jeanie used to tell me of it? The Faerie Rade in all its pomp and splendour, so that mortal dare not look upon it? And when I first saw this crew, riding out so gallant in their armour all gold and jewels, and their blazons of every colour, I thought of it. I wondered what in G— what in any man's name I was doing, setting myself at their head. But now I'd as soon have, oh, Bide-i'the-Byre Croser and Gyte Willie Gilchrist and even Fat Heckie Laidlaw at my back, let alone Gawn and my own good housetroop.'

Michael chuckled. 'Old Bide-i'the-Byre? Him that Storey of Eskdale's cowmen found up to his neck in the cow-slurry? Is he not hanged yet? Aye, well, there's hope for us all, then. But as to these folk, have no fear. Set your knights on firm ground and you'll see them fell and fierce. As for the noise, don't fret too much; have you not felt a greater hush about us since we came among the fens?'

Walter listened, and it was true. Somehow the sound had changed, swallowed up in the soft susurrus of wind on reedbed, the piping of small birds in the trees, the soft continual bubble and wallow of the boggy stretches around them. 'Odd,' he mused. 'Is it some quality of the place? Or the air?'

Michael smiled. 'Not till I came among them. The Fair Realm and its folk have each their proper measure of power, but that of mortals is all the greater here. Did not Jeanie tell you how the Fair Folk fear it? It was thus I was of service to Laurin before. I doubt we will be heard, so long as no man out and screams at full throat, until we are close upon them.'

Walter regarded the older man with a wry admiration. 'Is there no end to your tricks? But you might have told me.'

'I wished to be sure the charm was working, first. It hangs above us like a canopy, and moves with us. And it is no absolute protection, to make men careless – these hot-blooded squires of the Fair Folk especially.'

Walter nodded feelingly. He had never realized how arrogant

he must seem himself till he came among these lordlings who looked down on mortals as he might the lowest of his swineherds. Nothing less than the word of Laurin and the command of Astrafiammante could have made them follow him, and at every bickering he went cold lest they break and turn on him. Only honour held them, and their awe of Michael, whom they seemed to view as somehow their own. Their pale cold faces, handsome but long-drawn, Walter was finding less and less human, more and more nightmarish. He really felt as if he were in the company of fallen angels, spared Hell but nonetheless banished from bliss as the old tales told. Yet they were living creatures, capable, it seemed, of birth and death, though they still scorned men as mortals and affected to make less of dying. He dared to broach the question with Michael only as they scouted ahead, dismounted and far away from the rest, slipping through the reeds to skulk behind a stand of bent trees like a pair of Border lads after fish.

'Yes, they are mortal, after their fashion; perhaps that is the condition of their banishment, if the tale's true. But they live immensely long, and about their death there is a mystery I have never dared penetrate. Certainly their numbers scarcely change. I could say more, but I will not – not here especially.'

'These others, these Otter-folk—'

'I know less of them. They are not human, though they speak and stand and live as men. They are what the Danes call *vaettir*, children of Nature, creatures of the ancient wood and water in the north before the coming of the Fair Folk, and ever jealous of them. From them they have learned the arts of horsemanship and war, yet they live much in their old wise, between land and water. Of man, beyond the simple hunters and trappers of the human lands that neighbour theirs, they know little or nothing; and no doubt you and your ways will come as a great surprise to them.'

'Let's hope so!' grunted Walter, peering cautiously about a stunted willow. 'By what Laurin said, their encampment should be somewhere – there!'

It was hard to see, against the smoke-green hills that bordered the river plain; but Walter had taken his marks from their summits, and his eyes were keen and well used enough to peering into dim distances. They caught the wisps of fires, and the glimmer of colour others might have missed. 'Now what might that be?' he murmured. 'Bright like flowers, lifting above the reeds like crowns – pavilions?'

Michael's eyes were closed, yet Walter could see the deepset eyes behind the lids questing restlessly this way and that. The wizard's tight lips shaped soundless syllables. 'It is them,' he said at last. 'The heart of their force, their great lords and knights in camp of war.'

Walter knew better now than to ask if he were sure. 'There's no denying you have your uses, wizard. Could you not have spied them from further back and saved us this long crawl?'

Michael's eyes flicked open, glittering as dark as any in this realm, and as furious. 'No! And I wish you would not call me that! I am a scholar, and that is *all*! I – have my *uses*? If I know certain things beyond the usual, it is because I learned them in the course of my study, in pursuit of better! Uses? Believe me, I hardly thought that my best use was to be knee-deep in a marsh alongside a bone-brained young barbarian with barely sense enough to break heads as thick as his own!'

Walter grinned. 'And he's your kith and kin. Never mind, respected sir, I did not mean to piss in your well! Even your inkwell. A scholar I believe you are, and a mighty one; but here you play a wizard's part to such perfection I could not but pay tribute to't, that's all!'

Michael grumbled and fidgeted, but it was clear he was not unpleased. 'I hanker for the calm of my scriptorium in fair Palermo! And for dry feet! I had told myself I was finished with such things forever, and where did it get me? This is a part of my penance, no doubt; or I hope it shall stand so. But no, I could cast my mind's eye only as yours went; I have not the strength to search a whole countryside so. You had to find our target first!'

'I understand, after a fashion,' said Walter, and clapped him on the shoulder. He felt far more at ease with Michael in this tetchy mood than with his usual polished calm. 'Come then,

Master Scholar, we'll back to the column! Haply this'll be all over soon and your toes toasting at a fine fire.'

'Pray to the Powers it will not be for an Otter-man's dinner!' said the dark man lugubriously as they scrambled and splashed through the pools.

Walter paused. 'They're – what's the word? Anti—' He grimaced.

'Anthropophagi? Aye, why should they not? Our flesh is none of theirs.'

'Agh! I don't even know what they look like.'

The sorcerer grunted as he pulled his boot out of the mud. 'You will, I do not doubt. Inside as well as out – soon enough.'

'That's so. We attack at sunset.'

Michael looked up sharply. 'Here? Is that wise?'

'You'll see.'

There could be no surprise attack, such as Walter would have mounted on intruders in his own Marches. That was more than Duce Manfredo and the lesser lords would stomach; they would attack only in due and honourable form, with trumpets and flourishes to give time for their enemies to arm. But under all the bluster they were avid to make use of whatever advantage Walter could win them, and for the first time their complaints were stilled as they listened eagerly to his plan. The column moved forward, under benefit of Michael's quietening art, creeping up to around three hundred paces from that bright clump of tents, as close as they dared – some hundred and fifty tents, with rougher bivouacs around for the commoner sort. Those hardly mattered; it was the knights who would decide the day. Walter, lifting his head cautiously above a screening bank of water sedge, peered at the tall shadows that came and went among the tents, and cursed the poor light.

It was a beautiful place in its way, this land, but an eerie one because it was always so hazy and twilit. By day the sun was never to be seen, and the only earnest of night was that now and again dim stars shone through the wreathing greyness, in constellations he did not recognize. He had striven to grow used to it on their ride north, telling himself it was no worse than the lead-black overcast of a Marches winter; but it weighed on his spirits and oppressed them. Only twice, at its rising and at its falling, did the sun become visible beneath the mantle of cloud, a blood-red orb that balanced an instant on the world's rim and then slid away. Walter lived for that moment of light like a message from home, meagre and strained as it was; but he had noticed that the Fair Folk, as Michael found it best to call them, would shade their eyes, or avert them altogether.

He could go no closer, that was clear, not with the horses. He came slithering back to his troop and gave them their dispositions. 'We form rank of battle according to precedence of honour!' said one of the older lords, Monforte, in a tone that anticipated opposition and scorned it. 'The Constable of the Centre being foremost under the pennon argent, which is on this occasion myself, followed by the Captains of Left and Right beneath pennons of chequer—'

Walter surprised him. 'Form it as and how you will, so long as you do it quietly and where I bid you! And let no man mount until I give the signal – then mount as one! Is that understood? The rest is as I commanded.'

Mollified somewhat, they accepted his commands with only a token grumbling and squelched away to either side, leading their horses with extra care.

'The presence of an enemy makes a difference,' observed Michael, as he helped Walter buckle on his borrowed armour.

Walter scratched his unshaven chin – not that he was in danger of growing much of a beard yet. 'So it does to me,' he admitted, shifting in the unfamiliar straps, flexing his arms to test their freedom. Plate armour of this kind, artfully jointed and loricated in a strange light metal threaded with foliage of silver and gold, was new to him, though already he preferred it to his mailshirt, heavier and less well crafted. 'It seemed so obvious, when Laurin told me of the lie of the land and the problems he's faced. Just stage it like a Marcher cattle-raid! File through the fenland where no great army can make its way, and fall on them from behind. But now . . .' He swallowed. 'This is real war and no skirmish to be forgotten tomorrow.'

'So it was with de Soulis' ambush, though you were not expecting it, and you bore yourself very well. Any man may make war with pomp and formality and restraint. It becomes little more than a tourney then, in which the common men perish forgotten and the great hold each other for ransom, to be recouped tomorrow. But Marchers fight for their livelihood, and do not scorn to use their wits and whatever else they are given, even though it means crawling through mires and riding rough rivers in unlit blackness. You have the makings of a better war-marshal than any of these, lowly though they hold you.' Michael's face was as usual composed, but there was something like concern in his voice. 'What you do here will forward your revenge, the cleansing of the Marches, the rescue of Margaret.'

'And Astrafiammante will hear of it,' mused Walter, riffling the bright white crest of his helm.

Michael raised his eyes to the grey clouds. 'Persephone! Pomegranate seeds! . . .'

But then there was no more time, for the westernmost line of the clouds brimmed suddenly with molten gold. Walter waved to the trumpeter, who paced forward. *'Sound the mount!'*

The notes thrilled in his blood, ascending; and with them, in a unison which startled and pleased Walter, a hundred knights of the Fair Realm raised plated boot to wide stirrup, clapped glove to pommel, and swung themselves into the saddle with a jangling ring. Above the featureless reedbeds a double line of armoured knights appeared as if by magic, in a great half-moon formation bristling with lance and banner. Among the distant tents to the east there was a sudden flurry of motion.

Walter himself mounted then, patting the neck of the charger Laurin had given him, and took his place in line beside the Constable. He raised his arms in a sweeping wave. The trumpeter sounded again, and the line moved forward at a slow walk.

Behind them, like a banner of nemesis unfurled, fell the blinding curtain of fire that was the setting son. Across the landscape it sent its beams like lances already bloodied, and turned the armour of man and horse to a shimmering mass of fire that hurt even Walter's eyes to look upon. The trumpets flashed a flame of sight as well as sound. The land was growing dryer and more even underfoot, as he had guessed it would at a chosen campsite. The line advanced easily, with measured tread, but along the ground their shadows, unwontedly firm and black in this land of twilight, went racing on before them, impossibly gigantic, until they were already among the pavilions ahead and blotting out their gaudy stripes.

Give the strange intruders their due, they were not slow to take up the challenge. Behind the opposing line a tall hooked horn arose and vented an answering call, deeper and brassier like the roar of a beast. Others echoed it. Walter saw horses hurried forward and armoured figures mounting even as they donned their helms. He picked up his own, and unslung his shield from his saddlebow; they were well within arrowshot now, if there were archers over there. It was then he became aware that Michael was still beside him in the line, the black Algol keeping steady pace with that high-stepping gait.

'What d'you think you're doing?' he demanded, astonished. 'Get back, man! You've no armour, you'll be cut to collops—'

'I have armour enough,' said Michael, and smiled. His hand clenched in his lap. 'And against such a line of war you will need every man you have. For I count more than a hundred already mounted, and half as many at least coming behind, with more afoot. And these are strong folk. I think the odds should be evened a little more, do not you?'

Walter was about to argue when he saw Michael raise his hand and thrust it out, fingers wide as if to throw something; but his palm was empty.

Out of that emptiness flame spurted, a blasting, spreading flare of smoky light that enveloped a knot of the opposing knights. An explosion made Walter's helm ring. The sheer force of it shot two bodily from their saddles; another was flung by his rearing mount. They fell and did not move, smoking, and the line was slow to close. Horses balked and whinnied at the sulphurous, acrid fumes.

Walter stared, aghast. Then he yelled to the trumpeter to sound the charge, and clapped on his helm, cold leather and metal clasping his head, muffling his ears. The two sides' horns sounded as one, a discordant, shrilling bray, and the other line began to move. Knights in mail mostly, and heavy helms of bronze on their shoulders, crude-looking bucket-shapes that took little light and hid the faces within. But by the Lady he dared not name here, they were tall! Their lances looked like young treetrunks, and the heads were great dull jagged things, as big as swords; clumsy, perhaps. He would need speed to outbalance their weight; speed, and luck, and grace. No use crying *God defend the right!* here, though. Only spur, and hope.

The horses were gathering pace, the line opening up a little; he seized his lance and brandished it lengthwise, and by a miracle they obeyed and closed again. A canter now, slow at first then opening up to a bounding, leaping onrush, making his armour jolt and chime about him. In the opposing line a long lance swung down to face him, hanging there unwavering at the centre of his vision, however the figure behind it moved. At last, then, at the lightest touch of his spurs, came the change in gait, the sudden thrill, the great back flexing and stretching beneath him with a strength that seemed to flow along his own arm. The neck outthrust, almost as straight as the lance he lowered, raising his shield and marking his man among a mad jingle and squeal of metal. The windrush through his visor, flaying his eyes with tears—

The impact!

Fearsome – every joint in his body aflame with pain – a jarring, scraping, squealing clash along his shield-arm—

In the same skipped heartbeat, a thudding, crashing judder on his lance-point that all but lifted him from his stirrups, his lance tearing from his hands with sudden weight—

Then it was weightless. The opposing horse flew past him wild-eyed and riderless, broken stirrups swinging, and – there! – other lances from the second rank were swinging round at him. From somewhere at hand came the crash of Michael's spell once again, and Walter muttered '*Scholar!*' to himself. The oncoming lances jerked with shock. He batted the nearest aside with his shield and struck out one-handed at arm's-length. The lance-point screeched over armour, found a joint and stuck. He heaved and heard a hoarse cry of pain as the other rider rocked back. The lance bent and snapped, and swinging his horse about he struck out with the truncheon at the bronze helm above.

Another cry, a crash and he whirled his horse, flailing out at the dark eyeslots of the helms that were closing in about him, lances clashing, saw them halt – and then, forgetting all else, he flung down the raw shaft and drew his sword.

The last ray of sun caught the steel with a blinding glare as he raised it, flashing across the marsh. The tall bronze helms turned and twisted away, the horses reared and bolted, and the Constable, riding to his rescue, gave a shrill scream and bolted in the opposite direction. The Otter-folk seemed made of sterner stuff, yet even they flinched from the blade as he swung it, and he was vaguely aware of a tide of figures on foot bolting through the reeds. Then one of the tall knights ducked under and hewed with a long-handled axe. Walter scythed it aside, struck out at its wielder but caught him only a glancing blow on the helm, striking it off. But at the face revealed it was his turn to yell and flinch.

It was wholly unhuman. He had seen nothing like it save the face of the heraldic lion on royal banners, wholly animal. Clad in sleek brown fur and surrounded by a backward-flowing mane, longer than a horse's, it was thrust forward on the neck rather than carried erect. That was why the helms were so huge! Long predatory jaws led to a muzzle, not a mouth, whiskered and catlike beneath the moist black nose. Shorter whiskers blossomed above the brilliant eyes, wild and rolling from the force of Walter's blow, human enough in proportion but still strangely feline. The thin dark lips rolled back, uncovering long white teeth, and the axe swept back at him.

Gasping, he cut at the hilt, turned the blow and struck hard in his turn, overhand at the unprotected head. The other, ducking back, thrust up the long haft in both hands to meet the blow, and stopped it with a jarring clang that rocked them both in their saddles. The axe sang about, one-handed, straight at Walter's visor; he swung up his shield. Head-on, it would have broken the metal and his arm with it; but Walter had seen long-axes used before. He rolled with the blow, deflecting it, and sent his swordarm snaking out beneath. It caught his enemy's heavy ringshirt in the side, digging it into the leather beneath and through. The impact lifted the other from his stirrups, or it would have impaled him. His axe flew wide; he toppled and fell after it into a bush, landing with a crash and an agonized cry. Walter spurred forward, ready to cut the creature down if he rose, but he lay there hugging his side and twisting, and when Walter pointed the sword at him he moaned feebly and threshed the harder. Only gradually, as he stilled his sobbing breath, did Walter notice the silence. He looked up, and saw a ring of knights staring at him, his own and the enemy's, mounted and dismounted, and many more sprawled and silent beyond.

He glared at Monforte, shorn of his elegant crest and bleeding a little over his mail at one shoulder. 'What's this?'

Monforte shook his head a little, having difficulty speaking. 'The day, my lord – is yours.'

Walter stared around, dazed. The tall Otter-folk stood empty-handed and dejected among the bending reeds, their weapons strewn on the damp ground before them, while his own knights seemed almost as amazed. The sun had barely gone, its glow still lingered over the hilltops and among the clouds. 'Mine? So swiftly? How—?'

'I hardly know myself, my lord! You – we – broke their line in the first moment! Many hurt, but none of us fell – and *Messer* Michele's fires – and that sword—' He shook his head again. 'I beg of you, my lord, sheathe it! It pains my head and blinds my eyes, the cold iron—'

Walter looked down at his captive, who had stopped threshing and was beginning to sit up, slowly and painfully, obviously no menace. He wiped his sword on a bush and slid it into the scabbard. The whole gathering seemed to loose a relieved sigh. 'And,' concluded Monforte, still dazed, 'then you, my lord Gualtiero – you felled their fiercest captain, my lord. That unmanned them, completely. The foot-men never came near us, but turned and bolted like rabbits. The rest – you see.'

From behind them came a sudden beat of hooves, and heads turned to see Michael ride up, dishevelled, sulphur-scented and glaring. Both victor and vanquished stepped hastily back. The wizard swung himself from the black beast's saddle and stooped down by Walter's captive, seized him by the mailshirt. 'You!'

he snapped. 'You were the marshal here! Where is Andvari? Where is your King?'

The creature winced, and the whiskered brows tightened in a frown. Then Walter jumped; he had not imagined these things would be able to speak. But though the accent was harsh, the voice was as clear as his own. 'Far from here, *ja*! Or you laugh not so loud, maybe even with your man-magics and swords out of man-lands – you there, Skinshanks with silver pennon, you stand against that blade a moment, eh? You shrivel up like in fire, *pffpt*!' The long red tongue sprayed contemptuous spittle at Monforte and the Fair Folk. A gauntleted hand thumped his chest. '*I* stand! *I* fight! Man bests me – not you! To man only I bow the knee!'

'And man shall ransom you,' answered Michael smoothly, 'if you say where your King is.'

The Otter-marshal chuckled harshly, rumbling deep in his chest, then winced and clutched his side. 'Where you not come on him, you with these dungfolk! Word you send, if herald brave – no knight, no horse! At fen's far rim King fishes, where only small boat pass, where armour your coffin. Go, take boat of ours upriver northward one, two day, seek falls at long mountain-root, tall falls of five stairs, pool below with lime-trees. If lucky, he spare you while you speak! It is said!'

Walter looked at Michael as he straightened up. 'We have to find this – Andvari?'

The wizard nodded. 'We do. And for the first time I am out of my reckoning here. I had not thought he would leave his people.'

The marshal laughed again. 'Grow bored, no Skinshanks to eat!'

Michael made a musing noise. 'I doubt that. Indeed I do. I thank you for your directions, Marshal; I think we shall take them. At once.'

Walter grunted. 'I might have known. Very well, wizard, I go as you direct. My lord Constable, guard these – men – against our return.'

Manfredo came running forward. 'Don't go, my lord! Don't go, they set snares for you!'

'He is right,' put in Monforte anxiously. 'But I see that will not dissuade you. Every instant you are gone, a halter is round these necks. If you are not returned within – five days, beast? – the other end is round a high branch. And, at need, a fire beneath.'

'No!' said Walter, though their new concern surprised and touched him. 'Deal with them as honourably as you can – though beware lest their foot-men return. Withdraw downriver to the guardposts, and if we are not there in six days . . .' He shrugged. 'Take what ransom is offered for them.'

So it was that as the light shifted from the pale dimness of day to the bluer dimness of night, scarcely less light, a small boat glided northward among the reedbeds on a following breeze. It was gentle and warm as a woman's breath, but the river flowed broad and sluggish, heavy with the debris of the mountains, and the current hardly opposed them. Small birds piped sleepily in the bushes as they passed, little scurrying things dipped and splashed about their own busy concerns along the muddy banks, or came splashing out to snatch an apple-core or crust of bread thrown from the boat. But now and then a white shadow would drift past, soft as a tumbling fragment of cloud, and they would dive and cower, and a deathly hush would fall, broken only by the cold owl-cry. Now and again bigger creatures, strange shapes limned only in shadow and soft sound, would come down to the water to drink. He heard their breathing, swift and nervous or deep and rasping, the lapping or sucking at the turbid river, the satisfied grunt and squelch of footprints at the edge.

Around the single small lantern that burned by the tiller heavy moths butted and blundered, foiled in their own destruction, only to be scooped up by the bats that flittered effortlessly about. Walter trailed a hand in the warm water and stretched luxuriously, surprised how easily he had put off the strains of the day with his borrowed armour. It was hard to feel ill, somehow, in this land. The thought of their mission, and of what they must achieve, weighed on his mind nonetheless. He stirred uneasily, and looked to Michael, sailing the little shell of a craft with practised ease. 'These Otter-things – what are they? Where do they come from?'

'Whence,' corrected the sorcerer absent-mindedly. 'You are a lord, you should study high speech and lofty expressions. Whence come they, these creatures? From the fount of all creation, for they bleed as we do, eat and sleep and couple. But beyond that I cannot say. In this land that Laurin claims as his they are incursors, newcomers who first appeared from the far north at the time that Theodoric, he whom the romances call Dietrich of Bern, brought the Goths to colonize Italy.'

Walter looked at him very hard. 'This,' he said with grim accusation in his tone, 'is *not* Italy.'

There was a faint glint of teeth in the darkness.

'This is Laurin's land,' said Michael easily, 'and he must have whatever gold there may be in it. Many people see it in different ways; this is how *he* sees it. Andvari's folk terrorize the rivers, waylay travellers and fishers, but worst of all – as Laurin sees it – they have cunning ways of sifting the fine gold particles the rivers carry down from the heights.'

Walter smiled to himself. The wizard was usually better at evading a question than that. To his own surprise he found he scarcely cared about the deception, anyway. Let him be where he might be, he felt a great measure more happy here than in his Marchlands, and scarcely less at home. If the day was less light, the night was less dark, and he felt as sure in the one as the other. He thought of those ringing blows that had ended the fight, clenched his fists and relived each jarring impact, each sweep of the opposing axe. It made the life he was living now taste all the sweeter, and sparkle in his blood like wine, or the light of Astrafiammante's eyes.

For much of the night he slept, blanketed boards ease enough for him with the gentle rocking of a cradle, and while he woke next day he was still lost in dreams. It was only a sudden jolting of the boat that brought him to his senses, hand to hilt in abrupt chill. Michael was standing, lowering the sail; and as it fell it showed him a looming wall of rock behind.

'We're here?' he gasped.

'Sooner than I expected. Distances are deceptive in these flat lands, and the marshal did say a long mountain-root. This must be it, and we shall scull from here.'

So it seemed, a long spur of land outthrust into the wetlands from the still distant heights, so that the river wound sharply away like a snake from a footfall. Thick undergrowth clustered around its root, and trees climbed to its crown. In the Marches they would have been windstunted, on such an exposed slope, but here they grew tall and rippled gracefully. The breeze was in the wrong direction, but it seemed to Walter, as he took a turn on the sculls, that he heard their distant rush even from here – or was it something else? A moment of listening confirmed it, and he saw Michael nod.

'The high force the marshal told of. It must be on the hill's far flank somewhere. Not so very far.'

Walter listened more intently. 'You can hear it against the wind, and the sound of the sculls. The fall must be vast!'

'Taller than the Marches can show, aye. Our hills have seldom the height or the crags. But it's not the falls we've come to see. Leave your sculls now, I'll take them. Better you look to your arms!' He leaned on the sculls with an easy strength that sent the little boat bobbing onward, and the sound of soft thunder grew louder in their ears.

They came upon the place within the hour, when a stronger current plucked at the little craft as they rounded a wooded outcrop, and water bubbled and boiled about their bows. Pulling past it, they found themselves facing a high wall, an embracing arc of raw, craggy rock that fell sheer into a wide dark pool through which the river here passed. Its stillness contrasted eerily with the hissing vigour of the water that came tumbling down a jagged crack in the rockface, stair after stair just as the marshal had described it, spurting clouds of spray at every facet of the glistening rock. Some halfway down it burst out and plummeted straight down the cliff into the pool at its further edge with an endless drumming roar and a boiling fury of foam and spray. Somewhere far below that fierce current was born; but across the body of the pool the water's surface was dark and smooth, mirroring the rock's blackness rather than the sky above, or the thick mass of trees and tangled greenery that stooped and nodded over the brim. The scents of leaf and weed hung heavy in the breathless air.

As the little craft began to draw around the great shallow curve of the river, with its sprawling half-moons of gravel, the wizard pulled swiftly on one scull, and turned the bows inward towards the shore. Walter unpacked his borrowed plate from the oilcloth parcel beneath his feet, and began, rather awkwardly, to strap himself in.

Michael looked concerned. 'Look to your arms, I said – but armour? You heard the marshal – it can be your coffin in this boggy land. Plain leather will be better for a swift strike.'

Walter pursed his lips. 'The marshal told us his King's whereabouts to send a messenger, not betray him. I'll not go secretly against him.'

Michael snorted. 'This from the son of four generations of cattle-lifters? Monforte and his kind are giving you ideas. Still, have it your own way. A shame we did not think to pack a trumpeter or a herald.'

Walter picked himself up, balancing gingerly in his armour to step ashore. 'Can't you conjure one up? I'll step ashore and hail him fairly. A voice should carry well between these walls—'

'*Only too well!*' barked a voice like footfalls in gravel. From beneath the curve of the boat a huge hand struck upward, its brown fur spraying, and clamped about Walter's ankle even as his foot touched the ground. Another hand caught the gunwale and rocked the little craft. Between them a head lifted, a huge head, lips parted in a predatory grin over the inhuman teeth. It surveyed Walter a moment as he froze there; Michael it ignored. 'I could have overturned this cockleshell any instant since you rounded the point, and held your round little heads under, together. Overhearing your honourable sentiments made me hold my hand. We can dispense with heralds, the like of you and I! Am I to understand you wish to issue a *challenge*? To the lord of this land, by any chance?'

Walter swallowed. He had more sense than to reach for his sword. 'To Andvari, Lord of the Otter-folk, who claims it – yes!'

'Mmnh,' said the head reflectively. Water fountained suddenly, spraying in his face, and the grip on his ankle was loosed.

The little boat rocked violently. Walter blinked away the water, and found himself looking up, and still further up, at the creature that overshadowed him, though it still stood ankle-deep in the river. The Otter-marshal had been tall, but this was almost a head taller and broader in proportion, its muzzle heavier and scarred, its body massive and bow-limbed. It wore a close-fitting coat of metal rings over a high-collared jacket of greenish leathery stuff that shed the water, and breeches of the same; winged metal shoulderplates and heavy swordbelt made the body seem even wider. Thick sleek fur covered the bare arms and legs, rippling at the play of muscles beneath. And strangest of all, fur and mane, even the paw he rested on a heavy swordhilt, glittered in the dim light, shone and sparkled with a dusty golden aura that lent a strange kind of beauty to this nightmare shape, like the memory of sunlight from a kinder world.

'Now,' inquired Andvari with ominous courtesy, 'are you altogether sure?'

Walter's words stuck in his throat. Man or animal, he had never set eyes on a living thing as big as this; it looked like the lions out of the romances. What had that by're— what had that thrice-damned conjurer got him into this time? But running was unthinkable. Here, if Michael was to be believed, was his revenge. Here was honour to lay before one who had believed in him. 'I am, yes,' he said, rather incoherently. 'Lord of Branxholme – me, that is. To mortal combat, in the name of King Laurin and of Astrafiammante – unless,' he added with all the nerve he could summon, 'you would rather save us both trouble by surrendering now.'

'Oh dear,' said the creature mildly. 'Still, you will not be the first to perish in such circumstances. Astrafiammante. Hmm. Neither of us are mounted, so if swords and bucklers will suffice, and this grassy strip here? Armoured as we are, but without helms? Very well.' For the first time he shot a direct glance at Michael. 'But *he* stays where he is, in the boat, and does not interfere. His honour I do not trust! He has the odour of tricks and stratagems, the stink of sulphur about him!'

'You don't know the half of it,' said Walter feelingly. 'Well, Master Michael?'

The wizard shrugged. 'If you want my word, you are welcome to it. I never planned to do more than watch, and perhaps shout some opportune counsel.'

'Unless you are very quick,' said Andvari, still mildly, 'you will have to shout exceedingly loud indeed.' He stretched out his long arms, plucked a small shield rimmed with loose bronze chains from the water by the boat, and the golden light danced in his fur. He caught Walter staring, and bared his teeth in what Walter devoutly hoped was a smile. 'Ah, yes. The fair seed of the river. Laurin's folk must gather it with sordid labour, sluice and pan, even by setting fleeces and skins in the flow. But we harvest the sandgold with our very bodies as we swim and hunt, drawn fast by the oil of our fur. Is it not thus much more rightfully ours? Although I admit we do not scorn swifter methods. Well—'

His sword swept from the scabbard with a slight sucking sound, a long bronze blade clouded with sinister dark stains here and there. Walter stepped into the grass, testing his footing, watching out for snags and holes. Andvari, watching him with interest, scythed the heads from a few thistles. Walter took a couple of deep breaths, muttered a prayer of sorts and drew. Andvari stiffened as he saw the sword; his casual manner vanished. He lifted his own, took two long strides forward on his massive legs and aimed a frightful slashing cut that looked completely unstoppable. Walter met it with his shield, and the blow echoed off the embracing walls. To his surprise he turned it well enough; the strength behind it was alarming, but that great sword was lighter than a steel one would have been. At once he lunged beneath, skidded off Andvari's shield – and barely missed catching his blade in the chains as the Otter-Lord twisted it quickly, and kicked at him with a heavy blunt-clawed foot. He sprang back, watching the giant warily. Andvari, eyes narrowed, struck out – in a feint, catching Walter's counter against his shield and chopping down hard above it. Walter sprang sharply sideways; the blade shaved his vambrace and thudded into the earth. Andvari thrust out the flat of the shield and knocked him sprawling, hauled his sword free and slashed again. Walter rolled away, and dashed his shield against Andvari's hairy ankle. The huge creature hopped and howled, and among the eerie echoes Walter creaked upright and swung at him. The bronze sword turned his blow, twisted with appalling strength and forced it against the shield; the chains snagged and all but tore the sword from his hand.

'*A double main*, Branxholme!' shouted the wizard. Walter let his shield swing, grabbed the hilt with that hand and yanked it free. He took a two-handed cut that twisted Andvari's shield on his arm in a shower of gold flakes, and caught his sword on the return stroke. The double clangour filled the walls. Andvari staggered, and Walter pressed home his advantage with a steady rain of blows which the giant could only block, not counter. That was how it would have to be; strength wasn't going to win him this fight. Nor would endurance; it would have to be soon.

'Into the water!' shouted Michael, over the ringing echoes. 'Force him in!'

Of all manners of suicide, fighting this water-monster in his own element seemed the nearest and easiest. But Michael's advice usually had something behind it – and Andvari was forcing his shield into play, to free the blade again. He was slower than Walter, but he was regaining the advantage. Walter let his attack falter an instant, saw the sword come up to slash at him – and hopped nimbly aside. The cut sang right past him and his own blow struck it on its way. Andvari's own strength spun him around – and Walter crashed into him, shoulder on. With a startled roar the giant positively flew sideways, off the little strip of grass, through a waterside bush and crashed sidelong into the pool. Walter ran down the gravel after him and splashed in, struck – and staggered at the force of the counter.

'But this,' said Andvari, rising up in the deeper water, 'is very foolish. You might as well have fallen on your clumsy sword, young mortal, and saved me the trouble. You may return to the land if you wish . . .'

Walter, knee-deep, fought down his panic, and shook his head mutely.

'So be it,' said Andvari, and struck. Walter caught the blow, and staggered – but it was Andvari who fell, his legs skidding out from under him in the loose gravel. Walter, weighted by his armour, stepped waist-deep and hewed at Andvari's neck. The shield turned it – almost. The water slowed the broad shape just enough; Walter's blow skidded and bit lightly into Andvari's shoulder. Black blood spurted, and Andvari roared. He hacked out – and skidded again, and sprawled to his knees. Walter's blow drove the bronze sword back to jar against the Otter-Lord's own head. He hurled Walter off by sheer main-force, snarled and suddenly plunged forward in a jack-knifing dive. Black water boiled where he had been.

'Back, Walter!' cried Michael. 'Along the shallows, towards the wall! He'll seek to take you from below!'

Walter had already guessed that, and slashed at the water around him as he backed away. In front of him a fountain of glittering gravel erupted as something struck the bottom. He reached knee-depth, dodged a sudden swirl and ran clumsily for the rockwall where it fell smoothly into the gravel. With the thunder of the water shaking him he put his back to the cold wall and waited, watching the deep pool to his side. Water poured down a thousand little crevices and into his armour, but he found the chill invigorating in this misty heat.

'The shield!' called Michael, swinging the little boat about in his haste. 'The wall! Pinion his shield! Jam—'

The roar of the falls suddenly took a deeper tone. Out of the crashing column of white marble itself Andvari came lunging, fangs bared, shield raised and sword already swinging down for the killing blow. But it was the very poise of him that showed Walter what the sorcerer meant. His own shield swung up, though it could hardly stop that onrush. His sword stabbed out – not at the creature, but at his shield, straight into the ensnaring chains and on through, carrying it sideways into the deeply creviced wall. It stuck, with the shield along it, jarring his arm. But it jarred Andvari far more. With all his strength the Otter-Lord ran into his own shield – and fell over it, as Walter plucked back his hand. The iron sword bent, and snapped under the weight. Andvari, winded, fell to his knees, the broken shard raking at his unprotected shoulder. His blow went wide – and Walter brought his shield down with a resounding clang. Not on the unprotected skull, as he might have, but on the outflung arm. The bronze sword fell, and Walter snatched it before it broke the surface. When the gasping face looked up, the blade was levelled at it, unmoving.

The silence was long.

Andvari finally broke it. 'The challenge was mortal. I suggest you do whatever you must do, before rust sets in.'

Walter fought not to grin. 'What I do depends on you. By rights I should probably take your head to Laurin the King, as whose champion I stand, but equally the choice is mine. For you and your folk I will accept a ransom that is of use to me.'

Andvari coolly fingered the chin he did not have. 'I appreciate the gesture. Well, you have broken that wretched iron instrument of yours. You may take mine. It will turn any weapon in this realm or yours, and it has considerable power against malignant sendings and shielding spells.'

Walter frowned. 'It is mine by law of arms, and as gild for my sword that I had from my father. You give me what I hold already! As I do your life. But I would gladly grant you it, if you can help me. I serve Laurin and his daughter, but I have a mission of my own to fulfil. I have to defeat one whom no weapon will touch nor ill destroy.'

'Oh dear,' said the gravelly voice again. 'Evidently you have been well prompted – and I can guess by whom,' Andvari growled, glaring at Michael, who sat calmly in the bobbing boat a little way off. 'Go ahead. Kill me, then. Tan this elegant fur of mine, and wear it. As you have guessed, it will make you as invulnerable as your enemy.' Walter hesitated. Could that be what Michael had meant? He found it very hard to hate this splendid monster. He didn't want to strike him down in cold blood; and the thought of wearing his skin . . .

'On the other hand—' said Andvari questingly, '*if* you should choose to exercise a certain mercy – taking, say, the sword, a decent portion of gold to warm Laurin's chilly heart – I and my folk will withdraw under oath from this country here.'

Walter's mind raced furiously. Andvari had trapped him neatly, between his honour and his own needs. The Otter-Lord sighed. 'Oh well, you drive a hard bargain, mortal.' He had mistaken the hesitation for cynical obstinacy. 'The sword, the withdrawal, the gold – and something else.' He rose in the water, as if unconscious of the blade that followed him. 'I am not without powers of my own, and the spells of one realm are redoubled in force in the other. I shall grant you a greater hold over your destiny.'

'What?' said Walter, surprised.

'Call it the granting of a desire, if you will.'

Walter scoffed. 'How can you do that? You cannot pass my destiny to me in a purse! How will I know you do not cheat me altogether – or that some greater evil will not come upon me through such unhallowed aid?'

A spasm of pain flickered over the Otter-Lord's strange features at the mere mention of hallowing. 'I cannot convince you, but perhaps your counsellor there may?' He gestured at Michael.

But the wizard, though he was obviously listening hard, simply shrugged. 'It is your victory, Walter, and your choice. I cannot choose for you.'

Walter's mouth worked. Impulses warred within him; but at his heart was his own honourable standard and that of his line. To kill the creature would be lawful, but to profit so hideously by its death . . . And somehow Branxholme and all about it seemed very far away, in a deep and distant dream. He would be shedding blood here and now. 'The choice torments me,' he said, 'but maybe the sword will be enough, if it has such power. And maybe your wish will be worth a little at least, as you claim. I accept your terms. Live, Andvari.'

The explosive cry from Michael startled him. '*Bravo! Molto mi guardo, ragazzo!* You did not fail at the test, as I had hoped you would not.'

Walter stammered. 'I – did right? My choice will serve me?'

'Both choices would have. But the other would only have made you de Soulis' equal and – who knows – perhaps too much like him. This way, the way of mercy, makes you his superior.'

Two huge hands landed on his shoulders, and he turned back in alarm. But Andvari's face was genial, and he made no move to strike. 'May you go forward as you have begun, young lord.

You are no longer my enemy. Say what you wish, and the ways you tread shall lead you towards it. I do no more than set a purpose in your feet.'

Walter looked at the creature reflectively. 'Well – for what it is worth – I suppose I seek the power to right the wrongs done by a sorcerer of black intent, by name de Soulis, and to avenge my father whom he has slain. That will do.'

'Nothing about rescuing the lady Margaret?' demanded Michael, surprised.

Walter shrugged. 'That is included, obviously. I want to release her, of course, but – well, as I would anyone in such straits. I've no special feeling for her – to be honest, I can scarce remember what she looks like.'

'A common complaint among mortals, they say,' said Andvari tolerantly. 'Well, young sir, you have your desire.'

'I do?' Walter considered. 'I feel no different. I know no new secrets.'

'Why should you? In time you will know much. Meanwhile, the sword you have, and – shall we say three boatloads of gold?'

'Five,' put in Michael. 'You have gathered the greater part of the gold there is here by now, anyway. And, painful as it is to mention, we hold a strong party of your knights against it.'

Andvari shot him a look. 'Assuredly. Five. It will be delivered to the guardpost by the time you return. Upon that, and upon our leaving this land the day following, you have the solemn oath of Andvari.' He put a claw to his torn shoulder, and then touched Walter on the forehead. 'Sealed in his blood. Wear that mark in Laurin's court and you shall have honour beyond your dreams. Do I have leave to depart?'

Walter looked to Michael, who nodded. 'Go then,' he said. 'And . . . thank you!'

Andvari flashed him a sudden grin, twisted and dived in one fluid movement. Sand boiled in his wake, and a rain of tiny gleaming flakes danced in the dark water and settled swiftly. Walter watched him go, a little sadly. 'I never thought I could like such an ogre. Will he keep his word, do you think?'

The dark man nodded. 'You may be sure of it. You especially, who bear his bloodsign. Andvari is by no means the worst of creatures, and a man may often find sympathies where he least expects them. It can be inconvenient, at times.'

Walter snorted. 'That's a damned cold way of putting it! A scholar's view, I suppose! And that reminds me,' he added, as he peeled off his armour and laid it on the bank to dry, 'you and your damned Mongol powder! There was no powder in your hands when you cast those levin-bolts, nor naught else either! That was plain sorcery you used, back at the ford!'

Michael's smile was guileless. 'There is such a powder,' he said, 'and easy enough to make – though most often it yields only an undestructive fizz and a pop, if the proportions are not thus and thus exactly. It provides a convenient cloak. After all, suppose I had admitted it was sorcery – where would I be now? And where you?'

'If I knew where I was now,' grunted Walter, 'that would be a sight easier to answer.'

'You are on your way home,' said Michael, 'in all honour, and with what you need and desire in hand for the storming of Hermitage, and your vengeance. How many can say thus much?'

Walter looked at the long bronze sword, weighing it in his hand. It looked strange, that yellow metal with its clouded stains, but it flexed and sprang with a feeling of strength; and its edge was fearsomely sharp. Sharp enough, maybe, to sunder more than mortal things.

'Yes,' he said dully. 'Home.'

8 ♜ Gold at Sunset

There was great stir when he and his strode into Laurin's cool halls, voices and running feet. Now Walter walked with calm pride, knowing it was no empty swagger; and though he looked neither to left nor to right, his mind cast about him. When the train of gold passed there was silence; and when it was brought before the dais the cold-faced King of the Fair Folk half-rose, gaping, as carrier after carrier of pale gleaming flake, bar and ingot, chain and ring and rough coin was laid before him. He came to dip his hands in it, and its reflecting gleam put warm light in his hair and colour in his skin. He beckoned to his daughter, who stood beside him as ever, to come rejoice in it also; but she held back, standing in the shadows of the throne. 'Young mortal,' Laurin said, 'you have done that which the great of my realm have not in many hundred years. And Andvari and his folk? Do you have his head or fell?'

'I won their submission, Lord. They quit your land under blood-oath, sealed by this mark upon my brow.'

Laurin regarded him narrowly, among the rising clamour. 'You took naught for yourself?'

Walter held his gaze. 'This sword, Lord, to replace my father's, which was broken in single combat with Andvari. And he gave me the granting of a desire. Naught else.'

Laurin shook his head. 'You put me under great obligation, young sir. How can I, your lord in this place, be any less generous than my enemy?' He looked around at his court. 'Know all, then, that Lord Gualtiero of – of Branchia'olme, who has served me with faith and valour, is my chosen champion and commander, the first mortal to command in the Realms since Huon of Bordeaux cast off his shackles of human destiny. And to mark the occasion I also will fulfil a desire of his – be it for all the gold he has won me this day. He has only to name it!'

Michael strove to catch Walter's eye, but he ignored it. He bowed deeply, his heart thudding in his ears. 'Lord, I am unworthy. Yet I was taught to be honest and speak plainly. What I will have may not be mine to ask. I seek the hand of the lady Astrafiammante, if she will have me.'

Manfredo dropped his shield. The noise sparked off a terrible hubbub in the court; yet no young men dared put themselves forward, or set hand to blade. Only the wizard drew himself up, looking darkly anxious.

Laurin looked coolly amused; and Walter realized with a sudden chill that his request had come as no surprise at all. '*Fiat!*' said the King. 'Provided that you undertake to stay and be my champion – for my daughter cannot long leave this land – your desire accords altogether with hers.'

Walter's heart skipped beats, leaving him breathless. 'My lord, I always wished to travel and see other lands. I have seen no place fairer than this, and Astrafiammante is its flower—'

Michael seized his arm. 'Do you realize what you're about, man?'

With a clangour of armour Walter brushed him free. 'Better than yourself, maybe! And if I do not, remember it was you who brought me here! But I am lord of my own life, and of my own love! Here—' He looked up at the dais, and saw the dark girl step out of the shadows, her long hair curling about her pale shoulders and uplifted breasts, her lips strangely scarlet in the colourless gloom. 'Here I find what I truly sought! Say no word against me!'

Stepping forward, he seized her hands in his, and drew her down to him. Her eyes were bright, her body feather-light against him, yet full of a warmth he felt even through his armour. 'Is it your will that we wed, lady?' he demanded breathlessly. 'You could have the pick of blood-princes born to great palaces such as these, where I am only a rough young man out of a poor country!'

Even as he spoke the sinking sun traced its fiery image on

the walls, high above the sight of those below, and he saw the image of it in her eyes, brighter than all the gold. He breathed a perfume of heady flowers.

'Yet the strength of it is in you,' she whispered, 'and the courage! And the will which could one day grow to mortal greatness when we and all our princes are but shadows of memory. I would have my share of that now. I would have you, my champion.'

'Did I hear you say something, Master Michael?' inquired Laurin politely.

'Only *Persephone!*, my lord.'

'It has brevity,' said Laurin. 'But it lacks clarity. Meanwhile the matter seems to have been decided. Lord Gualtiero, stand before me; daughter, by his side. Kneel, both; for I pronounce you wedded, my lord, and henceforth a prince of this realm. Let there be festivities, feasting, music, dancing – but before that, let my Lord Treasurer find room for all this gold, or the dancers will be falling over it!' He fingered his chin, with a gesture very like Andvari's. 'A great deal of room!'

The palace, for all its deep shadows, was a place of life that evening, of revels the like of which Walter had never seen. Much of it delighted him, the unforced honour with which Monforte and the other lords treated him, the fine garments he wore, almost impossibly soft against his skin, the strange and exotic foods he feasted on and the fine wines like liquid silk that seemed to become vapour upon his tongue and rise to his brain directly. He took particular delight in the unceasing music, always varying, one delicate sound or a ringing sinfonia of many instruments; in the songs and ballads, though he had to struggle to understand so much of them; and above all in the dances Astrafiammante danced before him, delicate as windblown web, or dragged him into, laughing. Yet some of the revels startled him, and what he could make out of many songs; and some of the near-naked dancers' cavortings genuinely shocked him. Astrafiammante only laughed. 'They are traditional for a wedding, such songs! The people expect them, they wish us much bliss and many children!'

'And a lot of goats, too,' he said sourly, 'to judge by what those satyrs are about!'

'You have nothing of the kind in your land, my lord?' she giggled, her long fingers tapping out the rhythm of the dance on her stomach as she sprawled on their common couch.

'Well . . . the night before a wedding things can get pretty cheerful, aye. But nothing quite so . . . out in the open.' He recovered his good humour. It was odd. Here, before all this throng, he felt completely at ease with her; or would have, but for the sense of anticipation that intruded, too taut to be entirely pleasurable, like an overtightened harpstring. 'It's a cold country, after all.'

She leaned close on their common couch, lifted a beaker of wine to his lips, followed it with her own. 'But you have women to keep you warm, do you not?'

'I . . . uh . . . like anywhere, I suppose. But before you, nobody I . . . Astrafiammante, this – this is my land now. And you the only woman I want.'

She lounged back, smiling at him, sipping the wine in turn. 'How can you be so sure of that?' Delicately she lapped a stray speck of ruby from the rim. 'You have not put it to the test. Perhaps you should. Shall we not slip away and be by ourselves?'

'Can we?'

She slipped a hand in his. It felt impossibly tiny and fragile, and cool against his warmth. 'It is expected. Nobody will miss us.'

He cast a quick glance around the hall, red-lit by braziers and leaping firelight in the great chimney. Lute and chitarrone chimed gentle chords to a beat of sistra; lords and ladies laughed and sang. Laurin sat with a court lady by his side, playing some elaborate game of chess that seemed to be punctuated by long and meaningful glances. Dancers postured and plunged against the light, young girls from Libya Major, wherever that might be, in headdresses and little aprons that made the merest pretence of concealment. There was no sign of Michael Scot anywhere—

He stiffened. Astrafiammante had slid his hand into the

bosom of her gown. 'Would you rather watch them, my lord,' she inquired, 'or me?'

It took him an instant to recover his voice. 'My lady, I am at your pleasure.'

'Not yet,' she said, her own voice no less choked. 'Let us go.'

Walter stood up, carefully, and raised the girl to her feet as he had seen other men do. She did him a courtesy and then, laughing, flitted off before him into sudden shadow, and he followed, feeling earthbound and leaden. Up long silent stairs she led him, and through long corridors hung with gloomy folds of drapery, and at last through heavy doors she fastened softly behind her. The draperies here were of gauzy stuff, many-coloured and pastel-pale, many layers thick so that he must push between them as through foliage. The room was wide and open to a great balcony, high over the strange city; and in the centre of the floor before it, surrounded by more drapery, was a great bed hung about with garlands of flowers and sweet herbs whose savour hung on the air. She turned to him, her dark eyes wide, and stopped his halting impulse to speak with a quick kiss whose fierceness startled him. Only a second later, as her hands flew down the parting of his robe to pull his sash away, did he realize it had excited him also. She pressed close, and pushed the robe from his shoulders, leaving him in tunic and hose. His arms closed around her, feeling the sudden warmth of her through the tissue of her dress; his hands slid on the slippery fabric and closed where they fell, clasping.

They kissed, long and deep, drinking a shared breath, darting tongue against tongue in a game of exploration that was teasing on her part, burning on his. Her hands slid upward, raising his tunic to press hotly against the skin of his back, her long nails digging gently into the flesh like delicate claws. His hands slid to her side, rose to stroke across her breasts. She drew breath sharply, broke her grip, stepped back. Her black eyes blazed, and he feared he had been clumsy, hurt or offended her. But with a sweeping, whirling serpentine writhe she twisted out of her dress and stood, panting, in a mere transparency that barely reached her thighs and shimmered as she breathed.

He stood also as she retreated towards the bed, staring,

drinking in both the beauty of her and the more than mortal poise, and wondered if this was how men had conceived the heathen goddesses of old. She was delicately young; she was ageless as the starlight she was named for. Nakedness became her as naturally as her courtly dress; and the marks of her state, her parted lips and lifting, shivering breasts, the hands that stroked and clutched at her flanks, were both things exciting and carnal and things unearthly, exotic mysteries a man might explore at his peril, and only with reverence in his soul. He strode forward, aflame and eager. But he did not pull her to him; he hardly dared. Slowly, astonished at himself, he sank to his knees before her, pressed his hot cheek to her belly almost in worship, his lips to the brief tangle of black curls. Her hands caught at him, held his head as if for support and acknowledgement in one. She shivered, gasped, sank back across the cushion-strewn coverlet and pulled him with her, writhing, wrapping her legs about his shoulders. Her hands clutched in the tunic and with convulsive strength tore it asunder off his back, then drew him up across her, sliding, caressing from chest to back and finally down to his thighs, drawing, compelling and at the last enveloping. He was vaguely aware of the cushions scattering as they rolled and plunged like fish in a dark pool, of her long hair damp and wrapped around him, entangling him as weed does a drowning man, of the sharp sea scent of her as she held his head tight to her breast. At last he felt as if his pounding heart split him open, pulsing head and heaving breast, as if his soul burst out of him in an endless moment of searing, ecstatic release; and at that moment he would have counted it well lost.

Later, much later, when he was drained beyond restoring even by the supple subtleties of touch and tongue, he rose, afire, leaving her sprawled and half-sleeping. He walked to the balcony, letting the warm night breeze dry the many moistures on his naked skin; he wore them like an anointing, a benison. He stood and stretched, gazing out into the misty greyness over the strange city that was now his home, and at the single star that blazed through it. The balcony stood high and isolated, outthrust on a promontory wall from the hillside, looking down upon the roof of the palace itself. He listened to the revelry that still arose from there, and smiled.

'You need only be licking your chops to complete the picture,' said a sardonic voice from behind him.

He whirled about. There stood Michael Scot, in red robes richer than the ones he had come in, and hung about with gold. There stood his damned horse!

'How – how did you get up here?'

Michael only bowed, as if at some deft compliment. He surveyed Walter's nakedness with an amused lift of his eyebrow. 'It is time, Branxholme.'

'Time for what? And how long have you been here, damn you?'

Michael bowed again. 'Time to go, of course.'

Walter choked. '*Go?* Where – go?'

Michael's dark face grew deepening lines of anxiety. 'Go home! Home, where deep concerns await you, in case you had forgotten! Concerns to which I have bent great efforts on your behalf!'

'Aye, aye, so you have! And don't think me ungrateful for that much! But you've done other things as well, wizard! You've opened my eyes! Did you not expect that, did you not mean to? You've shown me things I could never have dreamed of, you've led me into dangers I'd never have passed and honours I'd never have gained, and – and – other things, glorious things! You've shown me these, you've let me enjoy them – and now you say I must leave them all and return to my old bleak corner of a mortal world, to live and die in squalor as my fathers did? Would you give a damned man a taste of Heaven, only to hurl him back into Hell?'

Michael shrugged. 'I thought you felt you had duties. And, believe it or no, I who have lived in the rich court of Palermo, where the Emperor keeps his harem like the caliphs he crusades against, a place of fountains and fair architecture and deep wisdom – even I yearned for something that lay among the bleak bones of Oakwood, my land, my home. You may, too, one day.'

'Never!' said Walter passionately. 'Never, while I have—' he cast a glance back to the bed, unsure whether Astrafiammante slept or woke, hearing this. 'While I have love!'

A sardonic grin twisted the wizard's face. 'Silly of me. I had assumed your catship was sufficiently gorged upon the fleshly cream. You stink of it like a stableyard with the mares in season. Has it caused the matter of a certain Lady Margaret to slip your mind altogether?'

Walter's anger blazed. 'She? What's she to me, what was she ever? A chit of a child, who flyted and scorned me with never a civil word, who never missed a chance to pour out her pride over me like her stale pisspot! A pretty match we'd have made of it – she her uncle's pawn as I my father's, and yet forever thrusting her loftiness home upon me!' Unable to shout for fear of wakening his wife, he let the words stream out like furnaced metal, hissing. 'The Douglases would sell her, would they? And drive me to my death in the name of barren honour, for a deed they feared to do?'

Bitterness swelled in his throat. 'And, to be sure, to lay hands on my lands! Well, let them rescue her, as they're better able to! Or simply sell her to de Soulis as they'd have sold her to me! I wish the maid no ill – I would help her if it were my part to do so – but as you said yourself, de Soulis will do to her no more than he has done already. If the Douglases, with all their might, first try to release her by force or ransom, and fail – then let them send word to me! But not before!' As if to echo him, there came a flurry of festive trumpets from the palace below. 'If they demand compensation, let them eat up my lands indeed, and may they choke upon them! The honour of the Scots will grow in richer soil!'

More sardonic than ever, Michael inclined his head in the merest formality of a bow. 'If that is your mind, my lord, so be it. But I will extend you a courtesy still. I shall return to ask again if you are still so minded, in a year and a day.'

'Come in a century and a day if you will!' shouted Walter. 'Even by then I'll not be weary!'

A sleepy voice spoke from the inner room. 'Dearest, with whom do you dispute? Hero, come back to your heroism . . .'

Walter turned. 'I come!' he said fervently, alive again at the very sound of her. 'But as for you, old man . . .'

He stopped. The balcony was empty. Michael Scot had vanished as he came.

So it was that in the year that followed the former Lord of Branxholme settled happily in the land of shadows as the greatest champion of King Laurin, prince of his household, sharer of his counsels, captain over a hundred among his knights. A war was fought that year, against intruders from the East in bright fantastic armour with fluttering banners at their backs, and fierce facemasks beneath their spreading helms. On the wide plains before Cleopolis, Laurin's lesser capital, the Lord of Branxholme led the company that broke their greatest assault, leading a bold surprise attack across the very line of their charge to strike at the centre. He and his men were among the vanguard that some days later drove the invaders back into their own wagon-lines, cutting the guys of their silken many-tiered tents and the fetters of their slaves. He himself bested their imperial standard-bearer in a fiercely chivalrous riding of spears, striking through the wide plates of his armour to dash him from the saddle, and cut down the silken balloon in the form of a serpentine dragon that was their standard, raising in its place Astrafiammante's veil. But as he stood there panting over his fallen foe, watching the fluttering wisp add one more shade to the infinite variety of greys that painted the clouds, he thought suddenly of his own racing Border skies, and the many-shaded play of light over heather-purple moorland and brown heath and bright green forest. He caught his breath, sharply, suffocating in the twilight. Then the trumpets sounded, and the triumphal roar of his fellows rolled over him like a cresting wave, and memory was overwhelmed. Acclaimed with honour now by all, he gained command over a thousand, a captain-general of the Right Flank.

Other triumphs were won within doors, in struggles no less heated. At that first year's end the lady Astrafiammante bore Gualtiero their first child, a son and heir with traces of his own brown hair, rare among these black- or blonde-crowned folk. In pride and delight the young general sat by the cradle while the mother slept and the nurses went to their refreshment. As he rose from it to summon them once again, a tall shadow fell across the child; and there was Michael Scot awaiting him.

Walter laughed, quietly, for at that moment all the world was his friend, and offered the wizard wine, which he drank. 'But I assure you,' he said, 'you need not bother me with your question once again. Here I am, here I stay. Would I leave at this moment? I would needs be mad to even dream of it! But I owe this to you, I would give you some better reward and reparation than hard words.'

Michael shook his head. 'Young man, I want nothing of yours that is here.'

'Not even my reverence? Come, I was seeking a name for the child – shall I give him yours?'

The wizard shuddered horribly. 'No! That – no! Only let me return in a year and a day, and ask once again!'

Walter shrugged. 'You're easily contented – a licence to waste your time! Come, then, for how could I prevent you? But I could give you your answers now.'

In the next year there was no strife, and Walter made it his task to see the ravages of war made good. As he watched road and bridge restored, field and orchard new-planted and cot and village rise from ruin and ashes, it often came to him that there was less ill done here than in any war of men he could imagine. Even the fierce Easterners, though they took slaves readily, seldom slew except honourably under arms. He remembered then his father's tales of when the English had passed over the Marches last, under John Lackland, setting every town to the torch. In Berwick the king himself set light to the very house he had slept in, while his hated guard of *routiers*, Brabantine mercenaries, put the townspeople to the torture. In retribution King Alexander and his troops, Robert among them, had done almost as much to Carlisle, and then struck south right the length of England to Dover, where they received the King of France. He had thrilled at the story, once; but now he could guess at the cost in human misery and the trail of bitterness it left.

Only at the memory of his father did his blood flare. He thought of returning then, even for a while, to his own lands, dreamed of leading a host of the Fair Folk against Hermitage, and the shock that would be to the creature which lurked within it like a gross and evil slug. But that, he knew, could not easily be brought about, nor would Laurin permit it. Not now, at all events; not even in a year. The King trusted his son-in-law, no doubt of that, but there were still barriers between them, and if ever he spoke of his own land Laurin would deftly turn the subject aside. Astrafiammante would listen, as she always did; yet he felt less and less inclined to speak of it to her. Somehow he felt ever more earthbound and clumsy at the mention of his origins, as if they were dungy clay clinging around his boots, and ever more unworthy of her. He idolized her, called her a child of light and air, and it seemed to him that she lifted him out of his fallible mortality and made him capable of extraordinary, superhuman things. But, though she denied it when he demanded it, he felt always that there was something more she wanted of him, something in him which disappointed her, yet for which she would never blame him. It made him want to please her all the more, and fearful of offending her. He could not dream of returning, not now. One day, perhaps; the fall of de Soulis would be all the greater then. Meanwhile he was winning honours that would have delighted Robert, and he had concerns no less pressing, a son named Roberto to bring up.

And at that second year's end another child was born, a daughter. Once again on that chosen night Michael was on the balcony, and once again he took the same answer back, without recrimination or complaint. Of the affairs of his own world he said nothing, and it never occurred to Walter to ask. He had all but forgotten it.

The next year was a threatening one for Laurin, for many other great lords of those realms were inclined to make common cause against him. In need of a stronger command than his own, he made his daughter's husband Grand Marshal of his wars. It was a choice few doubted by then, and those who did were swiftly silenced. His victories were many, his defeats few and never costly or final, for he was not afraid to retreat, and always prepared for it. It was one of his few boasts that he never wasted a life in his service, and he was honoured for it. In all that time he had little thought to spare for anything but the here and now, the welfare of his forces and the folk they shielded taking every waking moment, save the few he could spare for his family. Only briefly did the past awaken in him, in a sudden flash as he sat ahorse, watching a great army file past him into misty fells like those above Ettrickdale, or when the blaze of sunset momentarily sketched the triple coronet of the Eildon hills into a starker skyline he scanned – then he recalled, briefly, that he had not been born to endless twilight, that there was a world of light and shade elsewhere. He wondered then vaguely why the thought plucked so at his heart, and dismissed it all the more angrily, burying memory and feeling alike beneath the rubble of a life discarded. He remembered beauty of a strange sort, warm hues alien in a land where even the flames exhaled by the brightscaled firedrakes, quicksilver strands wriggling beneath the dark green forest boughs, flared green or icy blue. Even ordinary firelight shone redder here, and duller; only gold mirrored a brighter light, and 'gold at sunset' was a proverb for any sight that tormented the eyes.

Home? Home was where his wife and children awaited him. That home was all he yearned for now; he had little thought to spare for any other. Home was their palace, built in elegance and graced by art and culture, and not the limewashed stone hovel he half-recalled in a bandit land. And when the horns sounded the sight, or a knot of dark hulking shapes burst out of the darkness and fell upon the Marshal's guard, such memories could only rend like a veil before the here-and-now. When Michael returned that third year, it was the Marechale Gualtiero he met; the boy Walter was no more. And the answer, as always, was the same.

Another year passed, and Gualtiero grew in stature and in wisdom. He came to know Laurin's realm from end to end, from the riverine fens of the North, out of which he had chased Andvari, to the stifling southern slopes that yielded great quantities of dark strong wines, and the castles that dominated the river that was the Southern border, crossed by the brazen bridge

King Elfinor had raised. He crossed and recrossed the Eastern plains, where you could ride through the hot wind from dawn to dusk and see never a living soul save some few cattleherds and the occasional herd of wild centaurs, breasting the tall grasses like a green sea as they ran, or, solitary and perilous with its moonlight coat, a unicorn. He rode westward, to where a dark sea breaks beneath long banks of green and high chalk cliffs; but there, for reasons he only dimly realized, he found he had no desire to linger. From that way alone, it was known, no enemy could come; and the mists hung heavy about his heart. So as the year advanced, and a kind of autumn came to the land, he returned, down pale roads along which his following glittered like a silver thread in the skein, to the heartland of the realm, and the palace Elphicleos had raised. He returned in time for the birth of his latest child, and, wearied by his long riding, slept early and at peace that night. He woke unwillingly with a hand that shook his shoulder, and stared blinking with disbelief at Michael, hardly recognizing him. Yet when roused he answered, more patiently even than before; though in the morning he remembered it only briefly, as in a dream.

In the year that followed he went abroad, in embassy rather than in war, to many of the realms that lay around his own. He attended the court of Midir beneath the hollow hills of the Sidh, held grave converse with their lords and followed their wild stag-hunts among the glens and woodlands. He descended into the mountain realms of Alberic the Black, down endless cavern-ways into sulphurous airs, and saw there in the feeble light the denizens that swarmed like ants over a mighty jewelled crown they worked on, to grace a head some twenty times the human span. He walked the fields of Arcady, where peace still reigned unchallenged in clement climes but no great art or science could thrive, and was received beneath the vine-trellises and feasted with rough plenty by rural lords in laurel crowns and flower garlands. In all he was met with deep respect and not a little wonder, for his victories and his presence had changed much. The bronze sword of Andvari had become a symbol of fear to the enemies of Laurin, and a lodestone for allegiance. Even Huon, who had once been a mortal knight of King

Charlemagne, chose the path of discretion and held back from confrontation with the young newcomer, sending embassages of amity and respect. But Huon sent no invitation to the Marechale, as others had, and it was thought that he would not willingly look upon the face of one whose origins were as mortal as his own, some four centuries earlier – one who still had a soul. The idea made Gualtiero laugh; but he returned fair words, and was glad of peace. He busied himself with the charges that Laurin set him, and with raising his family, and adding to it. When Michael returned that fifth year Gualtiero was ready with his answer, and threatened cheerfully to have it set in a plaque on the balcony so Michael could simply read it. The dark man smiled at that, with a faintly pained air, and promised to return once more.

So it was that in another year and a day, being the end of the sixth since his coming, Gualtiero went out from his wife, if anything more beautiful for the passing of time, and his dark-eyed children, and stood on the balcony of the great bedchamber to greet his visitor. For he was a courteous, good-natured man, and mindful that Michael was in some sense doing him a kindness. Also, rather to his own surprise, he desired this time to ask of his old world, of how things progressed, and of someone called Lady Margaret, who had suffered some misfortune he could not right. It was the merest shadowplay of a dream to him now; but, with the power and position he had achieved, his conscience had if anything grown more keen. Even such a dim memory was a trouble to him. Its very faintness carried a hint of failure, and though he was ready enough to spare others, he found failure harder to tolerate in himself. His wife seemed to be aware of his trouble, and had been strangely silent all that evening.

At the sound of hooves on cool marble he turned, smoothing the wings of his moustache in a considering gesture that had long ago become habit with him. As befitted such an occasion, he wore a fine robe, with the bronze blade belted beneath.

'Welcome, wizard,' he said genially. 'Ask your question, for you will find the answer ready to hand as ever. And then stay, if you please, and take some refreshment, for there are some matters of which I wish to ask you.'

Michael Scot stood before him. 'I do not come to ask, Lord of Branxholme,' he said flatly. 'Enough, my lord, is enough. Your time here is at an end. Now you must return with me, now upon the hour, and linger no day longer.'

The Marechale, as befitted a counsellor and courtier, no longer took anger easily, but outrage swelled in him. 'You forget yourself, wizard, in presuming to give me orders! Are you mad, that you think me the same way? Go, now, and never return!'

The wizard's look was strange, but there was no anger in it. 'I give you no order. I only tell you what must be, and leaves you no choice. You must come at once, and without fail, and leave everything – *everything!* – behind! For otherwise you will lose it in any case, and much more as well. You have learned much here, my lord, but there is one thing that none would dare tell, not those nearest and most deeply bound to you—'

'Astrafiammante would tell me anything that affected me!' said the Marechale calmly.

'Not if she knew I would spare her the pain,' said Michael softly. 'You must not blame her. These people are less like mortals than they seem, Walter; but it is only at such times that the differences appear. They are neutrals, as once we spoke of, and for that neutrality there is a price – many prices. Every seven years the land must pay what might be called a teind, a tithe, to Hell. There are other, better prices, but that is the one that concerns you. Any mortal souls who have found their way here are in danger of it, inevitable danger. Not even your wife, your children, the King's true gratitude, can shield you from it.'

Against the dark conviction in that voice Gualtiero felt the strength drain from him, and a bleak devastation take its place. A shadow stirred among the breeze-blown draperies, and he turned, clutching the balustrade for support, reaching out to her. 'Astrafiammante – *mia carissima* – *negate*—'

'My lord, I cannot deny what you have heard. I have known what must be since the first moment of our eyes' meeting. I have gained, knowing all the time I must lose. You are a mortal, and that pain I spared you.'

Walter sagged. 'Is there no way—?'

Michael's voice was relentless as iron. 'Only to give up your soul, as Huon did.'

Walter clutched at Astrafiammante, gasping in the delicate scent of her. 'You are my soul!'

'My lord,' she said sadly. 'If you could have given it up it would have already left you. For that I have watched long, and know that you cannot. For you, my lord, the price is too great. I am not your soul. You must forsake me now, and all our children, and go.'

He convulsed, like a man stabbed to the heart, and bowed his head. There were tears in her voice, but none on her face, not one; and to his own inner horror he found that he also had none to shed. Like a man walking in his sleep he turned away from her.

But Astrafiammante, like a last vision of loveliness, ran lightly across the cool stone, and as he stepped towards the black horse waiting she clutched at him, one swift embrace. Into his hands she thrust a weighty burden, and pressed upon his brow, where the blood of Andvari had rested, one swift kiss, that burned with the icy clarity of starlight.

9 ⚑ The Burning Lance

Up and into the night they rode, and the mist closed around them like the chill clasp upon Walter's heart. Again the black horse sped faster and faster beneath them, and the air lashed at his eyes. Numb, uncomprehending still, he saw the bleak fells flow by, smelt for but an instant the sweet savour of the lilies on the verge of that nightbound sea, heard the dark waters hiss and surge beneath the thrusting hooves. And once again, as meaningless time went by, the terrible stench of the river rose around him, and the hot blood lapped around his legs in sickening currents. All passed, all fell away as he sat dazed and griefstricken, dead to all feeling, too aghast even to contemplate throwing himself off into oblivion. He reeled and grew faint, but he did not fall; perhaps he was held in some fashion – he neither knew nor cared. His senses all but left him, till only a thin thread of consciousness remained, and the incessant rhythm of the ride.

Light beat upon his eyes, fearful, searing light like an iron-kiln thrown open a hand's breadth away. He sat up with a start, shielding them against a brightness he had not endured for so long. He blinked, once, and suddenly it was no longer agonizing redness, no longer searing but pale, watery greyness before dawning, on the margin of drizzle-dripping woodlands with a wide vale beyond. Out of the trees onto the track they rode beneath a weeping sky, and below them yawned the half-ruined gates of Branxholme tower, the village around it just stirring at the foretaste of dawn. Walter stared dully at tower and townlet as they drew nearer, neither elated not downcast. They hardly seemed to have any meaning for him, the home he had once admired and so easily forgotten. The chill seemed to have sunk into his very bones.

'What have you done to me?' he demanded, and his own voice and the rough accent of it sounded strange in his ears. 'All gone, all lost— Wizard, what have you done? This is a miserable place, a stall, mean, savage – despicable! I need never have seen it so. What have you *done*?'

Now, at last, his loss brought him close to weeping.

'It seemed very much the same to me,' said Michael Scot quietly, 'when first I returned from fair Italy. But all the same, Lord of Branxholme, it is in this soil that our roots lie, and our destinies entwine with those of others. Come now, re-enter your rightful home!'

They rode into the courtyard through gates that had still not been repaired. Together, limping and weary, they passed the nodding sentries and entered the hall. It seemed to have changed very little; it stank. Few of the sleepers were stirring yet, only the lowliest servants, and they spared the newcomers little attention. Walter stalked on into the kitchen, but the fire was barely alight, and the sooty drudges shambling around it were too cold and sleep-eyed to pay heed to anything much else. He sank down on a bench at the great table with all its clutter, and put his head in his hands, utterly void and despairing, ignoring his companion. The first pale sunbeams spread along the walls, touching the yellowing greasy limewash with a tinge of warm gold. Walter looked up, aware suddenly that he was killingly thirsty. Flies buzzed round the congealed platters on the table. Not without a shudder, he reached out for a half-finished jug of ale, around whose rim a fly was circling hopefully.

'Are you so ready? Now.'

The fly landed.

Walter swatted at it and overturned the jug. Then he stared, and sat staring, eyes wide, mouth slack, and spoke no word.

Ale frothed across the scarred ash-grain. After a moment Walter laughed, a little crazily. 'You mean – no time has passed? God alive – *none at all*?'

He dug his fingers into his hair. 'All that distance, all those years – my love, my children, my honours – all in less than a heartbeat of time?' He was practically sobbing now. 'Away for so long? Till my own home became a hovel to me! Till I forswore my own heritage – and yet it was all, *all* just more of your glamoury? All that I did, all that I won, all – I loved? All – no more than just another of your damned trumpery *illusions*?'

The dark man seated across the table shook his head, and there was stern fire in his voice. 'Not all!' His gesture swept down Walter from head to foot. 'See!'

Walter followed it with his eyes – and half sprang from his seat, violently. Here in this squalid kitchen, from which it seemed he had never stirred, he sat still clad in the rich robe he had donned to welcome Michael, fine weave of darkest blue shot with embroidery of delicate silver by the hands of Astrafiammante herself. And by his side, scabbard scraping along the trodden floor as he rose, was the great bronze blade of Andvari. The heavy bundle she had given him, which he had clutched all this time, half forgotten, almost fell from the seat beside him. He touched it, and knew what it was from the feel of the metal beneath, the soft chiming resonance within.

With a soft oath of awe on his breath he caressed the ornate figures of the broidery on his robe an instant, and sank back on his bench, fixing Michael with wide astonished eyes. Instinctively he reached up and smoothed down the wings of his moustache – and froze again. He was staring into the polished base of a pewter ashet from the great dresser, held inches from his face. The blurred image that floated before him was that of a boy of seventeen no longer, but a young man in his middle twenties, though the grave and settled countenance of authority made him seem somewhat older. Walter stared at the image of the Marechale Gualtiero, and whispered: '*Astrafiammante!*'

He sat there, stark stunned, after Michael laid down the plate, hardly hearing the hubbub in the outer hall. The door bounced back, and in strode the hefty figure of Sir Andrew Ker of Cessford, balding head agleam with sweat, face a mixture of anger and anxiety. 'Young Walter!' he rumbled. 'What's this—?'

He stopped dead, and the blood ebbed in his florid cheeks; his blue eyes almost started from his head. 'Holy Mary Mother of God defend us!' he whispered, and crossed himself. '*Robert?*'

Then he shook his head like a drunken man struggling to

clear it, and stared again. He came forward and gently seized Walter by the shoulders, half lifting him. 'My lad, I beg your pardon – Branxholme, I mean, rest your poor father!'

Walter smiled, a little wearily. 'You may always call me what you will, Sir Andrew.'

Ker nodded, absently, and released him. 'It's past all believing. I could have sworn it was your father sitting there as I remember him, when we were young men together.' He shook his head again, and thumped his chest. 'It sent my heart stottering, lad, and I'm not so young as I was! Ach, laddie, I'm sorely sorry to see grief and hard times put the look of years on you.'

'It appears,' said Walter acidly, 'to be an effect also of consorting with sorcerers. But—' he added, with malice aforethought, 'they have their uses . . .'

Ker blinked. 'With—?' Then he noticed Michael for the first time, and started again, in anger now. 'You! You by're lady bogle-raiser! It was you sent word to me this night gone! What've you been leading this young man into, in his grave distress? You said that you've been and gone and paid a call on de Soulis, by're Lady!' He blew out his cheeks. 'What in God's good name did you hope to achieve by such infernal meddling?'

The dark man shrugged. 'My lord warden, you yourself suggested—'

'Aye, on your own account! You being knowledgeable in such cantrips and cavals, and in sufficient good odour with popes and legates and Percys and whatnot, it would seem, to risk it! Small loss, to you who have already foresworn heirs of your blood! But this young man who's sole lord and heir of his line, to risk his life and limb and soul—'

'I was more than willing!' interrupted Walter, irritated by remembering how ready the sole lord and heir had been to toss away his birthright – and for what? 'As you would have been in my place, Sir Andrew. If I'm to beard the lion, better I learn the lie of his den and the colour of his mane. And do you not want to hear what passed there, and what we were able to learn, Master Michael and I?'

Recovering himself, he called for ale for his guests. They told Ker what he needed to know, of Michael's visit to Hermitage and Walter's disguise. The Marchwarden seemed to assume that accounted for the outlandish clothes, no doubt from Michael's store; but he kept darting confused glances at Walter's moustache.

When Michael recounted the discovery of the deep dungeon and the maid held there as a rumour overheard by his servant, as in a sense it was, it set Ker bristling with new anger. 'All the more so, because it makes little odds!' he rumbled. 'I have not been idle these past days, either. When I heard of the attack here I sent swiftly to court and to those with whom I have some voice there. The answers are come back – the King is obdurate, will hear nothing against his lieutenant in Liddesdale who is supposed to suppress raiding there, both from and against the English, for it is them he is most concerned with for now. Indeed, the word is that without iron-clad proof any interference with him, even if it did not break like water against the walls of Hermitage, would most certainly be construed as treason, and bring down the royal wrath.' He stared bleakly into his ale. 'And Alexander is a man of little patience in such matters. I'd get nobody's support at such a hazard. I may not credit de Soulis' nonsense about being invulnerable; but for all I can do he might as well be.'

Walter stirred. Hermitage had daunted him, but that was a night since – or seven long years. How many strong castles had he laid siege to since then, and stormed by all manner of stratagems? Things were bubbling up in his mind, ways to deal with impregnable walls . . .

'Suppose,' said Michael, so conspiratorially that they all leaned forward. 'Suppose you could lay hands on the man himself, in the act of doing some dark deed? Some delict of sorcery, say, or secret murder, committed in person against a man or woman of consequence. Then you could lay hands on him *in flagrante*. The King couldn't possibly protect him. Everything could be done in due form, the man imprisoned, an application to Alexander for a warrant of execution in such terms and with such strong testimony he could not avoid the issue!'

Ker contemplated him with dour distaste. 'Oh aye, maybe. But who'll buy the bearskin before you've caught the beast?'

'Exactly right!' said Michael, with suppressed force. 'Caging the beast, that's the first thing. Hatred surrounds de Soulis throughout the land, does it not?'

'Aye. Even in Liddesdale his name reigns through fear, not love. A good many of the dale's riders could be persuaded to turn against him, if that way the tide flowed.'

'Then how many men could we get to join a siege of the Hermitage, do you think?'

'Devil a one. They're not mad in these parts.'

'But suppose,' said Walter quietly, 'we had a sound stratagem against the Hermitage, and they knew it?'

Ker shook his head. 'No. What they know, de Soulis'll know a few hours later—' He stopped, mouth open. 'You have something? A slip of a lad like you?'

Walter rose and looked down on him sternly. 'I believe I do. And do I seem like a slip, only? I have looked upon darkness since my father died, and learned more than I wished to, perhaps, through the agency of this . . . scholar, here. You could say he has made me old beyond my years. I believe there is a way into Hermitage's walls, for men who are brave and fast enough. And more than that, there may be a chance to turn that stratagem to serve Master Michael's suggestion. A perilous chance, but—'

Ker twisted his beard. 'Even if de Soulis expects it?'

'There are means to make sure he does not,' put in Michael smoothly. 'To gather men and inflame their hearts, to make them move swiftly and become a tide which carries others along, drowning doubt and fear and treachery in its stream. All the elements of this we have to hand!'

Walter's swift mind grasped almost at once at the core of what Michael proposed; Ker was more dubious, needing each point explained to him at length. That was understandable, for it would be his duty to call the trysting that was needed, and on his head would fall its failure. Walter's mind wandered again, back into the warm shadows of the land he had made his own. He could not even wonder where Astrafiammante was now, or his eldest son for whom he had had such hopes, or his laughing daughters. What meaning had time, when a man could be hurled through a great slice of a lifetime between one heartbeat and the next? His family, and his youth – seven years of his life, that might have been good years even in his own mundane world, with nothing to show for them.

Nothing save a sword, a robe, and sorrows.

Walter watched Michael, counting off points on his fingers to Ker, his eyes hooded as ever, and boiled with the cruelty of what the man had done to him. Hatred shot through him like a draught of poison, bitter, corrosive, stinging the very marrow of his bones. During their brief quest he had come to respect and depend on Michael, even to feel a kind of guarded affection for him; he had felt that Michael returned the regard, to some extent. And then he had kicked the ground from under Walter, like the hangman on the ladder. What manner of man could do such a thing, so lightly, without warning or apology?

He was persuading Ker, that was clear. The warden's eyes were alight now, his nostrils flaring like an old hound on the scent; he gave a short harsh laugh and slapped his thigh. The plan would be accepted – and where would that leave Walter? He shuddered. It was one thing to propose a daring plan, another entirely to find yourself committed to carrying it out. Even the warm morning and the good fire at his back could not banish the cold knot in his stomach. But play the part he must. Michael's work, again – what was it drove the man so?

'But once we have the carl!' exclaimed Ker. 'Prison walls have a way of melting around men of influence, as you know. If there's truth to this spell about him, as you affirm – then even if we do gain the royal warrant, what're we to do with a miscreant we can't string up or shorten by a head, eh?'

Michael stroked back his hair, as if to brush the grey ones deeper. 'Only gain the warrant,' he said quietly, 'and that you may safely leave to me.'

The tone of his voice set Walter's teeth on edge, so predatory it was; and he remembered how Michael and de Soulis had exchanged dark references, like rivals in love outboasting one another, prowling and sniffing like two circling panthers. They were too much of a piece. Ker was growing excited now, slapping his thigh again and promising every man jack answerable to him at the trysting; but Walter sat cold and grim. This Imperial scholar who had near-warlocks as servants, and rode upon something that was more than an earthly horse – could he be helping them against de Soulis only for his own purposes? Even, as Robert had once suspected, to set himself up in the other's place?

It hardly seemed likely, given what he had seen of the man. But then it would not, of course, if he were cunning enough – and Walter had no doubt of that. Why was a man so tainted with eerie associations, so capable of terrifying callousness, thus ready to spend his labours in helping those unlike him, for no apparent reward? Walter could find no answer. But it came to him that, in all fairness, he had after all gained something from his experiences. All that had been done to him, devastating as it was, had had one effect. He was no longer a boy, to break under such a burden. He would endure, if only for the sake of the happiness he had thought was his. Even if all was lost to him, he would live in honour, shield his folk, avenge his father – even free the maid Margaret, if he could. He fingered the hilt of Andvari's sword, and felt the grim resolve grow in him. Even if she were no more than the shadow of a shadow, Walter of Branxholme would not fail his lady.

He could do none of this if he was ready to murder his only helper. With a conscious effort of will the young Walter would never have made, he shifted the focus of his hatred as a man might shift his glance, from Michael to the Lord of Hermitage, and he cursed that beaming mask of geniality. For, after all, the blame for all of their sufferings did lie squarely with that evil man. If they were but pawns in Michael's power, who after all had delivered them there?

The old woman Jeanie came bustling up to the table with a board laden with ale and oatmeal and buttered eggs and strips of salt smoked pork griddled for the noble guests' breakfast. But as she laid it down before them she caught sight for the first time of Walter's face. She opened her mouth wide in a silent shriek, and let fall the board. A bowl toppled off and burst upon the floor. Almost at once she collected her wits, bobbed her apologies to the gentry and set slaveys to picking up the pieces and fetching another; and Walter, who knew her voice well, caught the words she was muttering to herself all the while. 'Aye, aye, it is for the best, for the best. Not for a' the kine in the Marches would I be in the seat of the Laird Soulis the now! No, nor a' the red gowd neither.'

So it was that, that self-same day, riders went forth from Cessford to the other Scots of the Buccleuch line and the other family lords of Teviotdale and Ewesdale and lands further north. The Kers of Ferniehirst were summoned, and the other Warden families, the grim Maxwells of Annandale and the Humes of the East March, all with their associates and dependants of many names. Even into England the riders went, to men who could be trusted, Musgrave and Shaftoe, Ridleys and Dacres, Collingwoods and Charltons. To each a warning went, to prepare armed force and all needful supplies against a trysting day and ready to ride; yet no day nor place was made known. That word would reach them by a later messenger, whom they must be prepared to follow. Such a tryst as was preparing had never been seen in the Marchlands since the late wars; but Ker's name was held in reverence enough to see his bidding done and his command kept firm. Besides, his summons had more than hinted at profit to be gained. When at last the second messengers came, riders in the night, most men were ready, as their practice of reiving had made them; they mounted up and set forth at once with few words spoken. The same night-riding skills kept them on the dark and winding ways, the secret reivers' paths across the rolling hills, towards a destination they only gradually became sure of, the Jedward region and the mighty abbey of Jedburgh.

No doubt by then the Lord de Soulis knew something was afoot, for word had been sent even to the more reliable lords of Liddesdale. But that very action meant he could not be sure of the mustering's purpose, whether it might not be for some new stroke against Northumberland, or rebels in the north and west, or whether it was some crazy move against him. It would have caused him little enough concern, in either way; for his own strong housetroop of outlivers and northern outlaws acknowledged no other master than himself. If Ker came up against him, he would be discredited, and then there would be a new warden in this March – perhaps in all the Marches. If the muster were for some other cause, his raiders would have all the freer reign. He could sit tight within his well-provided walls and await the outcome with a considering smile.

As the morning of the tryst dawned, cool and moist but promising sunlight, it was the Scots and their neighbours of Teviotdale who were earliest upon the scene, having least far to ride, Pringles, Davisons, Youngs and Rutherfords among them, and men of Roxburgh. Taits and Halls and Robsons rode in from the Cheviots as the daylight grew, neighbours and associates of the Kers, and from Tweeddale the Humes with Dixons, Grays and Trotters. From Eskdale in the west, a little later, came more Scots, with Turnbulls and Crosers, Elliots and Laidlaws. But time enough had been left so that even the furthest-flung could arrive more or less together, Maxwells and Johnstones from Annandale and Nithsdale leading a fine cavalcade of Bells and Irvings and Carlisles and Burnses; there were Armstrongs with them, kin to the Liddesdale families. And though not all those summoned from Liddesdale dared heed the call, there were some who welcomed the excuse to evade their Lord's eye awhile. All were gathered, with many lesser men besides, while there was still food and ale enough, and none went altogether without; which was important. No man had brought many of his household troop, for nobody would leave their homes undefended; but that had been allowed for. So many households had been summoned that even a few from each made a strong force. And it was best that no lord or kindred have overwhelming strength, so that fallings-out and feuds could be more easily overlooked.

In that regard it helped, too, that they met upon holy ground. The fashion of the abbey at this time was that it stood upon a low hillslope above the Jedburn, with its farms around it and a wide pasture by the river at its foot. Though a simple building compared to what it was to become, its great church was still the largest in that region, and of a strength and grace that seemed to stem from another way of life. The men who rode in that dawn were hardened warriors and practised thieves, and their horizons were narrow enough; yet they were becoming aware of concerns beyond them, a wider, deeper life with different demands. They themselves might not aspire to it, but their sons could, and their sons thereafter. So it had been with Robert Scot, and so to a greater or lesser degree it was with many of these, and their followers. The Church was part of that life, and not even thieves could prosper without the indulgence, at least, of the Lord. A gathering at Jedburgh must have upon it the Church's blessing, in which they would share; and a blessing at Jedburgh had to be worth a lot more than anything merely local. To them it looked halfway to Rome itself. And it had not escaped the wiser among them that, though the abbot at that time was from Lothian or some such region, the prior was a Ker, and the sub-prior a Scot. When the commoner men found that food and ale and even wine were provided, their spirits also were greatly raised, and most of them, lord and man alike, were more than ready to await what would follow.

They had not long to wonder; but the manner of it surprised them greatly. They expected an address from the warden; but the trumpet that sounded was before the doors of the abbey itself. As the single challenging note faded the doors fell open and were flung back with a creak and a dull boom.

In the dark gap there appeared a strange figure. A knight it seemed, riding a great dapple-grey warhorse richly bridled; but it was no knight of any fashion they knew. His armour was of gleaming dark plate such as few had seen, shining with traceried foliage of silver and gold, like a reflection of some unearthly forest. The lance he bore was long, and at its tip there burned a great ball of pitch and smoking peat, like the embodiment of spitting wrath. This was the ancient custom at market-days and such by which a complainant or challenger drew attention to his proclamation; yet never had they seen it delivered in such a manner and from such a source. Slowly the knight rode out into the day, and they saw that he was bareheaded, his brown hair and moustaches gleaming in the early sun. Down onto the path that led among them he made his slow and ceremonial way, his shield at his saddlebow shining with the device of

Branxholme. That was how they first knew him; and even those who had shared his schooldays might not have known him otherwise, so grim and hardened did he look, and so upright and sturdy a man among men. In such a manner, and in so strange an armour, Walter seemed unearthly himself, a champion out of the elvish lands ridden into the brightness of morning. His eyes were bright, yet he looked neither to left nor right till he reached the margins of the trysting field.

Then he shouted, in a great voice as clear as he could make it, and it carried loud over the hushed morning air. 'Be it known to all that I am Walter Scot of Branxholme, knight! And that I cry grievance most dolorous, by open voice and fame, as our sovereign Lord's true liege against a common traitor, reiver and thief! I declare him a weak thing and a coward, that skulks behind high walls and sends others to work his evil deeds! I declare him secret and stealthy murderer of honest men, ravisher of maidens, despoiler of honest matrons! I denounce, proclaim and declare him outlawed and accurst, in going and in riding, at board and at bed! I spit upon his honour and spurn his arms beneath my armoured foot!'

A little ripple of cheering went up as he drew breath. This was a style well known to them as bauchling and reproaching, the ritual cursing and insulting of an enemy to force a single combat; it was a popular art. They waited eagerly for the usual less stately afterthoughts.

'Dweller among filth I name him, haunter of middens, wallower in dung to drown the lice the good Lord sends to plague him! Leprous master of foulness I name him, so full of filth that his bowels have risen to contaminate his brain and flavour his speech! I name him sapless seeker after debauch, abuser of women, bugger of boys, rascally whorer after bitch and beast of every shape and gender, sheepbiter, scabby bestial pimp and master of sins unimagined! Coupler with decayed carcases I name him, burrower among maggots! Lurker in shadows I name him, lest the clean sun scorch the raddled hide from him! Hider of his face, lest men read his filthy deeds in it and scorn him from their doors in disgust as they would a diseased cur!'

More cheering, and some judicious nods. This wasn't anything like as inventively obscene as usual, but it had a literary ring they respected. Only the more alert ones hesitated, as it began to dawn on them just who this enemy might be. But the ring of command in Walter's voice held their ear regardless.

'For his open reiving, saikless slaughter and shedding of innocent blood I call down upon him both the temporal sword and the sword of holy Kirk, that shall hound him to his determined end! I name him Nicholas, called de Soulis, malefactor, sorcerer, murderer and coward, and call for the verdict of the Lord upon him! And if I am allowed I shall prove it upon his corrupt carcase!'

There was an instant's horrified silence from the crowd. Then into it, from the abbey doors above, came the tolling of the greatest bell, a gift of the Scots, and the throbbing echo of voices in deep chant, on a single note, a baleful, resonant monotone. Into the doorway, austere and resplendent in habit and staff, strode the abbot, with swinging censers before him, and a great processional cross. Its jewelled arms flashed as it was raised high on its staff; men crossed themselves, and some men knelt uncertainly. But it was no prayer or blessing that was spoken over them, for the abbot raised his voice in the ordinary tongue all men could understand, echoing the Latin of the chant behind him, while the solemn bell tolled.

'The malediction that lighted upon Lucifer and all his fellows, that struck them from the high Heaven to the deep Hell, must light upon him!'

Domine maledice! sang the dark voices.

'The fire that stopped Adam at the gates of Paradise, the maleson that lighted upon accursed Cain, must light upon him!'

Domine maledice! came the echo, and the bell kept pace.

'The thunder and fireflaught that set down as rain upon the cities of Sodom and Gomorrah, with all the lands about, must light upon him!'

Domine maledice! out of the vaulted dark.

'All the malesons and waresons that ever got worldly creature since the beginning of the world to this hour must light upon him, upon the Gigantis for their oppression and their pride, upon Pharaoh and the people of Egypt, their lands, corn and cattle, upon all the cruel tyrants that murdered Christ's holy servants, must lie upon him from this day forth!'

Domine maledice! Domine maledice!

'And by the authority of Holy Kirk I, Lord Abbot of this most sacred house, do call upon all men present to stand firm against such terrible evils that walk among men, and to lend their aid to Holy Church and her servants! If this they fail to answer, their own precious souls they set in peril! And if this they answer well, in letters of gold shall it stand against their sins in Judgement, be they e'er so black!'

The choir's chant swelled high in sudden radiance. *Domine defende eos! Defende, defende!*

All this Walter had rehearsed at length; yet even now his hair bristled at the sound. So might the call come to the Crusade he had dreamed of following. He knew that in truth the abbot had said little, adding only one more curse to those the Church had already heaped around de Soulis' head since his excommunication many years since. It was the most he could be persuaded to do, for he feared the King's wrath, and perhaps also de Soulis', over anything more positive. So the curse had been carefully constructed. Recorded coldly on paper it bore little enough weight; yet pronounced aloud against such a backdrop it had the effect they needed. Most men still standing fell to their knees, crossing themselves; those already on their knees shouted and beat their breasts, for such was the fervour of the age. The abbot raised his crook and chanted his benediction over all their heads, and then over Walter by name and title as he bowed in the saddle and crossed himself in answer; then, no doubt well pleased with promises of gift and tithe, he and his retreated with ceremonial calm within the gates, while the bell marked their paces. But as the doors boomed shut behind them, Walter tilted his lance and hurled it quivering into the earth before them, where it stood blazing and crackling with the pitch at its tip.

'You have heard the voice of holy Kirk!' he shouted into the awestruck hush. 'What de Soulis has done to me and mine, you know! You hate him, all of you, that I know! But some of you fear him also! I do not blame you – for any day now he may decide to despoil your fields, steal your land, your chattels, your womenfolk and your very lives! Aye, fear him! But consider this – what have you to fear that he will not very soon do anyway? First it was Liddesdale – and who now there can call his land his own, except on sufferance? Now it's to Teviotdale he reaches out his greedy fat paw, and the land of my people. Ewesdale and Eskdale suffer – where next, if an end is not called to his ambitions? Tweed and Annan, Ettrick and Yarrow and all the wide Marches, all yours – to lose! And very soon you will – for he will not overlook what lies unresisting in his path!' He paused, while the pitch spat and flared along the lance.

'But look around you! Your neighbours and mine, all in the same plight, facing the same loss – and free to give the same hard answer. Free, to flout him with a closed fist! Look at such numbers! So gathered and so roused, can the mere stones of Hermitage stand against us! With so many of us together, will we submit to such rapine? For when comes such another gathering, or a greater? When shall we put a stop to it – when, if not now? And if we do not, my lords and liegemen all – shall we not deserve it?'

His gaze swept them as they stood open-mouthed; and from out of their ranks Ker of Cessford rode to Walter's side, though remaining silent, leaving the last words to the young man.

'So then! By the authority of the King's true warden in this Marchland I call upon all here present to join me, Scot of Branxholme in Teviotdale, that we may ride against the fastness called Hermitage; that we may demand in due order the surrender of its walls, the stolen goods and unjust prisoners within, and the delivery of its lord to justice!' Walter drew the great sword that hung at his side, and the bronze burned in the morning sun as he slowly raised it aloft. 'This is no ordinary weapon! Whence it came is not my part to say; but it has power, ancient power against such as our common enemy, and has been given to us to wield against him. Our counsels are taken, our stratagems are made; we have the wisdom and the means to use against him. Delay, debate, and all that we hold is lost! Together, if we act now, at once, we can scour this evil from the Marches, and save all that is ours! The voice of the Church is with us – who shall withstand us? This is our moment! Shall we grasp it – or fall? *When comes such another?'*

Slowly, very slowly, the abbey bells began to toll for the solemn mass Walter had commanded, and the sound of the opening chant echoed out over the meadow. There was a breathless moment when even the voices of the monks seemed to falter, as if the whole assembly drew a single uncertain breath. Men glanced at one another; hands moved to swords, hesitated – and then clasped them decisively. Then the roar that went up was deafening.

Some distance away, within the margins of the Jedwood overlooking the abbey, Michael Scot heard the wine-slurred roar, and smiled to himself. He saw the crowd stir and mill around Walter, ahorse and afoot. 'Come!' he said out loud, and flicked the reins. 'It moves, all – and so must we.'

Men slapped Walter on the back till he was glad of his armour; they seized his hands till it felt as if they would tear them from his wrists. To all he nodded, or smiled grimly; but all he said was, 'Go within! Hear mass, be shriven and prepared! We ride this noontide!'

Thus he directed them all, before their wine-fed enthusiasm waned, and the whole great gathering went streaming into the abbey chapel till it seemed the walls must burst, and lesser men were obliged to kneel outside in the sunshine and hear as best they could. Walter knelt in his allotted place before the altar; but there was no fervour in him. He prayed; but between prayers he brooded. His heart felt cold. All he had done and said today, the fire and the oratory, had been in cold blood and by careful direction of Michael, who had seen the ceremonies of popes and emperors. For him there was little true wrath left in it, only a great sickness and revulsion at driving men so, like swine to a slaughtering. Yet the Marechale knew it must be so, and reminded him that the feelings were true, however they were used, and the end good. Nevertheless he felt soiled and dishonest, and in need of absolution all the more.

The solemn chime of the bells drifted across the empty, trampled meadow. Michael absent-mindedly patted his fretful horse, and smiled to himself again as he dismounted some way from the gate. Walter, standing by his own mount, looked up at him sourly. 'They're mustering on the road below. They stay only for me, and I for you.'

'I know. I am ready. Are you happy now?'

'Happy?' Walter shook his head. 'These men hang like lead about my neck. Some of their lives will be forfeit at my behest. What if—?' He stopped. 'No. A man could ask too many such questions.'

'You are grasping the rudiments of philosophy, I see. But you are pleased with the outcome, at least?'

'I suppose I am. I didn't enjoy it, but you prepared it well.'

Michael's calm smile broadened. 'One day, perhaps, you will see – and enjoy – the puppet theatres of Sicily. They have puppets of Paladin and Saracen almost lifesize and in metal armour, swinging on their strings across a painted backcloth and roaring and beating at one another in the most approved martial fashion. His Highness the Emperor is very fond of them. I have often thought that if I were not a scholar I would make a passing good puppeteer. Here was my cloth, and my puppets await you. Best, I think, that you and the good warden get them on the road before their ardour cools, and that I wait to join you until much later, when they're committed beyond turning back. I might perhaps put some of them off.'

'As you will,' said Walter curtly, clambering into his saddle. 'As usual, Master, you're wise. I'll look for you upon the road.'

Michael watched him go, and patted his horse's neck once again. His voice was low and in some wise mocking. 'There goes a work of great virtue to our account. Out of the Realms we mere men bring chiefly what we brought in, though more refined and rarefied if we are fortunate, or well guided. In that one there has arisen true nobility, for all his angry demeanour. He will be a good Lord of Branxholme in his time. But in some wise he is still an innocent. Did you know he sought to borrow you for his grand entrance? Imagine – coming out of an abbey, *you*!'

He laughed quietly but heartily. There was no answering laughter at all.

10 ♖ Fire in the Dale

So great a riding could hardly be concealed for long, even if de Soulis had no more than human eyes to serve him. They were over a thousand spears that took the road southward that day, many of them knights of proof. Ker and Walter drove them outward at speed, outwardly for the sake of surprise, but for other reasons they did not speak of. They had no illusions about their followers. They had won them over with wine and words and crusading fervour, and the further they rode, the sooner these would fade. The blood would cool, the men remember their destination, and the black dread of it would clench about their hearts.

For the Border lords it was a point of pride to fear no man; yet like all such boasts this was apt to turn against them. A man cannot face what he does not admit; it grows like a canker within him, till of a sudden it breaks out and batters down the reason which has never needed to defend itself. All the more likely, this, if these men were called upon to face some terror beyond the common run; they had little fancy, the most of them, little breadth of mind. They would be ill prepared. And the Marchmen's very independence made it hard for them to unite, hard to swallow old feuds, hard to follow a lord on loyalty alone. A quarrel might provide too many convenient excuses to withdraw, and so weaken or split the force. Ker and Walter kept watch, made note of likely waverers and weathercocks, blowhards as swift to sway one way as another, and as suddenly. Those who showed signs of straying were swiftly detached into smaller bands under a few good men who knew the Liddesdale, to close off escapes through its treacherous hills and marshes. Thus they were kept of some use and their honour salved, while removing them from the fellows they might dishearten.

In the body of the main force he gathered the most reliable men, but in the vanguard he set those who had suffered worst at the hands of de Soulis, the dispossessed and disinherited, bitter men of Liddesdale, Esk and Ewesdale, of the Bewcastle Waste and Englishmen of the Upper Tyne. Small men most of them, farmers and yeomen who had had little enough, and now had nothing, reduced to sweating for their bread from other men; even their arms were borrowed. Some were bad men, hardened brutes and gallowscheaters, for de Soulis in his first days of office had been careful to sweep out the worst first – those he did not employ – and so give a fair complexion to his black greed. But bad men and good, misfortune beat them into a common purpose as hammering tempers a spearhead.

These were Walter's plans, for the most part. More and more he took the lead from Ker, though always in the warden's name. Ker was content in that, although often he wished his own sons could be here to share in the excitement, as was young Hugh Ker of Ferniehirst, their cousin. So did Walter at first, till chill remembrance came to him that he might be leading his closest followers to their deaths; better his friend's sons were safe abroad. Yet he dared not let that worry show as he rode among the column, speaking to all he could, nor let it darken the quiet confidence in his voice. The most he could do was prepare them to face strange and sinister assaults, but add that a protection was promised them, no less strange but more hallowed, a fire to fight fire.

'And I pray to the good Lord,' added Ker in a whisper, 'that you're right!' All the while Walter was scanning the skyline, after a sight of the familiar figure on the high-stepping black horse; but there was no sign. Doubts grew in him, till it began to seem as if he had been decoyed into the venture; but he repressed them sternly. Decoyed or not, there would never be a better chance – any other chance at all, most likely. And for all his anger at Michael, and the sense of utter loss and emptiness that still burned at his heart, Walter found he had a curious trust in the man. Michael had, after all, given him seven years of a happiness few ever knew in their lives, of love and honour and riches – no small gift, surely? But it did not satisfy him.

'Better never to have known it,' Walter muttered to himself, 'than ache as I do now. Better to have been blind from birth than have your eyes plucked out!' Or was the gift subtler? Had he been given a sorrow so great that he would no longer fear death in his purpose? He caressed the fluted curves of his armour, and thought of Astrafiammante, and mused upon the wizard, and on death.

As the second day of the march went by, the land changed. They were approaching Liddesdale not by the Scot country of Teviotdale, but from the east over hill, by the Liddel Water in a pass between high fells. The trees grew thinner and swayed in clumps and copses, bent to the lash of the prevailing winds like workworn serfs. The hills grew barer and bleaker, as if shorn of greenery; the gorse was dark and stunted, the grass scrubbier and grey and so windflattened on the lee slopes that the horses had to mouth the stony soil to crop it. The sky above faded to a leaden roof, and over the rounded hilltops clouds massed, frowning, like a mustering army. 'It grows late,' grunted Ker, signalling a halt. 'And we near the dalemouth. Maybe we should camp here the night, and wait to ride in for the heartening morning light.'

'And if there come storms by night – or worse?' Walter hesitated. He knew better than most how much easier it would be to face the gaping jaws of Hermitage in the warm light of morning; but he also knew what some fearsome sending might do to his force. He saw with annoyance that men were already kindling fires from the bundles they had brought with them, as if to ensure a camp. 'We might better . . .'

He stopped, and threw up a hand for silence. Men heard it then, a sudden pulse in the air, a deep drumming tremor that grew slowly nearer. It was the sound of hooves, of a horse hard-ridden, and throughout the column hands fell to swords. But it came not from the mouths of Liddesdale ahead, but across the hills from the north, where the deep forest still reigned; and there was only one horse. Very soon it crested the rise of the knowe above. Beast and rider stood out an instant, deep black against the twilit heavens, like the pagan ancestor-god that still, as many peasants believed, rode the nightwind to hunt down souls for Hell. Walter drew breath faster; those lineaments he knew, and the urgent voice that came ahead of the rider down the slope confirmed him.

'Fools!' roared Michael as his great horse came charging into the centre of the column, scattering the fires unheeded with its hooves, its mane and his hair flying wild. 'Have you so little fear you'll sit and griddle your dinners at the gates of Hellmouth?'

Up to Walter and the warden he rode. 'Aye, kindle fire enough! But not to sit here by! My lords and knights and common kerns, all, are you so eager to be slaughtered in your blankets? D'you think your enemy marks not your coming?'

Walter snarled. 'D'you tell me so? Then we'll give him the wherewithal to see us better!' He stooped from his saddle to snatch a torch from a startled footsoldier, reared his horse high to catch men's eyes, and whirled the brand aloft. 'Up, vanguards, and ahorse! Gather up the fires! Light brand and torch, light our road! *Into the dale!*'

He reined in his impatient mount while the vanguard formed up, and shouted to Ker: 'Get them ahorse, in God's name! No telling what'll come upon us if we linger!'

'Or if we don't, maybe,' muttered the older man. 'But at least we'll shift them for now!'

Walter nodded curtly and spurred his horse out into the dark. The vanguard, following him like their last spark of hope, fell in behind; and as they went, their torches gleaming like coals, Ker rode in among the main force, shouting, 'Up, Marchers, and after! Will you hold back while others lowp at the leash? Are you base limmers, to flee before the first blow's fallen? Take fire, and follow! Into Liddesdale!'

He came face to face with Michael, leaning panting on his dark horse, sides heaving, while around him men flowed like a river in gathering spate. He stooped over the dark man. 'You came timely, or they'd have set here the night! Are we espied, indeed?'

'We are,' panted the scholar. 'I was watching, and was detected somehow. There were flashes of light from the hills, signals I could not read. But the place was already on the defensive, the flocks called in or dispersed, the palisade closed, the battlements manned. A patrol was set on my trod – and something else also, that hunted like a beast, swiftly. I barely outran it with my hide intact.'

Ker blew out his cheeks. 'It was to be expected, perhaps. But you, wizard – you're coming too! We'll need you all the more sorely now. *Ride!*'

Like a fiery serpent, picked out in points of flickering light and roaring with a confusion of many voices, horses whinnying and clangour of arms, the mustering rode out in haste, and the barren soil shook beneath them. Like the sudden backwash of a tide they rolled down the winding river's edge to the mouth of the lesser dale, hard on the heels of the vanguard. The rumble and ring of their passage echoed off the steep face of the Arnton Fell, and rode before them as the roar of a breaking wave into the open bleakness of the Liddesdale itself. Down towards the Hermitage Water they turned with the stones cracking and scattering under their hooves, and across the ford by Toftsholm in a great splashing and crashing of water and rock; so that the cottagers, accustomed enough to armed men riding by night, fled their homes into the uncertain dark. But there was no thought of reiving this time, and the little farms were passed unharmed. Along the river they rode, to avoid the worst of the treacherous mosses, and the banks crumbled as they passed. It was not long before the keenest among the vanguard, Walter among them, made out the shape outlined against the sky's faint gleam, square and hard and grim between the roundly weathered hilltops, the battlements of Hermitage.

There was no gain in secrecy now. Shouts went up, and they rode all the harder. But as they rounded the curve of the river and came out of the meagre tangle of stunted oaks and brush onto the open knowes they slowed, and at last were halted by Walter's upraised hand. The castle stood louring before them, a sullen slab of darkness like the offspring of night and stone. Not a light showed; not a head was silhouetted upon the battlements, not a gleam of blade or mail. They reined in beneath that blind maw of a gate, baffled by the black strength of stake and stone, weathered palisade and close-chiselled wall, a massive mockery of all assault.

As they hesitated there in that daunting shadow a sudden chill breeze wafted over them, and a faint misty drizzle, like weeping. Men started uneasily, then laughed harshly to kill the shame of fright; was this the storm they'd heard de Soulis could summon up? But all at once the castle stood out against the night, a slab no longer but a solid shape of implacable strength, shining eerily as its stark stones grew slick with moisture and caught the faint skygleam.

'That'll make them slippery, by're Lady!' puffed Ker nervously as he stood in his stirrups at the head of the main force.

'It will,' said Michael, so flatly that Ker grabbed his arm.

'Christ's blood, man! You don't think the bastard—'

'It's a reasonable precaution. It was allowed for.'

Ker looked at him murderously. 'Grand for you to say! It's not you who must carry it out!'

The dark man pulled the hood of his cloak over his head, and stroked down his beard. 'Day will come. It cannot rain forever.'

But day was slow, a pinched famine-face peering feebly through the sullen cloud. The walls of Hermitage glistened now like a slug's trail; and still no man showed his face, while the thin rain blew through cloak and cotte, through rings of mail and joints of armour, chilling as it went. Men hugged themselves and shivered; horses stamped and bowed their heads. Tents sagged; fires sputtered and would not light.

'We must do something, man!' raged Ker. 'I couldn't hold the siege a week in this state!'

'So long?' grinned Walter. 'Well, for a start we'll force the palisade. That'll at least give us a windbreak, and some more firewood.'

'And lay us within close range of the wall,' growled Ker. 'But it's as you say, young man.'

They had brought a ram, knowing there was no timber solid enough in the dale; and they had its tackle slung between horses in minutes. They dragged the huge pine trunk up to the gate swiftly, for they feared a sudden hail of arrows from the wall; but there was nothing and nobody. At the third swinging stroke, reverberating off the silent hills, the gate cracked and sagged aside; and in the same instant the castle's narrow door slammed smartly shut, leaving the open ground within the palisade empty and undefended, as if mocked by those manmade cliffs.

'He plays us like trout!' raged Ker. 'Luring us to hand with a tickle and a prod—'

Walter caught his arm and pointed up above to the battlements. One figure alone stood there, leaning over, looking down at them. It threw back the hood to reveal a close-cropped head of silver hair and a beaming, puff-cheeked face. Was there another beside it, shorter, topped with red?

'Well, gentles? What leads you to knock so early of a morn?'

'Nicholas de Soulis!' raged Ker. 'I charge you as a King's officer and in the name of God to surrender yourself and your trust into my—'

'But the Lord of Liddesdale is also a King's officer,' said the voice from above in reasonable tones. 'Perhaps even ranked more highly than the wardens. Would you care to put it to the test?'

'Enough of this, man!' raged Ker. 'Surrender your prisoners and hand yourself over to us, or we'll pull the place down stone by stone!'

'A curious argument for the unco' righteous!' boomed de Soulis genially. 'Well, that may prove to be rather a long undertaking. And I counsel you, gentles, you stand upon ground where it is not always wise to linger. Many old wars have passed over these lands, and many deeds of blood. I counsel you to take care lest you awaken some memories long-buried.'

'De Soulis!' shouted Walter, and all heads turned at the bleak and bitter wrath of his tone. 'Scot of Branxholme speaks! You have despoiled my land and had my father slain! Yet for the sake of mercy, and to save lives, I will give you one last chance for grace. Surrender your prisoners, your keys and yourself to us and you shall have life and freedom in exile. Refuse, and I shall give you only one choice more – whether it is from your own battlements I hang you, or from the tallest tree by the river here!'

'There is no Scot of Branxholme now,' rumbled de Soulis with genial contempt. 'The old lord died a fat fool, and the son is become an Italian body-servant, I hear, or catamite. The honour of Branxholme is mine for the asking from the king. Now get you from my door, for I do not entertain landless beggars. Stay, and I shall shortly extend the same courteous choice to you!'

'I hear you,' said Walter evenly, and turned away.

'You made him a very noble offer,' murmured Michael at his side. 'That was not in our plan. What if he had taken it?'

Walter shrugged. 'Lives would have been saved, as I said. I cannot bring my father back, however many more I throw after him. Muzzling the man and hounding him out—'

'It was a dangerous moment.' Michael's voice remained soft, his expression all but unreadable. 'He would have chewed through that muzzle, and we could never have slept quiet in our beds again. Free and resentful, he would be twice the peril. The end of all this can be nothing but his death! Nothing else serves.'

'Serves who, Master Michael?' demanded Walter coolly. 'Are you so eager to see a fellow-sorcerer fall? Well, fall he will now. And, if you will permit, I must go see the camp set in order.'

So began the brief siege of Hermitage. Walter knew how camps should be laid out, after the old Roman fashion, but here on this damp ground men took little heed. They pitched their tents casually on undrained soil, or built crude shelters against the broken palisade, taking little care where they threw their waste and filth. 'They know we're not going to be here long, whatever,' he told Ker. 'They'll grow weary and uncomfortable too quickly. The sooner we strike, the better. Tonight, maybe.'

Ker twisted his moustaches. 'God, so soon? Will you not first spy out the lie of it all? But then,' he sighed, 'a day'll tell you all you can learn. Tonight let it be, if you have your men; but it will have to be late. And I feel in my guts that de Soulis may not bide so patient.'

All that long day Ker's words were belied. From the walls of Hermitage no sound was heard, save voices raised in merriment. De Soulis' men seemed to share his confidence, and were content to do nothing. Many hotheads among the besiegers were eager to try the ram against the castle gate, but they cooled off remarkably when Walter pointed out the arrow-slots above it, and told of the defended way beyond. He rode around the area with Ker and Michael and other men of repute, spying out the walls from every angle. Up to the Nine-Stane Rig they rode, and from the slopes beneath the ancient stone circle that gives that hill its name they looked down upon the distant roof. Nothing stirred, no sentry or picket, save one small figure that paced and prowled through the drizzle. They could make out no more of it than the red cap it wore, though for Walter that was enough; but more than once it stopped and seemed to return their gaze, as if it could see them more clearly.

'And one watcher's enough!' grunted Ker. 'Sleepy as a wasp's byke in summer, but one shake and out they all come swarming!'

'What chance flame?' demanded a fierce little Roxburgh reiver-knight, swigging at a jack of rough barley spirits. 'I've smoked out wasps enough ere now!'

'Not from within those walls,' said Walter. 'Or from under that slate and lead roof. There's no wood exposed save the walkways of the battlements, and they've water enough within to quench any little fires that arrow or tarball might start. If we could get a siege-belfry up it might be different, but not on that soggy rolling ground.'

The Roxburgh knight eyed him keenly. 'Siege-engines, eh? You're too young to have seen them in the wars. Now when I—'

Walter smiled. 'I've read of them. And . . . Master Michael has, um, afforded me some experience.'

'Books!' grumbled Roxburgh. He took another copious swig, broke wind loudly and scratched his balding pate. 'What by'relady good ever come of those, eh? Naught but for kindling, aye, and scholars too! More profit to be had from a bed or a barrel than a book! Should've known all those hare-brained plans were dreamed up between boards!'

'But we are agreed,' put in Michael Scot easily, 'that, hare-brained or no, they are the only ones likely to succeed?'

Darkness came early beneath that shrouded sky, and with it a change in the rain. At first men thought it was growing finer and more showery, till the hidden sun sank and the shadows deepened. Something came with them: cold fingers that touched the neck or cheek like things almost material, and made a man start and turn and snatch for weapons. But the fingers were mist, thin streamers of it drifting up on a sullen breeze from the river, playing about the palisade, twining like ghostly foliage around the walls of Hermitage. It grew thicker, carrying with it a clinging dew as wet as the rain. Campfires were lit, but after the day's soaking they spluttered and fizzed and burned low. Men gnawed at leathery smokemeat and half-griddled oatcakes, and shivered beneath their dripping cloaks, and cursed the whole enterprise.

Then, gradually growing on their ears, came a faint disturbing sound, sourceless at first in the sodden air. It swelled and faded, but always, slowly, it grew more intense, a soft tuneless thudding like a heavy-footed dance, or the uncertain pulse of a faltering heart. 'What in hell's that?' demanded Ker, peering out from under the front of his dripping leather-topped tent. 'A drum? Who sounds that?'

'No drum of ours,' said one of the Maxwell lords, peering about. 'Not a soldier's drum at all. Not crisp.'

'Mair like to an Erseman's skin drum,' agreed one of the northern Elliots, who had travelled. 'Or among the wild Hielandmen and Islemen. *Bodhrans*, they call 'em, and beat them tae their endless by'relady ballads; but by the dint o't yon drum's a sight bigger!'

'There're Irish outlaws aplenty within those walls,' said a Liddesdale man. 'And Islemen.'

Ker shook water off the tent, and listened uneasily. 'I feared he might have reinforcements marching in. But you wouldn't get men to march to that!'

Walter nodded. 'A dreary sound for this dreich weather. And – hark to that!'

'I hear nothing more,' said Ker after a moment.

'There is something,' put in Michael Scot. 'A sound like a whisper of wind, or steel drawn over steel, very soft—'

'I hear it!' said the Maxwell frowning.

'And I!' added Roxburgh. 'There's words in it, though damned if I can—'

A sudden yell rent the air of the camp, and a spreading hubbub. The lords came spilling out of their tents to see what was the matter, and found men in turmoil, staring around them with bared swords and bows drawn. It seemed that some great beast had run through the camp; a wild pig, said some, others a stag. But they came upon two of the pickets they had posted near the castle gate, kneeling now by the fires, shaking and scarcely able to speak. They had seen the shape first; the scream had been theirs.

'It was a stag!' said the first, when he had had some spirit forced down him. He coughed violently. 'I wis' hearkening tae yon damn' drum, and – I saw the antlers first, comin' out of the rain – and the eyes—'

'Aye,' wheezed the other. 'The eyes – first naething, then the eyes—' He choked. They were hard-faced Grahams out of Eskdale, but they were white in the cheeks now, and shivering.

'A stag loose in Liddesdale?' laughed young Ker of Fernie-hirst, the warden's cousin. 'As soon find a virgin with a gold ring in her ear!'

'Could you not've just passed your good spears through it, man?' demanded Roxburgh, patting his belly.

The pickets stared at him in horror. 'We did!'

'They jist went through it like smoke!' added the other. 'Like it wisnae there! And then it pushed past us – and we saw, we saw—'

'It had the limbs and body o' a man!'

The drum thudded and stuttered.

'Ach, away with you, churl, you're seeing things!' barked the warden.

'I'm not so sure,' said Walter softly. 'The storm he sent, when we pursued his men, there was some awful thing of the sort in that. If—'

There was another outcry. Turning, they all saw it, passing around the margin of the firelight but shimmering with its own luminescence against the dark. It had the head of a boar, a huge beast; but it ran on human limbs, the limbs of a naked woman. The head she wore, with the skin trailing like a cloak, but otherwise her sallow skin was bare save for streaks of bright ochre paint, and darker streaks that trailed from the arrow at her shoulder, the stump of another in her side, and many lesser wounds. She passed by close enough for them to see the sheen of sweat and grease on her heaving breasts; she strode with dreamlike slowness, as if barely touching the ground, yet it seemed she was running fast, and faltering. At her heels loped another figure, a man naked and painted in a wolfhead cloak, his face shadowed between the gaping fangs; and he raised a spear for the kill. A grey stone edged with sharply glinting facets gleamed at its tip. Even as the watchers sprang up in horror, the bestial vision faded into the uncertain night, full of drumming and whispering.

'What was that?' stammered Ker wildly. 'What was that? A vision of Hell?'

'No!' said Michael Scot grimly. 'A rite of it, perhaps; a hunted sacrifice. A vision of what must have passed on this land among its ancient dwellers, the builders of the Nine Stanes and others – ages since, long before our ancestors came here. De Soulis threatened as much, and I should have hearkened. He is summoning them up.'

'Phantoms?' muttered the other lords uneasily. 'Evil spirits?'

Michael shrugged. 'Not evil in themselves, perhaps. But fell and savage, and full of hate for the usurpers of their tribal land. Celt, Saxon, Norman, Norseman, you stand in their children's place, as the Roman legions and *colonias* once did.'

Walter dug his thumb into his swordbelt. His air of unconcern was not altogether a pose. In his long sojourn with the Fair Folk he had grown blunt about such night terrors. 'Even if it's so, what harm could such sad old shadows do?'

'They can terrify!' warned Michael. 'And maybe more, I fear—'

Now the alarum was general; the scream cut off suddenly and the camp erupted in shock and turmoil. Walter and the rest ran to the fore with torches, and found the pickets gathering around a man struggling on the ground.

'It was naught but air!' one of the pickets was repeating. 'See through't you could, like smoke! Struck at Jockie as though it wouldna' break a bubble – but he skelloughed and fell—'

Michael's knife sliced the straps of the man's jerkin, and the grubby shirt beneath. The watchers drew breath sharply as the torchlight showed them the great black bruise which crossed his chest. It was red at the edges, and still slowly spreading; but the skin was unbroken and the bones whole. The man's breathing roughened suddenly, his back arched violently and he sagged; a ghastly bubbling began in his throat. The drumbeat thumped and lumped with maddening tirelessness. Walter's eyes met Michael's an instant; then they sprang up together. 'Back!' roared Walter. 'Back to the firelight, all, and face outwards! Take torches!'

'Iron!' shouted Michael. 'Iron or steel, hold it before you! Or the Cross, if you have it! Kindle more fires!'

Yet even as they called there were more cries, more yells and screams. The watchers by the firelight stared out in horror. It was as if the darkness had come alive, churning with half-glimpsed movement which would abruptly resolve into shadowy figures that ran and leaped at the edge of vision, or acted out little incidents bestial enough to shake even the hardened reivers. The unwary man who could not get close enough to the fires, or peered too far out, or let his iron weapon sag momentarily, would see only a sudden rush, the flicker of a ghostly arrow, and fall in unexpected agony. Few lived; phantoms the hunters might be, but their aim was deadly. And they were growing in number all the time. It sounded as if the wind were rising, but the mist lay undisturbed, and it came to them suddenly that they were hearing a host of voices crying out of the distances, out of the deeps of time, wolflike and hungry, crying to the deadly pulse of the drum.

Every way they turned the skin-clad figures pranced to the howling chant, circling and bobbing in a savage, menacing dance that encircled the watchers. At every pass the ring seemed to close, and more men died. Stone-tipped spears shook and stabbed, stone axes swung and smashed, drawn bows were brandished with jagged points agleam. They danced the hunt to the yammering drum, and the sight struck cold terror into men; hearts weakened, guards faltered, and they fell.

Walter alone stood firm, but his armour was not of any steel or iron. The bronze sword of Andvari he brandished, and wherever he came the deadly ring gave back for a moment and grew dim. Before Michael, too, when he went out with flame, the hunters gave back; but they could not be at every corner, and there were not enough fires to guard everyone. Ducking back from one more futile sortie over a handcount of bodies, Walter seized Michael Scot's shoulder as if it was his throat. 'We must do something!' he screamed over the hubbub. 'And now! Do you hear my men die? Are you hearing them, damn you?'

Michael's eyes showed very white in the darkness. He plucked down Walter's hand with little effort. 'I can essay. I have thought of a sending to match his. It will not be easy. And it will tax the strength that might help you later.'

'There'll be no later, otherwise! Do it, man!'

Michael nodded curtly. He stooped to earth, spread his hands wide over it, murmuring. With swift care he cut away a little space of soaking turf, raised it to his lips, murmuring still. Clots of earth dripped and splashed through his fingers as he closed them slowly, squeezing; Walter could hear him breathing hard, very hard, like a runner in the last stages of a race. Then, abruptly, with a savage gesture he flung the turf far out into the darkness, and pitched forward on his face, drawing in air in shrieking gasps.

Walter stooped to him, heard him still mumbling between breaths.

Venite, Valerii! Victrix, ad vincere! Hispana adeste! Valerii, Hispanii! Adiuvandum est!

Over and over, barely coherent, fading into nothing.

Another sound came to Walter's ears, as if out of an endless depth. A strange inhuman roar, remote and terrible, a brassy, echoing roar as harsh as justice. He felt a tremor in the earth he knelt on, a faint swift shiver, a pulse quite unlike the drum high above, yet still more regular and unvarying. The roaring cry came again, and with it a thinner, purer call that made his skin prickle; for it brought back the timbre of Laurin's war-trumpets, and the crashing stride of a great army on the march, a force of foot and horse ten or twenty times the number he had brought to this siege. Even as he heard it again in his memories, that massive singing stamp and swing, the ring and jingle of armour and weapons and gear, he heard them with his own ears, clearly, swelling in the night. He sprang up, hoping for an instant that it was his old host summoned to his aid; but there was nothing of their music in the harsh voices crying the pace. And there was a grim note to that stride that did not belong in his memories, a measured, inexorable pace like the action of some arcane engine that could roll with the same relentless fervour over land and sea alike to the wide world's end, sweeping all from its path.

The other lords drew closer around Walter as he stood over the prostrate Michael, gabbling questions. 'What's happening? Have they got the sorcerer? What'll he do?'

Walter silenced them with a quick gesture, and then they all heard it – a fearsome bull's bellow, a flare of trumpets, and behind it, shivering up through their very feet, that ruthless, crushing tread. Out of the darkness it came, inexorable, almost upon them; and one man cried aloud and pointed. The demonic dance around them was faltering.

The ring broke; shadowy heads turned, as if hearing a long-remembered call. The blackness they moved across was no longer empty; it seemed to quiver with the rhythm of that relentless march, ever louder and louder. Points of light swayed there, and specks of colour, flickers of gold and red, flashes of bright steel that hurt the eye, half-glimpsed images of bronze and copper that spoke with those fearsome voices. Suddenly, as if the eyes of the watchers found their focus, the chaos resolved at one single, swaying point. At the top of a tall shaft a golden eagle, wings outstretched, swooped to catch the lightnings in its grasp. And, like those lightnings, the eye leaped from one detail to the next. From below the claws blood-red streamers, tattered and stained, fluttered in an unfelt wind, twined around a wreath of gilded laurels and a row of insignia, tarnished and earth-clodded. Behind the eagle fluttered others of its kind, above a host of dully shining spearpoints, swaying like cornstalks in a harvest field, and as uncountable. Bronze helmets gleamed, cuirasses and shoulder-plates, tall oblong shields and short swords held bared and ready for action, rust-mottled and age-notched as they were. Below the standard nodded plume and crest, torn and battle-stained, yet upright still and unbowed. And above them, between the battered eagles, the wide copper mouths of the carynx horns and battle trumpets lifted and shrilled a timeless challenge out of the jaws of death itself.

'Behold immortal Rome!' The stern voice at their backs made the watchers start. Michael Scot, risen to his knees, spread his robed arms wide. 'Behold her undying might!'

The dance was broken. Like the animals they embodied, the skin-warriors whirled aside, raising ancient weapons against the brutal impact of that horn-cry and the shadow-column that trod in its wake. Blackness swirled, the mist convulsed. Chaos whirled around the startled army, and a sudden waft of screams and cries, a bitter clash of metal. Amidst all the confusion visions came in sudden flashes – a hail of glinting javelins arching across the darkness; a long phalanx of soldiers suddenly swinging their shields before them, transformed instantly into a rippling wave of glittering, blade-bristling steel. More javelins, like a shower of needles; a legionary dragged down with a pack of the naked warriors clawing at his limbs like hounds, as if to tear away the living flesh; an antlered warrior staggering and swaying, plucking futilely at the spearhead that transfixed his chest, a flash of a swordblade that sent another kicking and writhing into darkness. A myriad of the same, swift and bloody; and at last the shieldwall again, surging forward into a series of arrowheads with the standard-bearers at their apex, themselves clad in the skins of great pard-cats, driving forward into the churning mass of warriors, into and over with the sweep of a reaper's blade.

'Man!' sighed Ker. 'Yon's discipline for you, is it not?'

All around them roared the insanity of a thousand ghostly conflicts, of men cut apart, or trampled underfoot, of helmets smashed by stone-axe blow, scream and groan and gibbering release of madness, horses whinnying and women weeping. Tumult and the clash of arms filled the air, till living men cowered from it and hid their heads in pain.

Walter turned on Michael Scot. 'What have you done?'

'That which I might not do lightly.' His voice was harsh and effortful, and at times it shook. 'When de Soulis summoned up the ancients of this land as forces of terror and slaying, he tipped

203

an age-old balance. That allowed me to level it once again. From the grip of the earth that held them it became possible to summon up the Roman legions who broke the ancient sway with order and law, according to their way. The Ninth Legion, the Hispana, that for over a century stood in garrison over the northern lands, and at the last vanished into them, never to return; and the Twentieth Legion, Valeria Victrix, that when the Empire crumbled was last to defend these shores against the advancing dark. They are long departed, but their bones and blood mingle with the clay. From that they were called forth to battle again with their shadow-foes. It serves. Hark!'

Even as he spoke, all in the space of two heartbeats, the unnatural tumult faded and was gone. Above the darkness, invisible, one solitary trumpet sounded, warlike no longer but elegiac and lonely, remembering and pleading for remembrance, remote and infinitely sad. Then that also was gone, and Michael spoke.

'One outrage to nature annuls the other. It is ended. Let them sleep!'

Slowly, accepting that the threat was gone, men bowed their heads, or sank to their knees. Walter felt as they felt. He turned to the wizard again. 'Well? Will that suffice? Is he spent yet? You know how much depends on it!'

Michael heaved a painful breath. 'The rain – and now this. He may well be. Certainly I am, very nearly! But we must wait a little longer.' He coughed. 'Give me wine!'

The wizard was just lowering the leather jack from his lips when he looked up suddenly.

'What's the matter?' demanded Walter.

'Something stirs!' said Michael. 'Be alert—'

His warning was forestalled. Out of the night, darting down upon them, came a gout of something like pale fire. Pooling and pulsing, crackling as it fell, it was hardly bright enough to blind the eyes, a ghostly yellowish phosphorescence. Yet it landed against the palisade where the leaders had pitched their tents, and burst in that instant into a rocking, blasting spurt of fire. The tall logs bent and shattered where it struck, throwing out gledes upon trails of smoke. Walter and Michael hurled themselves aside; others were thrown from their feet. Two tents flared as they stood; others sagged, smouldered and collapsed amid the screams of those inside. Most horribly, one man blazed against the night, ran a few steps and rolled, screaming and gibbering as his fellows fought to smother the flames. Across the camp to the west another pale gout flew over the sky and smashed into the palisade amid a chorus of screams and yells; stones and earth rained through the air, and men became stick-figures in its glare, dashing this way and that like ants in a disturbed nest. From above, in the instant of shocked and ringing silence that followed, there sounded two laughs, one a robust, deep-bellied chuckle, the other a high, dry snigger. Young Ker of Ferniehirst sprang up from where he had thrown himself, and screamed obscene defiance at the towertop; but Walter's voice overrode him.

'*Out!* Get out, all of you, out beyond the palisade! Leave your tents, leave your gear, take only your weapons and get out! Out for your lives!'

Another bolt came sizzling down, this time to the northward; and as Walter, running with the rest, looked up at the shaking crash of its impact he saw to his horror that a kind of spectral glow filled the sky behind the tower, a great rippling curtain of coldly glowing greenish light rising to Heaven alone knew what heights. The tower stood out clearly against it, and on the battlements, momentarily clear, a bulky shape Walter recognized, and beside it, stooped and eerie, a lesser. But, even as the light glared, a great voice shouted a summons, and he sprang aside with the rest as the huge black warhorse came plunging through the rout.

'*Algol! Algol, ad magistrum tuum! Veni, venite!*'

Into the crowd ran Michael Scot, thrusting men heedlessly aside. To the stirrup he sprang, and into the high saddle, and, hauling his gold-hilted sword from its sheath, he brandished it aloft. Again the sky filled with that terrible glare, this time directly in Walter's path, and men threw themselves screaming around his feet; but the black horse reared, and the light struck home upon its rider.

For an instant the wizard looked as if liquid fire ran in his veins, tracing every line of his face, every fold of his robe; the horse's mane and tail flared like a field alight. The swordblade burned and sizzled with the balefire seamen called St Elmo's, or the corposants; pale light crackled and sparked on silver-chased bridle and carven bit, leaped and fizzed from stirrup to spur. Michael's hair rippled as if in an invisible gale, his heavy eyebrows lifted with the force of the fire; the very eyes beneath glittered like jewels in deep mines. The earth quivered at the impact, the damp soil steamed and hissed. Walter, wincing, thought to see him blaze and blacken and collapse in ruin. Yet he was not consumed, and the fire ran off him in streams of coruscating specks, trickling away to earth in an instant like rain.

He shouted defiantly then, and the huge horse pawed the air and sprang away, racing to the tower's far side even as another bolt of light speared earthward. Again it struck the racing figure, again as it blossomed he stood out in that hellish glare – and again it smashed around him into a spray of harmless, aimless sparks. Smoke filled the air, and a hellish stink of thunderstorms; the shroud of sky light seemed to shake itself, and another bolt came leaping from the towertop. And again the black beast was there, neighing its defiance as the flare burst around its flank and rebounded to earth in a steaming, jarring explosion. And again, as more bolts flew; and again, circling the tower in a tireless, dizzying course, drawing the fire as a rod draws the wrath of the storm, diverting it from the stumbling soldiers as they fled the walls of Hermitage.

How long it lasted was hard to say, that shattering assault. It could not have been long, mere minutes, perhaps, though to the running men it felt like an eternity. The blasts shook the ground beneath their feet, till it seemed that even the mass of Hermitage must shake and shatter. At last they realized that no more bolts were falling near them, that the horse was running free just beyond the smoking ruins of the palisade, and that the bolts were aimed now only at its defiant rider.

'So it has a range, that hellfire!' cried the warden. 'And we're beyond it! Stand your ground, men! Stand firm!'

Men heard him, and stopped; yet it was less in obedience to

him than in falling to their knees in shock. And Walter saw with a sudden thrill that the bolts were growing dimmer and smaller now, mere spattering fireballs, and gradually less frequent; and the sky above was quiet and dark once more. Already soldiers were standing and shouting, cheering the rider on, screaming defiance at the walls. Then, as he slowed to a canter, they saw that there were no more, and they raised a great howl which would have scared any mere pack of wolves. By the light of the still-burning balefires they saw Michael Scot ride casually around once more, ignoring the occasional arrow from the slots, and, pulling his hood over his head, turn away. From the upper walls came the sound of furious voices. The rain seemed to be beginning again.

The officers ran to greet him as the black horse bore him out past the palisade and into the clearer dark. Head bowed, he seemed to ignore them at first, and it was only when he tried to dismount and could hardly free his foot from the stirrup that they realized in what case he was. They half-lifted the scholar from the saddle, carried him to a small fire they had built, and tipped some of Roxburgh's raw spirits down his throat. He coughed most of them back up.

'In God's name!' he protested when he could speak, 'are you trying to do what de Soulis could not?'

Walter, eyes gleaming, seized him by the arms. 'You think he's spent, then?'

Michael grimaced and coughed again. 'If he had any more real power he would have used it, depend on that! Even over the levin-bolts I could hear the rage shrieking out of him.'

'A shame you couldn't turn them back on him,' said Ker of Ferniehirst reflectively. 'Or launch a few of your own!'

Michael glared at him. 'Each one would weigh upon my soul like lead. In serving you I walk a great brink as it is. Would you make it worse?'

'But you think it's time?' persisted Walter. 'Time for our stratagem?'

'As much as it will ever be,' said Michael muzzily. 'Give me some more of that madman's barley juice!' He coughed again, and gave a sardonic little laugh. 'After this night's work they will probably credit me with scouring out the falls of Tweed and splitting the Eildon Hills into three! For the moment you are safe. If de Soulis can do more than light a farthing dip, I am no – scholar. But whatever you do now, you will have to manage without me. I also am utterly . . .' He could not articulate the last word, but let his hood overfall his face and slid slowly backward to the ground.

'Find him a blanket, somebody,' said Walter as he rose, grimacing at the gathering rain. 'See he's looked after.'

The warden confronted him. 'You're not going ahead? Into that devil's den without him?'

Walter smiled a tired smile, and began to unstrap his armour. 'Is this the man who didn't believe in sorcery? Sir Andrew, I've scant choice. How long before de Soulis can launch even one of those bolts again? No, summon my party, and the archers; we have only minutes left us!'

Ferniehirst looked doubtful. 'You should take more men along. Me, at least!'

Walter snorted. 'What for? More corpses? What'll your new lady wife say to that? Your part is not easy either, you and Sir Andrew. Look to it well, and leave mine to me, and to the others who have . . . nothing.'

The men of the vanguard were quickly gathered, and from among them the twenty or so Walter had picked out, the worst and the most thrawn. Quickly he outlined the plan to them, and the peril, and gave them the chance to draw back. They laughed, cold little laughter; and one or two slavered like hounds, for their tongues had been torn out. With the rest of his band they stole quickly within the palisade again, staying out of the firelight that not even the sharpening rain could quench, and under the very shadow of the walls. Walter and his men chose their spot and ducked down, while the rest slunk quietly around the far side, waiting. It seemed that the defenders were sheltering from the rain again, daunted by that thunderous encounter, perhaps. As in the daytime, no sentries walked the ramparts, and the single watcher was gone.

They were beyond any ordinary scaling ladders or belfries, beyond the reach of thrown grapnels; but not beyond picked

Border archers with twine on their arrows. Walter, feeling naked in a mailed leather jerkin, checked the knots and lines once more, and the white shafts, for there would be no second chances. Then he bade his archers draw and sight, and at the word they loosed, not at the ramparts but over them. Their arrows soared high in the air so that the many fathoms of twine were jerked up into a sudden trailing arch. Right over the Hermitage they shot with a soft hiss, thudding to earth in the soft bank opposite so that the twine they drew draped over the roof. As quickly as that the watchers on the far side sprang out from the shadow, having tracked the arrows by their white glimmer, and began to reel in the twine with maniac speed. Across stone and slate it ran, and after it the lengths of knotted line hissed out of their coils like so many serpents, up to the roof and over. To ears still ringing from the earlier blasts it seemed to happen in eerie silence. Walter hoped the defenders within those echoing walls had been even worse deafened, for whatever slender advantage it might give.

Already it was going better than he had dared hope. He had planned for the presence of rooftop sentries, intending his archers to harry and distract them; but he had always expected perhaps half of the twenty lines to be cut, nevertheless. Now, though, each one hung steady, meaning the watchers on the other side had got them in hand. There was not a second to waste. He flung himself to the first line, and the other men followed, swarming up by the knots. As the watchers on the far side felt the weight, they pulled, and even as the storming party climbed, they were drawn up still faster. But that meant the heavier lines were drawn taut across the roof, making a noise; and the climbing men swayed and swung, scraping their boots on the wall-stones as they climbed. That was bound to happen; and a moment later the long-delayed volley came whistling up from the archers below, meaning that sentries were coming out.

No matter. It was too late now. Walter hung steady with one hand free, unwound the light grapnel from his waist, and threw – an easy shot to the rampart from here. It clattered home. He leaned on the line and felt the hook bite into the wood. Beside him other grapnels flew. He spun crazily some sixty feet up in the air, and fought not to look down into the firelit chaos below; but he was doubly supported now, and able to swarm up the last few feet. He got one leg over the wooden crenellation, drew one great gasping breath and drew his sword. From the door to the stairs, some way along, an indistinct figure rushed at him, then ducked back as another sleet of arrows burst around him. Walter yelled down to the archers, grabbed his neighbour and hauled him in; but they were not the first. All along the parapet the stormers were piling over, though one lay dead with an arrow in his throat, perhaps one of their own. Others pushed past Walter and fell upon the men at the stairhead with swords and a great battleaxe. The defenders gave back almost at once into the stairwell and slammed the door. They knew that was easy to defend, being wide enough only for one enemy at a time.

Let them! Walter grabbed another axeman, pointed, and saw the blade smash down into that costly fireproof roofing, breaking slates free and tearing up the lead sheeting. Other blades bit, slates went slithering away and a gaping maw opened in the lead. Walter and the others threw themselves onto it and tore more away, peeling it back like a beast's thick hide, grabbing slates and hurling them down like lethal missiles at the startled faces far below, till a wide hole was opened and the beams laid bare. There was shouting at the stairheads, but that narrow stair was a two-edged defence, for no more than one defender could get up; a few men held it without trouble. Meanwhile the other stormers were hauling up the lines they had climbed, and tipping them over the roof-gap, fastening them to the beams. As swiftly as that they swung themselves through after, and went slithering and swarming down, straight into the heart of the Hermitage.

The stairhead men came plunging after; but by the time they touched floor their fellows, with Walter at their head, were already in furious fight with the startled defenders, striving to cut their way through to the main gate. It was a stratagem utterly unexpected; and so startled were the defenders, and so demoralized already by the unheard-of challenge to their sorcerer-chieftain, that it came close to success. It was an attack that de Soulis could have undone with one spurt of fire; but he was not to be seen. Right through the main hall drove the attackers, battering and goring surprised men from their path like savage bulls, so that they were in sight of the great door, and few defenders between them. Out of the hall they poured, yelling like fiends, and even the fierce Islemen faltered at the force of their charge. The defenders gave back, stumbling aside, and a shout of triumph went up – only to change to a howl of dismay.

Out of the tower stair, running, came the hefty shape of de Soulis, bare head gleaming silver. He wore no armour, only a sweat-drenched shirt and breeches; but in his hands he bore a massive beardaxe, and swinging it high with no thought for defence he fell upon the stormers from the flank. His axe crashed down on one; in the same instant another axe and a broadsword cut at his unprotected side. They should have met in his spine; but instead, as they touched his ribs, both blades balked and broke asunder. Like brittle glass they shattered all at once, into a cloud of shards.

His men bayed triumphantly and stood their ground. The attackers' rush was checked, their line broken; they swayed and milled, trying to dodge the sweep of de Soulis' axe, while Walter cursed and stormed, trying to struggle his way through the crush. Two more whistling cuts, and two men fell; and from the hall behind the startled defenders were gathering. The attackers were surrounded, and by overwhelming numbers. Spear and sword stabbed from every angle, and in seconds half Walter's remaining men were down. Walter yelled at de Soulis, an incoherent challenge; de Soulis saw him and turned, his plump face creased into an unholy, gloating grin.

Men sprang aside as they came together, circling. The axe hewed down at Walter's neck; but Walter was faster. With both hands clutching the long hilt of Andvari's sword, he swung a blow that met the oncoming axe head-on – and sliced the iron-bound haft like a twig. To the disbelieving yells of de Soulis' followers, and the man's own howl of disbelief, the bronze sword neither stopped nor broke. Across his arm slashed the

211

point, cutting a scarlet line, and over the barrel chest, trailing a spraying banner of blood in the air.

The axeblade flew across the court. De Soulis screamed aloud, as well he might. He staggered back, letting the useless truncheon fall, half-fainting as he clutched at his wound. It was the turn of Walter's men to jeer and yell; the defenders stared in abject horror at what had happened to the lord they had thought invulnerable. It was evidently no mortal wound, little more than a scratch in fact; but in the Sorcerer-Lord of Hermitage it was a deadly rift.

His face slackened, and great childish tears rolled down those ruddy cheeks. Suddenly he looked like a very old man; yet within those little eyes, screwed up in pain, a glitter of fearful malice still shone. Walter moved swiftly. Even this terrible creature he hesitated to cut down so, wounded and disarmed; but he sensed the truth behind Michael's words. And most of all he remembered his father.

He took one step and struck. It was a clean stroke such as an executioner might make, a scything cut at the neck with all the wielder's force behind it, so that the bronze sword sang in the air. It touched de Soulis' thick neck – and with a terrible shattering ring it flew up. The blade of the Otter-Lord, before which even the dead had quailed, exploded into a cloud of needle-sharp fragments.

11 ![tower icon] The Waving of the Branches

De Soulis staggered with relief and shock. Walter, thrown off balance, skidded and fell, striking his head on the filthy stones. The amazed defenders stood gaping. But from the tower stair the little old man called Redcap came running, and screamed at them; and they jerked into sudden awareness. De Soulis, recovering, was shouting too, and that decided them. With gloating cries they closed in around the remnants of Walter's men. Hot blood sprayed around him as he struggled to rise, and dimly he heard choked screams, felt bodies falling and writhing across his legs. He managed to struggle to his knees, half-blinded, groped about for a weapon but felt hard hands seize him. One clamped in his hair and jerked his head back. The cold sting of a sharp edge bit his throat.

'No!' That was de Soulis. The sting faded, though he felt a warm trickle down his neck. A heavy hand half-wiped, half-slapped the blood from his eyes. He blinked them clear, and found himself staring into de Soulis' face, cherubic no longer but twisted by pain and fury into the semblance of a demon. A tic worked all down one side of the face, his eye winked grotesquely and his mouth worked; a trickle of foaming saliva dribbled down his jowl. There was desperation in that look also, a desperate need to know.

'What manner of trick was that you used on me, brat? *Answer!*' A knee jarred hard between Walter's thighs, and again, in an explosion of agony. A hard fist thumped into his stomach. Walter shook his head, grimacing, unable to speak. 'Answer, by Hell, or I'll burn them off over hot coals!'

There could be little harm in any answer, not now. The chill sickness of betrayal welled up in Walter, worse even than the pain. 'I . . . Andvari . . .'

De Soulis' anger faded, and he stood very stiff and straight, though he still clutched his chest painfully. 'You met – Andvari?'

'I . . . fought him . . . in the service of Laurin . . . won his sword . . .'

The rage drained from de Soulis' face as he stared at Walter, and for a moment what lay beneath it stood out, quite naked. He was terrified. 'Laurin,' he repeated softly. 'Well, the sword's gone; and there'll never be another like it, not in this world, anyhow. He can't help you now. Nor that overweening busy-body Master Michael.' Clearly he was speaking to reassure his followers, but also, guessed Walter, to steady himself. 'I shall turn my attention to Oakwood next, and make him wish he'd stayed playing dice-tricks for the young Emperor. A shame you'll never see it – eh, boys?'

The noise that went up was somehow loud but dispirited; edgy, uncertain men trying to convince one another. De Soulis turned quickly to Redcap, in obvious anger. 'You! About time you made some good use of yourself! Have you been watching? What're this puppy's deluded friends about – preparing another assault, I suppose?'

The little man showed his yellowed teeth, in grim mockery of a grin. 'No' them! They're well oot o' it, and they know! Turning tail, the most of them!'

De Soulis grinned fiercely. 'Already? You're sure?'

Redcap's answering smirk had something even less pleasant about it. 'D'ye ask *me* sic a thing? Speir for yourself, if ye've eyes tae see in the dark! They melt like ice in the sun. There's some already oe'r the knowes and away, and a pack more that's takin' horse the now! Come dawn I'll wager you'll see never a one o' 'em left i' the dale!'

De Soulis clapped his hands together forcefully. 'As I thought! A last desperate throw, this! Twenty dead of theirs for a couple of ours, and all the sorcery they can summon – what's it cost me? A scratch! I might send a little something after them to singe their tailfeathers!' He laughed uproariously, then choked and winced, hunching over his torn side. He was obviously unused to pain, anxious to get it tended, but not to admit it. 'Still, why waste effort on the broken? Better I give our wee squab here some time to think things over. Throw him in the dungeons!' He turned away, then back, as at an afterthought. 'The deepest! Can't say we bear a grudge, boys, can he? We'll at least give him some sweet company in his last hours – eh? In the bosom of his family!'

This time the laughter was less forced. He rounded on the little servant with a sudden blaze of angry contempt. 'Go call the chirurgeon – about time he earned his pay! And I'll say as much for you also, Redcap! Get you back on watch, it's all you're good for! Or I'll have the hide off you for sure!' He spat deliberately in the little old man's face, turned and stalked away.

Walter sagged. He had torn more than de Soulis' flesh; he had made a rent in his esteem, and the awe in which his men held him. But that, he guessed, would be best mended by his own sufficiently awful death. He found himself hardly able to care. He was grabbed, cuffed, dragged across the court and into the stone stair he had slunk down only days before; a door was thrown back, massive and creaking, upon a stinking cell. He saw white bones on the floor – de Soulis' idea of company, he supposed; but it hardly concerned him. He was dead to all feeling save betrayal and despair. He was surprised, though, when his guards, instead of slamming the door on him, pulled up a massive flagstone in the floor to reveal another very narrow stair. Down this they manhandled him, and flinging back a heavy door at its foot they more or less threw him in.

He hit a trodden earth floor, and rolled bruisingly. The door did slam now; the bolt shot and a minute later the flagstone fell. Far above, muffled, he heard the boom of the upper door. Then there was nothing more, save silence.

Gradually he became aware of something in the chill air, a faint but perceptible whiff of corruption, worse than anything he'd ever smelt. He could almost taste it. It called him back to himself, a little, and he raised his head dully and looked around. The cell was not entirely dark; a faint smoky glimmer of light crossed it, coming in through some tiny grille set high in the wall, and evidently a long shaft above that. And as he stared dazedly at the light he became aware of two faint glimmers in the deeper dark beyond it. Two eyes, watching him.

He caught the slight sound of an indrawn breath, and raised himself sharply. There was a faint choking sound, and suddenly the watcher leaned forward, almost into the light. The hair bristled on Walter's head; he knew the face, none better.

'A–Astrafiammante?'

'W . . . Walter? *Walter!*' She could hardly speak. 'It's m–me! *Margaret!*'

Walter heaved himself up on one arm, gaping. Margaret Douglas was there. Margaret, her hair no longer tightly pinned beneath a coif and headdress but long and flowing, tousled and gypsy wild. Margaret, her mouth tight and pursed no longer, her eyes not downcast and narrowed but wide and desperate, gasping with startled surprise; her dress was torn above her heaving breasts. He saw her clearly – as he had seen her every day of their life together, as the Marechale had remembered her when campaigns dragged him from home. *Margaret?* This was no smirking chit of a child, all primness and sharp manners and nasty humiliating tricks. This was the princess of the Fair Folk he had loved from first sight, who had loved him as fervently and borne him children.

He spread his arms wide, and with a strangled cry she rushed to him and flung herself against him, burying her face in his chest, her whole body heaving with the force of her sobbing. He knew that body, the feel of it against him; his very hands knew it. Everything was the same. The feel of her soft cheek was the same as he bent his head to clasp her tighter, the very scent of her – and the tiny mole on her neck that he kissed. This was his only love, whom he had deemed for ever lost. This was Astrafiammante.

And it was also Margaret.

And it was only then, as he held her tighter yet to his heart and she him, that Walter began to conceive of the strangeness that Michael the enchanter had brought about.

'I didn't know . . .' she whispered, her voice weak and dry. 'I couldn't believe that you – that you would – that you cared—'

'Heart, heart, never doubt it, never doubt it!' he whispered incoherently. 'I dreamed of this—'

'I dreamed also,' she whispered. 'Oh, the strangest, silliest dreams – I can hardly recall now. But you were there and you loved me – no, I can't hold on to it any more—'

'I can,' he said softly. 'One day I'll remember for the two of us. One day—'

With that, as sharply as a lash of cold storm-rain, the awareness of where they lay came back to them, and they pulled apart sharply. 'Oh no,' she said softly. 'Oh no . . .'

She reached up to the caked blood on his brow. 'None of that's mine,' he said sharply, turning away. 'Well, not much. You? Are you—?'

'Me?' She laughed bitterly. 'Oh, I am well enough. Fed, watered, enough – just. And not violated, not harmed any other way.' She shook her head violently, as if to cast off a thought. 'In the body, anyway . . . And you?'

'A few scratches. But what other cruelties—?'

She looked away. 'You'll not wish to know.'

'Tell me!'

She looked down. 'We're not alone in here. Can you not nose it? They said they'd give me a companion – and they carried in—' Her voice shook. 'They set it in the corner. I've never dared go look.'

Her tone told him how much she had imagined, though. Walter released her, and rising unsteadily to his feet he groped along the encrusted wall, icy cold beneath his fingers. He could follow the odour himself now, and an awful fear grew in him. He forced himself on into the deeper gloom, accustoming his eyes . . .

Then he saw it, and he recoiled with a shriek he could not help. Propped up on a crude stone bench in the far corner, naked, grossly bloated, and streaked with blackened blood, sat the riven corpse of Sir Robert Scot, his shrivelled eyes glaring, his lips curled back in a fearful grimacing grin. The skin was dark with near-corruption; only the chill in here must have preserved the body thus far. Walter whirled away from the awful sight, struggling not to vomit, scrabbling at the wall till his nails tore. And miracle of miracles, the girl was on her feet, running to him, ignoring that fell vision and drawing him to her in comfort, drawing him away.

It was a long while before he spoke, and that thickly. 'If I have to hunt him through the very halls of Hell for it . . .' He seized her hand then. 'Not harmed? Christ, not *harmed*?'

She clutched his hand. 'I never went to look. They never made me. The dead would not harm me, I knew that. And I was not so afraid of *him*, either – not for the moment, anyway. He'll not suffer real harm to me or have my maidenhead, not yet. Not while there's a price to be gained for one or the other.' She looked away suddenly. 'Was it that brought you storming to this Hellgate?'

'You know it was not!' said Walter fiercely. 'I – it's a sore tangle, so much has happened! I sought you, out of duty perhaps – or maybe I just didn't know my own mind – but what does it matter? The moment I saw you, I knew.'

'Yes,' she said tightly. 'The moment I saw you . . . Too late. You are here, and the doors closed upon you. Oh, you were gallant, I don't doubt it, but—'

'I wounded de Soulis,' he said tightly.

'*What?*'

'I wounded the bastard. I wounded him with a blade out of the elflands, that the enchanter Michael Scot – you heard us talk of him – helped me win. If I had only hit de Soulis squarely with that first stroke – but the blade shattered on the second. I despaired then – but by the good God above I'll not despair now, not now I've found you again!'

She shook her head. 'I felt that, at first. But if that devil lives, he'll never let you be. He'll put you to a terrible end, one way or another. At the very least he'll leave you here till – till you rot!' She choked, but steadied her voice again at once. 'Shall we not sooner . . . end it all, the two of us together, and thus cheat him altogether?'

'Would you?'

Her voice quivered. 'I . . . have thought of it, yes. Often! But if my life is all I have, I'll hold on to it till it's torn from me. It's you I'll not see suffer!'

He held her at arm's-length and laughed fiercely. 'There speaks a Douglas! There speaks my princess! We'll live until we die, together! And never, *never* give up hope, even if it seems I do!'

She snorted. '"Douglas" be damned! And all my daft pride with it. I'm unworthy the name. Just a silly wee carline that never saw true worth, though it was thrust under her eyes! You, now you seem so grown, so – so noble, I could almost believe you'd grown older somehow. And yet it must have been there, all of it, and me who never gave you the chance to show it. Who dreamed all manner of things, but never that.' She shook her head again. 'And who's forgetting her manners! I've no food left, I wasn't expecting company, you understand, but I've some water—' He gulped at it thirstily. 'And I'll use the lees to clean your wounds. I'll not leave them festering in this place, whatever else befall!'

He lay back on the rough mats she had been given, leaning his back against the stone wall as she dabbed at his cuts and grazes with a wad torn from her gown, letting all else be. His mind whirled with questions, and he allowed it, detaching himself from the horrors and terrors surrounding them. Those realms he had wandered in, through the power of Michael, in which he had grown seven years without ageing so much as a day – was it through the eyes of Michael he had seen them somehow, that they had seemed so much of Italy?

And, if so, had they some truer shape – and, if so, among what manner of beings had he really dwelt for so long? The dull pain receded, and he drew breath more easily. Could it be that they had no single true form, and that each man wrote upon them the forms his own mind conjured up? It was true that he had always wanted to see Italy. But that conjured up a strange and terrifying thought. What shape was Astrafiammante's? Did she exist at all? Was it Michael who had given her that form – or was it his own will? Had he shaped her in the image of the woman he really wanted, but would not admit to himself, would not even see?

He had no answers. She mopped away the last of the gore from his eyes, and sank down by him, in the crook of his arm, to rest. Her in his arms, that was an answer. That was enough.

The crash of the door seemed almost immediate; but the angle and quality of the light was greatly changed. And de Soulis, as he ducked under the low lintel alongside two guards with lanterns, had been bandaged and had changed his clothes. He had found no rest, that was evident; his mouth was still twitching, his eyes looked red-rimmed and feral and his puffy cheeks seemed ashen. He leaned on a long white staff, and winced as he straightened up. Walter realized he must have been asleep, and deliberately prolonged his awakening, stretching and yawning.

'How touching!' De Soulis kicked him in the ribs. 'Up, carrion's child! I'm quite in your debt.' He tried for his usual bluff geniality, but on that face it looked ghastly, like paint bubbling and peeling to reveal the half-maddened wrath beneath. 'You'll be interested to hear that your rabble of so-called friends has cleared the dale, indeed! For once that idiot Redcap spoke the truth! So all your splendid riding has achieved is to demonstrate the sheer folly of assailing me – *me*!' His face worked feverishly. 'And, incidentally, deliver to me the last of the Branxholmes. And perhaps also a new lever to bend the stubbornness of this little Douglas bitch! You'd have wed her? I may be doing you a mercy, boy!'

He booted Walter again, harder. 'You need not think this will be forgotten, though, or forgiven. Oh, I've brave punishments in store for the pair of you! You, Lady Margaret, you will witness Sir Walter's; but you, sir, will just have to imagine hers, I am afraid, while you undergo your own. Of course' – he turned to Margaret – 'you cannot save him. But if you have the wit and heart you might buy him an easier end. Do you want to hear how?'

'How?' she echoed tonelessly.

'Why, by writing a letter in your own doubtless excellent hand consenting to a full form of marriage, with all rights and dowries appertaining, to the Lord Nicholas de Soulis. Write that, and he'll have the plain hanging he promised me, with a good quick drop to cut it short. I'll be sorry to let it go at that, but it's worth it to me. Speak now!'

Margaret rose to her feet, pale and still as a statue, neither weeping nor fainting, but fixing de Soulis with a clear eye. She would not look at Walter, but he turned and looked her full in the face. 'You must agree to this!' he said gently. 'Believe me at all costs, you must! Trust my judgement!'

She met his eye with a wild look of horror, and he prayed she would not break down. She looked away rebelliously at first, and then back at him – a guarded, considering look that lifted his spirits in relief. Abruptly, dashing a hand over her eyes, she nodded as if she did not trust herself to speak. De Soulis gestured, and a servant, his nose wrinkling at the smell, hurried forward with a board and an inkstand, and a few sheets of very fine vellum. 'Write, then! Address it to your noble uncle. Choose your own words, but nothing of duress or ill will. Keep it simple and clear.'

Still white, still with her eye fixed on de Soulis, she sat and wrote, quickly and without crossing out. De Soulis looked over her shoulder and nodded approvingly. 'Well then! Sand it and sign it!'

'No,' she said, and rose. 'Not till I see your end of the bargain carried out. If I cannot save him, I will at least not see him suffer.'

Walter gritted his teeth. De Soulis glared. 'When he dies I lose my hold on you. You could cheat me, refuse to sign. I might have some trouble in making you.'

Margaret blazed up suddenly. 'You smirking – you stinking, filthy-mouthed old spewing of Hellmouth, d'you think I care what happens after – after that? Do you think I bandy bargains? I'll sign faithfully, and you may do with me what you will, I care not! Or,' she added contemptuously, 'what you can, which is little, I guess! Oh yes, that would be why you take so much delight in paining others, it's all the pleasure you *can* take, that's clear as day! But there's no need to be so afraid, is there? You would still have the letter, so why should I not sign? May it hasten my own end, that's all!'

All trace of geniality had dropped from de Soulis' face. His plump cheeks sagged. 'It will,' he said, softly. 'I promise you, madam, it will. Well, you have your way, let us be about it if you're so eager. Your lover has left ropes enough on my walls, at least.' He half rose, but Walter lunged forward angrily right to the points of the guards' swords.

'No! That's a filthy trick! You'd try to break your word by stealth! Such a drop would half-tear a man's head off, a felon's end!'

This time Margaret did blanch and sway, but she caught herself on the wall. 'That – will not suffice to discharge our bargain, de Soulis!' was all she said.

Walter cheered her on, inwardly, with fierce intensity. 'I offered you a choice, my lord – remember? And you made the like promise to me!' He clicked his tongue. 'I hold you to it. I had always understood, not from any vast education, you understand, that the keeping of a word meant something, even in the matter of your – arts.'

'Not so very much,' said de Soulis mildly. 'The breaking of a pledge can be an act of potency in itself. But you have the right of it, I did so promise.'

'I choose to be hanged from a tree, then, if I must,' said Walter, 'away from these befouled walls and out in the sweet air.'

'Do you now?' De Soulis considered. 'Well, that may be granted – if there's no more tom-o'-bedlam trickery in it. We'll see.' He tapped the floor with his staff a moment, and then very suddenly scratched a perfect circle in the filth, and within it a many-pointed star, and several ill-shaped characters. Then he struck its rim, hard, and stamped. *'Redcap! Ad dominum!'*

A sizzling steam leaped up suddenly within the circle, glowing as if with an inner light. Margaret skipped back with a half-stifled scream, and even the guards and the servant gave back, retreating hastily to the stairs, backing up them as far as they dared. The steam heaved, coloured, coalesced into a swift and horrible procession of half-formed, stomach-turning shapes; and then it hung steady an instant. Within it, halfway to the apex, two eyes appeared, glittering green and slanted, fastened with a fierce intent upon the sorcerer-lord, the same cat eyes that had gleamed at Walter in the darkened tower. De Soulis hissed something, and stamped his staff at the circle's edge, and the haze shimmered and sank inward to reveal a figure in the circle. It was solid and material to all appearances, nothing monstrous; but Walter felt sick at the sight. He had suspected; but now he felt a sickening chill in his heart, an icy, creeping revulsion at the intrusion de Soulis had allowed into the world of nature. Even disguised as it was in human shape he could scarcely endure its presence, now he knew; the mere sight of it seemed to contaminate something deep within him, some place where all his deepest beliefs and feelings lay. How could de Soulis suffer the thought of this thing he had unleashed, even for a moment? Let alone its constant company.

In the circle, wizened and bent, stood the shape of the little old servant in the dirty red bonnet.

'Well?' he demanded in his rasping voice. 'What would ye of me the now? Why the circle? Am I not to be free, to walk about upon the Earth, and to go to and fro upon it?'

'Sneck up your tongue, serpent,' barked de Soulis, 'or you'll find who holds the sting now!'

The little man hunched down into his bent shoulders and snarled. 'Crach and crab upon me, aye, and still go callin' upon me to leap to your petty purposes! What is it now – has the fair young sprig scorched your arse for ye this time guid and proper?'

'Last night you failed me, you miserable little bauchler!' grated de Soulis, raising his arms as if to grab and shake his gadfly. 'Led me on to squander all my force to small purpose! Left me spent, left me vulnerable before a weapon out of the elvish lands! Left me to be weakened and wounded – me, wounded! Before my men! It pains me still! Henceforth I'll have you in the circle where I can hold you, fast!'

The old man sniggered, and broke wind with a disgusting stench. 'Haud hard on this, then!'

De Soulis stamped his staff again.

The old man hunched down still further. His snarl became more like a whine. *'Ne weapoun of alle this worlde*, they were the words o' the bond. Yon sword was of another, yet even that could do no more than scratch. That's faith kept and more!'

The sorcerer's voice almost cracked with the effort of control. 'Don't split hairs of law with me! Hold you to the spirit of the bond, not the mere letter, or I'll abrogate it if I will – oh aye, never sneer at me! I could! Absolutions are bought easily enough. If you keep not to your side of the pact, they'll have effect, will they not? And why then should I not repent in earnest, even? The austerities of a monastery and the discipline would not terrify me, who has endured so much!'

'*Thou?*' mocked the creature. Suddenly it was a vast thing, eyeless and glistening, towering with a mouth of serpent's teeth bellowing, right over his head. The servant fell in a swoon, the guards leaped for the door – but de Soulis, though he flinched, stood firm at the circle's edge. The thing fell away from it, and was the little man once more. 'Sae calm an' brawly stands he there!' he cackled, half-singing. 'But the lordie's shat his britches, has he no', has he no'?'

De Soulis' face was slack now, but a red madness lurked in his eyes. 'I'll not trade abuse with you, bestial abortion! I curse the pilgrimage I took. I'd spit out the fiend's bargain that ever saddled me with you! So now, upon pain of breaching it forever, do you tell me in strictest truth if any weapon yet remains that can hurt me – or if I have anything to fear beyond these walls now?'

The little man fleered, but he said no more, only glanced about like a mean thief casting for likely prey. As his gaze crossed Walter's he leered horribly, as if over some unguessable gloating; but from Margaret, pale yet unmoved by the awfulness before her, he glanced hastily away again. At the last he spoke, his voice no longer rough and mocking but thin and clear and venomous.

'I have speired, I have scried, I have looked about. There remains now no blade to pierce thee, no bar to bruise thee, no halter to choke thee, no fire to burn nor water to drown thee, nor cold clay neither. Nothing worse needst thou fear than the waving of the branches, and thine own roof covering thee, and the King's word over thee. Thus much, and no more. That is Redcap's promise!'

Walter felt a deep shiver start through him, and forced it down. The change in de Soulis was dramatic. He straightened up, not without wincing, and bellowed with laughter. 'Your best counsel's always what I beat out of you! I'll fear no more, and hold our compact kept – for now.' He turned to his guards, hovering pale and awestruck by the door. 'But we'll be sure of this, nonetheless. Send to the sentries on the roof, send out scouts at speed to the hilltops around. I'm sure the young lovers are in no great haste.'

The scouts came back within the hour, by which time Walter and Margaret had been led, bound and chained, up into the light. Sitting under the swords of a dozen men, dirty and wild but fierce and alert, they heard it told that the horse-sleuth of the host led right out of the dale north and westward, and that for a good mile round at least there was nobody to be seen; even the cottagers had fled. De Soulis thumbed his chin, and nodded. 'Very well, then. It would amuse me to have you dangle awhile as a warning, and I care not for something so noisome upon my clean walls. So you shall have your way, and be damned to you! Take them out!'

With many a kick and a curse de Soulis' men led the pair through the narrow way and out by the gate on to the open slopes, with most of the garrison laughing at their heels. The air was clear, save for the tang of smoke, and there was even some thin sunlight. It showed all the land around the Hermitage looking as blasted and scorched as if the gods of old had rampaged across it with their thunderbolts; the palisade was no more than a few standing trunks, the rest fallen in piles or burned to charred stumps. All across the land lay tents and weapons and gear abandoned, and some of the defenders began rifling these already; but they left even their profit meanwhile for the promise of sport. The wilder men and the worse pawed and slobbered at Margaret, and tore her clothes and shouted threats in her ear, made obscene display in her sight; but she walked as tall and as proud as chain and rope would allow, acknowledging nothing and no man. Walter longed to call to her, to offer her some reassurance; but he did not dare. That might only make things worse.

The highest tree was not hard to find; it was in the nearest copse, down by the river, one of the oldest and strongest oaks along the bank. De Soulis contemplated it with bared teeth. 'I trust it meets with your approval. That limb there should serve our turn. *A Roin Ban! A Ruaraidh!* Untie this precious pair, and throw me a line over there, with a noose – very good! And now' – with a sudden snap – 'make it fast around this young bastard's ankles – and hoist him up!'

The world whirled around Walter as he was whipped off his feet and dangled, head-down and helpless only a few feet off the earth. He heard Margaret cry out, and be silenced by a sudden slap. De Soulis' face swam into view, bland and cherubic as ever. He leaned down, peered into Walter's face, then struck him a casual blow that sent him spinning. 'Now,' said de Soulis with deep satisfaction, 'haggle with me like a damned chapman, would you?' Another cuff, and a kick. 'Hold me to my promise, would you?' A powerful punch burned agonizingly in Walter's overstretched stomach muscles. 'We'll see, my lad, we'll see!'

He grabbed Margaret and threw her to her knees with a cuff. 'And you, my haughty wee bitch, will watch him smoked like a herring, then roasted nice and slow. And the longer you wait to sign yon letter, why, the longer it'll last!' He kicked her on to her face. 'That for your high words and your wills and won'ts! You chose a wrong man to meddle with in me!' He turned to the jeering men clustered close around him. 'Fetch me the dryest branches and some kindling, and pile them up here for a burly fire. We're going to give this insolent wee pup a taste of Hell even as we send him there!'

Not a yard from Walter's ear a dry voice spoke. 'There's wood enow already!'

With no more signal than that, and a mighty rustle and waving of branches, all the line of underbrush along the river seemed to come alive. For hundreds of paces on either hand barely more than the front row of bushes still had their roots in the earth; all the rest had been cut, and rose now like an avenging wave. The men who had held them for so long, the steadiest of the steady bulk of the force, who had prepared these positions under cover of the darkness, and sat hunched in them since before dawn, sprang to their feet at last, and flung down their concealment to reveal the bows and crossbows they held. Walter, swinging helpless in their path, winced and shut his eyes, giving thanks that Margaret at least was already on the ground.

The air cracked like a whip. A rushing, whistling breath sang in Walter's ears, and something plucked sharply at his sleeve. The screams came hard upon it. His eyes flew open. Where de

Soulis had stood in the midst of his men there stood he still; but he stood alone. Arms outstretched, eyes wide and staring, he gaped like an idiot at the arrow-quilled bodies kicking and quivering around his feet, as if ordering them to rise. Then he turned to run; but there was a sudden flurry of movement, a feral scream and a wild-haired figure rammed into him at the knees. Caught utterly unawares, he staggered, tripped over his assailant and crashed down in a tangle of limbs and long gown. A dagger flashed. There was a crack, and another yell . . .

Then Walter's view was cut off as hands bore him up, and he felt the ropes about him slashed free. The world whirled, and suddenly he was on his feet, tottering, in a ring of grinning faces, Ker of Ferniehirst among them. He pushed them aside. '*Astra*— Margaret?' he shouted, and was face to face with her, hair wild and eyes staring, nose streaming blood, lip split and cheekbone scarlet with bruising, her breasts spilling out of her ripped gown. In her hand she brandished the hilt of a shattered dirk.

'Well?' she screamed, eyes flooding with tears. 'I had the coward, I had him but he ran! What d'you stay for? Must I run him down myself?'

Walter drew breath, then thought better of wasting it in answering. He held out a hand, and a swordhilt was slapped into it – as smartly as all else he had planned. He and Michael – for, though he had rested his hopes on the sword of Andvari, they had agreed there was still a chance he might fail and be taken before he could reach the gates. They had laid a plan to answer it. But this had been a last resort, a final desperate dice-throw he had never really expected to achieve; and it was almost a shock to see how well the cast had fallen. One ambush had paid for another.

That first astonishing volley had taken the men of Hermitage utterly aback, cutting down many, wounding more, striking terror into the rest. As one they had fled like skittered sheep, many hobbling along with bolt and arrow still in their wounds, up the bare brown slope towards the safety of their walls. Behind them, clutching at the bandages half-ripped from his chest, ran the bulky figure of de Soulis. But even as he screamed at them in some incoherent attempt at a rally, the piles of the demolished palisade were pushed aside, and the men who had dug in beneath them sprang forth. There were not so many; but they too had bows. And between them, out of nowhere as it seemed, rode one tall rider on a black horse, his greying hair streaming in the breeze. He raised his hand as if to hurl something; that alone was enough. The foremost in the flight saw him, the man who had withstood their master's flame, and recoiled in panic. Those who came behind balked, hesitated, turned back uncertainly and blocked the way to the gate. De Soulis, red and raving at the sight of Michael, screamed at them to turn and fight like men. It was too late; the watchers were already upon them.

Men fell then and died in many ways; but their lord was not among them, though his garments bore the mark of a dozen arrow-strikes at least, and within minutes as many cuts more from sword and axe. Not all were from his enemies; for, finding his way blocked by his own embattled followers, de Soulis drew sword and sought to cut a path through struggling friend and foe alike, to the gate perhaps, or to the tall man who sat ahorse, watching and doing nothing. Many of de Soulis' men, even his most trusted, rounded on him then, yet their blades could make no more impression on his body. Every one that touched him shattered, and every man left weaponless he cut down, merciless. But even as he hewed down his most trusted sergeant and burst through, howling, to confront his foe, he heard the shouted challenge of Walter Scot, and turned furiously to strike.

No man came near him. The sorcerer-lord found himself penned with long spears, like a boar at bay, and as fast as he hacked at the shafts they sought to knock the sword from his hand. He howled for rescue, but his own men threw down their arms and spat at him, and made no move against the besiegers. They sent no more arrows; it was ropes they threw, with wide nooses, as deftly as they snared their enemies' cattle by night. With a maddened bull's bellow he cut the first; but there were always more. They closed around his arms, they plucked at his ankles, and then there were weighted nets flung, that spun and spread out in midair, entangling his sword and swordarm even as he lashed about. The ropes sang tight, and hauled. Like an ogre of old tales brought low, the dark Lord of Hermitage toppled and crashed to earth, and rolled roaring and kicking and growling, foaming at the mouth, upon the mould.

'Well, then, Nicholas,' said a calm voice beside him, and he quieted at once. 'Your star, it seems, is no longer quite in the ascendant – Pisces, is it not? In the House of the Sun? Indeed. Small wonder your redcapped friend betrayed you! But be still, you shall have justice at the King's own hand.'

De Soulis shrieked like a maddened beast. '*You? Justice? The . . . King?* He has betrayed me, you've betrayed me! But I defy you! Do your damnedest, and I shite on the whole pack of you! Bring anything home upon me if you can – and if you dare! I'll live to see every whore's get of you gutted like fish! I'll flay—'

Walter prodded the netted bundle with his foot. 'Bind him fast!'

He stretched wearily, wincing at a thousand small aches and cuts, and looked around at the field. There was fighting enough, but there was little doubt of its ending. Only a small part of the force had actually quit the vale, leading the horses with them; and outside the castle walls the garrison was still grossly outnumbered. Without leadership or order they scurried this way and that, like ants kicked from a nest, unable to flee, unable to reach the gate, harried and cut down in their tracks if they faltered. Soon, leaderless, they would tire and surrender, or die on the spot. Meanwhile it was a brutal business, and Walter took little pleasure in the sight. He felt numb and weary, little else.

He turned to Michael again. 'Did he say right? We have the beast, but cannot bring it home?'

Michael folded his arms, smiling thinly. 'Did I not promise you I should find you the means?'

Walter choked back an oath. 'Aye, you did. And what am I to make of that, after all else? That sword, that I went through so much to gain, aye, and lost so much to bring back – one fair blow it struck him, then its power was gone!'

The dark man shrugged. 'Indeed, for by that stroke it came

to be a thing very much of this world also, and so subject to the ban he bears.'

Walter grabbed the front of his robe. 'You mean – you mean you *expected* that? But you promised me! After all that— You said that was the weapon to defeat de Soulis! You said nothing of having only one stroke to do it! And Andvari – he promised me the means, too! Your word, his promise – neither worth a damned jot more than that demon's was to de Soulis, that drew him out to his doom! Christ alive, does every bastard sorcerer break faith?'

Michael took hold of Walter's big hands and easily forced them away. 'That I would get you the weapon to defeat de Soulis, that was what I promised you. And that promise I kept – in full. The sword was not it. Did I ever say it was?'

Walter felt as if he were going to burst. 'You – you said – you let me think – I lost so much in search—'

Michael smiled, and Walter did not like that smile at all. It was not evil, but nor was it kind. It was an inward smile, and a bitter one. 'I said only that it would have much power over ill spells. As indeed it did. Oh, it was worth the winning, well worth. A fortunate blow just, might *just*, have put an end to the man; but we could not rely on that, could we? No, I promised you only this, the means to defeat de Soulis, and you won it honourably and in full measure. It was the courage and the skill you found for yourself – that was the head-ransom you won from Andvari. *Those* were the means!'

Walter was beyond speech. Michael shook his head. 'You needed them. And, I will admit, the small extra assurance that believing in the sword gave you. Without them, without the Otter-Lord's gift, you could never so have steeled yourself to carry out this plan – the one you thought was a last resort of utter desperation, when I knew that it was the only one that stood a fair chance. The boy you were could never have done it. Oh, you had the makings of what you needed within you, aye, no doubt of that; but it seemed somewhat unlikely you'd live long enough to bring it to flower. So that time I gave you, at no cost to yourself; for though you are older in experience, and it shows in your face, your body aged not one second.

Callow youth is small loss, and your life will be none the shorter.'

Michael's smile was thin and one-sided. 'A long life can be lived thus, many lives. Believe me, I know. Have I not lived them, to the length of utter weariness? Lived, and loved, and lost, many times and many places, over and again. But you – now you have found her, and seen, and you understand. As much as is good for you, anyhow! So what can you tell me you have really . . . *lost*?'

The mask was shattered. He looked no longer the suave courtier but, for almost the first time, truly like an ancient sorcerer, consort of demons, beset by perils, all the more blackly perilous in himself. His hair and beard trailed wild and tangled, exposing more grey hair than before; his teeth gleamed in a twisted smile of weariness. Years descended upon his face, caught at his mouth, drove deep furrows into his brow. His shoulders seemed to bow under the weight of too much knowledge, too many memories, too few illusions. Over him hung the exhaustion of a man who has striven to know life, and taste it from the depths to the heights, and peer behind the curtains of birth and death; and in all of that succeeded only too well.

He snorted in contempt, and his deepset eyes stabbed through Walter like darts of light. 'Don't prate of loss to me! I know what loss is! Consider rather what you have gained! And will gain! And be thankful, damn your hide! Be thankful!'

12 ♜ The King's Word

The King's court was in session, which meant that the great hall
of Falkland Palace, aslant with dusty sunbeams, was crowded
with ambassadors, courtiers, hangers-on, ladies and lapdogs.
Walter decided it was hard to tell the difference between them.
Except for the ladies, that was; and he found he had only a
casual eye for them now. It seemed to him that the King had
dealt with each and every petitioner, however petty their
business, before finally, graciously, making a little time for his
own Marchwarden. Now Walter was stalking up and down outside the door of the King's council chamber, feeling as if any
moment his head would boil off, bubbling like a pot-lid. For the
last three hours they had been closeted in there, with Ker and
Michael Scot arguing their case. They had called Walter to bear
witness, and the sworn statements of many other lords – too
many, Walter had thought, to be ignored. He should have
known better. Finally he had pleaded the need to consult, and
stamped out with Michael in his train.

'You must be patient yet!' counselled Michael, stroking his
beard. 'Politic, calm, persistent. Surely you learned enough of
the courtier's art with Laurin?'

'I did that,' said Walter between his teeth. 'But by God it has
its limits! I swear if I'd been in there a moment longer I'd have
pushed the sleekit bastard's quibblings back down his gullet!'

Michael shook his head gravely. 'That is something you do
not do with kings, as a rule, and especially not Alexander – not
more than once, anyhow. Besides, it would be unfair.'

'Unfair! He's doing this deliberately! Penning us like beasts
in a stall!' He had been in such haste to be rid of his burden, of
the raging fiend he had caged. He had taken only the hastiest
farewell from Margaret, slaking the fiery confusion in his heart

with no more than a brief embrace, a touch of lips; it burned within him yet. He felt stained by his charge, contaminated by the burden of de Soulis and his fate. When he could shed that, then surely he would be free. Free to live and love again, in this second life he had been given – no, that he had won, and she too, by her steadfastness. That thought had sustained him all through the long and rainy ride to Edinburgh, that stern and ancient fortress with its tall houses clinging about it on the high rock like children round their mother's skirts. And from there to find that the King was gone to Falkland, a long and stormy sail across the mighty firth of the River Forth, and a nightmare ride along rain-lashed cliff paths. All that urgency, all that in readiness to discharge his burden at the door. And then to have to spend a week in dancing idleness, kicking his heels in antechambers and eating at lower tables, watching Alexander come and go in a bee-swarm of counsellors and petitioners . . .

'And this the last day before he's away to Scone to gather his land-taxes and stamp on the Highland unrest! Where of course he'll hear no Border business, then!'

Michael shrugged, an impressive gesture in the ballooned sleeves of his crimson and blue silk robes. He was dressed in the grave splendour of an Imperial courtier of Sicily, his tousled hair repressed under a gold-embroidered skullcap, his beard neatly combed out and oiled; the tall staff of glossy African ebony he leaned upon was topped with the Imperial eagle in Spanish gold, as was the heavy chain of office around his neck. He was by far the most important-looking person in the court, and attracted many inquisitive bows and greetings, which he returned with grave detachment. He tapped the flagstones with his staff. 'The King is in a cleft stick, Walter. Put yourself in his place, and consider – if you pardon de Soulis, you show yourself to have not only favoured a criminal but endorsed his crimes, and their odium sticks to you also. Yet should you abandon him too openly you will lessen the confidence of other lords who must often act harshly in your name – even the good warden himself, perhaps. What if Sir Andrew finds himself forced to string up, oh, say Gibbie Forster of Coquetdale on slender evidence but for the undoubted good of the King's Peace? When the other Forsters come bitching with the English sheriff behind them, will they not cite de Soulis as an example? No, I do not envy Alexander!'

'You mean, we should be helping him find a just solution, rather than demanding one?' Walter twisted his moustache thoughtfully. 'Well – I haven't any ideas, so far. But why should I, if you cannot? You promised you would find one – and aye, I know, you've helped us well enough. But can you not complete the task?'

For a moment the older man's grave manner faltered, and his face became haggard and haunted. 'It may be that I can. But it would be better coming from Ker or you, or anyone else. I have enough burdens on my soul already.' He braced himself, visibly. 'Now come you back, for Sir Andrew needs all the support we can give him. And perhaps the King does, also!'

He pushed aside the age-darkened French hangings at the door and they went back in. It was obvious how matters stood. Alexander the King sat slumped in his carven chair, scarcely concealing his lack of interest. The two Writers who stood ready had put down their desks and quills and were quietly studying the ceiling, while Ker stalked up and down much as Walter had been doing, white hair bristling, huffing and puffing and gesturing furiously. Clearly he was running out of arguments, and had began to bluster.

'But, my lord, my lord, it runs counter to all conscience! What will come upon us if you allow a flouting of the King's peace to go wholly unpunished—?'

'The King's peace is the King's concern, warden!' Alexander had seen a chance to silence Ker, and seized it. 'True, it is a trust I must keep to justify my kingship. But since you broach the subject, did you bother to ask my leave before storming the Hermitage in my name? You did not. And is that not a breaching of my peace? Oh, I agree de Soulis' means have been . . . drastic, far in excess of any word I gave him. And his associations, aye, very sinister – if all that's said to me is true. But it might not be, and you gave me no chance to look into the matter for myself, now, did you? You deprived me of the opportunity to make judgement in my own good time!'

As if you would have! thought Walter, but he kept his thought to himself.

'So that way goes the game,' mused Michael quietly. 'Then let us play it so.' He stepped forward, tipping Ker a quick wink, and gave Alexander an elaborately graceful bow. 'Your Majesty, if I may—'

'Aye, aye, do and welcome,' grunted the King with a weary grimace. 'Sir Andrew has shot his bolt, I think. Only say something new, by God's good blood, or I'll settle the case with no more ado!'

Michael bowed again, less floridly. 'I was actually about to offer your Majesty the counsel I might have given to my Imperial master – namely, that he could do exactly that, without loss of honour.'

Alexander sat up. He was still a youngish man, nearer Walter's age than Ker's, and not very impressive at first sight, quite short of stature but stalwart and heavy in the arms. The features beneath his dark blond curls were regular enough, but marred by protruding grey eyes, heavily shadowed. It was his voice that carried the crisp tang of command, and the weariness also; he looked and sounded like a man who did not sleep easily. 'Imperial-quality counsel, eh? Not often I get offered that. Let's hope it would please him. Tell me more.'

Michael smiled. 'It is no very complex thing, your Majesty. Justice must be seen to be done, true; but if, as you seem to be saying, Sir Nicholas has exceeded your orders—'

'Exceeded?' Alexander's eyes seemed ready to pop out. 'Exceeded? Carrying off a noblewoman and an heiress – though admittedly the Douglases were slow to complain – and murdering this young fellow's father, and damn' near him as well? Amassing an army of outlander bandits and cutthroats? Not to mention God knows how many other villainies – no, those were none of my will! Let there be no doubt of that! My warrant to him and all my letters speak of peace and order!'

Walter smiled inwardly. As Michael had predicted, Alexander could not be seen to countenance de Soulis' crimes. He had to say that, to shield himself; and up to a point it was true.

'Well then,' said Michael, 'he must be seen to be punished,

in some wise. The penalty laid down by law and custom is death, that is clear. But need that matter? Whatever warrant your Majesty makes, Sir Nicholas by his own incessant boasting ought to be proof against it. You have heard the statements—'

'Aye, aye, over and over. So you're saying—'

'That, sadly, all we can in fact do is confine this evil man in prison – his own cells, perhaps – pending an execution we probably cannot carry out. We could wall him up, but he claims he cannot even be starved to death. We regret this, but we would accept it if there is nothing better. And the formal necessity of punishment would be fulfilled.'

'Yes!' said the King emphatically. Walter could practically see the thoughts streaming through his mind like banners. Making a death warrant for de Soulis, yes – that would preserve the royal justice. It would keep the Church off the royal back, too, howling for an inquisition into alleged wizardry. But if the warrant couldn't be executed, he could be quietly pardoned after a decent span of time, a few months even – perhaps even reinstated, with somebody to keep a close eye on him. That would avoid the appearance of betrayal, without creating any destructive precedents for later on. De Soulis would have a bad time, no doubt, but Alexander would lose no sleep over that. Serve the old swine right, for causing such upheavals. Walter could practically predict the next question.

'But if this famous . . . charm of his doesn't work?' demanded the King. 'If something actually . . .' He made a chopping gesture.

'Then it is no fault of yours, your Majesty,' replied Michael Scot, with his gravest face. 'And my Lord de Soulis is the victim of his own foolish tongue.'

Alexander considered a moment. Then he gave a bellow of laughter, nodded and rose. Swiftly Michael clicked his fingers to the Writers. 'Your Majesty's decision, then?' he prompted as they came forward, proffering the desks, dipping their quills, twisting the sealing wax in a handy candle. 'In what form shall we make the warrant out?'

Alexander glared at the commitment in two copies dangled where he could not ignore it, and decided. 'Oh, anything, God's wounds, anything you please!' He laughed. 'Here, I'll sign now! Pen – sand – just there! And wax, there, and my seal – there! And there! Boil the bastard if you please, but for the love of our Lady let me hear no more of him!'

Michael's eyes fluttered closed, and for a moment he looked weary himself, horribly so, and very haggard and pale. *'Heard,'* he whispered. *'And witnessed!'*

The King pushed past him without listening, thrust the hanging aside, shouted for wine and stalked out into the shifting quag of courtiers beyond.

Ker and Walter took one deep breath to let him go, then rounded on Michael Scot. 'What in hell was all that about? You promised you'd find something, yet here we are, come all this way, and what do we get?' Walter snatched the first copy from the Writer, who stood blinking uncertainly. 'A warrant only fit to save appearances for the King? A warrant that you admit we can't execute? Water won't drown him, nor fire burn—'

They stopped dead, and the Writer shrank back. Abruptly the sorcerer raised his arms to the sky beyond the window, his staff all but touching the roof, commanding and terrible as an ancient god. And in a dark voice, half chanting like a sombre litany, he declaimed:

> *Wound shall he have, but from no blade,*
> *Bruised shall he be, but by no barre,*
> *Choked he shall be, but not in rope,*
> *Burned he shall be, but by no flame,*
> *Drowned he shall be, but in no water,*
> *For by the waving of the branches was he taken;*
> *And the word of the King upon him.*
> *And the roof of his house shall be above him,*
> *Thus it was made promise to him,*
> *Thus shall it be brought to fruit.*

He sighed. 'The demon knew it that betrayed him, seeing him over-mastered. A terrible fate awaits de Soulis. But he has no man to blame but himself alone. *Alea iacta est!'*

★

237

The door of the dungeon slammed back, and the men winced uneasily at the stink that rolled out, Walter most of all. It smelled still of the corpse that had been carried out many days since, and lay now decently beneath the chapel floor of Branxholme; and it smelled of the confinement of a man in chains. Yet there was another odour still, a sulphurous waft that brought shudders to them all with its hint of sorcery and secrets, of strange company recently departed. They all of them glanced uneasily into the dark corners. When they unlatched de Soulis' chains from the wall and dragged him forth, he was streaked with his own filth, but hale and laughing at them with the force of snarling rage.

'What's it to be now? A heading? I hope it's not too costly an axe! Or would you use fire? I'd welcome one – not that I feel the cold, you understand, but it cheers the heart of a man so.'

'Fire enough where you're bound, my lad!' grunted Ker of Ferniehirst, examining the chains. 'Will you look at this! He's practically bent the manacle from his wrist! Another day and he'd have pulled free entirely!'

De Soulis' face creased up, and he chuckled deep in his belly. 'Amazing what a man may do, isn't it, when it doesn't hurt? The iron's not made that'll bind me for long, nor the door enclose me! Or,' he added more quietly, 'keep my fingers from your gullets, or your children's! Best make fast your chamber doors in the nights to come – little though it will serve in the end! You cannot kill me, and you cannot hold me. Starve me, and I am fed as the ravens in the wilderness fed Elijah. And when I am free, then you will all die.' There was no bravado in his voice then. It was a simple statement of what was and would be.

'We'll see,' said Walter shortly. 'Hale him up and into the air!'

For only a moment did the big man resist as he was pulled up the stairs, long enough to half turn and shout back into the shadows. '*Redcap!* Hold what was consigned you!'

Nothing returned but echoes; yet de Soulis smiled, as if hearing some message, and suffered himself to be drawn away. He glanced around him curiously as they took him out of the castle gate into the waiting escort of horsemen and pikemen, headed by the Kers, Roxburgh and other local lords. 'No crowds? I'd have thought all Liddesdale would be out. Or do you fear failure so much, you do it in secret?'

'There'll be crowds enough at the Nine-Stane Rig,' said Walter dully. 'That is the appointed place.'

De Soulis nodded. 'A place of power,' he said, half-approvingly. 'That will be Master Michael's counsel, no doubt. But I tell you now, it will not be enough to break the force that is about me, or the promise I have been given. Still, I shall enjoy the walk.'

'Enjoy what you may,' said Ker of Ferniehirst, tightening a rope in the metal collar, 'while you may. Come!'

So it was that they led the late Lord of Hermitage from beneath its yawning gate, fettered like the felon he was, led like a beast. But he bore all with an arrogance which went beyond courage, for at every glance he seemed to promise worse to his captors, and with every word he threatened it. For their part, they showed him no violence or mockery, but used him with a wary watchfulness, tight-lipped and tense. Had he been less sure of himself, or less consumed by hate, he might have read more into these signs, perhaps made some bid to escape. But it was not to be.

'It pleases me,' he said, contemplating the waiting throng around the grass-grown stones, 'that they should see me thus, and the futility of challenging my power! So much the easier to cow them once more, when the time comes!'

Walter shook his head in grim forbearance. 'You would be better occupied in seeking what grace and mercy you can. There is a priest for you, if you want one.'

'What, to kiss my arse?' wheezed de Soulis. 'That's all they're good for!' He held his head high as the murmur of the crowd reached him. Walter quickly sent pikemen to hold them back, lest the prisoner be accidentally loosed in a riot. He need not have worried. As they drew nearer defiant screams erupted, filth and rotten food flew, and some stones; but de Soulis cast his glance on the crowd, and gave his harsh chuckle. Under that chill blue gaze the voices faltered, the arms fell; one woman shrieked and fell down in a foaming fit, legs kicking. One or two men began to turn away. Walter was about to say something when it seemed to him that he half-heard words muttered behind him, or in the back of his mind, indistinct but menacing. He whirled about, but met only de Soulis' cherubic smile.

'Now what foolishness have you prepared for me today?' he inquired, peering vaguely between the tall standing stones. 'Fire, from the smoke; a large one, lit already, so you're either going to put me on a griddle or drop me into it. Or – what's that, a cauldron?' He gave a great guffaw, and rubbed his bound hands as if he hoped to warm them. A rough drystone hearth supported the huge squat cauldron there, already sizzling and singing, and the grass and weeds around were curling brown with the heat.

'Oh, you're going to *boil* me? Well, that's all been provided for, fire and water, you know, fire and water. But I'll allow I'd welcome the bath!'

Walter's mouth worked. He looked to Ker, who snapped his fingers to Gawn the sergeant. As de Soulis passed between the first of the standing stones, sturdy men-at-arms stepped out and seized him fast. He laughed. More men came trotting up, survivors of Walter's vanguard carrying sheets and strips of a heavy dark stuff that clunked dully as it was bent. Kneeling before de Soulis, they wrapped the strips around his legs, pinioning them, then began to enfold him bodily in the dirty-looking sheet. 'What in the name of – what's this bloody nonsense?' roared the Lord of Hermitage. 'What's this stuff that stinks of pitch? What're you clowning about with, you witless bastards?'

Beyond the fire men seized the levers of a smith's bellows, which filled with a sound like a spent man's breathing. It was Sir Andrew Ker who answered, at last, in a cold and even tone. 'It's lead, my lord. The lead torn from your own roof.'

'Lead? *Lead?* Are you clean reft of your senses? D'you think it'll drown me any the sooner, or hold me under the earth, or – or –' He made a strangled sound; and then he sucked in air in a horrified gasp.

Walter gestured quickly to Gawn. The sergeant slapped the sheet lead closed, hiding that blood-drained face, and bound it with the rope. But so absolute was the hush within the ancient stone circle that de Soulis' hoarse screams were barely muffled. His furious twisting and writhing strained the bonds, even as he was thrown down and rolled like an obscene chrysalis in another great chunk of lead.

'Get on with it, man!' said Ker of Ferniehirst through tight lips. The executioners stooped and seized the shapeless thing, staggering under the weight and the force of the struggles within. They half-dragged, half-carried it towards the fire. Already the base of the cauldron glowed cherry-red under the bellows' blast, and at its heart a faint yellowish-white was spreading. But the bellows-workers let go as they saw what was coming, and ran back, turning away their eyes.

With a hoarse gasping shout the bearers swung their burden shoulder-high. The screaming redoubled. Then, with another savage heave, they tipped it forward.

Walter had meant to shut his eyes, but he could not. Fascinated, he saw the thing land upon the cauldron's rim, rocking it, and then, writhing still, slide forward and fold and fall inward with a dull kitchen clatter . . .

The cauldron righted. Out of it there erupted an explosive, ear-searing sizzle that narrowed to an intense volcanic hiss; but louder yet was the shriek, echoing around the stones, around the hills, off the walls of Hermitage itself, till the birds erupted out of the distant wood in mortal terror. The horses balked and had to be reined in; Gawn seized Walter's by the bridle and quieted it. An obscene bubbling and crackling mingled with a demented animal noise. Smoke and steam puffed out of the cauldron in great heaving spurts, like a porridge-pot, but the shrieking did not stop. The hair rose on Walter's head, and his horse stirred and shifted under him. The crowd to the lee of the flames fell back with a cry of disgust as the first stench reached them. A waft of it came to Walter; it was mostly burning pitch.

Then there was a strange, quiet gurgling, and the screaming rose to a thinning wail and bubbled away to nothing in an instant. There was a moment's threshing in the cauldron, then it quieted, vibrating on its stones like a boiling kettle. Sir Andrew Ker sagged in his saddle, looking down at nothing. Ker of

Ferniehirst passed the back of his hand over dry lips. Walter twisted his reins in his fingers.

'For the waving of the trees came upon him,' said the warden softly, 'and the word of the King is upon him. And the roof of his house is over him, indeed. No promise was ever made to him of boiling lead. *Domine gratia—*'

Then without warning, as the crowd pressed closer, there was an appalling sound, a veritable thunderclap on the earth. The cauldron burst asunder, and a jet of smoke and steam spurted and screamed skyward at the clouds. Men shielded their faces as a mist of molten lead spewed all around. Yet there were some, Walter among them, who saw in that spear of steam a momentary shadow-form, capering and grinning like a twisted ape, in the likeness of the little old man he knew as Redcap.

Two men died on that field from the first blast of the cauldron. Many others were horribly burned from the falling lead, commons and lords alike, and women and children also; though bringing children to such an execution was beyond Walter's understanding. Ker of Ferniehirst, blown from his horse, would bear a streaked scar on his cheek to the end of his days. So de Soulis was not without his last stroke, even in unlooked-for death, and a futile vengeance.

Yet the hardened Marchmen rejoiced, cheered when the warden's banner rose again above the walls of Hermitage, and returned merrily to their old and time-hallowed ways. And though the thieving and feuding were not to end in the dales of the Borderlands, they grew far quieter for many long years, for ambitious men had the model of de Soulis as a dreadful warning before them. It did not deter them entirely from their ill-doing; but it set a tinge of fear in their dreams, and a hint of a retribution that defied even the strongest sorcery and the blackest alliance. In time, to placate de Soulis' kin, Hermitage was made over to them once more, under the warden's eye, and others of the line held it, some in decent honour. One at least was a black cruel villain, who starved his tenants in the same lightless dungeons; yet even he never sought to become more than a man.

In good times and in bad, nevertheless, there was an atmosphere that never quit those walls, a feeling of dark and sinister presence. Even many hundred years after the de Soulis line was extinct and the castle had been partly rebuilt, this lingered on. Many evil destinies were worked out there – that of Queen Mary, for one, and the Earl of Bothwell, who was her lover. Both she and that Earl James, who had had her husband Lord Darnley murdered, met sorry ends in exile and misery. Hermitage passed to Bothwell's nephew and heir Francis, and he led a career that was a vile echo of de Soulis', of reiving, murder and black magic, till in the end he was dispossessed and died in exile, a penniless half-mad mountebank. It made men think, and tell again of de Soulis' last command, and wonder if in some hidden chamber beyond sight and discovery his blackest secrets remained to be found, all ready to ensnare and lead astray other overly ambitious minds – guarded, perhaps, by a little old man in a dirty red cap. Certain it is that, where the tides of time have ruined or swept away altogether many other strong walls throughout the old Marches, those of Hermitage stand strong and grim to this very day.

Perhaps Walter felt something of this. Certainly there was no rejoicing for him, for with a few curt orders to Gawn and only the briefest farewell to his fellow lords he turned his nervous mount and hastened away. To the others he left it to bury what remained where it lay, and have the priest say mass above it; he was not needed for that. He spurred swiftly for his home, by the shortest route. It took him up to the clearing where his father fell, and many bones still strewed the grass and the heather; but he paused there only briefly and would not let his horse graze. Back through the woods he cantered, along the path of their retreat, still visible among the thorns, and out over the fells to the green vale of Teviot and the welcome walls of Branxholme.

They still looked poor to him as he rode through the village, but cold and bleak no longer. This was his home again, and the soil in which his hopes were planted. He had no great ambitions left for worldly fame and honour; how could he, who had already risen higher than most men ever rise? He had served well in the courts of a different world, and, whatever it was in truth, a better and a higher one. The human court he had seen paled by contrast. He wanted no more of it. He would be content to live within these bounds, safeguard his people and his herds and flocks and fields, and raise a fine family and a strong line, and that would be more than enough. Except that one day, perhaps, he would make a pilgrimage, as many lords did, and see the flowers that grew upon the banks of Italy, and walk among its palaces and holy places; and Margaret would go with him.

She was waiting for him there within the tower, now. Yet it was not to the tower he went, but to the chapel, straight away; and it was kneeling there that she found him, before the altar but also by the slab that enclosed his father's coffin.

'They said you were returned,' she said quietly, neither challenging nor questioning. 'It is over, then?'

'Over,' he said thickly, rising. 'And more terribly than I feared, even. I could not face you at first, not without trying to clear the taint of it from my soul. Margaret, heart, we who hold ourselves honourable and Christian, have we not made ourselves as evil as de Soulis, this day?'

She embraced him quickly, and shook her head. 'I asked myself the same, when I watched you ride out. He had to die, as we all have to. He made it sooner by his own actions; and in trying to cheat his death he shaped the manner of it. He wove his own destiny, no other.'

Walter held her a moment, looking at her as a man looks at some incredible and unexpected gift. She was his lost love, and yet she was more; there was a force, a life to her that the lady Astrafiammante, for all her loveliness, had not had. Astrafiammante still burned in his memory, but it was a cool blue flame, cool as moonlight, and as bound to the night. Everything about Margaret seemed stronger and more complete. She was as squarely of this world as he was, and all the fairer for it. He kissed her, a timeless kiss that ended only for breath. 'Heart, you bring me healing. But you are not quite right. There was another had a hand in the weaving, and that is what burns

244

within me still. I do not want to leave you now, but I must ride out again today – not too far. I shall be back late tonight.'

She smiled, only a little tremulously. She was, after all, a Douglas, and a wise one. 'What you must, Lord of Branxholme, you must. But take great care! And do not tire yourself too much, for remember, tomorrow is your wedding day – and,' she added without any undue coyness, 'your wedding night, my lord.'

'Could I forget it,' he murmured, holding her tighter, running his hands around the lithe body that was new to him, and yet so well remembered, 'Astrafiammante?'

She pulled away, eyes like gems in deep water. 'My lord, you forget yourself! This is holy ground! A kiss is one thing, but such carnalities—' She sniffed in mock disdain, and prodded his chest. 'And why will you be forever calling me that strange name? In mistake for some old abandoned love, no doubt?'

He chuckled. 'Yes indeed. One that by a strange coincidence looked like you, every inch like you, from head to toe.'

'And how would you know so much of how I look, inch or ell?' Margaret demanded suspiciously.

'I know,' he said, and smiled into her pugnacious face, healed now from de Soulis' blows. 'We lived long together in perfect love, and she bore me many children. Seven, in fact.'

Margaret gave a low hoot of derision. 'Seven? Not the one to rein in your hopes, are you? You'll be lucky, my lad; we'll see. But that name—'

'It's Italian,' he said, taking her in his arms again. 'It means *Starblazing*. And it belongs to no woman in all this world, but you.'

It was later than he intended when he rode out, and the shadows were already deepening on the hills. Summer was coming, but it was not here yet, not quite, and the evening sun was low and red, the light over the green fields long. Soon they would be golden and heavy, those fields; but not yet. Trees cast strange lacy shadows along the earth, and the slow clouds drifted easily from horizon to horizon as if to rebuke the fierce haste of the rider beneath. He might have lingered to savour the land he loved; but he could not. A fresh horse bore him easily over the long miles; he rode armed but without escort, though it would be a brave footpad who would challenge the terrible young Lord of Branxholme upon his own land. The man who had brought de Soulis down was already becoming famous throughout the Marches, though he did not know it. And at that moment he would hardly have cared. His mind was on what lay ahead, and on the words she had called after him: '*Give him Godspeed from myself!*'

He wondered what dreams she had been having, and just how much she truly understood. Maybe one day, when they knew one another better, he would be able to ask her.

Along the forest tracks he galloped, for there was no mist at this hour, and out between the tree-crowned hills, until at last he came to the shoulders of Ettrickdale, and the ancient Roman walls from which he could see the ruinous turrets of Oakwood.

He kicked on the doors, and they swung back. The spidery servant Ghismondo admitted him with a conspiratorial bow and grin, as one man to another who has worn his clothes. Walter strode past, looking about, and, seeing the light in the tower room, he did not wait to be announced but went striding in, clattering across the creaky floor and up the low staircase. He glanced sharply to one side, and saw Gilberto, looking more hunched and deformed than ever, perched on a stool by the dying fire, rocking back and forth. He too grinned, a nasty grin that seemed to delve into the turmoil in Walter's soul. Walter swore beneath his breath, took the remaining steps two at a time and threw open the tower door.

There was no splendour in the room, real or glamorous; indeed, there was little of anything save three large lamps, a small fire in the hearth and a mass of chests and trunks, some closed, some open, half-full of robes and books and other paraphernalia. In the middle of them, leafing through a weighty tome in a strange crabbed script, sat Michael Scot in a dilapidated but comfortable-looking chair.

'Greetings, cousin!' he said, rising without haste and laying the book back in a chest at his side. 'I regret I have little cheer to greet you with, beyond my goodwill—'

Walter kicked the side of a chest, so that the lid fell with a slam. 'Going somewhere, wizard?'

'Obviously. But I intended to see you before I left.'

'That's good, because I want to ask you some questions, wizard – questions I want answered, and fully!'

Michael Scot spread his generous sleeves. 'I am at your service—'

'Are you?' spat Walter. 'Or at another's? You, you ruthless warlock, you've toyed and tangled so deftly with a whole sheaf of lives, haven't you? You've torn and worn the strands of our destinies every way, all of us! Why, wizard? Because you wanted to help – because you're good, and de Soulis isn't? Is that why you wanted to help us? Are you really *good*, wizard? Or—' He swallowed, struggling for words. 'Or have you only ever acted under the cloak of doing good?'

Michael shook his head wonderingly. 'Why should I—?'

'To serve yourself? To put a cruel end to a potential rival? I saw a man perish today, wizard, as horribly as a man can, I guess. Where were you, *scholar*?' He smacked hand into palm. 'Yet that was your doing, your shaping, that was what you tricked Alexander into permitting! And I went along with it! I shared in it, I am dragged down by it! How does a good man conceive such a horror? A man who's forever claiming to be a scholar and not a black sorcerer in the Devil's leaguing, fit only for the tar-barrel or the stake? Why should we not thrust you in a cauldron also, Master Michael Scot, with all your books for kindling? I'll have an answer, I warn you! And one that satisfies me – or by the living God, wizard, and for all I may owe you, there must be another case set before the King!'

A sick feeling grew upon Walter as Michael sat slowly back in his chair. He did not look at Walter, and spoke no answer directly; but his face grew dark and old, and an unhealthy sheen stood out upon his brow. 'At least your scruples and sensitivities may make you a better man than your father!'

He reached down into the chest, and took up the book again, opening it to what looked like the same place. 'There is an Italian,' he said slowly, 'a Florentine who will one day consign me to the Inferno, in the bitterest pains. This I have been told.

247

I most fervently pray he will be wrong. And to that end I have recanted, done penance, given rich alms, received absolution at the highest hands of man – and ever I strive to do all the good I can.' A sudden fire burned in his glance, and he stood up, and spoke with no less vehemence than Walter. 'You, you of all people, dare ask whether I do good? Would you be Lord of Branxholme now without the things I have done? Would you even be alive? Are your scruples grown so fine you'd regret that?'

Walter made as if to seize the collar of his robe, then let his hand fall slowly. 'I was grateful beyond words. Until I saw the end of what I had won. Was it bought with tainted coin, wizard? Will such an evil beginning not spread and corrupt all that you have given me?'

'That was not a beginning,' snapped Michael. 'It was an end. For you, anyway. It has no power over you now. What you make of your life is up to you, and how many can say as much? Look at your state now! At your wife of the morrow, at the children you will have, fair and healthy and hopeful; then, and only then, will you have the right to judge! Ask yourself whether or not I have succeeded. Ask yourself then whether I am – *good*. But . . .'

He hesitated, and sighed deeply, and bowed his head.

'Well?' prompted Walter softly.

Michael's eyes burned in their deep sockets, reflecting the firelight. 'As anyone else must – anyone! – I can only use all the talents I have, the means at my disposal. Who can do otherwise? When there is no other way? Means I have acquired at great pains, after long and anguished studies throughout the length and breadth of our world and in worlds that are not our own – aye, at the Scholomance itself, in the hills above Trasimene's dark mere, that terrible night-long circle of learning in which the Black Man himself claims the last scholar of ten as his fee, in the instant before dawn.'

A great chill grew upon Walter. 'Twice,' he whispered, 'I remember . . . you said to de Soulis, and it daunted him – you sat through that once, waiting, not knowing – and then the lot fell on another – and you went *back*?'

Michael's voice was a thin protesting edge. 'I had to *know*! There was so much I needed to know!'

Walter swallowed. 'The others – the two – what happened to them? Death and damnation? Torn apart?'

'Not quite. They . . . enter service. They are . . . changed.' Michael gave a snort of laughter. 'You should know. You have seen them. Gilberto, Ghismondo—'

'*Your* service?' demanded Walter, aghast.

'Oh no,' said Michael sadly. 'Not mine. But they are mine to command, and apt to the hand, they and . . . others. They, and much knowledge, keys to many locks in many doors that men do not even dream of, doors to which those you have passed are the merest outer wicket-gates. That knowledge I won when I was young and foolish and in love with the understanding of this world, afire to reshape it for the better. Now that the means are mine, I know how foolish I was – yet I cannot be rid of them. But to use those means, as I have for you, boy – that may be to damn me further.' He snapped the book shut, and made as if to hurl it from him; but instead he laid it gently down.

'Yet I am faced with such as de Soulis – and what can I do but use them? Shall I sit back and let evil roll over you and Margaret and Sir Andrew and all the other innocents? Surely that would damn me in itself! And yet, if I do use my power, somehow the end, however good, is always coloured by it. There is always evil in the outcome – oh, not for you, boy. Ultimately for me. Do you wonder I was not there today? That was my own flesh that boiled from the bone. I cast my penance and my absolution away.'

'I'm sorry,' choked Walter. 'I didn't know—'

'You were so concerned with good and evil,' said Michael, and then something like a frenzy entered his tone. 'You come marching in, you demand that I tell you whether I am good or evil?' He never raised his voice, yet anguish hammered each word like hot steel, spoken as a man might speak who clings to a crumbling clifftop by his fingertips alone. 'The brave young knight confronts the wicked sorcerer – straight out of the romances! God, God, God! Me, tell you? You young fool, will not *you* tell *me*?'

Silence fell. Walter could not have spoken if he wished. Michael Scot dropped into his chair, and rested his forehead on his fingers an instant. His voice was deep and hollow. 'And now I cannot rest in the home of my fathers, but must set out for the south again, a weary pilgrim, to pursue my salvation once more. And what now? Shall I find it? What if I miscarry by the way?'

His voice had sunk to a whisper. 'I am in fear, for not many years are left me . . . I fear! And I am never alone . . .'

From below, from the stable outside the window, came the sudden neighing of a great horse, as if impatient to be off on a journey, and a crashing stamp of hooves that made the ancient walls of Oakwood tremble. The neighing sounded like laughter.

Author's note

Michael Scot, as the name was then spelt, was a very real person, who emerged from the obscurity of medieval Scotland's Border country to become one of the greatest scholars of the age. All this region is a remarkable hotbed of tales and traditions of legend, magic and mystery, and Michael's story seems haunted by them. He had no direct descendants – he had taken minor priestly orders, then obligatory for scholars, though he wore them very lightly; but among the descendants of his line were Sir Walter Scott, and my mother's forebears.

Michael went from Scotland to study at Oxford (where I followed him) and then at Paris, Bologna and most of the great universities of Europe. Boccaccio's *Decameron* mentions him as having recently lived in Florence. At Toledo he became one of the translators who first introduced the works of classical thinkers and Arab philosophers to medieval Europe, laying the groundwork for the Renaissance. He produced the first European editions of Aristotle and Avicenna, among others, and pioneering – for their time – works on physiology, natural history and many other subjects. But he was also an earnest student of the occult, and produced a remarkable (and daring) textbook of ritual magic and necromancy, the *Liber Introductorius*. Later he recanted, but by that time his popular fame as a mage was well established. It did not hinder his career; Pope Honorius even offered him the bishopric of Cashel in Ireland, which he declined on the grounds that he did not know Gaelic – meaning, it seems, that he didn't want to treat it as a non-resident sinecure.

In around 1220 Michael became counsellor, physician and court astrologer to the Holy Roman Emperor Frederick II in Sicily; many of his books on philosophy and natural history for the cultivated and open-minded Emperor survive, one in the form of a personal dialogue with him. He served Frederick for the rest of his life, but it is almost certain that he returned to Scotland during this time – bringing with him, according to legend, the true formula for calculating the date of Easter, which had been mistimed until then. Interestingly, the histories agree on the manner of his death, in France around 1236, struck down by crumbling church masonry as he was about to take communion – a fate from which some drew dark conclusions. The more so, when the Emperor Frederick quarrelled with the Pope and was excommunicated; vitriolic church propagandists found a ready-made evil genius in Michael. Some seventy years later Dante consigned him to the Inferno's Eighth Circle, among the sorcerers.

In Scotland he gained the name of the Border Wizard, later given to Sir Walter (who also depicted Michael in *The Lay of the Last Minstrel*). Many tales grew up around him, both in Scotland and Europe, one or two of which I have worked into this story, along with other Border legends of the time. While I've tried to reflect the historical background, I haven't striven for minute accuracy. The story reflects the feuding and cattle-thieving Border life recorded in the sixteenth century; it is sometimes thought this was a recent result of the brutal scorched-earth tactics in Scotland's wars of independence, but more likely it was there all along, inherited from the region's Viking settlers. It is by no means certain whether Branxholme was in Scot hands this early; and some legends name a slightly later Lord de Soulis, William, who, however, is known to have died relatively peacefully in prison. Nicholas is a more likely candidate. In one version of the story Thomas the Rhymer – another real person – plays Michael's ambiguous role; but this is harder to believe of the gentle poet-lord of Ercildoune (today's Earlston), even though he too was carried off by the Queen of Faerie. Maybe Astrafiammante had acquired a taste for mortals. Neither Walter nor Robert are historical figures, but the name Walter was frequently given to eldest sons of the family, as for example Wat of Harden, the archetypal Border reiver, a Falstaffian rogue who is said to have observed of a neighbour's haystack, 'Aye, if ye had four legs ye wouldna' stand there lang!'

At any rate, it is of Walter Scot of Branxholme, his bride Margaret, and the first Lord de Soulis that the legends speak, and of Michael Scot, and it is these I have chosen to follow. The landscape of this book is real, and all the Border places in it; I've known many of them from childhood, though the great forests have long gone. Some, like Branxholme Hall and Oakwood Tower, though largely rebuilt, still stand today – and most of all Hermitage itself, one of the most sinister places I have ever seen, even from the bleak winding roads that lead to it. Judge for yourself; it is open to the public during the summer. Even the sunniest day cannot dispel the aura that clings to those immense and threatening walls; in their ancient shadow it is all too easy to feel legend and history mingle, and to believe in both.

It's not every fantasy author who has the good start, as it were, to have a genuine wizard for an ancestor and namesake. I feel immensely privileged and grateful, and I salute the memory of both the real and the legendary Michael Scot.

CRITICAL WAVE

THE EUROPEAN SCIENCE FICTION & FANTASY REVIEW

"CRITICAL WAVE is the most consistently interesting and intelligent review on the sf scene."
- Michael Moorcock.

"One of the best of the business journals... I never miss a copy..." - Bruce Sterling.

"Intelligent and informative, one of my key sources of news, reviews and comments." - Stephen Baxter.

"I don't feel informed until I've read it."
- Ramsey Campbell.

"Don't waver - get WAVE!" - Brian W Aldiss.

CRITICAL WAVE is published six times per year and has established a reputation for hard-hitting news coverage, perceptive essays on the state of the genre and incisive reviews of the latest books, comics and movies. Regular features include publishing news, portfolios by Europe's leading sf and fantasy artists, extensive club, comic mart and convention listings, interviews with prominent authors and editors, fiction market reports, fanzine and magazine reviews and convention reports.

Previous contributors have included: MICHAEL MOORCOCK, IAIN BANKS, CLIVE BARKER, LISA TUTTLE, BOB SHAW, COLIN GREENLAND, DAVID LANGFORD, ROBERT HOLDSTOCK, GARRY KILWORTH, SHAUN HUTSON, DAVID WINGROVE, TERRY PRATCHETT, RAMSEY CAMPBELL, LARRY NIVEN, BRIAN W ALDISS, ANNE GAY, STEPHEN BAXTER, RAYMOND FEIST, CHRIS CLAREMONT and STORM CONSTANTINE.

A six issue subscription costs only eight pounds and fifty pence or a sample copy one pound and ninety-five pence; these rates only apply to the UK, overseas readers should contact the address below for further details. Cheques or postal orders should be made payable to "Critical Wave Publications" and sent to: M Tudor, 845 Alum Rock Road, Birmingham, B8 2AG. Please allow 30 days for delivery.

Pasquale's Angel

PAUL J. MCAULEY

Florence, 1518: a city riven by scientific and sociological change caused by the wonderful devices of the Great Engineer, Leonardo da Vinci.

Pasquale di Cione Fiesole has come to Florence as an apprentice painter. He is witness to an assassination attempt on Raphael; worse, his own brother seems to have fired the shot, and the weapon has fallen into his hands. Soon Pasquale must prove his own and his brother's innocence, while on the run from both the engineers and the artist as civil unrest mounts towards open warfare.

'A suspenseful murder mystery' – *Sunday Telegraph*

'Conceptual wit, inventiveness and [a] capacity for enjoyable but upsetting mayhem' – *The Good Book Guide*

£5.99   0 575 05917 6

A Dangerous Energy

JOHN WHITBOURN

London, 1967. In an England where the Protestant Reformation failed, and in which magic is an integral part of the mighty Catholic Church's armoury, there are plenty of opportunities for a talented young necromancer like Tobias Oakley. From his early initiation into the dark arts by an elvish witch, he progresses steadily into a career as a Church magician.

In such an exalted position, Tobias finds not only the power he craves, but also the time to indulge in other, secret, and more satisfying, pursuits – such as drug-running, debauchery, demonology – and murder.

A Dangerous Energy was chosen as the winner of the BBC Bookshelf/Victor Gollancz First Fantasy Novel Competition by a panel which included Terry Pratchett, Mary Gentle and Nigel Forde.

'He doesn't soften the edges. A well-textured alternate history' – Mary Gentle

£4.99   0 575 05576 6